LINDSEY KELK

I Heart Paris

HARPER

Harper
An imprint of HarperCollins*Publishers*
77–85 Fulham Palace Road,
Hammersmith, London W6 8JB

www.harpercollins.co.uk

A Paperback Original 2010
This production 2012

A catalogue record for this book
is available from the British Library

ISBN: 978-0-00-792952-8

Set in Melior by Palimpsest Book Production Limited,
Grangemouth, Stirlingshire

Printed and bound in Great Britain by
Clays Ltd, St Ives plc

MIX
Paper from
responsible sources

FSC
www.fsc.org

FSC® C007454

FSC is a non-profit international organisation established to promote the
responsible management of the world's forests. Products carrying the FSC
label are independently certified to assure consumers that they come
from forests that are managed to meet the social, economic and
ecological needs of present and future generations.

Find out more about HarperCollins and the environment at
www.harpercollins.co.uk/green

I HEART PARIS

Lindsey Kelk is the author of *I Heart New York*, *I Heart Hollywood*, *I Heart Vegas*, *I Heart London* and *The Single Girl's To Do List*. When she isn't writing, reading, listening to music or watching more TV than is healthy, Lindsey likes to wear shoes, shop for shoes and judge the shoes of others. She loves living in New York but misses Sherbet Fountains, London and drinking Gin & Elderflower cocktails with her friends. Not necessarily in that order.

To find out more about the *I Heart* series, sign up for the newsletter, read exclusive extracts and much much more visit www.iheartparis.co.uk

Follow Lindsey on Twitter @LindseyKelk, and find out more about Lindsey at www.lindseykelk.com

By the same author

I Heart New York
I Heart Hollywood
I Heart Vegas
I Heart London

The Single Girl's To Do List

Jenny Lopez Has a Bad Week
(novella only available on ebook)

For Mabel, Kara, Joel and Chloe – hope you're
not too ashamed of me when you're old enough
to read this

Massive thanks enough to everyone at HC, especially Lynne, Victoria, Claire and Sarah. Kate and Lucy, you're amazing. Lee, thank you for making the covers so incredibly beautiful that people pick the book up in the first place. Wendy, thank you for convincing buyer-types to put it in the shops so people can see the pretty cover. Liz & Kiera, excellent work ladies. And to everyone else, as an ex-HCUKer, I totally appreciate what amazing stuff you're doing for me and I'm so proud to work with you in any capacity.

I also want to say super special thanks to Sam 'The Butcher' Hutchinson and Jane 'Gaga' Griffiths for making our Parisian research so much fun but then, I always say that, don't I? Thanks to Jenny Jacoby and all her friends for their hints and tips and 'a sparky young monger named Hugh' and to the man on Rue Oberkampf with the bottle of vodka . . . That answer's still no, thank you.

To everyone that helped me make New York feel like home; the World's Best Roomies, Ro and Shirin, Beth, Janet, Kari, Sarah (B/HS! B/HS!), Erin, Brenna, Rachael, the America's Next Top Model Watching Collective and everyone who has laughed with me, instead of at me. Appreciated. And finally for all the red-headed Texan poets in my life. I would like to acknowledge their abundant inspiration, encouragement and physical attractiveness. And the fact that they had the balls to suggest I put this in here. Ask and ye shall receive.

CHAPTER ONE

New York hadn't even attempted to cool down in the three days that I'd been away. When my friend Erin had suggested we get away to her beach house for a long weekend, I almost threw myself out of her eighteenth-storey office window to get there quicker. But three days beside the seaside only made it harder to be back in the sticky city. I'd only walked two blocks to the subway and my heel had slipped into the melting, sludgy tarmac between the paving slabs three times already. Ick. It almost made me long for a wet summer Saturday in Wimbledon. Almost.

In this cloying heat, the only way I could cope was to wear as little clothing as possible whenever I had to be outside, and spend as much time worshipping at the altar of the air-conditioning unit as humanly possible. Today's survival ensemble was pretty much nothing more than a really long pale pink vest from American Apparel and a bangle. The bangle was to show I had actually put some thought into getting dressed and hadn't just wandered out in my under-wear. Back in London, I would never, ever have left the house in something so skimpy, but it was just too hot to worry about bingo wings. When I left the house, I didn't feel as if I'd forgotten to get dressed. Right now, I was one towelling headband away from the crazy lady that liked to sit outside the twenty-four-hour deli opposite my apartment in her dressing gown and bra.

Once I was safely on the air-conditioned train, I flailed around elegant as ever, hanging from the pole in the centre of the carriage and swapped my shoes for the ever-present flip-flops in my Marc Jacobs satchel. I thought back to the precious moment when the bag had come into my life. I had treasured it more than anything else I'd ever owned, I never put it on the floor, always checked that pens had their lids on, lip glosses weren't leaking and there was no way on God's green earth, I'd have ever put a pair of dirty street shoes in it. Rummaging around for my left flip-flop, I wanted to shed a little tear for the unravelled stitching and the used subway cards, crumpled napkins and dozens of half empty packs of chewing gum that now littered the lining. Classy.

Changing from the Six train onto the L at Union Square, I felt myself begin to smile. The same nervous flutter started to pick up in the pit of my stomach that always attacked me when I stepped onto the train towards Brooklyn. So, maybe there was an upside to being back in the city. Alex. Of course, I wouldn't have the L train flutters nearly as often if I would just move in with him, like he kept asking. According to my friends, it was ridiculous that I was keeping our rela-tionship 'bi-coastal'. I'd spent an awful lot of the weekend trying to explain to uber-Manhattanite Erin, who didn't even venture below 14th street unless she positively had to, that Murray Hill to Williamsburg wasn't exactly bi-coastal. And besides, I just wasn't sure

I was ready to take that step just yet. Yes, I loved Alex, yes, I wanted to spend time with him but did that mean I should shack up with him right away? No.

After I'd shuffled off the train and hauled myself up the stairs to the street, I paused for a moment to let my eyes readjust to the sunlight. As always, Alex was propped up against the corner of Bedford and North 7th, bobbing his head to whatever was coming out of his iPod, his thick, black hair pushed back off his face, messed up at the back as though he'd just got up. Which, given that it was only one in the afternoon, I guessed he probably had. Sticky August weather or not, Alex's wardrobe never changed. Skinny black jeans clung to his legs, his T-shirt was tight to his chest and he was sipping from a steaming cup of coffee.

I shook my head. How could he drink anything hot on a day like this? Just looking at the cup made me break out in a sweat. Just looking at Alex made the flutter in my stomach graduate into a full-body shiver. I ran my ring fingers under each eye, clearing any potential mascara smudges – not even the most waterproof of mascaras could survive ninety-five degrees of New York City heat – and pulled my sunglasses out of my handbag before I started over.

'Hey.' Alex dropped his coffee in the bin beside him and leaned his head down to mine for a kiss. 'How was Erin's?'

'Amazing,' I replied, reaching back up for another slightly longer kiss that made me catch my breath. 'You should come with us next time. Provincetown is beautiful.'

'I'm not really beach people,' he said, catching my hand in his and pulling me down the street. 'And from the look of those shoulders, neither are you.'

'Oh, I know.' I shrugged the strap of my bag back on to the narrow strap of my dress, revealing my attractive lobster red skin. 'I should just stay inside until September.'

'Hmm.' Alex squeezed my hand. 'That's not going to play exactly into my plans, but I'm not entirely against the idea.'

There was that shiver again.

'And what plans are these?' I asked as we walked up the block to Alex's apartment. His place was only five minutes from the subway, but in this heat, they were five minutes too many.

'So the band has been asked to play a festival,' he said, forcing his hand into the skin-tight pocket of his jeans, feeling around for a key that wasn't there.

'Really? That's great,' I dipped my hand into the tiny pocket inside my bag and produced my key to Alex's flat as we reached the door. He took it from me with a heart-stopping grin. It was sickening how much I fancied him. It was like, I'd see him every day and after a while I stopped seeing him. And then, out of nowhere, I'd just get a sidelong glance at him and the wind would be completely knocked out of me, as if I were seeing him for the first time.

'See? This is why I need you to move in,' he slid his hand around my waist and pulled me in for another, deeper kiss as we staggered sideways into the apartment building. My skin prickled with goosebumps from the shock of the air conditioning.

'Or you could just remember to take your key out with you,' I whispered, pulling away with stinging lips. Must remember to buy lip balm with a higher SPF. 'Tell me about this festival.'

'Tell me you missed me this weekend,' he whispered back, running his finger over my bottom lip.

I paused, looking down at my flip-flops for a second. It was moments like this that made me feel like a complete idiot for not running back to Manhattan, throwing all my belongings in a bag and pitching up at the apartment in Brooklyn in a heartbeat.

'Of course I missed you,' I took the key from his hand and opened the apartment door. 'Did you cry yourself to sleep every night?'

'I cry myself to sleep every night you're not here,' he shot me a grin and walked over to the fridge, producing two icy beers. 'But since you won't move in, I've had to find a way through it.'

I dropped my bag onto one of his knackered old sofas (better for it than the floor) and took the beer. This was the perfect time to have The Conversation. To say, "I really do want to move in with you, but I'm ever so slightly shit-scared." But I didn't.

Alex vanished into his bedroom and I didn't follow. Instead I looked around the apartment. The tiny open-plan kitchen, littered with take-out boxes and empty coffee cups. Two huge, squishy sofas faced the huge floor-to-ceiling windows with all of Manhattan laid out in front of us, sparkling in the sunlight. It didn't look sweaty, hateful and oppressive from in here. It looked beautiful. And whenever I got bored of looking at the New York City skyline, if that was in fact possible, there was always the massive flat screen TV shoved in the corner, with the DVR already set to record all my favourite shows.

Was I being completely ridiculous? What was the worst that would happen? I'd move in, there would be fewer takeaway cartons in the kitchen, more products in the bathroom. We'd go to bed together every night, wake up together every morning, go out, come home, watch TV, cook, shop, clean, moan, bitch, stop

5

having sex, stop talking, start cheating and end up hating each other.

Wow. I followed my bag down on to the sofa. Now that was not a healthy internal reaction to the idea of moving in with my lovely, lovely boyfriend.

'So, the festival,' Alex called from the bedroom. 'It's pretty cool, we've played it before, but they've asked us to come back and play again, it's like the second headline slot.'

'That's amazing,' I yelled back, trying to wipe those horrible thoughts out of my stupid head. 'So when is it? Next summer?'

'Uh, it's kind of next weekend.' He appeared in the doorway. 'Yeah, it's not that amazing. Someone else dropped out and we were first runner-up.'

'But still,' I let myself be distracted by the biceps peeping out of his T-shirt as he stretched against the door frame. 'It's better than a slap around the face. Is it in the city?'

'That's the other thing,' he let go of the door and came over to the sofa, 'it's in Paris. France.'

'Paris, France?'

'Paris, France.'

'Is there another Paris?'

'Paris, Texas?'

'All right smart arse.' I rubbed my forehead. 'So you're going to Paris next weekend?' At least that would buy me another couple of weeks to try and get over this whole moving in nonsense.

'We're going to Paris next weekend,' he corrected. 'You'll come right? I figure I can't leave you alone in the city after what happened in LA.'

'Nothing happened in LA.' I slapped his thigh. It didn't matter how many jokes he made about my ill-fated work trip to LA, I still wasn't OK with it. As much fun as an all-expenses paid trip to Hollywood to interview an up-and-coming Brit actor who turned out to be gay and tried to convince me to be his professional beard might sound, it almost cost me my job, my work permit and Alex. So I thought it perfectly understandable that I might still be a little bit sore about it.

'OK, OK.' Alex grabbed my hands to hold off the attack. 'So how about you look at it like a romantic trip to Paris. We've never taken a trip before.'

'True.' I nodded, letting him slide his hands up from my wrists to interlink his fingers with mine. 'And I have always wanted to go to Paris.'

'You've never been?' he asked, looking surprised. I shook my head. 'But it's so close to the UK.'

'I missed the GCSE trip after I fell down a pothole on the geography field trip,' I admitted. 'Not my finest moment.'

'I don't know what a pothole is, but it sounds like something you would do.' He kissed me lightly on the lips. 'You know I love you even though you're a walking disaster zone, right?'

'Thanks.' I couldn't really be offended, it was true. I'd already broken two glasses in a week. 'Won't Paris be super expensive though? I'm still broke from LA.'

Broke, but beautifully dressed, I thought, just not today.

'You don't need to worry about anything.' Alex started to plait a section of my hair. 'I'm hardly gonna ask you to come away with me and then expect you to pay for it.'

'But I want to.' I frowned. 'I don't want you to have to pay for everything. You know I'm really not that girl.'

'I thought every girl was the "let my boyfriend take me to Paris for the weekend" kind of a girl,' Alex said, pulling my hair. 'Or is this just an excuse for you to weasel out of the trip the same way you're trying to weasel out of moving in with me?'

'I'm not weaseling out of anything,' I pulled the loose plait out of his hands. 'I do want to go to Paris, I just don't want you to have to pay for me to go to Paris. I'll find a way to make it work. And if it's next weekend, we'll be away for your birthday. Your big three-oh.'

Alex's thirtieth birthday had been looming on the horizon for months and, while he was pretending to be super cool about it, the official line was that I wasn't allowed to 'make a big deal out of nothing', which I had translated from boy-speak to mean 'if I don't acknowledge it, it won't actually happen'. Typical boy-logic that could be applied to many, many of his actions.

'Yeah, well, who doesn't want to be in Paris for their birthday?' he shrugged. 'The record company want us to play a couple of warm-up shows, the festival is on Sunday, but I'll keep Friday night free so we can do dinner or something. What could we do in New York that we can't do just as good in Paris? Or even better?'

He kissed me lightly on the lips and waited for a response. Sneaky tactics, he knew I wasn't at my full mental capacity when there was kissing involved.

'I don't know, I told you, I've never been to Paris,' I managed to get in, between kisses. 'When would we leave?'

'Monday?'

Untangling his hands from my hair, I pulled away slightly trying to remember what day it was. That was the problem with working from home, I had absolutely no sense of time. 'Today's Tuesday, there's too much to organize with work and the flat and, really, Alex, it's only six days.'

'It turns me on when you are so smart.' He persisted with the kissing, moving on to my neck and pushing me backwards against the sofa. 'There's nothing to freak out about, Angela. You pack a bag, you tell work that you're blogging from Paris for a week, you leave Vanessa in the apartment, we go to Paris. And if you're gonna go all feminazi on me paying for your flight, you can make it my birthday present. Seriously, how many times do I have to tell you to stop over-thinking everything?'

'At least once more,' I said, giving up. I reached my arms up around his neck and shifted around on to the sofa as his hand moved up my thigh and under the thin cotton of my dress-slash-vest. 'So you say you missed me this weekend.'

I felt his breath against my ear, giving me an altogether different case of goosebumps.

'Like you wouldn't believe.'

CHAPTER TWO

'What is that noise?' Alex groaned from underneath his covers.

'My phone,' I staggered out of bed the next morning and rolled into the living room, swearing and following the beeps. 'Go back to sleep.' I plunged an arm into the darkness that I hoped was the sofa until I felt my vibrating phone.

'Yeah?' I answered eloquently.

'Hi, Angela?'

'Muh?' I mumbled, rubbing the sleep out of my eyes. What time was it anyway?

'Angela, it's Cici? From the office? Were you still in bed, sleepyhead?'

There was no wonder I was shocked. If I had to name a New York nemesis, it would be Cici. She was my boss's assistant at *The Look*, tall, skinny, loaded, desperately 'On-Trend' and, God bless her, she might hate me with a fiery passion, but at least I could rely on her to be consistent. Until today. Shit.

'Erm, I was in the shower,' I lied for absolutely no reason. I pulled the phone away from my ear. According to the clock flashing on bedside table, it was eight-thirty a.m. There was no conceivable reason why I wouldn't still be in bed. Was there? Had I forgotten something? 'What's wrong, Cici?'

'Nothing's wrong,' she giggled. Actually giggled. 'Mary just asked that I give you a call to see if you could make an early lunch meeting today. Well, not really a meeting, more of a get-together. Twelve? Pastis?'

I almost dropped the phone. Mary Stein, my editor at Spencer Media, had never so much as walked me out of her office let alone taken me to lunch. 'Yes?' I asked as much as confirmed.

'Awesome.' Cici giggled. Again. 'Oh, Mary said to let you know that Mr Spencer, as in Spencer Media, will be joining the two of you. So . . . and I just want you to know that I say this with love, you should dress up. You know, just don't wear what you usually wear here. Or anything you've ever worn here. It's kinda fancy.'

And there was the Cici we all knew and loved. Before I could even sigh in reply, she'd hung up. Sitting in my knickers on the cold laminate flooring, I stared out of the window at the city in front of me. Lunch with Mr Spencer as in Spencer Media? What was that supposed to mean? Surely it had to be good though, there was no way it could be a bad thing.

What was a bad thing, was the state of me, I thought, peering at my reflection in the window as I pushed myself back up. I couldn't really show up at Pastis in a vest and flip-flops with just-shagged hair. Bedhead was great in theory, but in reality, it just looked as though I hadn't showered.

'Do I have any clothes here?' I asked a sleepy-looking Alex, as I dropped to my hands and knees in the bedroom to search for a stray dress or errant smock under his bed.

11

'Pretty sure you came in clothes,' he mumbled, throwing his forearm over his eyes. 'I know you lose shit all the time, but surely you haven't managed to lose your clothes in a one-bedroom apartment overnight.'

'You're hilarious.' I pulled the slightly worse for wear strappy dress from yesterday out from under the pile made up of Alex's jeans and T-shirt. 'Work just called, I have to meet Mary for a meeting at Pastis at lunch. I have to go home and get changed.'

'If you lived here you wouldn't have to,' he replied without moving.

'You make a fine point,' I said, wriggling into my dress. Leaning over the bed, I gave him a quick kiss and a gentle slap around the head. 'I'll call you later.'

'Yeah yeah,' he smiled, still with his deep green eyes closed. 'I know I'm nothing more than a booty call to you. You callous, British heartbreaker.'

I paused in the doorway, slipping my feet into my Havaianas, and watched him shuffle back under the thin white sheet on his bed. I was being stupid. Imagine waking up to that messy black bedhead every morning. And imagine not having to leg it back to Manhattan to use a decent brand of shampoo, conditioner of any kind, and find something to wear. How did boys keep their hair so soft without conditioner? Was the whole industry a sham? I shook my head and tried to concentrate. Now was not the time to worry about the effectiveness of Pantene.

'You planning on going soon or are you just gonna stand there and freak me out all day?' Alex asked from under his covers, making me jump.

'Going,' I said, grabbing my handbag from the sofa. 'Gone.'

'I'll come over tonight? We'll talk Paris?' he called.

'Tonight,' I agreed, closing the door behind me. Shower and Pastis first. Alex and Paris later.

Putting myself together for my lunch meeting would have been a lot easier if I hadn't started running through a million different terrifying scenarios in my head on the way home, during my shower, through every wardrobe change and while applying the few scraps of make-up that might not melt off on my way downtown to Pastis. I hailed a yellow cab outside the apartment in my LA-purchased dandelion yellow Phillip Lim dress and gold strappy flats, and tried not to think about all the reasons Mr Spencer might want to see me. Maybe he just wanted to meet the girl that had interviewed and inadvertently outed James Jacobs. Lots of people did. Mostly women, young and old, who wanted to give me a really, really filthy look and then ask me incredibly inappropriate questions about his boyfriend.

Or maybe he was a fan of my blog. My slightly random English-girl-living-in-New-York-rambling-on-about-her-everyday-life blog. Yes, that would definitely appeal to a sixty-something media magnate. Or perhaps he was a massive fan of the Shakira album review I'd just filed? Or perhaps he was a massive Shakira fan and didn't like the album review? Surely not, I'd been super kind. No, there were just too many possibilities even to begin guessing.

I hoped and prayed all the way downtown that Cici would have booked us a table inside the restaurant, very near an air-conditioning unit, and not one of the see-and-be-seen tiny tables outside looking out on to the cobbles of the Meatpacking District, but as the cab swerved across the street, I could see Mary's steel-grey bob sitting opposite an equally authoritative head of icy white hair. Not only was I the last to arrive, I was going to be stuck sweating like a pig in the street. Fantastic. Attempting to get out of the cab in a lady-like fashion and failing, I stumbled forwards, snagging the front of my sandal in the cobblestones. I caught myself at the last minute, stood up, straightened my skirt and gave Mary a half wave. I couldn't see behind her massive black sunglasses, but I was fairly certain the smile she gave me in return did not make it all the way up to her eyes.

'Angela Clark, this is Robert Spencer,' she said, rising out of her chair as I hobbled around the table.

Mr Spencer held out his hand and gave me a very, very firm handshake. Ow.

'Well, hello Angela,' he said, gesturing for me to take a seat beside Mary. 'I have to say, I've been looking forward to meeting you for a while. And please, call me Bob.'

I gave Mary a quick sideways look, but she was too busy spitting her water back into her glass to respond.

'Thank you, uh, Bob,' I replied, setting my handbag between my feet, underneath the table. 'It's really lovely to meet you. A real privilege. An honour, really.' Mary kicked me sharply under the table before I could carry on. It seemed fair.

'Not at all,' he said smoothly, nodding to the waiter at his elbow to pour three large glasses of white wine. 'I always like to take time out to meet our rising stars here at Spencer Media.'

He held up his glass. 'To you, Angela.'

'Thank you.' I tried not to think about what could happen if I started drinking wine on a completely empty and panicky stomach and took a small sip.

'So, Mr Spencer wanted to meet with you and talk about some new opportunities,' Mary said, folding the menu with which she was clearly very familiar. 'Things you might do outside the blog, outside *The Look*.'

'He did?' I asked, staring into the opaque glass of her sunnies. Was she serious?

'Ladies,' Mr Spencer folded up his own menu and placed it in front of him. 'Shall we at least order before we talk business?'

'Of course, Bob,' Mary smiled tightly and sipped her wine. It was so strange. I'd never seen her outside her office and she did not look comfortable at all. In fact, nothing about this entire scenario was comfortable. I was starting to feel as if I were at dinner with my mum and dad while they were in the middle of a particularly nasty argument. And no one who's ever argued with my mum would want that.

'Have you eaten at Pastis before, Angela?' Bob asked.

I shook my head and chugged my wine. I had a feeling that it was just going to be better to avoid talking whenever possible.

'Then I'd recommend the scallops to start and then maybe the *pasta puttanesca*?' Bob folded up his menu.

'You know *pasta puttanesca* means whore's pasta?' I dropped in casually.

Mary coughed into her wine glass.

'I mean, it's what whores would make after they'd you know, worked.' I looked from Mary to Bob and back to Mary again. Yep. Should have stuck with the no talking plan.

'Perhaps the *moules frites*,' Bob said quietly.

Before I could agree, someone's mobile started to chirp. Bob pushed out his chair and took a tiny phone out of his jacket pocket. 'So sorry ladies, that's me. Excuse me for a moment?'

'Of course, Bob,' Mary said again, this time through gritted teeth as he left the table.

'How is he even wearing a jacket?' I asked, turning in my seat to watch him walk out into the street. My head span as I turned back around. 'It is so bloody hot.'

'If I were you, I wouldn't drink quite so fast, Angela,' Mary said, pouring me a glass of water. 'This isn't a social lunch.'

'Arses. I was really, really hoping that it was,' I reluctantly swapped my, wow, more than half empty wine glass for a tumbler of water. 'So what is it?'

'It's a pain in my ass, is what it is.' Mary drained her wine glass and returned my raised eyebrow with a look of her own. 'I can hold my liquor, don't you worry. This, Angela, is a "Big Deal For You". Apparently one of Bob's granddaughters is your "biggest fan" and she seems to think you should be doing more, I don't know, "legitimate journalism" for some of Spencer's other magazines like *Icon* or *Belle*.'

'Legitimate journalism?' I didn't enjoy the number of times she had made air quotes during her last sentence. '*Belle*? They want me to write on a fashion magazine?'

'Apparently so. I don't know what though, so don't ask me.' She poured herself more wine. 'I'm only here because I heard about this through Cici and called Bob to find out what the hell was going on.'

'Hang on a minute, how did Cici hear?' Now I was really confused.

'Cici Spencer. She's one of Bob's granddaughters.'

I was sober in a heartbeat. 'Of course she is.'

'You don't think I employ her for her charm, do you?' Mary gave me an understanding grimace. 'Bob and I are old friends.'

It took everything I had not to raise an eyebrow. Old friends. That old chestnut.

'But Cici hates me,' I said, swapping my water for wine. Definitely time for wine. If I was going to stay in control of my facial expressions as well as my mouth though, I had to stay off the booze. 'Why would she tell her grandfather to give me more work?'

'Cici doesn't hate you,' Mary said, topping up my water again. 'Cici is jealous of you. She knows she's only my assistant because of who her grandfather is. She's been trying to get on the writing staff since she finished college, but even Bob knows she can't write for shit.'

'Oh. Wow. That's awful.'

'Don't start feeling sorry for her Angela, she's a bitch. And she'd get rid of you without a second thought if she thought she could take your job.'

'Fair enough,' I said, packing away any blossoming Cici-sympathy. 'But then why would she recommend me for more projects?'

'I keep waiting for her to lose interest and embrace her trust fund like her sister, but that girl just will not give up,' Mary nodded towards Bob as he strode back towards the table. 'I'd be impressed at her tenacity if she were working for anyone else, but me. And don't be a fool. She didn't, it was her cousin.'

Bob took his seat opposite me as our starters arrived. The food looked delicious, but I really wasn't very hungry any more.

'Apologies ladies, I've asked my secretary to stop my calls for the next couple of hours, so I'm all yours,' he said with another beaming smile.

'What a relief,' Mary replied, spearing a scallop.

I looked nervously from one to the other, Bob's benevolent grin clashing with Mary's openly pissed off expression, and reached for the wine. Sod it.

'Let me,' Mary said, snatching the bottle from my

17

hand and splashing a mouthful of wine in the bottom of my glass.

This wasn't going to be awkward at all.

'I don't know if you're aware, Angela, but you have a great fan in one of my granddaughters,' Bob finally got around to business over coffee. After Mary had refused dessert on behalf of both of us. Bugger.

I blew on my cappuccino and smiled nervously. It was still far too hot for coffee, but this really didn't feel like a Diet Coke kind of situation. 'Really? I didn't know that,' I lied, hopefully convincingly.

'Oh yes. And Mary speaks very, very highly of your writing.'

'She does?' No need to fake surprise this time. 'You do?'

'I do,' Mary replied, grudgingly. 'Your blog is very good.'

'And the piece you did for *Icon*, I read that one, Angela. Very good. You have a fun style, very personable.' Bob set down his coffee cup. 'I understand from Mary that you're only with us on a part-time basis at the moment. On a freelance arrangement?'

'Well, I don't work in the office,' I explained, trying to read Mary's face, which she was hiding behind her poker straight bob. 'But my work permit is tied to my writing the blog for *The Look*, so . . .'

'We own her ass, Bob, so just get to where you're going,' Mary interrupted. 'You're taking her off me, is that right?'

'Not at all,' he shook his head and covered one of her hands with his. 'You know I'd never tread on your toes. Although I do think it would be in Angela's interests to spread her wings a little. Get a broader experience of Spencer Media. Does that sound like something you'd be interested in, Angela?'

I bit my lip and nodded. I was worried that if I actually made a noise, Mary might throw her espresso in my face. And there might not be a lot of coffee in that cup, but it looked really hot.

'Fantastic, maybe you could come in and meet the *Belle* team next week,' Bob suggested. 'Maybe think of a couple of ideas to bring to the meeting. I know Emilia is very keen to meet you.'

Mary and I choked on our coffees in tandem. Emilia Kitt, editor of *Belle* magazine, Spencer Media's fashion monthly, was notoriously not keen on meeting anyone. As in anyone. I had been in for a meeting with Mary a few weeks ago and saw Angelina Jolie waiting in the lobby. And she was still waiting when I left. For Emilia.

'This is probably a really stupid thing to say, but I'm actually going to be in Paris next week,' I said, not sure whether or not I was making a huge mistake. 'From Monday. For a week.'

'You are? Since when?' Mary asked.

'I only found out yesterday.' I turned to give her my best 'help me out' face. Bob's expression really hadn't changed all through lunch so I had no idea what he was thinking. 'It's my boyfriend's thirtieth birthday.'

No one looked particularly impressed.

'He's in a band and they've been asked to play a festival in Paris.'

Still not impressed. And now Bob was looking at me as if I were a groupie.

'And I thought it would be really good for the blog. Didn't the visitor numbers go up when I was in LA?'

'Yes, but you were plastered all over the gossip pages when you were in LA,' Mary reminded me, unnecessarily. 'Are you planning on making an international spectacle of yourself in Paris?'

'Wasn't planning on it the first time, so who can say?' I defended myself pathetically.

'I think this all sounds great,' Bob said, finally breaking the stony silence that had built up between me and Mary. 'Emilia is planning a European issue in a couple of months. Perhaps you could put together an insider's guide to Paris for *Belle*? Off the beaten track, show us all the underground hotspots?'

'I could do that,' I agreed slowly.

'Then you'll come in and meet the *Belle* team tomorrow.' Bob suddenly got up from the table. 'I'll have Emilia's assistant call you later today, Angela.'

Mary stood up just as suddenly and, not knowing what else to do, I followed suit and accepted Bob's overly dramatic air kisses.

'Lovely to meet you, Angela, and Mary, always a pleasure.' He smiled and walked over towards a long black town car that had just pulled up beside the restaurant. Mary sank back down into her chair and emptied her wine glass.

'Cheap bastard didn't even pick up the bill.' Mary shook her head and pulled a huge wallet out of her even bigger bag. 'Well, I hope you're happy, Angela Clark.'

'Shouldn't I be?' I asked, trying to work out what had just happened. And whether or not Mary was sleeping with Bob. Because she most definitely had been at some point.

'Writing for *Belle* magazine is not going to be the same as writing a blog for me.' She called over a waiter and passed him a black American Express card. 'You're going to need to know exactly what you're doing.'

'But I can do this, the travel guide to Paris,' I said. 'It'll be fine. Won't it?'

'You know I like you, Angela,' Mary said, putting

her elaborate signature on to the credit card slip. 'But if you fuck this one up, there's no way I can help you. The girls on *Belle* are not the girls on *The Look* or *Icon*.'

'But they want me to do this, don't they?' This did not sound promising. 'I mean, it was their idea?'

'It was Bob's idea,' Mary corrected me. 'Worse, it was Bob's granddaughter's idea. Just, before you go in to the office, know that the girls on *Belle* make Cici look like a labradoodle. Each and every one of them has destroyed the career of someone else, or slept with at least three different married men to be there.'

'They sound nice.'

'Then I'm underselling what a pack of bitches they are.' Mary tucked her wallet back into her bag. 'They're not going to love that you're waltzing through the door with a Paris assignment without ever having so much as broken a nail at Fashion Week. Not that any of them have actually ever broken a nail in their lives. Unless it was to scratch someone else's eyes out.'

'Oh bloody hell,' I said, breathing in deeply. 'Any way I can get out of this?'

'Not now Bob's involved,' Mary said, standing up again. 'Look, I don't want to be too cynical, this could be great for you. Just keep your eyes open, OK? And you might want to get a haircut before your meeting.'

Well, I thought, pinching the ends of my bob, checking the split ends and sighing, at least Paris will be fun.

CHAPTER THREE

Three hours later, after a hastily arranged trim and several buckets of iced tea, I'd found the last shred of shade in Central Park and was halfway through my *Rough Guide* to Paris, with the *Lonely Planet* and *Wallpaper* guides well thumbed beside me. I scribbled down address after address in my notebook, but somehow my mind kept flitting back to an image of me and Alex skipping along the banks of the Seine, him in a black polo neck, holding a cigarette, and me in a very fetching stripy sweater dress and beret. Sometimes I was clutching a baguette. Sometimes I relocated us to the top of the Eiffel Tower. It was all very Tom and Katie. Except less creepy.

An irritating beeping snapped me out of my fantasy. I looked around, but for some reason, everyone was staring at me. It took me a couple of moments to realize that it was my phone ringing and a couple more red-faced seconds to find it in the bottom of my bag.

'Hello?' I answered, eventually.

'Is that Angela Clark? This is Esme from *Belle* magazine. You have an appointment with Donna Gregory tomorrow at nine. Please be in the *Belle* reception at eight forty-five a.m.'

'Uh, OK?' Esme from *Belle* magazine was all business. 'Will Emilia be in the meeting?'

'Sorry?' Esme from *Belle* magazine sounded confused.

'Emilia. Bob, Mr Spencer, said she was keen to meet me,' I explained, feeling a little bit like an idiot.

'Oh. No.' Esme from *Belle* magazine confirmed I was in fact, an idiot. 'Do you need directions to the offices?'

'No, I actually work on *The Look* so—'

'Oh, cute. Then we'll see you at eight forty-five,' Esme from *Belle* magazine confirmed. And hung up.

I lay back on the grass and stared up at the sunshine. This was going to take some thinking about. Writing my blog was great, but writing for *Belle*? It could just be incredible . . . Everyone read *Belle*, it was global, it was massive. And surely Mary was just throwing a hissy fit because she was pissed off that Bob had gone over her head. It made sense, she didn't like having her writers poached for bigger publications. She was the online editor at TheLook.com. With *Belle*, we were talking the printed pages of the world's biggest fashion monthly. There was way too much at stake here for me to worry about offending Mary's ego, that wasn't going to get me anywhere fast. She had offered me the moon on a stick when I'd pulled off the James Jacobs interview and so far I'd seen an awful lot of the stick and not very much else. Where was my monthly column in The Look? Still 'under discussion.' This was an opportunity that I would not cock up.

My phone was still hot in my hand from my brief chat with Esme when I felt it vibrate into life again.

Did u get ur hair cut yet? It looked like shit last week xoxo

Of course it was Jenny. I checked my watch for the time difference between LA and New York, five p.m. here, two there. Knowing her, she'd probably just woken up. My best friend and first New York roommate, Jenny Lopez, had been out in LA for the last five months, and from the look of the constant stream of photographs she sent over, she was having a fairly good time. If you considered partying with pop stars, hanging out with celebutantes and twenty-four-seven shopping with someone else's credit card for 'work' having a good time. Which I was fairly certain she did. And while it was much easier to get my work done without Hurricane Jenny in the apartment, I missed her horribly. Even with the continuous flow of text messages, emails, phone calls and, ever since she'd bought her new laptop a month ago, video calls, New York sometimes felt empty without her. And America's Next Top Model marathons just weren't the same without her screaming 'Smize, bitch!' at the top of her voice. It was good to know I could always trust her to be worried about the big issues at all times. Rolling over on to my stomach, I quickly tapped out a reply.

YES. Guess what? Going to Paris with Alex next week!

I checked to make sure my skirt was still covering my knickers while I waited for her reply. Maintaining your modesty was never easy when your skirt only just covers your pants in the first place.

GOOD. And Paris? 4real? Yay-we're-movin-in-together trip?

I paused to tie up my newly chopped hair. The loss of my split ends was great, but it was just too hot to have my long bob flopping around the back of my neck.

Just a trip. Talk later x

Having managed to get myself into a relatively uncomfortable, relatively non-knicker flashing position that was, for the time being at least, out of the sun, I flipped through my phone book, looking for someone else to talk to so I didn't have to move.

Hey Lou, you still up? A x

Before I could send another message, my phone started to buzz again and Louisa's name flashed up on the screen.

'Hey!' I answered happily. 'How are you? What are you up to?'

'Hello you,' Louisa replied over a crackly line. 'I was just online. I'm trying to book a caterer for our wedding anniversary.'

Louisa had been my best friend for ever, but I hadn't actually laid eyes on her since I'd accidentally ruined her wedding reception. It wasn't like I'd meant to break her new husband's hand, but I was a little bit upset having just found my fiancé shagging some tart in the back of our Range Rover. Of course I'd upped sticks and run away to New York the very next day. Who wouldn't?

'Oh my God, it's been a year already?' I couldn't quite believe it. So much had happened. 'It's gone so quickly.'

'It's been a year,' Louisa said. 'Think you're ready for a repeat performance?'

'Maybe not just yet. You're having a party?'

'Er, yes. Tim thought,' she sounded as though she was picking her words very carefully, 'it might be nice to have a bit of a do what with last year's . . . fireworks.'

'Right,' I pressed my lips together in a tight, thin line. 'Well, you can tell him not to worry about me. I'll actually be in Paris.'

'You're going to Paris?' Lou squealed. 'But that's so close by! You have to come to the party.'

I held my phone away from my ear. 'Oh, I'd love to,' I was lying a lot today. 'But Alex is playing at a festival and I'm reviewing it for *Belle*, so I just wouldn't be able to get away.'

'Really? *Belle*? Wow!' Louisa made a small mewing noise that I chose to ignore. 'But you can't be so close by and not come and visit. What did your mum say?'

'My mum hasn't said anything because I haven't told her yet,' I said quickly. 'And I'm not convinced I'm going to so please don't say anything if you see her.'

'Oh, Angela,' I could feel a lecture coming, 'I know your mum can be hard work, but she does miss you.'

'Playing the mum card is the wrong way to guilt trip me into coming home. You of all people should know that,' I warned. 'Besides, since she and dad took that internet course I can't bloody get rid of them. Did you know they have Skype?'

'I had heard,' Louisa said. 'She's always on about it to my mum in the supermarket. So Alex is playing a festival? I can't believe you're going out with a rock star. Is it amazing? Has he written any songs about you?'

'He's not a rock star,' I gave my official line. 'He's just Alex.'

I felt myself flush from head to toe. It wasn't entirely true. I absolutely loved that Alex was in a band. I loved

26

that I got to watch him get all sweaty onstage, singing songs he'd written for me. I loved to see a room full of chin-stroking hipsters and doe-eyed girls with ironic tattoos in vintage dresses staring at him while he did something he loved, something he was amazing at. But really, day in and day out, it wasn't about him being a rock god. It was about him buying tea bags for his apartment without me asking, even though he hated tea, the way he always Tivo'd *Gossip Girl* for me, even the repeats, and how, when he was writing a new song, he would sit cross-legged on the living-room floor with his acoustic guitar, fringe flopping into his eyes, tongue stuck out of the corner of his mouth, always with a Diet Dr Pepper. Everyday life really wasn't rock and roll, but it was sort of wonderful.

'Yeah, right,' Louisa said, entirely disbelievingly. 'You love it.'

'Well, maybe.' No point even trying to lie to Lou. 'He's actually asked me to move in with him.'

'Wow, really? Already?'

'It's not that soon, I've known him for a year,' I said, surprised to find someone who wasn't jumping up and down with joy while simultaneously packing my bags for me.

'But it hasn't exactly been smooth sailing, has it, honey?' Louisa said diplomatically. 'I just don't want you to rush into anything. You're not lonely out there, are you? You know you can always come back. Any time. Just say the word and I will have your room ready.'

'Louisa, calm down, everything is fine.' Bless her heart. 'I'm fine and I'm not rushing. Honest. I haven't even decided if I'm going to move in yet.'

'I just worry about you, that's all,' Lou replied. 'Anyway, if you can't come to me, how about I come to you? Will you have an afternoon free for lunch or something? Are you there on the Saturday?'

'That actually sounds brilliant,' I said, suddenly excited at the idea of seeing Louisa, not in a wedding/wedding reception/wedding anniversary/anything to do with weddings situation. 'I would love that.'

'Fantastic!' Louisa squealed again. 'Let's be really cheesy and meet under the Eiffel Tower or something.'

'Yeah, OK.' I smiled. That was just the sort of thing Jenny would want to do. God forbid the two of them should ever be in the same place at the same time. The universe might implode or something. 'I actually cannot believe it's been a year.'

'I know,' Louisa said. 'I think the longest I'd gone without seeing you before you abandoned me was something like four days.'

'Surely not more than three,' I was surprised at how upset I was all of a sudden. I really hadn't been that homesick since I got to New York. When had I had time? 'I'll text you when I get to Paris. Love you, Lou.'

'You too honey. Can't wait to see you and maybe you could bring this non-rock star of yours for my approval?'

I pursed my lips. 'Yeah, if he's not rehearsing or something, then yeah, definitely.' Was it weird that I felt a bit queasy at the idea of mixing my two lives up like that? 'Talk to you later.'

I hung up and smiled. It would be amazing to see Louisa. It would be amazing to go to Paris. It would be amazing to write for *Belle*. It would be amazing to take a trip with Alex. Really, this wasn't turning out to be the worst Wednesday in the world ever.

After another hour of lounging in the park, the sun finally worked its way around to my safe little spot and forced me to drag myself home. Vanessa, my temporary roommate, was at work at The Union and so the apartment was eerily quiet and ridiculously hot. I bashed the air-conditioning unit sticking out of the living-room window and grabbed a Popsicle out of the freezer before sitting down at my laptop. What would the *Adventures of Angela* reveal today? I logged into TheLook.com, clicking through the links until I got to my blog.

When I started writing, almost a year ago, I'd found it so hard to put my thoughts well, not exactly down on paper, but it was tricky to write about what was going on in my life and then post it online for all the world to see. But now I found it so cathartic. Writing the blog really helped me clear my head and make sense of things. I'd learned what was safe to put up there and what wasn't, how to share what was going on without spilling anyone's secrets, and for the most part, I only got nice comments and emails, at least no one had ever chased me down the street with flaming torches and pitchforks. And apparently, my mother had got bored of reading it some time ago. Thank God. I started tapping away into the empty white box.

The Adventures of Angela: Ooh la la

Today has been one of those days when everything happened at once. My boyfriend asked me to go to Paris with him next week, I had a really important work meeting which has led to a really, really exciting new project, I arranged to meet up with my best friend from London, oh, and I got my hair cut. It's been a big day.

But aside from the massively dramatic event that was taking half an inch off the ends of my

*bob, how exciting is Paris? I know I'm a bit rubbish
for not having gone before, especially when I lived
in London for five years, but yay, I'm going now!
And sigh, with my boy. And that's the only way
to do Paris isn't it? It'll be all romantic walks down
the Left Bank, holding hands outside Notre-Dame,
watching the sunset from the top of the Eiffel
Tower. I am a little bit concerned about the
wardrobe though – my experience of Paris is more
or less limited to* Funny Face, *Gentlemen Prefer
Blondes and the last third of* The Devil Wears
Prada. *So it's either black turtlenecks and pedal-
pushers or haute couture. Hmm. And bugger.*

*So, while I try to resolve my sartorial crisis,
please let me know if you have any Parisian advice
– I want to know exactly where to sip my* chocolat
chaud *and bag the best* baguettes. *And obviously,
any shopping suggestions are more than welcome.
My heart says Chanel, but my head and credit
limit says flea market. Why don't you send both
and I'll work it out once I get there . . .*

Before I could really start thinking about actually
getting to Paris, I had to get through my meeting at
Belle. Maybe it would be a good idea to write out a
proposal for this Insider's Guide. Maybe it would be
a good idea to find some Parisian insiders. Maybe it
would be a good idea to spend three hours hunched
over my laptop, scouring the internet. I checked in at
all the usual places, *Time Out* Paris, Gridskipper,
Citysearch, and started to pull together my synopsis.
Several hours later, I had, well, something. For want
of further inspiration, I swapped my crumpled sundress
for a stripy Splendid vest and Hello Kitty knickers. It
was just too hot to wear anything else. I took an icy

can of Diet Coke from the fridge and draped myself across the sofa, rummaging around for the remote. Maybe just fifteen minutes of *E!* and then I'd do some more research. Or half an hour. And then an episode of *America's Next Top Model*. Two hours later, looking back guiltily at the sleeping screen of my laptop, I tried to convince myself that there was in fact such a thing as too much preparation. And turned back to the TV. It really is amazing what I can talk myself into.

The next morning, it wasn't quite as easy to believe that being over prepared was a mistake. Determined not to fall into my regular trap of waking up late and scrawling at my face with a kohl pencil, I woke up bright and early, washed my hair, did proper grown-up girl make-up and selected my most *Belle* appropriate ensemble, a simple vintage sky blue shift Jenny had guided me towards at a vintage store in Williamsburg. I figured that even the biggest fashion bitches would struggle to find fault with it. It couldn't be the wrong designer because it wasn't designer in the first place. Anyway I wasn't worried about what these girls thought of my dress sense. It didn't matter. I wasn't going to pitch an article on the hottest trends coming from the catwalks of Milan, was I? Besides, I thought, slipping my synopsis into my bestest swankiest bright blue Marc Jacobs handbag (OK, so I was a little bit worried), I'd seen *Ugly Betty*, I'd seen *and* read *The Devil Wears Prada*, there was no way these girls would actually be like that. Yes, Mary had been fairly snippy about them, but then I'd never seen Mary out of jeans and Converse. She probably just didn't like the fashiony types. It would be absolutely fine. And I had Bob's backing. My good friend Bob. Bobbity bob bob. Oh shit, I'd gone mad.

With one last look in the mirror, I smoothed down my hair and wiped away the tiniest smudge of mascara.

I could do this. I'd been writing for *The Look* for a year. I had my column in the UK magazine. I'd interviewed a movie star for God's sake. All they wanted was a tourist guide to Paris. A city that hardly anyone who was going to read this magazine would ever visit. This was going to be brilliant. Easy even.

'What this isn't going to be is easy,' Donna Gregory barked at me, my synopsis crumpled up in her hand. '*Belle* readers have no interest in some tragically obvious tourist piece about visiting the Eiffel Tower and taking a boat down the Seine. Our readers want to know the most exclusive, most stylish, secret sides of Paris. Not where to get the best *crêpes* according to Gridskipper or *Time Out*'s top ten scenic parks.'

I flinched in my chair. As far as I could tell, during the ten minutes I'd been in the office, Donna hadn't even looked at my synopsis and yet she was still managing, quite adequately, to pull it apart, word by word.

'Why do you think you should be writing for *Belle*, Angela?' she asked.

'Well, I—'

'I mean, seriously, what makes you think that you –' she paused to hold her hand out towards me and then wave the hand up and down to make sure I understood her critique encompassed every last little thing about me. '– that *you* should be allowed to write for *Belle*?'

Silence. Allowed? Why should I be allowed?

'I'm waiting for an answer,' Donna said.

I was stumped.

Donna wasn't very nice.

'Well, I might not have written a specific travel piece before, but I write about a lot of different things in my blog and I interviewed James Jacobs for *Icon* earlier this year so I think that I could do this,' I said. Very quickly. All of my confidence had vamoosed and all I wanted to do was get out of the office, bury my face in a pan of chocolate brownies and cry, like the porky talentless excuse for a human being Donna so clearly thought I was.

It was fair to say that Donna Gregory wasn't the glamazon dragon lady you might expect to find sitting behind the features editor desk of a fashion monthly. She wasn't that tall for a start, her glossy (OK, very glossy) brown hair was pulled back in a ponytail and she was actually wearing jeans. Very skinny and presumably expensive jeans, but jeans nonetheless. But while she might not be wearing Prada, she was certainly proving herself to be the devil. From the second I'd walked through her door, she'd more or less done nothing, but insult me.

First, I wasn't allowed coffee because I looked like I needed a good night's sleep and the caffeine wouldn't help, then I was refused water in case I needed to use the bathroom, which was for staff only. The implication being that I was not now and would never be staff. But she did suggest I try drinking at least two litres a day outside of her office because I really did look a lot older than thirty. When I mentioned that I was only twenty-seven she actually made a little gasping noise and held her hand to her mouth.

Bitch.

'Hmm, I heard about the *Icon* piece,' she said, flicking through some printed out emails. 'You're the girl that turned James Jacobs gay, yes?'

'For fu— I mean, no, not exactly.' I wasn't quite sure why I was still sitting in the office. There was no way I was going to get this job. 'I'm pretty sure he was gay before I walked in on him and his boyfriend going at it in a public toilet. But I suppose you never know. It's possible that my extreme level of dehydration turned him.'

Donna paused for a split second and looked at me again.

'That dress, I don't recognize the designer. Where's it from?' she asked.

'I got it from Beacon's Closet, it's vintage,' I said with a modicum of pride. Vintage was cool, wasn't it?

'Right.' She sighed and leaned back in her chair, stretching up to let her tiny cropped Alexander Wang T-shirt reveal a couple of inches of taut, gym-toned stomach. And I knew it was Alexander Wang because she had gone out of her way to tell me almost as soon as I walked in the door. 'Of course it's vintage. And your boyfriend's in some band?'

'Alex? Yes?' I was confused. Which, to be fair to the witch, was pretty easily done. I didn't want her taking any sort of pleasure in that achievement. 'But I don't really see what that has to do with a travel piece?'

'It has everything to do with it, Angela,' Donna said, leaning towards me across her desk. 'I'm going to try and be as kind as I can when I explain this to you, but whatever, there's no point trying to sugarcoat it. You're really not the sort of person I would have write for Belle.'

'Really?'

This was just getting embarrassing now. How badly did I want this again? Oh yeah, really badly.

'Really.' Donna nodded, missing my sarcasm. 'But Mr Spencer is very keen for us to use you for something. And don't get me wrong, it's not that people who wear vintage don't have a place at Belle, it's just . . . it wouldn't usually be writing for me. One girl in the art team once wore this amazing Diane von Furstenburg original. To a fancy dress party. That's a beautiful bag though.'

'Thank you, it was a gift.' I lovingly stroked the soft blue leather on instinct, momentarily forgetting the torrent of insults that were coming my way.

'Of course it was.' Donna sounded almost relieved. As if the idea of my buying my own Marc Jacobs bag might cause the end of the world. 'Basically, the only way I can see this working is if we position this as a two part piece. I'll have someone else put together a high end Paris piece, a feature on the haute couture, the *salons*, the five-star hotels, and you, the quirky "vintage" girl with the boyfriend in a band, can provide the other side of things. The, oh, I don't know, the cool, hipster side of Paris?'

'Oh God, honestly, I'm not cool,' I said altogether too quickly. 'I don't have any tattoos. I don't even live in Brooklyn. I'm just very, very English.'

'Oh. Well that could be a problem then.' Donna leaned back in her chair. 'Because either you give me Paris's best flea markets, vintage stores, late-night cafés and dance clubs, or you don't give me anything.'

Meep.

After sitting through another hour of Donna's directions on exactly how she wanted the piece to come out – quirky, but not too quirky, edgy, but not too edgy, underground, but not grimy. Just very, very *Belle* – I was finally released from the office, none the wiser, but actually relatively chipper. I might not have received any compliments, but I had got the job. That was good, wasn't it?

There was only one person I could talk to about this. And that person better not be screening her calls.

'Pick up the phone, Jenny,' I said quietly, dashing into the shade of the nearest skyscraper and following it along 42nd street.

'Angie, baby, it's seven-thirty a.m.,' Jenny crackled all the way from LA. 'Are you dying?'

'No, listen, I just had this meeting at *Belle*—' I started.

'You're not dying, I only got in two hours ago, I'll call you back later,' Jenny interrupted.

'No! Jenny, listen, I have the most amazing news. Did you hear what I said? I've got a job writing for *Belle* magazine.' I hoped that dropping the name of one of her style bibles might keep her on the phone for five minutes more. '*Belle*. Your favourite magazine. B-E-L-L-E.'

'No offense, Angie,' Jenny yawned into life, 'but what are you going to write for *Belle*?'

'None taken.' I pouted. What about me was so fundamentally un-*Belle*-like? I had sorted myself out massively in the last year. Well, Jenny had sorted me out massively, but I could do my own eyeliner and everything now. I could do an entire evening out in proper heels if I had my roll-up ballet pumps in my bag. 'They want me to write an insider's guide to Paris. They're going to get some other girl to write the swanky high-end stuff, she's going to do, who did Donna say, uh, Balmain? Is that right? And you know, Chanel and whatever, and I'm supposed to write about the cool, underground stuff. But I could really use your help, I want this to be good. Do you know any stylists in Paris? Anyone who might know some cool second-hand shops or flea markets?'

'Balmain? Oh . . .' she breathed.

'Jenny, listen to me,' I said slowly. I should have known better than to start talking designer at her. 'Do you know anyone who can help me in Paris?'

'Oh honey, you know I think you've come a real long way,' Jenny snapped back, 'but you are so not ready to write a fashion piece, a fashion piece about *Paris* for *Belle* magazine.'

At least I had her attention.

'Firstly, thanks for your confidence and secondly, it's not a fashion piece, it's a travel piece,' I said. 'I've just got to write about a few vintage stores, a couple of cafés and then cover Alex's gig. It's going to be fine. I thought you'd be excited for me?'

'But it's *Belle*, Angie. And I don't want you to look stupid,' Jenny insisted. ''Cause, you know honey, some people know you know me.'

'Really, your belief in me is incredibly reassuring and I promise not to show you up in any way. Especially if you answer my bloody questions and tell me if you know any stylists in Paris.'

'Is *Belle* going to style you? Have they given you a list of places to go?' She carried on ignoring me. 'Are there going to be photos of you in the feature?'

'No they're not styling me, no they haven't given me a list of places to go – that's my job – and no of course they're not going to let me be in the bloody photos.'

'I guess that's a good thing at least.' Jenny sighed, audibly relieved. Cow. 'OK, I have an idea. I'm gonna pull some pieces together for you, OK? When are you leaving?'

This was the first part of the phone call I did not hate. Jenny being a million miles away in LA was completely shitty. Jenny being a stylist with access to lots and lots of beautiful free clothes was not shitty in the slightest. 'Monday, but really, don't go to too much trouble, you don't have to do this.' Yes she bloody well did.

'Honey, I got you covered. Skinny jeans, slept-in

eyeliner, beret, I'm all over it. I'll just take it up a notch. You'll be like, a *Belle*-hipster. A Bipster.' Her laugh turned into a yawn. 'Seriously, I'm freaking dying here. Email me the details, what you're doing when you get there and I'll send some stuff over. And I'm sure I must know someone in Paris. I'm on it.'

'Really?'

'Really. Angie, it's like, totally what I do. Now let me go back to sleep.'

'Like, totally go back to sleep.' I laughed. 'You've gone totally LA on me, Lopez.'

'Like, rilly. Screw you, Clark.' She yawned again. 'Go buy *Belle*, let the intimidation build a little more. Love you.'

'Love you too.'

Or at least, I'd thought that I loved Jenny until the three giant DHL packages arrived the next morning. It turned out, I really hadn't known what love was. Love was one box labelled 'evening', one box labelled 'day' and one box labelled 'I don't know when the fuck you'll wear these, but they're awesome'. I hacked into them desperately, using my keys to slit the package tape and carefully pull out one beautiful outfit after another. In each box was a manila envelope with handwritten (well, scribbled) notes along with gorgeous sketches of how each ensemble was supposed to go together. The Joe Jeans with the Tory Burch flats and Elizabeth and James blazer. The DVF royal blue silk romper with the YSL wedges. The beaded Balenciaga flapper dress with the Giuseppe Zanotti platforms. The Miu Miu purse with everything. After an hour and a half of playing dress up, I perched on the edge of the sofa in a pale blue silk Lanvin number, flustered, red-faced and grinning maniacally. At the very bottom of the 'Fuck Knows' box, under the Kenneth Jay Lane pendants and bangles, was a note from Jenny.

I know you said not to go to too much trouble, but you're going to Paris. For *Belle*. And people know you know me so there's no way I'm letting you head over to the fashion capital of the world, head-to-toe in American Apparel – don't tell me you weren't wearing it when you opened the box, even if you're in the Narciso Rodriguez jumpsuit by now—

I paused to look at all the outfits on the sofa, there was a jumpsuit? Had I missed it?

—because it's awesome. You're going to be amazing at this, Angie, I'm so proud of you. Just take the clothes, wear them, rock them, take photos and BRING THEM BACK, preferably in one piece and without ketchup all over them.
Love you, JLo xxx

It was only eight in LA, four hours before I was legally permitted to call Jenny without it going on her 'you're dead to me' list. Three strikes and you were out and I already had one from the time she caught me ironing the collar of a Thomas Pink shirt I had borrowed from her with my hair straighteners. Apparently, she had never done it. I did not believe her. What I did believe was that the collection of clothes, currently acting as a very expensive throw on my sofa, was a) amazing b) worth more than my apartment and c) going to make me the best dressed bargain hunter in all of Paris.

I tapped out a text to let her know that the package had arrived and that I would love and cherish the clothes as though they were my first-born child. Which I would be more than happy to trade to keep this stuff for ever. Clutching a pair of pale blue Stella McCartney wide-legged trousers to my heart, I stared at the assembled selection of swag. Truly, it was one of the most beautiful sights I had ever had the honour to behold. How was Paris supposed to compare?

CHAPTER FOUR

While the actual being-on-an-aeroplane part of flying had never been a problem for me, I really, really hated airports. The thrill of Duty Free wore off in approximately fourteen minutes when I remembered I was broke and the fact that I was left alone, slumped in an uncomfortable metal chair scarfing a soggy McDonalds while Alex was already up, up and away, didn't make me feel any better. Cici swore she had tried to book us on to the same flight, but his was already full. Even though his manager booked his flights on the exact same day she tried to book mine.

So instead of joining the mile high club with my boyfriend, I had a nine-hour flight sandwiched in between complete strangers to look forward to. Ramming a fistful of chips down my throat, I checked my (newly reinstated) Spencer Media-sponsored BlackBerry again only to see another message from Esme. Joy. I'd managed to avoid any further face time with the delightful people at *Belle* magazine, but there was nowhere to hide from Donna and Esme's terse, borderline bullying emails. And brilliant, here was another.

Angela.

French *Belle* magazine are sending an assistant to keep you on brief. Be in your hotel lobby to meet Virginie at ten-thirty.

Esme.

Oh dear God, no. They were 'sending me' a super cool, super hot French fashionista to make me feel inadequate. Mary had been right, the girls at *Belle* were really not happy at all with my being foisted on them by Bob, but I was determined to prove myself. I was a real journo girl with a real talent and I deserved this opportunity. My boyfriend said so.

And it wasn't as if everyone at Spencer Media was against me. Since everything about my assignment was a little bit last-minute, Cici had magnanimously stepped in and offered to help sort out my travel details. Even when she couldn't get me on Alex's flight, she did say she would ask a friend that worked for my airline to try and get me upgraded and she had couriered over a package with my BlackBerry, a corporate credit card, a map of Paris and even a DVD of *Funny Face*. And if that weren't scary enough, she had signed off the accompanying note 'xoxo Cici'. Either she had undergone some sort of complete personality transplant or Grandpa Bob had some serious influence on that girl.

Obviously, Grandpa Bob had some serious influence everywhere at Spencer. I'd had email after email from Donna Gregory checking on my research progress, reminding me time and time again what it was that she did not want from this piece. But next to no detail on what she did want. Not so helpful. I'd spent all week researching, but really, I couldn't wait to get to Paris, to really get stuck in. I couldn't help but feel that this was my big break. I mean, I'd thought the blog was my big break and I suppose it kind of was, it had got me the James Jacobs interview. And then I'd thought that the James Jacobs interview would be my big break, but that turned out to be a traumatic, potentially life-ruining pain in my arse instead. Although it had sort of lead to this. A piece for *Belle*. And a new Marc Jacobs handbag, so I suppose it hadn't been all bad. But this was definitely it. I could feel it in my waters. Whatever that meant. Actually, that was a bit gross, wasn't it? Hmm.

I waited impatiently to be called to board, flicking through the pages of the newest issue of *Icon* for the millionth time, wishing I'd left my Paris guidebooks and notes in my hand luggage so I could work on them on the plane. There was no way I'd be able to sleep on the flight, I was full of butterflies. Nervous about the article, nervous about not being able to speak French, nervous about getting to the hotel on my own and, for some reason, nervous about spending almost a straight week in another country with Alex. Good nervous, I was pretty sure, but still definitely nervous. Not as nervous as Alex however, who had spent the previous three days becoming increasingly uncommunicative and turning an attractive shade of pale green. He had explained that he didn't like flying at least twenty times and no matter how many times Graham and Craig, the bassist and drummer in his band, Stills, slapped him on the back and offered to get him shitfaced before they boarded, he never seemed to look any better.

I looked around for any telltale patches of puke at the boarding gate to show he'd been there, but it was clean as a whistle. But then, JFK airport probably sorted that kind of thing out fairly quickly. The Americans were pretty up on cleanliness.

It was really quite cute. Even when I was climbing

the walls about something, Alex was always so laid-back, and to see him panicking about the flight was sort of reassuring. So he *was* human after all. Even when I'd tried to reassure him with my 'more people die in hippo attacks than in plane crashes each year' favourite factoid of all time (not that I actually knew it was definitely a fact), he had just kissed the top of my head and gone back to pretending he wasn't flying anyway.

Eventually, the flight was called and I hauled myself and my wildly overpacked and battered MJ handbag over to the gate. I'd packed my beautiful blue number and decided to carry on my trusty old (well, I'd had it almost a year) satchel for fear of the new bag being scratched or stained or touched by human hands other than my own. And besides, I'd more or less convinced myself that the knackered satchel actually looked better for being worn in. Kind of. Shuttling down the windy tunnel on to the plane, a reassuringly bored-looking flight attendant took my tickets, checked my passport and then pointed down the right-hand side of the plane with a Joker-sized smile. I returned a tight grimace and shuffled down the aisle, trying not to wedge my bottom in the faces of all the club class passengers already boarded. One day they'd tell me to turn left, one day.

Predictably, I'd been blessed with a teeny, tiny economy seat in the middle of a row of four and all three surrounding seats were taken. According to an overly sincere Cici, it was Spencer Media travel policy to fly economy on all flights under twelve hours, but for some reason, I just didn't believe her. And besides, there was economy and there was the nine hours of living hell I was about to endure. Wedging my handbag under the seat in front of me, I glanced to my left to take in the extraordinarily large man currently crossing himself with closed eyes, a very large Bible in his lap. To my right, love's young dream sat giggling and holding hands. Catching my eye, a (not actually so young) blonde woman thrust her left hand under my nose.

'We just got married!' she shrieked, waving her hand around to give the ginormous solitaire sufficient opportunity to blind me. 'In New York! Married! We're from England. But we got married in New York. Not Vegas. Tacky, that is.'

'Right,' I stuttered, trying to pull my head away from the hard, shiny thing that could potentially blind me. 'Congratulations?'

'Oh you're English too! Dave, she's English,' my seat buddy went on, oblivious. 'It was just at City Hall, quiet, but very classy, you know? And we stayed at the Waldorf Astoria. We haven't told anyone at home. I mean, they knew we were engaged, but they didn't know we were getting married. Dave's been married before you see, so we didn't think we needed to make a big deal of it.'

'I've been married before,' Dave confirmed, leaning across to show me his massive, diamond encrusted wedding band. Mmm, tasteful. 'She was a right old cow. Not like this one.'

'Well, yeah, congratulations,' I said again, fiddling with my seatbelt as a polite 'leave me alone' signal, while seats 47 F and G began a rather aggressive PDA session.

'It was lovely,' Dave's wife said, pushing her amorous husband away. 'I got them Loobootin shoes, didn't I, Dave? Lovely.'

'She did,' Dave nodded. 'Loobootins.'

I managed a wan smile and tried not to start crying. How long was this flight again? Jenny would have actually slapped her around the face by now, my tolerance levels were most impressive.

'And now we're going to Paris for the honeymoon. Nice that, isn't it? He's a romantic, my Dave. Always said I'd marry a romantic. You married, love?'

'No,' I smiled, shaking my head. 'Not married.'

'Engaged?'

'Nope.'

'Boyfriend?'

'Actually, yes.'

'Well there you are,' she said, patting my knee. 'There's hope for you yet.'

I smiled brightly and speedily plugged my ears with my earbuds before she could start up again. Only to have the flight attendant tell me that I couldn't keep them in for take-off. Cow. Happily, Dave's wife wasn't a terribly good flier and had to bury her face in Dave's reassuring chest throughout take off and for a good fifteen minutes after, by which time, I'd got the earbuds in and was pretending to sleep. Not an easy task when the man to the other side of me was a) incredibly sweaty and b) reading out Bible passages under his breath, just loudly enough to convince me he might be a serial killer. Fantastic.

I squinted to see the screen on my iPod, trying not to open my eyes enough to be busted and I scrolled down to the play lists. Alex had promised to upload something 'other than Justin Timberlake and Gossip Girl' to put me in the mood for Paris. I smiled and clicked on 'Adventures of Angela: Paris Edition' and tried not to look incredibly smug that I had a wonderful boyfriend who had made me a mixtape – the internationally accepted Token of True Love from a Boy. I settled back in my seat for some *musique en français*, but instead was jolted wide awake by the sound of Alex's voice.

'Hey Angela, so I put some songs together to help you get through the flight although, I guess it's me that needs the help, right? Uh, anyway, I really wish we were flying out together, but I'll see you when you get to the hotel and I promise it's going to be a great trip. And yeah, this is a new song I've been working on . . .'

His quiet, smoky voice trailed off into a quick cough before his guitar took over. I closed my eyes quickly, not wanting to give The Second Missus Dave an opportunity to spoil this moment. Not that she could. I felt a hot flush in my cheeks while my stomach dropped and my heart pounded. It felt like falling off the kerb in my sleep, only in a good way. It felt the same as opening my eyes in the morning and seeing Alex's face. The same as getting off the subway and spotting him waiting for me. The same as I felt whenever I thought about him being within a three-foot radius of me. Honestly, what was my problem? He was amazing. And he wasn't my ex. My ex wouldn't have even asked me to come to Paris with him in the first place, probably because he'd have wanted to bring his mistress, but still.

Of course I should move in with Alex.

I felt as if someone had just slapped me around the face with the Great Big Stick of Obvious Revelations. Of course I should live with him, I loved him. Excitement bubbled up inside me, we were going to live together! And I could tell him on his birthday. Which would really help if he didn't like the watch I'd got him . . .

The rest of the flight passed relatively uneventfully, me struggling through fits and starts of sleep, the happy couple pawing each other throughout and only very occasionally grabbing my thigh accidentally (I hoped?), and my religious friend making it happily through a good couple of books of the Old Testament before the attendants came around with breakfast. Yawning widely and stretching as best I could, I shuffled from side to side and scraped my frizzy hair back from my face. Post long-haul was so not a good look for me. Across the aisle and past several people's heads, I could see land below us. I scarfed the World's Heaviest Danish Pastry as quickly as humanly possible, then slathered on a gob of Beauty Flash Balm and sat back, suddenly desperate to be on the ground.

'Oh, you're awake then, sleepyhead!'

Brilliant.

'I thought we were going to have to leave you on the plane,' Missus Dave said, giving me a jovial and yet oddly strong punch in the shoulder. 'So, are you meeting this boyfriend of yours in Paris?'

'Oh, um, yes,' I said, trying to apply mascara without poking myself in the eye. Give me some slack, I'd only just learned how to do this on the ground let alone in midair descent.

'Ahh, that's nice,' she said, fastening her seatbelt and settling back with Dave's arm safely around her. 'Who knows, maybe he'll propose.'

It really was an instinctive reaction. I really didn't mean to shoot my mascara-wand-wielding arm into the face of my Bible-toting seat buddy. And I really didn't mean to make him throw a scorching cup of coffee down his trousers.

'Holy Mary Mother of God!'

Oops. And I'd done so well not to offend or maim anyone for so long. I'd seen enough episodes of *Friends* to know that pawing at his crotch with napkins wouldn't help, so instead I muttered my apologies, leaned back into my seat and closed my eyes. If that was the worst thing that happened and I'd got all the way to Paris, I would be very happy.

*   *   *

'What do you mean my bag had to be "destroyed"?'

I stood in the baggage reclaim section of Charles de Gaulle airport, listening to an incredibly bored-looking official type person repeat himself for the fourth time.

'*Madame* Clark, as I explained,' he sighed, 'your suitcase failed our safety screening and was destroyed. This should have been told to you at JFK. In fact, you should not have been able to travel.'

'When you say destroyed,' I rubbed my temples and blinked a few times waiting to wake up, 'and you know, it's *Mademoiselle.*'

'*Pardon, Mademoiselle.* Destroyed. It is gone.'

I rifled around in my battered handbag, checking just what I had with me. Sunglasses, lip balm, two lipsticks, phone, camera, wallet, passport, laptop, *US Weekly*. Well, at least I wouldn't be stuck for some educational reading material. Thank God.

'But why?' I heard my voice start to crack. Apparently, I was starting to grasp the reality of what had happened. 'Why would it be, oh God, why would it be destroyed?'

'There are many reasons, *Madame*, security is very high right now. Possibly you have something forbidden in your suitcase? Something dangerous?'

'The most dangerous thing in there was a pair of shoes once involved in a case of GBH.' I pursed my lips together, determined not to cry. There had to be a mistake. 'Who can I talk to about this?'

'I am afraid it is me.' The officer sighed. Again. 'Perhaps there was something, ah, battery operated?'

'Battery operated?'

'Possibly vibrating?' he expanded discreetly.

'Vibrating? A vibrator?' I screeched. Wow, I could really be shrill when I wanted to. And given all the looks I was getting from every other passenger in the airport, vibrator was a word that translated globally. Brilliant.

'But when you say destroyed?'

'It has been securely detonated.'

'Securely . . .'

'Yes.'

'Blown up?'

'*Oui.*'

'I . . . what?' I suddenly felt very, very unsteady on my feet.

'I am sorry Ms Clark. I am able to let you pass through the airport as there is no security alert on you, but your baggage has been destroyed. That is all I can tell you. Would you like me to escort you to a taxi?'

'But really, how can it—' I tried once more as the officer took my arm and lead me out of the airport and towards the large double doors.

By the time I got in to the city I'd just about made it through to the third stage of grief. I had ploughed through disbelief by the time the airport official had physically tossed me into the back of a taxi and I powered straight on to anger halfway down the motorway. Once I'd finished swearing vengeance on the first-born children of every airport worker at JFK and Charles de Gaulle, I moved on to depression. My Louboutins. My beautiful blue Marc Jacobs satchel. All of my clothes. All of them. Oh God, all of the clothes Jenny had sent over. All blown to smithereens by a sweaty man in a short-sleeved shirt at the airport. Who probably had a moustache. They all had short-sleeved shirts and moustaches.

Somewhere inside my brain, a part of me tried to tell me about all the clothes shops and shoe stores and lingerie I would be able to buy on my research trips, but every time I closed my eyes, I just saw my dandelion yellow 3.1 Phillip Lim sundress flying up into the air and scattering into a million pieces while several French security guards stood around wearing berets and guffawing. Armoured berets. And the Lanvin. Dear God, the Lanvin. My fevered imagination preferred to imagine the case had been blown up in France.

According to the last text I'd received from Alex, he had to be at some place called Café Charbon by seven and told me to meet him there. It was way too late to get to the hotel first and besides, what exactly was I planning on changing into? This wasn't Project Catwalk, I wasn't going to be able to cobble together a Parisian evening look from the pages of *US Weekly* and a Lancôme Juicy Tube.

I attempted to explain where I wanted to go to the driver, but was eventually reduced to showing him Alex's text. He grunted and sped off down some tiny cobbled streets, lined with tiny tables and even tinier girls, all with extraordinarily long hair and pouty, miserable expressions. *Vive la France.*

Eventually the taxi pulled to a stop and the driver turned to stare at me. Even though I knew I couldn't be a pretty sight, I stared back. Had he just lost everything he'd ever owned that was shiny, pretty and beautiful? No. No he had not. As rudely as I could manage, I pulled out a fistful of Euros and handed them to him in what I hoped was a vaguely ignorant fashion. Although it probably ruined the effect when I awkwardly thanked him and told him to keep the change.

Attempting to compose myself before I saw Alex, I paused in front of a beautiful glass-fronted café and breathed deeply and slowly. Dozens of people stood outside smoking and laughing and all of them were beautiful. To be fair, I would have been overdressed in Jenny's Balmain sequined dress, but that didn't help me feel any less crappy than I did in my travelling clothes. Actually, my only clothes now. All of the girls were wearing blue jeans so tight, I was pretty certain that no matter how badly all the dark-eyed, dark-haired boys that were eyeing them up wanted to give them one, it would be physically impossible. How on earth did they get them on and off without specialized equipment? Standing around nodding and gesticulating with their cigarettes, I noticed that they all had perfectly dishevelled bedhead hairdos, as opposed to frizzy, flat plane hairdon'ts, and instead of mascara-stained cheeks and dark circles hastily covered up with too much Touche Eclat, every single girl looked as though she scoffed at make-up and was in fact, just a fresh-faced beauty. Bitches. And they had to rub in the fact that I wasn't allowed to drink red wine because I was incapable of drinking a single glass without spilling it all down myself. Or someone else in my immediate vicinity. Basically, there was no way I was going to be mistaken for being a French girl. Homeless French sixteen-year-old boy, maybe, but one of these sophisticated sex bombs? Not so much. Mew.

Eventually, I let out a huge sigh and pushed through the crowds and into the café. I spotted Alex almost immediately. Even in a sea of skinny, dark-haired boys stroking their chins and nodding, he was the first thing I saw. Unfortunately, the second thing I saw was an impossibly pretty blonde girl, sitting on his lap with her arms wrapped around his neck, laughing her arse off. And the third thing I saw was the inside of my eyelids because that's about when I passed out.

CHAPTER FIVE

'Jesus, Angela. Are you OK?'

'Yeah, go back to sleep,' I muttered, pushing away the familiar voice. I was so tired, couldn't he just let me lie in?

'Ahh, shit. Get me some water?' A hand brushed my hair off my forehead and, as I tried to roll over, I couldn't help but think the bed was very uncomfortable all of a sudden. And cold. And floor-like.

'Don't worry, she kind of makes a habit of this,' Alex said, helping me find my feet, then a chair and then a very large glass of water. 'At least she didn't throw up this time.'

'I'm not drunk,' I muttered into the glass, gulping down the water. 'I'm jet-lagged. And stressed.'

'Hi by the way.' Alex gave me a half-smile and brushed a chunk of frizzy hair behind my ear. *'Bienvenue à Paris.'*

I looked around, but the mystery blonde I vaguely recalled setting up shop in my boyfriend's lap had vanished. Had I imagined her?

'Muh?'

'Welcome to Paris.' His smile turned into a frown and

his green eyes peered closely into mine. 'Angela, are you OK? Do you need a doctor?'

'No.' I breathed in deeply. Really, no blonde anywhere. 'I'm fine, I just had the worst journey.'

'Bad turbulence?' An American voice across the table asked. Turning too quickly and getting a shooting pain through my temple for my efforts, I saw Graham and Craig, Alex's bandmates, waving from across the table.

'Great entrance.' Graham gave me a reassuring smile and pushed his glasses back up his nose. 'You could have just called if you couldn't see us.'

'I liked it,' Craig added. 'But uh, no offence Angie, but you might have changed? This is Paris, you know, not Brooklyn.'

'Thanks Craig.'

He wasn't nearly as polite as Graham, but then he wasn't nearly as gay either. I had almost, for one second, forgotten the fact that I'd been wearing the same clothes for almost twenty hours. And that I hadn't looked in a mirror for more or less the same amount of time. Although that one was through choice, not because all my belongings had been 'securely detonated'.

'You look great.' Alex gave Craig a filthy look on my behalf. 'But uh, you didn't have time to change? Not that you need to change. Cus you look great.'

Holding my head in my hands, I relayed the whole sorry story, pausing to let Craig laugh his arse off at appropriate points and finally ask if that meant I didn't have any underwear.

Graham shook his head. 'Angela, that's awful. But at least you'll get to replace your wardrobe in Paris, right? What a place to shop yourself blind.'

'Except my credit card is completely maxed from LA still.' I tried to smile.

'We'll sort something out, I'm so sorry you had to

deal with all this shit.' Alex put his arm around my shoulders and pulled my head down on to his shoulder. He smelled so good. Another reminder that I probably did not. 'Just relax now. You're here. In Paris. It's going to be awesome.'

'Yeah.' I closed my eyes and sighed. 'I guess. Although I do need to get some clothes. I have literally no clothes. But I honestly don't know when I'm going to have the time. I'm supposed to meet this assistant from French *Belle* tomorrow and I've lost all my notes and stuff.'

All of my notes, my camera, my laptop charger. All the research I'd carefully and painstakingly knocked off from other magazines and guidebooks, gone. Everything in my suitcase, gone. I could feel my second wind of grief coming on and there was nothing I could do to stop it. Tears prickled in my eyes as Alex stroked my arm and listened to Craig read out the menu. What was I going to do in Paris for almost a week without any of my clothes? Without my shoes? Without my hair straighteners? My stomach fell through the chair and hit the floor. And oh my God, Jenny's clothes. How was I going to tell Jenny I'd lost everything she'd lent me? I didn't want to get her into trouble, but there was no way I could pop into Balmain and buy a three-thousand-dollar sequined mini dress to replace the one I absolutely, one hundred per cent knew I shouldn't have brought with me in the first place.

'You're totally gonna want to get some nice shit for the festival, Angie,' Craig said. 'You should see some of the girls in the other bands, man alive they are hot.'

'Really?' I asked, looking to Graham for confirmation.

He half shrugged, half nodded. 'I guess, but hey, what do I know?'

Brilliant. Something else to worry about.

'Don't sweat it, Ange. You're probably as hot,' Craig

offered. He stopped eating for a second and squinted at me. 'In your regular clothes. And I guess you'll want to pick up some make-up or something.'

'Who died and made you Tyra?' Graham asked quickly. 'Ignore him. You look great.'

'Yeah you do. Beautiful, in fact.' My lovely boyfriend kissed the top of my head and stood up. 'Just running to the bathroom. You want to stay and eat or just go back to the hotel?'

'Hotel.' I nodded. 'I just want to sleep for a month.'

Alex nodded and bobbed off through the crowded bar. Even from the back he was gorgeous. Possibly I was biased and/or a bit mad, but really, he was hot from every angle. Being able to spot his slightly slouchy posture in a darkened room from twenty feet was one of my keenest talents.

'Sorry for being so rubbish.' I offered Craig and Graham a pained expression and glugged another mouthful of water. 'Not to go Yoko your evening, but I really do need to go to bed.'

'We totally get it, go get some beauty rest.' Graham waved away my concerns. And I elected to ignore his beauty rest comment. 'I'm sure Alex doesn't want to hang out with us anyway. Craig was a pain in both our asses on the plane.'

'Yeah, he won't want to hang out with his best friends when his best girl is here.' Craig sipped his beer and smiled. I wanted to be embarrassed, but instead I actually giggled. For shame, Angela. 'And y'know, he's totally pussy whipped again.'

'Again?' I asked.

'Like with that French bitch he used to date.' Craig nodded over his beer, ignoring Graham's warning cough. Which ironically, I picked up immediately.

'French bitch?' This was new information. Why

didn't I know about a French bitch? 'Alex never mentioned dating a French bit— I mean, girl?'

'Yeah?' Craig carried on ignoring Graham. 'Yeah, she was—'

'For ever ago. It was for ever ago,' he interrupted. 'He's so over it. Totally.'

'He dated her in New York?' I asked, flicking my gaze between the two suspicious-looking boys.

'Yeah, well—' Craig started.

'Yes. And it was a long time ago,' Graham said sternly. 'Which is why he never mentioned it. I'm sure.'

There were a million more questions swimming around my mind, but before I could form a coherent sentence, Alex reappeared with two large glasses of red wine.

'I know you want to leave, but Sam on the bar just gave me these and I couldn't say no – you want?' Alex asked, sliding into the chair at the side of me. 'I thought maybe a drink might do you some good.'

On one hand, this clearly was a bad idea. I was exhausted, I'd already passed out once and I needed a clear head in the morning. On the other, I could really, really, really do with a drink. But back to the other hand, it really was a bad idea.

'Sam on the bar?' I asked, nodding and holding out my hand for the glass. I could maybe just take a sip.

'Old friend,' he explained, pushing the glass towards me. 'Just this one drink and we'll make a move.'

I nodded and leaned against Alex, taking in the mirrored walls, high ceilings and racks and racks of bottles behind the bar. It reminded me of Balthazar in New York, except instead of posing as a French bistro, it actually was one. Every single table was full, and it immediately made sense to me that the guys had picked the café. There wasn't one ugly person in the place and I was pretty certain that none of them were bank managers or geography teachers either. Nothing so ordinary here. So this was where Paris's pretty people came to hang out. Note to self. And *Belle* magazine.

The boys talked band while I held my wine quietly, concentrating on not spilling it down my T-shirt. The odds were pretty good that I was going to have to wear it again. Oh, it had been a long time since I'd washed something out in a hotel sink – where was my mother when I needed her? Although her area of expertise was really knickers in a Mallorcan bidet rather than American Apparel V-neck in a Parisian boutique hotel. Much of a muchness though, surely? Maybe it was in my blood.

I clutched my wine, but just couldn't bring myself to drink it, so I people watched instead. I couldn't help but stare as four girls rose from a table at the back and started dancing around a raised DJ booth. They were laughing happily, pushing each other on to the dance floor, and just like everyone else in the café, they were all skinny jeans, long messy hair tossed over one shoulder and at least a fortnight's worth of eyeliner smudged all over their faces. But my God they were gorgeous. I'd never had so much as a same sex leaning in all my life and even I wanted to go over there and lick their beautiful faces.

The tallest of the four, a slender blonde with masses of Debbie Harry-a-like white-blonde hair hanging in her bright blue eyes, looked over at our table and then disappeared behind a door in the back wall. Was that her? The girl I thought I saw with Alex when I walked in? I looked back at the boys around the table. They were discussing their set for Sunday's festival and without meaning to, more or less ignoring me altogether, aside from an occasional arm stroke from

Alex or lewd grin from Craig. Once Alex was into 'work stuff', he was impossible to distract. I could have stripped off and performed an entire Pussycat Dolls routine and he wouldn't have batted an eyelid. It might have slipped into his subconscious enough to throw an ironic cover into the set, but that would have been about it.

Not having eaten anything in, bloody hell, I had no idea, the wine was making its way through my system fairly quickly. I slipped away from the table and followed the blonde girl through the door at the back of the room, hopefully to the toilets. Not that I wanted to give her the wrong idea, I wasn't nearly that drunk. Although maybe some girl-on-girl action would get Alex's attention back. Wow, sometimes I wondered if I'd been spending far too much time with Jenny. The blonde girl was washing her hands as I pushed through the door.

'Oh, sorry,' I said, bashing into her. Face to face, she was absolutely stunning. Her heart-shaped face looked to be bare of make-up aside from the lashings of eyeliner, and her platinum hair wasn't even dyed. I wasn't jealous at all. 'I was just looking for the loo.'

'*Pardon*?' she replied.

Right. I was in France. Completely forgot.

'Uh, *la toilette*?' I asked, pointing at what was very obviously the toilet.

'*Oui*?' She looked at me without quite the same reverence I'd sent her way. In that she looked at me as though I was slightly retarded. Which was probably fair.

I made some sort of laughing, oh-I'm-so-stupid snorting noise-cum-hand gesture and locked myself in the toilet cubicle. OK, so I couldn't even attempt to make myself understood when trying to get in the lav, but that wasn't going to be a problem, was it? Alex was practically fluent, and when I wasn't with him, I'd have my French *Belle* assistant. Surely she would be ecstatic to spend all her time translating for me. And lead me around town all day long. Surely the super trendy, young, hot, French fashionista would love that. Oh crap.

When I came out of the toilet, the gorgeous girl had gone. Reluctantly, I checked myself out in the mirror, trying not to compare and contrast. My light brown bob looked better for its trim last week, but without hair straighteners, a half-decent conditioner or even serum, it was a fluffy, bird's nest mess. Flat at the roots, puffy at the ends. My skin was dry and greyish from the flight, but for some reason, my nose and fore-head were so shiny, I could see a reflection of my reflection in my forehead. How could my skin be dry and shiny at the same time? For want of a better idea, I pulled down the V-neck on my T-shirt until I could almost see the edge of my bra. Admittedly, it wasn't my finest moment, but a girl had to fight with whatever weapons she had, and until I'd been to a pharmacy or something and picked up hair product, my 34Cs were all that I had.

But they weren't going to be enough.

Wandering back through the busy bar, I fought the fug out of my brain and tried to spot our table, but I couldn't seem to see it. Mainly because the tiny table populated by three very American boys that I was looking for, was now covered in four very French girls. Most notably, the beautiful girl from the toilets, who appeared to be compensating for the lack of chairs at the table by kneeling on the floor. At Alex's feet. I paused by the maître d's station and watched for a second. She took his hand in hers and cocked her head to one side, smiling. Alex was not smiling. Instead, he pulled his hand out of hers, took his phone out of his jeans pocket, stood up and walked out the door. And down the street. The girl laughed, said something hilarious to the others and hopped up, taking Alex's seat. I looked down, breathing deeply. What was that all about? *Was* that the girl I had seen when I came in? And why was there a number listed by the phone for 'Centre Anti-Poison'? Well, she'd be needing a number for an ambulance if she touched my boyfriend again. Not that she could, given that he'd completely disappeared out of sight.

I cautiously wandered back over to the table, standing awkwardly beside Graham and waiting for him to acknowledge me. Instead, he and Craig giggled with the other French girls, chattering away. Did everyone speak French except me? The blonde stared at me from Alex's seat, then picked up his wine glass and drank deeply. Colour me stunned.

'*Marie*,' she said to the brunette girl to her left. Who I was relieved to see was at least wearing make-up. Even if she was still hatefully good-looking. '*C'est la fille qui était dans les toilettes.*'

Now, even with my shoddy '*je voudrais un croque monsieur, s'il vous plaît*' GCSE French, I managed to pick up '*fille*' which was girl and '*toilettes*' which was toilet (she wasn't getting anything past me). She was totally talking about me. The other three girls stopped talking, put down their drinks and turned to stare at me. I felt like I was back in year nine, knocking on the common room door and asking the sixth formers if they wouldn't mind awfully turning their stereo down because we couldn't hear our recorders in the music room.

'Oh, shit, Angie, I so totally forgot you were here,'

Craig said, once he'd realized everyone had stopped talking. 'This is Marie, Lise, Jacqueline and Solène.'

The blonde raised an eyebrow and looked me up and down. 'Angela?' she asked Craig. He nodded into his fresh beer.

'Solène,' she said smiling and holding out a hand, but still not standing up or getting the hell out of my boyfriend's seat. 'We are playing the festival. Please, this is your wine?'

I really, really wanted to hate her, but her smile actually seemed genuine and her heavily accented voice made me want to curl up with my head in her lap. I awkwardly accepted my own drink, still standing by Graham's chair, trying to look casual, but actually bloody well waiting for him to get up and give it to me. He didn't. Some bloody gentleman.

'So, you're in a band?' I asked.

'*Oui*,' she replied. 'Yes, we are called Stereo. We play with Stills many times before.' The rest of the girls carried on laughing, the brunette kicking Craig under the table. Well, it certainly looked as though they had played together before.

'Right.' I nodded, not really knowing what else to say.

'You are not in a band,' Solène said. I wasn't sure if it was supposed to be a question or not. 'You are a writer?'

'Yes,' I said, relieved that she seemed to know who I was. 'A journalist.'

'You write about the band?' she smiled again. 'About the festival?'

Oh. She thought I was a music journalist. Was that good?

'Angela is here with Alex,' Graham said. 'She's here with us.'

'So you are not a writer?' Solène looked confused. 'You work for the band?'

62

'No, I am a writer, I'm writing for *Belle* magazine in America,' I explained, trying not to patronize her. I didn't want her to think I was an idiot. 'I am a writer, I'm just not writing about the festival.'

'I am sorry, I do not understand,' she frowned slightly, her tiny little, button nose wrinkling up, 'you write about Alex for a fashion magazine?'

'No.' I tried to think of a simpler way to explain myself, feeling completely inadequate. Why didn't I speak French? Why had I done history A level? No one cared about my knowledge of the Industrial Revolution right now. Or ever actually. And never in my life had I wanted another girl's approval so badly. Solène was beautiful and in a band and so, so cool. I was willing to bet she could play guitar and everything. She was like a blonde Carla Bruni except without the dodgy, short presidential husband. Jenny would hate her.

Before I could start again, we were all interrupted by a knock on the window. It was Alex. He looked at me and then at the table before gesturing for me to come outside.

'Sorry, won't be a minute,' I said, putting down my wine, picking up my bag and practically stumbling out of the café as fast as my jet-lagged legs would carry me.

'Hey, sorry, I had to take a call,' he said, taking my hand and leading me away from the café.

'Right,' I said, spinning around to look at the scene unfolding in the window. Craig was practically salivating over Marie while Graham was playing Lise and Jacqueline something from his iPod while they nodded intensely to the beat. Solène turned around in her chair, in Alex's chair and waved to me. I waved back before Alex pulled me around the corner. 'We're leaving?'

He nodded and kept walking.

'Are you OK?' I asked, stopping in the middle of the street, holding him to a standstill. 'What happened on the phone?'

'Sorry, just band stuff. The record label want us to play tomorrow night and I'm just so tired.' He draped both his arms over my shoulders and gave me a half smile. 'I was hoping we'd be able to do something tomorrow night. There's like, a million places I want to take you.'

'It'll be fine, we've got ages.' I pushed up on to my tiptoes and kissed him lightly on the lips. I pulled back suddenly and stared at Alex. 'Did you smoke?'

'Does it count if I took a drag off someone else's?' he asked sheepishly. 'Sorry, I was just kind of stressed. On the phone.'

I tried not to make a face. It was incredibly unsettling for me to feel physically sick from kissing him.

'I didn't know you smoked,' I said, feeling a little bit weird. Was it strange that I didn't know he used to smoke?

'I don't,' he said, fiddling around in his pocket for chewing gum. 'So there's nothing to know.'

'Good, because it's rank,' I said, taking his hand and squeezing it hard. 'And you're brushing your teeth before bed.'

'Whatever turns you on,' he said, squeezing mine back even harder.

CHAPTER SIX

'Alex, I'm not trying to be a bitch.' I yawned as we sailed into the Hotel Marais, Alex waving to the guy on the desk as we passed through reception. 'I just don't think you understand. I am ecstatic to be here. I am over the moon to be spending a week in Paris with you. But I have nothing. I'm in another country and I have nothing. No knickers, no phone charger, no carefully selected, one of a kind vintage ensembles. Nothing.'

'You mean those crazy eighties dresses you picked up in the thrift store?' Alex asked as I waited for him to unlock the bedroom door.

'One of a kind vintage ensembles,' I repeated. 'Honestly, it's like you've never read a single issue of *Belle*.'

'Is that going to be a problem? Because I haven't,' Alex said, kicking his own battered suitcase into the wardrobe. 'And until about three days ago, neither had you.'

'You're not helping,' I sulked, using every last ounce of energy to throw myself dramatically across what I took to be a normal bed, only for it to separate in the middle on impact, slide apart and unceremoniously dump me hard on the floor in a bundle of sheets.

'Angela?'

I popped my head up in between the beds like a very confused meerkat. 'Can I go home now?'

'It's going to be fine.' Alex tried not to laugh and pulled me out from between the beds before pushing them back together. 'You have had a bad day. I know you've been unlucky.'

'Falling down the bed was unlucky,' I conceded, collapsing back into the pillows. 'Getting my suitcase blown up was ridiculous.'

'Yeah, but ridiculous things happen to you, don't they?' Alex said, flopping beside me on the bed. Which of course did not part for him. 'Maybe this is one of those blessings in disguise things.'

'It's a bloody good disguise,' I said, rolling towards the edge of the bed.

'Where do you think you're going?' Alex asked, grabbing my arm and pulling me back on to the bed. 'Get back in bed this minute, Clark.'

'I have to take a shower,' I whined. His hand was warm and strong around my wrist and, without an awful lot of resistance, I let him roll on top of me and cup my face in his hands.

'You don't need to shower.'

'But I'm gross.'

'You're not gross.'

One warm, soft kiss that made my stomach flip and I was sort of over the idea of a shower.

'Did you like your song?' Alex asked, his voice rough and tickly in my ear.

'I loved my song,' I whispered back. It had been a very stressful day after all and wasn't sex good for jet lag? Hmm, I'd probably heard that the same place as the hippo story, but it sounded as if it could be true.

*　　*　　*

Apparently it was not true. I'd dozed for a while, coiled up in Alex's arms and thought I'd sleep for days, but by four-thirty a.m., after I'd checked the clock by the bed for the fiftieth time after just a couple of hours sleep, I accepted I was wide awake and in fact, completely jet-lagged. Alex had been snoring steadily for hours and as much fun as waking him up might be, it really didn't seem fair. Instead I slid out of the bed as quietly as possible and snuggled into the armchair by the window with my laptop.

The room was nice. Small compared to rooms at The Union and The Hollywood, but clean and pretty. I was so used to the stark white decor of chain hotels, the floral throw on the bed and patterned cushions on the couch seemed sweet and homely. A bit like something my mum might have if she had any sort of taste at all. Which, God bless her, she did not. She could cook a hell of a roast dinner, but she couldn't pick a coordinating cushion to save her life. With that thought in mind, I logged on to TheLook.com and started typing.

The Adventures of Angela: Can't Speak French

Hmm. I'm not very familiar with French supersti-tions and customs, but I would imagine that I'm right in thinking that airport security blowing up your suitcase isn't very good luck. Unless it's one of those mad things like when a bird shits on you and it's supposed to bring you good luck. It isn't? No, I didn't think so.

In that case I'd like to take a moment to mourn the passing of my beautiful things – the Louboutins, the Marc Jacobs satchel, sob, the GHDs. All gone. Seriously. Blown up. But anyway, I've decided not to dwell on it (having done nothing, but weep and wail for the last twenty-four hours) and to move on. I'm in Paris, it's beautiful and I have lots to do to keep me busy. Did I mention I'm writing for Belle magazine? I did? Oh. And did I mention that my boyfriend is playing at, no, headlining a festival here? Yes again? Oh dear, I'm shameless, aren't I? That wasn't actually a question, but thanks.

So here I am in Paris, any suggestions on where I should go/what I should do? It feels a little bit like everyone else in the world knows Paris like the back of their hand, so any suggestions are welcome. Also, any advice on how to achieve the effect of hair straighteners without actually using hair straighteners will result in you going straight to the top of my Christmas card list.

Having posted the blog, I opened up my email and stared at the blank page. I knew this had to be done and I really should have done it before now. I just didn't know how. I typed Jenny's email address into the To box and stared some more. Before I could start, a little box flashed up in the right-hand corner of the screen. Bloody G Chat.

Hey! How's Paris? What did you wear today? Did you take pictures? I'm so jealous. J xoxo

Bugger. For a second, my hand hovered over the keyboard, about to log off. But this had to be done. And done over instant messaging.

Hi Jenny. I'm OK, Paris is lovely, but there was a bit of a problem with my case.

It was delayed?

She typed back quickly. I'd forgotten that Jenny was a master of all forms of communication.

Not lost? A, is it OK?

I sat with my fingers resting on the warm keyboard for so long that the screen dimmed slightly. There was no getting around it, I had to tell her.

No, not OK. Security had to do a controlled explosion on it – don't know why. I am SO sorry, I'll sort it out. I'll replace everything.

Even on instant messaging, it was scary that Jenny was struck dumb. Silence was not a natural state for her, and it was not good. The screen dimmed again and started playing a slideshow of my photos, me and Jenny doing karaoke, me and Jenny having lunch on Rodeo Drive, me holding Jenny's hair back while she threw up in the street. Even my laptop was trying to make me feel bad. And scared.

Before I could freak out any more, the screen flickered back into life with Jenny's response.

You're kidding, right?

No, I shook my head while I typed.

They blew it up. Everything got blown up.

There was another pause, but it was shorter than the last.

WHAT THE FUCK DO YOU MEAN THEY BLEW IT UP?

I started to type out my explanation, as rubbish and pointless as it was, but before I could, a little box appeared on the screen. My computer was running on reserve battery life. Shit. I instinctively looked around for my charger before remembering that a) I wasn't at home and that b) my charger had of course, been in my suitcase. I didn't even have time to explain before the screen died and the laptop turned itself off. I carefully placed it on the coffee table as though Jenny could hear me somehow, and slinked back towards the bed, only banging my knee once on the frame. As I climbed back under the silky cotton sheet, my BlackBerry started to vibrate loudly on the bedside table. I grabbed it quickly to avoid waking Alex, but didn't answer. It was Jenny, of course. After what felt like for ever, the attempted call ended, but was followed by a text message.

ANSWER YOUR FUCKING PHONE

Strangely enough, after that charming message, I didn't really feel like answering my fucking phone so I turned the BlackBerry off and shut it in the drawer beside me. I'd talk to her in the morning. Or when I got brave enough. Or never. I rolled over and curled up against Alex, his arms instinctively wrapping around me while he slept. Maybe if I just moved in with him as soon as we got back, I wouldn't even need to go back to the apartment. Distracting myself from the Jenny situation, I leaned back until I could feel the full length of Alex's body against mine. We were going to move in together. With my eyes closed, my face broke out into a grin that would make the Cheshire cat look like a moody shit and waited patiently until I fell asleep.

*   *   *

'What are you looking so happy about?' Alex asked the next morning. 'I don't think I've ever seen you so pleased to be out of bed.'

I turned my back on him to try and straighten my face and pulled a longish grey T-shirt out of the chaos that was his suitcase. I would probably be arrested for indecent exposure, but this was Europe right? I should be able to mince around in a T-shirt posing as a dress with no problems. I turned to the mirror to confirm the sartorial situation. One look was enough to wipe the smile off my face. Crap. And without my full beauty kit (which was hardly sophisticated in the first place) I really did look like crap. Hotel shampoo and conditioner, handwash instead of cleanser and nothing, but a half-empty tube of Beauty Flash Balm to moisturize my entire body. Thank God I'd kept my mascara and pressed powder in my hand luggage, otherwise I'd have to be locked in my room like a shamefaced goblin.

'Hey, happy girl. What gives?'

'I'm just excited to see Paris,' I lied. The words 'I'm moving in with you' had almost burst out of my mouth a thousand times since the alarm had gone off half an hour earlier, but I was determined to keep it to myself. 'Anything specific I should save for me and you to do together?'

'Uh, I don't know.' He stretched and rolled over, his body still tangled under the covers. 'A lot of the regular stuff is kind of tacky. But, you know, do whatever you need to do for your article.'

'I don't see how anything about Paris could be tacky,' I said, throwing a cushion at him. I hated leaving him in bed. That was one of the biggest penalties of dating a boy in a band, he was almost always on night shifts. 'It's all so beautiful.'

'Yeah, maybe.' He threw the pillow back. 'But you also think that *Les Misérables* is beautiful.'

'Don't try and use my love of musicals against me,' I warned. 'Or I'll be asking why the episodes of *America's Next Top Model* I recorded at yours all say they've been viewed already.'

'So I'll see you tonight?' he asked, promptly changing the subject. 'The show isn't until ten so we should get a drink or dinner somewhere, maybe Le Dix?'

'I'd love to have an opinion on that,' I said, leaning over the bed and kissing him on the forehead. I pulled out the drawer beside the bed and took out my BlackBerry and wallet, slipping them into my bag. 'But I have never been here before, remember? How do you know so much about Paris anyway? Did you do a year abroad or something?'

'Kinda.' Alex's voice was already falling back to sleep. It was as though he wanted me to hate him. Or at least try to.

'So, I'll text you later?' I called from the door, checking I had my room key once more.

'Yuh-huh,' he murmured, lifting his hand to wave me off.

Arse.

Wandering through the hotel garden, out to the reception, I started to get nervous about meeting Virginie. What if she was all super hot and super cool like the girls from the bar last night? She worked for French *Belle*, so there was no way she was going to be, well, normal. The moment I stepped into the hotel lobby, it was impossible not to spot her. Lounging against a Perspex Philippe Starck ghost chair, was a tiny excuse for a girl, second-skin black jeans, black ballet slippers, long loose light denim shirt open over a tight black vest, masses of wavy brown hair spilling all down her back and most notably, a bored-shitless expression on her pretty face. It was almost reassuring to see some international consistency throughout *Belle*'s hiring policy. Stunning? Check. Too cool for the rest of the world? Check.

'Hi, Virginie?' I asked, holding out a hand in a half wave, half 'please-shake-my-hand-and-don't-stare-at-me-like-I'm-mad' gesture. For a second, she stared at me as if I were mad and then leaped up, poker straight, and grabbed my hand with both of hers.

'Oh, Angela Clark? Of course, I have seen your picture, it is you!' she gushed, the handshake disappearing into a flurry of air kisses and elaborate hugs. 'I am Virginie Aucoin, and I am very happy to be helping you.'

I pulled back slightly, not quite sure what to say. The miserable-looking *Belle* girl had suddenly morphed into an over enthusiastic puppy, all bright eyes and unable to stand still. She bounced lightly from foot to foot, all the while grinning at me madly.

'Um, well, hello,' I said, not wanting to upset her. 'Have you had breakfast? Do you want to get something?'

'I have not. What do you like to eat?' Virginie asked, turning very serious. 'Breakfast is very important. We are busy today, yes?'

'Yes?' I said, letting her drag me out of the lobby. 'And I would like coffee?'

She stopped short right outside the doors. 'Just coffee? Oh Angela, you are already so American. But you must eat also. Follow me.'

All the way down the narrow stone street, Virginie talked. Happily for uncultured me, her English was fairly brilliant, mainly thanks to the year she'd spent working at US *Belle* as an intern, which was apparently where she had first come across my blog.

'It was just beginning as I am leaving to return to Paris,' she explained, turning another tight corner and emerging into a beautiful open space, lined with rows of impressive mansion houses. 'This is Place des Vosges, very old, very beautiful. Many famous people are living here a long time ago. Do you know the writer Victor Hugo? And Cardinal Richelieu? I wish, one day, myself. It is my dream.'

'Victor Hugo that wrote *Les Mis*?' I asked, casting an excited eye over one of the fountains and the pretty trees in the square. 'No way.'

'*Les Misérables*? You like to read his books?' Virginie asked. 'Victor Hugo?'

'Let's say yes,' I replied, hoping we wouldn't need to get into a serious discussion on French literature. I would be outed as a musical theatre lover in a heart-beat. 'And it's good to have dreams. If you want to live here one day, I'm sure you will. Most of the girls at *Belle* in America already seem to be in their Park Avenue palaces. Shall we get a coffee?'

'But you,' she said, pulling me along and pushing me down into a small chair outside a coffee shop beneath a pretty archway. For a tiny girl, she was very strong. I was becoming more and more certain that she was actually Scrappy Doo. 'You live a dream already. I read your blog every day and it sounds so exciting. You leave London, go to New York, get a job, you are meeting amazing people, interviewing celebrities, you travel to LA, to Paris. I could not believe it when they ask if someone will help you here in Paris. I was so excited.'

'Well, you make it sound a lot more interesting than it really is,' I said, feeling like an enormous fraud. 'Most of the time I'm just sitting around in my pants staring at my laptop. Really.'

'But you are my hero,' she added shyly, looking up at me from underneath a ridiculous amount of hair. I had to find out what products she used. 'I would love to have your life.'

I really didn't know what to say. I was generally so busy trying to get on with things that I never took a step back to look at my life from the outside. Besides, I was pretty certain that most people only do that when things are going badly, not when things are going well. I'd long ago learned that the best way to deal with being happy was to get your head down and get on with it for fear of everything going spectacularly tits up.

'I'm sure your life is amazing, Virginie. Living in Paris, working at *Belle*.' I thought of Cici, stuck as Mary's assistant on *The Look* website and felt the briefest moment of sympathy. 'I know loads of people that would love to be doing what you're doing.'

'Yes, I know this,' she said, waving over a waiter and ordering for both of us. 'But, and I do not want you to think I am not happy about my opportunities, I am, but I am not really wanting to write for *Belle* magazine. I applied for the internship so that I could see New York and was so lucky to get a job there that I had to take it. But the girls there are not my friends. I do not really feel this way about the fashion they love.'

'Really?' I was so relieved. Was it possible that, against all the odds, she was normal? Aside from the whole hero worship thing, which I was fairly sure I'd be able to get used to. 'Well, that's OK, I'm hardly an haute couture obsesso and they've asked me to write for them. And you're getting great experience there, I'm sure.'

'This is true,' she agreed, taking a baguette from the bread basket that was placed between us, buttering it and then dunking it into her coffee, leaving a skin of butter and bread floating on top. 'And it has helped me to meet you. I am so happy that we are going to be friends.'

'We're not going to be friends if you do that again,' I gagged. 'That's disgusting.'

'It is?' Virginie immediately dropped the bread on to her plate. 'I am so sorry. I will not do it again.'

'Oh God, no, sorry, carry on,' I apologized immediately. 'I'm just not used to seeing people do . . . that.'

She smiled at me sheepishly and picked up her bread, nibbling cautiously, but not dunking it into her coffee. I smiled brightly, picked up my cup and looked away. Jesus, this was far too much power to have over a person.

Once the bread and croissants had all gone, we knuckled down to important business. The *pains au chocolat*. And the article.

'So you know what the piece is about,' I asked. She nodded in response, a notepad and pen in her eager hands. 'Right, well, we have two days to uncover the secret Paris, all the coolest shopping hotspots, bars, restaurants, that kind of thing. Are you up to it?'

'I am,' she cheered, jumping out of her seat. 'Let's go!'

'All right, calm down and sit for a minute.' I realized I had my hands up in the air, made quick little fists and pulled them back down to the table. 'That's not entirely all, I did have some notes and things, but there was a problem with my suitcase so now I don't have them. Or my camera. Or any other clothes. Or a Mac power lead. Or anything..'

I wasn't telling that story again.

'OK.' Virginie nodded seriously. 'I have some ideas of places to go, I am sure we will find you clothes in these places, notepads are easy to buy and I have a camera, I was hoping we would have a picture together. With the Mac power lead I cannot help, I do not know of a place in Paris for this.'

'Right.' I almost smiled. It was such a relief to have a friendly and helpful face by my side. 'I should call the office and check in. Maybe they can help out too.'

I pulled out my BlackBerry and scanned the contacts until I came to Donna. Oh, she was going to love this. Just before I pressed the call, button, I stalled. What was I supposed to say? She had already made it clear she wasn't my biggest fan. I scrolled down to Esme and paused again. Same situation. So who did I call? And at six-thirty in the morning? As much as it went against every instinct in my body, there really was only one person I could think of. Cici.

Instead of calling, even Cici's new camaraderie would have its limits, and six-thirty a.m. was probably one of them, I opened up the email box, skipping over the four emails I'd had from Jenny already (one problem at a time) and tapped out a short message. I outlined my main problems, avoiding the controlled explosion situation and opting for a 'lost luggage' explanation. Email sent, I slipped my BlackBerry back into my now extraordinarily precious, one and only Marc Jacobs satchel and smiled at Virginie. She returned it immediately, a thousand watts brighter.

'We are ready?' she asked, literally bouncing in her chair.

'We are ready,' I confirmed. And hopefully I will find the strength not to drown you in the Seine, I added silently as she took my arm and dragged me off down the street.

'*D'accord*, I am thinking of a store I know, not so far away, where they are making bags out of old leather jackets,' Virginie said, leading me further into the elegant, narrow streets. 'This would be very good for your article, *oui*?'

'Perfect.' I nodded, too busy staring all around me

to really concentrate. Paris really was beautiful. I just wished I had my camera. The sun shone down on to the cobbled streets, warming my bare limbs and helping me feel less conspicuous in my makeshift dress. It was almost as warm as New York, but not nearly as humid. All of the shop fronts had big glass windows with muted wood surrounds, and the apartments above them were almost all decorated with dollhouse-style window boxes, spilling over with colourful flowers. While I stood around staring, I felt my BlackBerry vibrate against my hip. I stumbled along behind Virginie, trying to catch up while I read the message.

Hi Angela,

Shitty news about your suitcase! You must be totally traumatized. I wouldn't know what to do with myself. Don't panic, everything will be fine. I've spoken with my grandpa and he says you should just replace the camera and laptop stuff with the credit card I sent you, same with your clothes. Since you're on a work trip, you're insured and Spencer Media are liable for your losses. I would say just don't go crazy – even *Belle* has a budget, I guess. LOL.

As for your notes, there's not a lot we can do about that, but I can send over a list of some of my favourite places to shop in Paris. I'm at the gym now and I have some errands to run for Mary first thing so I won't be able to get them to you until later, just enjoy Paris! I'll sort stuff, don't worry.

Cici xoxo

The first time I read the email, I almost fell over. The second, I just couldn't believe it. By the time Virginie had read it out loud to me to check I wasn't going mad, it had just about sunk in. LOL? Cici had 'lol'd' me? This was both unnatural and wrong.

'She seems very helpful.' Virginie held out my BlackBerry. I took it from her lightly as though it were cursed. Which for all I knew, it was. 'This is not how I remember her.'

'You knew Cici?' I asked.

'I did,' Virginie replied. 'She very much wants to work at *Belle*. I sometimes had projects with her, assistant things.'

I eyed her carefully. It was strange, she didn't have the look of someone who'd been tortured by a sadist. 'So you're friends?'

She let out a loud cackle and then clapped her hand over her mouth. 'Sorry, that was rude,' she said quickly. 'But no, Cici Spencer and I are not friends. She does not like the interns and assistants that work on *Belle*. I think maybe she thinks if she, uh, convinces us to leave, she will get the job?'

'Right,' I said. Phew. Bullet dodged.

'You are friends?' Virginie asked cautiously. 'With Cici?'

Without thinking, I gave her a matching cackle. 'No, not at all. Whatever that email might look like.' I took Virginie's arm in mine and smiled. 'I would not trust Cici Spencer as far as I could throw her. And that is actually probably quite far. Let's go and have a look at this bag shop of yours.'

The morning passed quickly and I felt as if we'd walked for miles. Which we actually had when Virginie showed me our route on a tiny street map I'd bought. As well as the addresses of lots of cool shops, I'd managed to pick up a couple of bits and pieces for my capsule Paris wardrobe. As much as it completely weirded me to use the company credit card to buy things for myself, I really didn't have much choice. I'd just paid my rent, Vanessa hadn't given me her share yet and it was a week until payday. And I was really badly dressed. At least now I had jeans that fitted (a Parisian staple), a couple of T-shirts (God bless the international plague of American Apparel), a couple of cute vintage dresses (definitely research) and some shoes that weren't the ancient and slightly skanky Primark flats I'd travelled in (just generally essential). There was a chance that I didn't need the two necklaces and several bangles I'd picked up, but I was writing for *Belle* now, it wouldn't be right if I was wandering around Paris badly accessorized.

The heat wasn't nearly as oppressive as it had been in New York, but I was still starting to wilt by three. Happily, it seemed as if even Virginie's puppy power was starting to wear off.

'I think we need ice cream,' she announced.

'Sounds like a plan,' I agreed, peeling some sticky strands of hair off my face. 'Where shall we go?'

'The Seine is just here, do you see?' Virginie pointed across a busy junction. 'Across this road is *Ile St-Louis* and there we will find the best ice cream. The best in the world.'

'I don't know,' I said, following happily. 'New York has some pretty good ice cream.'

For the first time, Virginie turned and looked at me with deadly seriousness. 'It is the best in the world.'

'OK.' I shrugged, holding out my hands. 'Whatever you say.'

'Fucking hell, this is amazing,' I mumbled through a mouthful of nougat ice cream. 'Sorry, didn't mean to swear.'

Virginie nodded at me with a satisfied expression. 'It is the best, yes?'

I answered by scraping my spoon along the bottom of my tiny metal dish. Ben & Jerry's meant nothing to me now. Without the distraction of the ice cream, I looked around me and realized my mouth was hanging open. Everything about the city was beautiful. The mid-afternoon sun beat down on the grey stone bridge that linked the island to the rest of the city and sparkled off the Seine. Across the river, beautiful apartments with rows of shuttered windows lined the banks, while spires, steeples and bell towers marked out the skyline. It couldn't have been more different from the stark, stylized view of Manhattan I'd got so used to from Alex's living room window. Everything looked so old and elegant, I felt as if I could sit there and stare out at the city for ever.

'There are many beautiful things to see in Paris,' Virginie said, interrupting my daydream. 'You would like to take a trip around the city?'

'I would absolutely like to take a trip around the city,' I said, visions of myself riding a bicycle along the Left Bank in a Brigitte Bardot inspired ensemble evaporating quickly. Sixties Brigitte Bardot, not crazy cat lady Brigitte Bardot. 'But I don't know, have we done enough work?'

I leafed through my notebook. It seemed as though we'd done loads of stuff, seen so many shops and cafés, but now that I looked at it, there really didn't seem like much there. Certainly not 10,000 words.

'We have done lots of work today,' Virginie said, closing up the notebook on my hand. 'You have many places already. And of course have tomorrow. And Cici is sendng you her list, *non*? You must see Paris, Angela, I insist.'

'And I do want to,' I said, whining slightly and

staring at a big boat full of tourists as it sailed by. 'But this is so important. Maybe we could do more research today and do the tourist thing tomorrow?'

'Tomorrow the weather is not going to be so good.' Virginie scrunched up her pretty face. 'But yes, if that is what you want. I thought tomorrow perhaps we would go to more shops and cafés on the other side of the city. Where it is better for the bad weather.'

'Bad weather?' I bit my lip and tried to ignore the nagging feeling in my stomach. I really, really wanted to do a good job on this article. But I had ages. And how was I supposed to give the article a genuine vibe if I didn't have an overall feel for the city? I couldn't. 'And maybe we'd see some places while we're going around, right?'

'Of course. I was thinking we would take the open-top bus? That way you will see everything all at once.' Virginie let out a little laugh. 'It is, how do you say, tacky maybe? But I think you might find it is fun.'

'I do enjoy tacky,' I admitted. 'Will we see the Eiffel Tower?'

'We will,' she pouted. 'You know that Parisians do not like the tower. That they think it is ugly?'

'You hear all sorts of things about the French,' I said, standing up and reluctantly walking away from the man with the ice cream. 'But I don't believe everything I hear.'

'This you can believe,' Virginie said, pointing back across the road. 'We must take the *Métro*.'

'But you do shave your legs, don't you?'

'I wax.'

'And you don't give wine to children?'

'I do not know any children.'

'But you would?'

Virginie sighed. 'The *Métro* is this way.'

Excellent. I'd broken her at last.

CHAPTER SEVEN

'And then we went on this open-top bus ride and I saw the Eiffel Tower and Notre-Dame, the Louvre, God, loads of stuff. And we went on the *Métro*, I got the *Métro* here, did I tell you?' I'd been talking at Alex for the last three minutes, not even pausing to kiss him hello. That was how much I loved Paris. A lot.

'You did,' he said, raising my hand up to his lips and kissing it lightly. 'I'm glad you had a good day. Did you get any work done at all?'

'Yes,' I said, pouting slightly. He wasn't nearly interested enough in my Parisian adventures. 'Virginie took all my stuff, I mean, the stuff we bought for research, back to hers. I told her to come to the gig tonight, is that OK?'

'Of course,' he said, leading me off the main road and down a steep staircase. I liked following him up stairs, it gave a great view of his denim-clad behind, but down stairs, I was always slightly worried I would trip and that he was too skinny to offer any real cushioning when I landed on him. 'I hate that you have to stand around on your own when I'm playing.'

'You don't have to make me sound like a sad groupie, it's not like I'm not on my own that often,' I said, my eyes adjusting to the darkness of the bar. 'Just since Jenny left, I don't have many other gig buddies, I suppose.'

'Good thing you have me then, huh,' Alex waved a hello at the man behind the bar and guided me to a tiny table at the back of the room. 'Also, did I tell you that you look super cute?'

'You did not.' I shuffled slightly in my seat, leaning forwards casually to show off my new Parisian cleavage, courtesy of my amazing new Aubade underwear, and waited patiently for my compliment. And if he wanted to throw in a little something for my slightly clichéd, but irresistibly soft sky blue V-neck T-shirt that Virginie assured me brought out my eyes, I would be fine with that too.

'You look cute,' he said, his hand gently resting on my thigh.

'Just cute?'

'Super cute.'

'Not *très chic*?'

Alex gazed into my eyes and clutched my hands to his heart. '*Vous êtes la femme la plus belle et la plus renversante à Paris. Aucune autre femme ne compare à vous.*'

'I don't know what you just said,' I breathed, 'but I'm pretty sure you're getting laid tonight.'

'Let's get a drink,' he laughed, nodding over at the barman. 'It's pretty much sangria or beer. And I wouldn't bother with the beer.'

'Sangria it is then,' I said, glancing around. The jukebox was loud and already, at six-thirty, the whole place was packed out with pretty Parisians. The cool, grungy kind, not the impeccably stylish ones I'd seen wandering the streets this afternoon. Even though it wasn't really what I was supposed to be researching, Virginie had promised to take me to the swankier parts of town the next day so I could sigh at pretty things through the windows.

The man from behind the bar, wearing a very interesting hand-knitted jumper with some sort of repeat animal pattern, scuttled over with two glasses and a jug of sangria. After splashing it all over the table, he muttered something in French to Alex and slapped him on the back with a big, hearty laugh. I gave him the raised eyebrow and sipped my drink. Bloody hell it was good. Bloody hell it was strong.

'Whatever he just said to you, I hope it had something to do with tonight's specials,' I said, putting the glass back down on the sticky table. 'I don't think I should drink too much of this with only half a baguette and an ice cream in me.'

'They don't do much food here.' Alex frowned a little, making his 'I'm thinking' face. I loved his 'thinking' face, it looked a little bit as if he was going to break out into a show tune. 'It's kind of just tiny bits of bread with cheese on top. There's a great *steak frites* place down the block though. We have time if you want to eat?'

'Right.' I tried to ignore the fact that my stomach wasn't rumbling, it was practically causing an earthquake. 'And you know this because you used to come here when you were doing what in Paris exactly?'

'Everyone comes here,' he replied, filling my glass up to the very top. 'Everyone meets at Odéon, it's like, I don't know, Union Square or Piccadilly Circus or whatever.'

'That's not strictly an answer to my question, is it?' I said, squeezing his leg. I was trying to keep things light, but the more evasive he became, the more annoyed I was getting. 'How come you know Paris so well? And not just tourist stuff. You know where bars are without looking at maps, you know where people meet at night. Spill it, Reid, how?'

'OK, so don't freak out,' he started, leaning back against the wall behind the table. 'I used to date a girl from Paris and we spent some time here. That's all. Paris isn't a huge city, you get to know your way around pretty quick.'

'And why do you think that would make me freak out?' I asked in a very, very high-pitched voice. 'I'm fine.'

'I guess because we never really talked about our pasts since, you know, the first time,' he said, his green eyes still cautious. 'And anyway, it was so long ago.'

'Were you here for a long time?' I asked, not really wanting to know the answer. I remembered this sick in the stomach feeling from the last time we had a conversation about exes. It wasn't pleasant.

'No. Not for long. And the reason I know the city so well is almost the entire time I was here, we were fighting so much I was out wandering the streets, making friends with bartenders. You pick up the geography pretty quickly that way. The language too.'

'Right,' I said, picking up my sangria and having another go at it.

'So you're gonna stop asking questions you don't actually want answered?' Alex asked, leaning forwards into my line of vision. ''Cause, I don't want to piss you off, but I know you and I don't think you want to know any more. Apart from that I ended it and then I went back to the States and I met you and I have never been so happy in my entire life.'

'Sounds fair enough,' I replied, taking a long drink.

Did the bit of dodgy chopped up orange count as one of my five a day? I chose to believe, yes. Yes it did.

'And you're not going to completely obsess over everything I've said?'

'No.' Of course I bloody was.

'I don't believe you, but OK.' He waited for me to set my drink back down and then took both of my hands in his. 'Because I was serious about this being a good trip. You don't think I would have brought you here if the place was all about some other girl for me, do you?'

I shook my head and didn't say anything, but I was shouting the words 'you better bloody not have' over and over in my head. And as happy as I was that he was there with me, there was still a tiny part of me that was fuming over the idea of him sitting at that very table with some other girl, whispering sweet French nothings and feeding her bits of cheese on bread. Well, maybe not the last bit, that wasn't very sexy anyway.

'Angela, I wanted you to come because I love Paris and I love you,' he leaned across the table and kissed me gently. 'And if it helps, I never came here with my ex.'

Brilliant. My boyfriend the mind-reader. The cheesy mind-reader.

'Well, I'm fairly keen on you too, so that should work out quite nicely,' I said, kissing him back, not entirely sure whether or not 'mind-reader' was a desirable quality in a boyfriend. Unless it was related to birthday presents and buying the right sized bra, I was definitely leaning towards 'not'.

Happily for my jet lag, Alex's gig was at a bar right opposite our hotel so it was just a short taxi ride back to The Marais and then straight on to the show. Virginie was waiting for us outside bar Pop-In, perky as ever in a T-shirt that just about covered her arse (way shorter than the one I'd been sporting – no wonder she didn't mention it) and a washed-out denim jacket. I tried not to be insanely jealous of how cute she looked, her thick brown hair scraped back in a ponytail that was on the verge of exploding all over her face, and her bright eyes that danced as I introduced her to Alex. And I knew air kissing was the done thing in France, but really, did it have to extend to my boyfriend? I was fairly against any sort of kissing in relation to Alex. After taking us through to the bar and ordering our drinks, Alex vanished into some tiny back room to get ready for the gig, leaving Virginie and I to try and talk over the loud rock music that throbbed out of the speakers.

'Alex, he is the Brooklyn boy in your blog?' Virginie asked.

'He is.' I nodded, sipping a truly terrible glass of wine. Wasn't all wine supposed to be amazing in France? This was like paint stripper. 'Do you have a boyfriend?'

'No,' she said, looking around. 'I did, but he is cheating on me when I am in New York and so we break up. Alex, he is very attractive.'

'Thanks,' I replied, not entirely comfortable with the compliment and massively awkward about her revelation. What were you supposed to say to that? The bar was tiny and dark, much smaller than the places I was used to seeing Alex play in New York, and the bright lights that lit the stage made his black hair shine, his green eyes even more vivid and his pale skin glow.

'Sorry to hear about your ex. Mine cheated on me too, not that it helps to know that,' I raised my voice slightly over the sound check.

'Really?' Virginie spun around so quickly, half her ponytail made a break for freedom. 'I cannot believe that someone would cheat on you. You are so pretty and funny and nice. And you have a lovely handbag also.'

'Well, I didn't have the handbag.' I clutched my beloved Marc Jacobs tightly to me. 'But to be honest, I don't think that would have stopped my ex from shagging his tennis partner.'

'He is an idiot,' she declared. 'Any man is very lucky to have you. I hope Alex, he knows this.'

I smiled awkwardly and sipped my drink. Ew, nasty. No one, not even Jenny I didn't think, had ever said that. Alex was lucky to have me? Hmm, radical concept.

'Well, don't tell him, but we're going to be moving in together soon,' I said as quietly as the music would allow.

'And he doesn't know?' Virginie sounded confused. 'Maybe you should tell him before you begin to pack.'

I laughed loudly, squirting wine up my nose. It was no better up there than it was in my mouth. 'No, he has asked me to, I just haven't told him that I'm going to yet,' I explained. 'It's a surprise for his birthday.'

'Then he is even luckier,' she said, knocking back her wine. 'This wine is terrible. Do you want a mojito?'

'That is one of my favourite questions.' I put my dodgy wine back on the bar. 'Yes. Yes I do.'

One and a half mojitos later, Alex was halfway through his set and I was standing in my favourite gig-watching spot. Leaning against the bar, behind the pulsing crowd, with a clear view of the band. I couldn't count the number of times I'd seen Stills play in the last year (actually, yes I could, it was seven), but every time I saw Alex get up on that stage I fell for him a little bit more. Seeing him up there, everyone in the room hanging on his every word, made it a little bit difficult to believe Virginie's words. How was he the lucky one? He could have anyone in the room, in any room mostly, and I was the one that got to take him home. And even though I knew that was what would happen tonight, and every night when we got back to New York, it was still sometimes hard to deal with the fact that every girl in the room was lusting after my boyfriend. Not to mention a few of the boys. Of course, I got a little rush of smug to know that they all wanted him and I had him, but it was still a difficult thing to get my head around. I hoped that made me human and not an arsehole.

The set was almost over when I spotted Solène at the front of the stage. Her blonde hair shone white under the bright lights that lit Alex, Craig and Graham, and I could see her dancing, holding another girl's hand high in the air and jumping around. The bar was tiny and they were only a few rows of people away from us. I could see her singing along to every word, her eyes closed, dress riding up dangerously high every time she threw her hands up into the air. In between songs, she would stop dancing, pull down her dress, brush her hair back off her face and smile blissfully. So, she was a Stills fan.

'This girl, you know her?' Virginie asked, pointing towards Solène.

I shook my head. 'Not really, I met her last night. She's in a band here, I think they supported Alex's band or something. I don't know, we really didn't talk that much.'

'She likes your boyfriend very much.'

I looked back over to Solène, her eyes weren't closed any more, this time she was looking right at Alex and singing directly to him, her hands clasped over her heart, tapping out the bass line. And I didn't love it.

Virginie tapped me on the shoulder. 'They were boyfriend and girlfriend?'

'Uhh . . . I don't know.' I didn't feel terribly eloquent as that theory flitted around in my head. Had they dated?

'I thought, perhaps. They look like friends.'

'I suppose,' I nodded, starting to feel a bit sick. And it wasn't from the mix of sangria, red wine and mojito. Well, it might have been, a little bit. 'He hasn't really told me anything about her.'

But he's bloody well going to, I added to myself.

At the end of the set, I waited patiently by the bar while Alex unplugged a million cables and put things back in boxes. I'd offered to help once, but when I'd shorted an amp within three minutes, it was suggested that I take on a more supervisory role. Away from the stage and the very expensive instruments. This time at least, I was glad about that. While he was occupied, and Virginie was in the ladies, I followed Solène outside. Swapping from wine to rum might not be a terribly good idea given the amount of work I had to do the following day, but it did make me much braver than usual.

'Hi, Solène?' I waited for her to finish lighting up a cigarette before she spoke.

'*Oui*?' she replied, looking at me blankly for a moment. 'Oh, Alex's friend! I am very sorry. I forget your name.'

'It's Angela,' I said, not sure how I was planning on managing this conversation. 'Solène, did you used to go out with Alex?'

'Go out with?' She blew out a long line of smoke.

It might have been a disgusting habit, but it was sexy. Bitch.

'Sorry, did you date Alex?' I asked again, starting to feel incredibly awkward. I noticed the other girls from her band heading out through the door towards us.

Solène nodded. 'He did not tell you this? Yes.'

'No, he didn't,' I said, a little surprised to have my suspicions confirmed so readily.

'I am not surprised.' She laughed and offered me a cigarette. For some reason, I took it. 'He is dating so many girls, why would he mention me?'

The other girls surrounded Solène and laughed along. Not really knowing what else to do, I laughed too. Wasn't it hilarious that my boyfriend had shagged so many beautiful women, he didn't see fit to mention to me that one of them was the lead singer of a French rock band who made the Victoria's Secret models look like a bunch of dumpy porkers.

'It was a very long time ago.' She lit my cigarette and carried on talking. 'Many years, we were very young, I was living in New York and it was just for fun. You should both come tomorrow, we are having a party. It would be good to talk to Alex again.'

'Your band is playing tomorrow?' I asked, my voice tight with cigarette smoke. Why was I smoking? Why?

'*Non.*' Solène shook her head. 'My boyfriend and I are just having a party. At our apartment, you must come. Here, I write the address.' She held her cigarette in her lips and scribbled an address on the back of my hand with a marker pen produced by one of her minions. With my free hand, I took another unwelcome drag on my cigarette. Seriously, it was disgusting, how did people do this for fun? I spluttered a little and tried to smile.

'You give me your number,' she commanded, holding

out a pristine white hand. Her nails were super short, just like Alex's. She must play guitar as well as sing, I thought with utter jealousy as I wrote my number out. I couldn't do either, despite what I might think after five frozen margaritas at Sing Sing karaoke on Avenue A.

'We begin at eight, please come.' She took a last drag on her cigarette, stamped it out and gave me two elaborate air kisses before turning on her chunky heel and leaving. '*Au revoir*, Angela!'

'Angela?' Virginie appeared beside me, concern in her bright brown eyes. 'You were talking to that girl?'

'I was,' I said, holding my cigarette behind my back. 'It's fine, but I think I should find Alex. And I think you should get home. You've been amazing today.'

'*D'accord*.' She gave me two quick kisses and hugged me tightly. 'Today was so much fun. I meet you in the hotel at ten tomorrow?'

'Ten.' I smiled tightly. I did not feel well.

I watched Virginie skip off down the road towards the *Métro* and leaned back against the cool wall of the bar. Staring at the half burned-out cigarette, I thought about Alex and Solène. So they'd dated. Did that mean she was La French Bitch? It hadn't sounded like it had been a serious relationship. Plus she said she was living in New York when they'd dated. I wasn't sure if that was good or bad, better the devil you know, after all. Either Alex had dated a super hot French singer ages and ages ago, who now had a new boyfriend and had invited us to her party as a couple, or he'd dated a super hot French singer and at least one other French girl whose level of hotness was a completely unknown quantity. Hmm.

'Angela, are you smoking?'

'Shit.' The cigarette had burned down to my fingers. That would teach me not to pay attention.

'Angela?' Alex put his guitar case down on the pavement and took the burned-out, butt from my fingers. 'Are you OK?'

'Yes?' I said, but even I didn't believe it.

'Come here.' He pulled me towards him, his brown plaid shirt all sweaty and hot from the gig. Performing always put him in the mood and to be honest, watching him wasn't terrible foreplay.

'No, don't.' I tried to push him away, but he'd caught me off balance and I fell against his damp chest. 'I'm disgusting. Again.'

'I don't mind that you taste like an ashtray,' he said, holding my wrists tightly. 'In fact, I kind of like it.'

'But I'm going to be sick,' I said quickly, the words not quite making it out before I spun around and vommed all over the street.

'And you didn't want to kiss me because I'd been smoking,' Alex said, picking up his guitar in one hand and scooping me up with the other. I clamped my hand tightly over my mouth and let him half drag, half carry me across the road and into the hotel lobby. 'I don't think anyone saw.'

I nodded. Wanting to say thank you, wanting to tell him I loved him, wanting to ask him about Solène, but I really, really couldn't take my hand away from my mouth.

'Wait here a second,' he said, carefully resting me against one of the chairs in the lobby and running back out through the door. I watched him go with my hand still firmly attached to my mouth. I looked around the lobby. It was awfully well lit. A soft coughing noise turned my attention to the reception desk. A tall, crisp shirt-wearing hotel worker stared at me. His disgust wasn't even thinly veiled. I took one hand off my mouth and gave him a thin wave. By my reckoning, Alex had about three seconds to get back before I was thrown out or I threw up. Again.

'*Madame*?' the man on the desk started.

'It's OK,' Alex ran back into the lobby and helped me to my feet. 'It's OK, she's a guest here. She has food poisoning.'

'Yes. Food poisoning from French food. And it's *Mademoiselle*,' I yelled back through my hand. '*Mademoiselle*!'

'You are such a freaking lightweight,' Alex said, picking me up and tossing me over his shoulder. A really bad idea given that I was about to puke again at any second. 'I can't take you anywhere.'

'Whatever,' I sighed, trying not to be sick on him. I lifted up my head to watch the concierge, night porter and other assorted staff pop their heads out of the door to follow our progress to our room before my eyes began to flutter involuntarily. 'And it's not the booze, it's the fags.'

'You are all class, lady,' Alex said, somewhere above me. 'You're not gonna pass out, are you? Angela? You still with me?'

'Nuh-uh,' I mumbled, desperately trying to keep my eyes open.

'Because I will be pissed if you don't at least give me time to return your anti-smoking lecture,' he said, stopping and rummaging in a pocket for room keys. 'And it would be better if you didn't choke on your vomit.'

Which were the last romantic words I heard before I passed out.

Asking Alex about his relationship with Solène at four a.m. the next morning while he was holding my hair out of the way so I could vom, might not have been the best idea I'd ever had, but to be fair, I was hardly in the right state of mind to be making my best decisions. Almost as soon as my eyes were open, I had to clamber over Alex and run into the bathroom. Dutifully, he followed, combing my hair out of my face and running cold water on a flannel to cool me down. I chose to take his loveliness as an admission of guilt for plying me with that cheap sangria in the first place, although I wasn't nearly as drunk as I should be to get so ill. Stupid jet lag. Stupid cigarettes. Stupid me. Throwing up sober was horrifying. And so it was with my forehead leaning against the cool steel of the radiator, knees tucked under my chin that I asked Alex the big question.

'So, Solène. She was the French girlfriend?'

Alex looked up from his spot resting against the sink.

'Yes,' he replied, staring straight at me.

Hmm. 'And you weren't going to tell me?'

'Kinda want to know who did tell you,' he said, unfolding his long legs and standing up. I felt tiny, all crumpled up by the toilet while he stretched in the doorway.

'You'll be pleased to know I worked it out all by myself.' I pulled myself up, using the radiator for leverage and trying not to fall down the toilet. Graceful has never been a word anyone has used to describe me. Rinsing my mouth out with water, mouthwash and then water again, I went in for the kill. 'And then I spoke to her tonight—'

'You spoke to her?' He cut me off verbally and physically, suddenly stopping and blocking my exit from the bathroom. 'Why did you speak to her?'

'Mainly because she was practically dry humping you onstage and, quite clearly, I had too much to drink tonight,' I half yelled, pushing past him. 'You don't have to freak out, she didn't sound half as bothered about the whole thing as you were anyway. I just wanted to know.'

'I wasn't trying to keep it from you.' Alex stood still in the doorway. 'I didn't know she was going to be here and like I told you, it was for ever ago. There's nothing to say.' The low bathroom light silhouetted his slender frame and broad shoulders. Why was even lighting against me?

'Whatever,' I said, turning to the wall. I was determined not to let my hormones betray me.

'Honestly, Angie, it's not like there are any feelings there, I just don't want my ex in my face.'

I felt the mattress give slightly with his weight and held my breath, waiting for him to touch me. But he didn't.

'I mean, would you want to hang out with your ex if he was in town?'

I breathed out. There wasn't a single thing I could think of in the whole world that would be worse than me, Alex and Mark hanging out together.

'Anyway would I want to spend a single second with her, when I could be with you?'

Begrudgingly, I rolled over to find that Alex really had assumed this argument was going to go his way. He was completely naked.

'Are you hot or something?' I asked, raising an eyebrow. 'Pretty sure it was my suitcase that got blown up, not yours.'

'Shut up,' he said, sliding his body over mine.

'Alex, I just threw up.'

'And now you're all minty and sweaty.'

'Sweaty?'

'Good sweaty.'

I highly doubted that. I knew what good sweaty was. Good sweaty was how he smelled after playing football in the park with his friends while I read on the grass, how he smelled when he came straight offstage from doing a show at the Music Hall and dragged me the three blocks to his apartment. Good sweaty was not me right at that moment. But I was oh so close to not caring.

I raised my arms above my head, helping him slip my T-shirt up and over, leaving us with nothing except sticky skin on sticky skin. Alex's kisses were always insistent, but tonight they felt deeper than ever, I knew he thought he had something to prove. It felt as if he was trying to tell me something important that there wasn't a word for. His hands moved over my body while we kissed, sending my senses into overdrive, I just couldn't keep up. And I didn't want to even try. After a while his kisses followed his hands, down my neck, my arms, my stomach, marking every inch of me.

I grabbed a handful of his thick, black hair and tried to pull him back up towards me, but he pulled away, disentangling my fingers and kissing them and running his tongue in between each finger, teasing, before getting back to the job at hand. My stomach jumped with every touch until I really couldn't bear it a second longer. I reached out for his hair again and found my hand resting against his cheek. I opened my eyes to see his long fringe swaying in front of his bright eyes, his pupils wide and dark.

'You OK?' he whispered, his head resting briefly against mine, his hair in my eyes, our mouths almost touching, but not quite. Between the, butterflies in my stomach, short, irregular breaths and the electric feeling on my lips, I really wasn't.

'I want you,' I managed to stutter in between ragged gasps. He smiled and combed a sweaty strand of hair out of my eyes.

It was always amazing with Alex, but I was ashamed to realize I'd got too used to tearing our clothes off and going at it like savages. We hardly ever indulged in each other like this. It was almost too good and I didn't know how long I could last. He didn't say anything, just held himself above me for another moment, the buzzing in my lips building until I couldn't hold it any more and pushed my face up to his, taking him in, tasting the sweet saltiness as sweat ran down our faces and into our kisses. My hands tangled themselves in his damp hair, before my nails scratched all the way down the length of his strong back, his lean, muscled arms, and slipped around to press against the hair on his broad chest that turned into the narrow black trail running down his tight stomach. My legs instinctively rode up and wrapped themselves around his narrow hips. Before I could lose my mind completely, he broke the frenzy and pulled away. It took a moment before I realized I was panting, my mouth open, my face scratched from his early-morning stubble.

'I want you too,' he said quietly. 'I will always want you. I love you.'

I stared at him hard, the, butterflies in my stomach turning into fireworks and the tingle from my lips spreading all over every inch of exposed skin. Nodding, I leaned up to kiss him again. It started gently, but it didn't stay that way. His words echoing in my ears, his mouth hard against mine, hands locked together above my head and our bodies synched. Everything else began to melt and he was the only thing in the world, in existence, until suddenly, there wasn't a him and a me any more. It was us, just us, and everything else slipped away entirely.

CHAPTER EIGHT

Reception seemed to take an uncommon amount of pleasure in ringing with my wake-up call ten minutes earlier than it was booked for the following morning, and it took me a whole three messy minutes to remember why that might be. Alex was already gone, off for an early morning radio show thing with the band, but that didn't make heaving myself out of bed any easier.

Standing under the shower, waiting to feel human again, I went over everything I had to get sorted out in my head. First things first, I had to talk to Jenny. It was only nine-thirty here, half past twelve there. Probably not the best time to try and catch her for a heart to heart. She hadn't tried to call or email since Tuesday night and with all the Solène nonsense going on, I just hadn't really thought about it too much. Which was, admittedly, pretty shitty of me. But I could only deal with one problem at a time, I'd proven that before.

After I'd spoken to Jenny, I needed to sort out this article. I'd convinced myself so completely that I was utterly capable of completing this assignment, the idea of that not being the case was a bit of a shock. Yesterday had been fun and I'd got the names of a couple of cool shops, well, I thought they were cool, but they weren't exactly super secret hipster vintage treasure troves. As sick and wrong as it was, I was really hoping that Cici would come through for me. Virginie was a teeny tiny Parisian angel, but *Belle* hadn't exactly helped me out by hooking me up with their least fashion inclined employee. I rang reception to see if there had been any calls, faxes or emails for me from Cici, but there was nothing. And she wasn't answering her cell. I was buggered.

Once all the research for the article was done and dusted (wishful thinking never hurt anyone) I needed to sort out the Alex situation. Given last night's activities, I was pretty certain things were at the very least OK, but I had completely forgotten to mention the fact that I'd told Solène we'd go to her party. And I had a not-so-funny feeling that he wasn't really going to be up for it.

And even worse, I knew it was tragic to admit it even to myself, but being without all my pretty things was still really playing on my mind. I'd forget for a moment and then a vision of my gorgeous gold Louboutins would shoot up and across my mind and it would be like a slap. And they would literally shoot up. In my fantasies, the airport security people had actually gone through the case and blown up each item of beauty individually. Sob. It had taken me a year to get comfortable with myself, with my new life, and it felt as if someone was testing me, taking it away bit by bit. Starting with my accessories. What a bitch.

I waited for Virginie in reception for fifteen minutes before I started to get worried. I'd parked myself in as dark a corner as I could find, dark sunglasses, black T-shirt, black jeans, hair in a ponytail, and had to wonder if I had been too successful in my plan to remain completely anonymous. It was the staff on reception that I wanted to hide from, not Virginie. Another ten minutes later, my phone trilled quietly inside my one-and-only Marc Jacobs bag.

'Angela, I am so sorry,' Virginie blustered down the line, not even waiting for me to say hello. 'I come to your hotel now. I had to go to the *Belle* office and collect the fax from Cici.'

'She sent a fax to the office?' I asked, confused, but relieved. Who would have believed it? Cici had come through, she just wasn't going to make it easy, obviously. How was I supposed to know she'd sent the fax to the office?

'*Oui*, I have it with me now. We will get coffee and read together?' Virginie asked.

'Coffee sounds amazing. How long will it take you to get here?' I was now dying for coffee. Possibly actually dying, my head throbbed and my mouth tasted like paint stripper. Not that I'd ever tasted paint stripper, but I felt I was making an educated guess.

'Perhaps you could come to Alma Marceau *Métro* station? We spent so much time in the Marais and Saint-Germain yesterday,' she suggested. 'It is a simple journey, you take a train at St-Sébastien, change at Bastille and then Roosevelt. Or walk to Bastille, it is not far. You have a map?'

'I do,' I said, checking my bag. I did. Phew. 'But really, I'm not really very good with maps – maybe we should meet here?'

Virginie laughed, all tinkly and reassuring. The opposite of a Cici cackle. 'Angela, you will be fine. I will see you in half an hour. Call me if you cannot find me.'

I really was not in any fit state to be navigating myself around the *Métro* system. And looking at the

Métro map on the back of the street map, it was not going to be as easy as Virginie had led me to believe. That girl had far too much confidence in me. I closed my eyes, dropped my head over the back of the chair and let out a too loud sigh.

'Everything is OK, *Madame*?' asked a very concerned voice at the side of me. 'You are feeling unwell? Again?'

Opening one eye behind my sunglasses, I saw the concierge from last night standing at a safe distance to my left. Clearly he was convinced I was about to chuck up all over his newly pristine reception. Again.

'I'm fine, thank you.' I clambered out of the chair in the most ladylike fashion I could manage (i.e. not very) and attempted to compose myself.

He nodded curtly and backed away slowly, not believing me in the slightest. I pursed my lips together. I wasn't having him going away thinking I was a horrible lush.

'My best friend used to be a concierge,' I blurted out. 'At a hotel.'

'*Pardon*?' He stared at me from behind the safety of his desk. 'Your friend works at our hotel?'

Why? Why couldn't I just leave things alone?

'Oh no, she lives in LA now,' I carried on, ignoring the tiny voice in my head that was telling me to shut up over and over and over and over. 'But she worked in a hotel for years. Have you worked here for long?'

'For three years?' he replied, still looking just as confused and now ever so slightly scared. 'My name is Alain. We are very pleased to have you staying with us, *Madame*.'

Now, there was no mistaking that for a very polite way of saying 'please get the hell away from me and leave me alone', but could I do that? No. Because that would be too easy.

'Wow, three years, that's a long time in one job,' I said, now leaning against the concierge's desk. The little voice in my head had blossomed into a full blown bellow now, begging me to get out of the hotel before my new friend Alain threw me out. 'Do you like it?'

He shrugged and stepped back from the desk. I couldn't help it. I hate when people didn't like me, or thought badly of me. Somewhere, buried not quite deep enough, was the feeling that somehow, my puking in the street outside this man's hotel would get back to my mother. 'Can I help you with something, *Madame*?'

Give up. Give up now, the voice demanded.

'It's Angela,' I said, reaching across to shake his hand. 'And no, I'm fine. Thank you though.' Giving him one last extra bright smile, I admitted defeat and legged it out the door. Note to self, try not to humiliate yourself in front of hotel staff when you're still a little bit drunk from the night before. And he was still bloody well calling me *Madame* when I was fairly certain I'd told him I was *Mademoiselle* at least twice.

At least I'd been right about one thing so far today, the *Métro* was not going to be easy. I'd found the first station easily enough, but had managed to go three stops in the wrong direction before I realized I was not on my way to Bastille. Every second I was sitting on that bloody train, I could see Donna Gregory's expression as she read my article, her eyebrow eventually rising so high that it fell off her face completely. I was fucked. Properly and completely fucked. The tunnels were bigger and brighter than at a Tube station or in the subway, but after I had navigated the dozens of short staircases, hundreds of different exits and a very confusing signage system, it was well over an hour and a half since Virginie had called me. I eventually emerged hot, sweaty and completely dehydrated at

Alma Marceau. Taking a second to try and work out where I was, I saw the Eiffel Tower and the river on one side of me and a huge roundabout on the other. Where on earth would Virginie be? Before I could throw myself in the Seine, my phone beeped again.

'Angela? Are you OK?' Virginie was apparently psychic. 'I have been calling and calling.' OK, maybe just concerned.

'I'm sorry, I'm fine I think,' I was not fine, I was very, very tired. As if my first solo mission on the *Métro* wasn't going to be bad enough, why had I attempted it hungover? 'Sorry, my brain isn't working right yet. Where are you?'

'I am in a café, just by the road. I am waving, can you see me?'

I did a slow turn, thinking how absolutely impossible it was going to be to find one tiny beautiful brunette in a sea of millions, before I spotted her, directly across the road and waving manically. At last, something was going my way.

'Stop waving like that, you'll have a stroke,' I said, waving back and hanging up, happily.

Thankfully, I was able to navigate crossing the road fairly easily and when I collapsed into the chair Virginie pushed out for me, she'd already ordered me fresh coffee, which I downed like a shot.

'Angela, I am so sorry,' Virginie buried her face in her hands. 'I think the *Métro* is so easy, like the subway, I forget you do not know it.'

'It's not your fault,' I said, signalling for more coffee, still too hungover to really reassure her. 'I could have just got a taxi, I suppose.'

'I did not even think of this.' She tucked a stray piece of hair back into the messy bun on the back of her head. 'You must be very angry.'

'Really, no.' It wasn't a lie. I was too exhausted to be angry. 'And you know, I'm sure I'll be able to use it in my piece, compare the *Métro* to the subway and all that.'

Virginie nodded eagerly. 'That would be very interesting.'

'No it wouldn't,' I said, downing my second coffee fractionally more slowly than the first one. 'But it will pad out a piece, which now I think about it, is slim to non-existent at the moment.'

'Well, we have all of Cici's places now.' She thrust a thick wedge of paper at me before delving back into her cotton shopper bag and producing more. 'For someone who is not your friend, she is making a lot of notes.'

I put down my coffee and tried to focus on the tiny type and little maps that covered the pages. There must have been half a ream of paper in Virginie's bag, there was no way I was going to be able to visit all of these places. Glancing at my watch, I realized it was already past twelve. I wasn't even going to be able to read all of these notes. Shit shit shit shit shit.

'Did you read it?' I asked, hoping she could help me tick off the highlights.

'*Non*, I thought I would wait for you.' Virginie winced. 'I am sorry, I should have read the notes.'

'No, no, no,' I muttered, flipping through the pages. 'But bugger me, I have no idea how I'm going to get through all of this before Christmas, let alone eight.'

'What is happening at eight?' Virginie asked, ordering me another coffee. Which was just as well because I wasn't going to have time to sleep.

'Oh, I erm, I told Solène we would go to this party she's having tonight,' I said, pretending to be especially interested in Cici's favourite massage café. Oh.

Ew. 'It's at about eight or something. Somewhere near the river.'

'The girl from the show?' Virginie slapped the papers out of my hand and on to the table. 'Angela?'

'Yes, the girl from the show,' I replied, studiously reviewing my coffee.

'But she is in love with your boyfriend?'

'No she isn't.'

'Yes, she is.'

Who needed Jenny when I had the travel version? Virginie packed just as much of a punch and would easily fit in a weekend bag.

'Well, she's not because she's actually his ex-girlfriend,' I said into my coffee cup. Why didn't they have mugs here? Couldn't we have found a Starbucks?

'What?'

'Solène and Alex used to go out with each other,' I said, trying to be OK with it, although hearing it out loud, illustrated by Virginie's incredulous expression made it really rather difficult to accept. 'It was ages ago. They're fine now. And I said I would go.'

'Alex wants to go to this party?' Virginie asked. 'With his beautiful ex-girlfriend who dances in front of him like a whore?'

'Wow!' I put the coffee cup down. 'Well, actually I haven't told him yet.'

'He will not go.' She folded her arms and stared me down. 'I do not believe he will go.'

'Right,' I said. What else was there to say? 'Well, I'll cross that *pont* when we come to it. We really have to work out where to start on all these places Cici has sent us. And I have to email my friend about . . . some stuff.'

I spread the pages out on the table and tried to make some sense of the addresses, but strangely enough, it was all a foreign language to me. Not quite Greek, but almost.

'I am sorry, I do not know your Alex,' Virginie said, reaching across the table and touching my hand lightly. 'I will look at Cici's emails and you can email your friend and call Alex? I can work out what is close by.'

'That would be amazing.' It felt a little as if I was cheating having Virginie do the work for me, but making up to Jenny wasn't going to be easy. It was still too early to call her, so a well-crafted email would have to do for now.

'And you are absolutely going to this party?' she asked, scooping up all the pieces of paper and taking a black leather notebook from her bag.

'I am,' I replied, although entirely uncertain as to why.

'*D'accord.*' Virginie gave me one short, sharp nod. And sighed.

Writing the email to Jenny took far longer than I had hoped. I was used to her moods, but we'd never rowed while we were on different coasts, let alone different continents, and I really didn't like it. Plus, this was entirely my fault whereas usually, I could more or less count on Hurricane Jenny taking at least fifty per cent of the blame. What was I supposed to do? Because of me, albeit inadvertently, about ten thousand dollars' worth of borrowed clothes had been destroyed. And who would believe what had happened to them? Jenny was still new at this whole stylist thing, her reputation, as she often told me drunk in the middle of the afternoon, was everything. Apparently the getting drunk part was actually essential to the process and not detrimental. But losing lots and lots of beautiful, expensive things was not going to help her out in any way. It wasn't as if she'd dressed someone who would at least have got the clothes on TV or something before she accidentally destroyed them, cough, Mischa Barton.

In the end, after writing four different versions of the same message, I opted for 'I am so sorry, let me know when I can call you and we'll try and work it out. I'll replace them somehow. Love you x'

Although I had no idea what somehow might be. And once I'd watched the email icon flicker and send, I took a deep breath and called Alex.

'Hey,' he answered right away which was unusual, but a relief. Pull it off like a plaster, Angela, I told myself. 'What's up?'

'Hey,' I began, biting my little fingernail. 'How did the radio thing go?'

If there was one thing I was good at, it was procrastination.

'It was fine, we played, we talked.' The line was crackly, but he sounded as if he was in a fairly good mood. Time to bite the bullet. 'Whatever.'

'So, I was just checking, we have no plans tonight, do we?' I turned in my chair to avoid Virginie's raised eyebrow. 'Because we've been invited to a party and I sort of said we'd go.'

'You got us invited to a party already?' He laughed. 'This didn't happen last night by any chance?'

'Maybe,' I admitted, turning a little bit more. 'You know I like to make friends when I've had a drink.'

'You like to do a lot of things I don't approve of when you're drunk. And some stuff that I do approve of.' Alex lowered his voice just enough to give me goose bumps. 'Sure, just let me know where I need to be.'

'Um, well, the thing is, it's Solène's party,' I said quietly. 'At her apartment.'

The line suddenly went awfully quiet.

'Alex?'

'We're not going to a party at Solène's place.'

He didn't sound that angry, just absolutely decided.

'It's just I said that we would, and she said that she really wanted to catch up with you, and for us to meet her boyfriend, and we would really only have to stay for a while, but I really think that, since I said we would, that we should go. Just for a little bit. Otherwise she'll think—'

'What?' Alex cut me off. Which was probably a good thing to be fair. 'What will she think?'

'That we're rude?'

'I'm pretty certain I don't care what she thinks about you,' he replied. 'And I'm completely fucking sure I don't care what she thinks about me. I'm not going, you're not going.'

'You can't tell me what to do.' It was weird to hear Alex swearing at me, and I really didn't like it. And I was trying to be as quiet as possible, pretty sure that Virginie was going to be ready and waiting with whatever the French version of 'I told you so' was. 'I don't know why you're making such a big deal of this. We only have to stick our heads in and say hello. And you might feel better about everything if you actually saw her. It's not good to be angry about something that happened so long ago.'

'Well thank you, Oprah,' Alex replied flatly. 'I figured you'd quit the self-help shit when Jenny left. And I don't want to tell you what to do, but I'm not going to this party. If you want to go to dinner with me, call me back later.'

I stuck out my bottom lip and stuffed my phone back into my bag.

'He does not want to go to the party?'

Looking up, I stared out across the river for a moment. Eiffel Tower, River Seine, lots of pretty people on bikes, yep, definitely in Paris. And yet still getting attitude from my girlfriend.

'He does not want to go to the party,' I confirmed. 'I get it, she's his ex. I wouldn't want to go to my ex's party. I shouldn't go.'

But the sick thing was, I wanted to. I wanted to see Solène's apartment, I wanted to see her boyfriend, and for some inexplicable reason, I wanted her to like me. And if not like me, at least see me looking awesome and know that I was good enough for Alex. As good as she had ever been. Hmm, I had to stop complaining that I didn't understand boys. I didn't even understand me.

'I was thinking,' Virginie tapped me cautiously on the shoulder, 'you have to go to the party.'

'What?' I did a full one-eighty in my chair. 'Now you think I should go?'

'I did not say you should not go,' she shrugged. 'I said Alex would not want to go. It is very difficult for a boy to see his ex-girlfriend. Very, very difficult with his new girlfriend there also. But you should go. And you should look fabulous.'

'Easier said than done,' I mumbled. 'How do you look fabulous without hair straighteners?'

Virginie outlined her plan as we crossed on to Avenue Montaigne. I tried to listen, there was talk of buying some amazing dress, her lending me some killer shoes and some sort of hairstyling extravaganza that would possibly negate the need for straighteners. I would have been more cynical, but luckily for my French Fairy Godmother, I was somewhat distracted. We were, in theory headed to the Roosevelt *Métro* station to get on with our research, but Virginie had failed to mention that Avenue Montaigne was home to almost all of Paris's designer stores, couture houses and general wonderment. I pressed my nose up against the window of Paul & Joe, lusting after a gorgeous grey silk dress and trying not to shed a tiny tear for the Paul & Joe Sister dress I had lost in Suitcase Gate.

'That dress would be perfect for tonight,' Virginie whispered into my ear. I nodded, she was right. It was short, silvery-grey with a white Siamese cat hand-painted on to the front. Slightly odd, but very cool. At least as cool as Solène. 'You should try it on.'

'I can't afford it,' I said, shaking off the vision of myself, all black eyeliner, messy hair and black opaque tights. In that dress. It was too hot for black tights anyway. Not that it wouldn't look awesome without tights. 'And it has a giant cat on it.'

'It would take a very stylish girl to wear it,' Virginie agreed. 'Perhaps someone like Solène?'

'I know what you're doing,' I said, pushing the door open. 'And luckily for you, I am very, very easily led.'

Happily, at least until the shopper's remorse hit, there was just enough room for the dress on my credit card. Or at least, the credit card company people were prepared to allow me to go over my limit to the same value as the dress. I liked to think I had a telepathic link to Barclays and that they understood my pain. I was pretty much able to convince myself of anything when a dress was at stake. But now, with this dress, I would definitely be able to face Solène on even terms. It was gorgeous and it fitted me perfectly. Besides, Virginie was right, I absolutely should go to the party, I wasn't having her, his ex, thinking that I was rude. Or even worse, running scared. Even if she was one of the most beautiful women I'd ever had the dis-pleasure to lay eyes on. And in a super cool band. And all sexy and French. It was OK, I had the cat dress. What could go wrong? Apart from Alex still being all pissed off.

I sent him a flirty (OK, dirty) text message about potential plans for the evening from the changing room at Paul & Joe, explaining that I would pop into the party, just to say hello and that he absolutely did not have to show. And then it was possible that I suggested we meet back at the hotel, go out for dinner somewhere lovely and then follow that up with a repeat performance of the night before. Obviously that would be back in the hotel. We might be in the world capital of romance, but I was fairly certain they still had decency laws here.

After Paul & Joe, it just got worse. Prada, Max Mara, Dior, Valentino and oh good lord, Chanel. For someone who wasn't into high fashion, Virginie certainly had an eye for it. I managed to keep my credit card in my wallet, but I just couldn't stop myself from pawing the windows or sticking my head inside. Aside from the delights of air conditioning, I couldn't help but feel a very pleasant tingly sensation for all the beautiful things. Chanel 2.55 bags, couture Dior gowns, Prada purses. It all just made the world seem a more lovely place. Until I looked at my watch and realized it was almost three.

'Shit, Virginie, you have to get me away from here.' I mentally slapped myself around the face. 'We have to do some research today or I'm buggered.'

'But you are having such a good time,' she said, squeezing my arm. 'And there are many more stores. This is not even the main area for shopping, we have to visit Colette and—'

'*J'accuse*!' I snatched back my arm and pointed at the sweet, innocent-looking brunette. 'You are an enabler. Honestly, I'm having the best time, but we have to do

113

some work. This is exactly the opposite of what *Belle* wanted. I'm sorry I got so distracted, but we should get a move on.'

'I am sorry, you are right.' She pulled out her note-book and flipped over to the notes she had been making while I'd been trying to figure out what to say to Jenny. Time not well spent given the crappy email I'd come up with. 'OK, Cici says we should try a store called Mim. It is not too far, near Les Halles.'

'Brilliant,' I took her arm again, all forgiven. 'There's a restaurant in New York called Les Halles. It's very swanky.'

'Once, Les Halles was the main market place for all of Paris,' Virginie explained. 'But not now. I am surprised we are going there, but she has listed many places that are good nearby. And Cici says this is her favourite store in all of the city, her secret fashion weapon.'

'And I have to give her credit, she does know how to put an outfit together,' I admitted, almost breaking into a run when I spotted the *Métro* sign. 'So let's see this secret weapon.'

'That fucking bitch!' I stood and stared. 'Pardon my French.'

'I do not think that is French.'

I couldn't quite believe it. 'She's screwed me over, hasn't she?'

Cici's secret weapon wasn't an awesome super secret vintage store. It was a crappy, mass market teeny clothes store. It made Primark look like haute couture. Actually that was an incredible insult. I would wear Primark to my own wedding before I wore any of this stuff. Actually, I had worn Primark to someone else's wedding before, but that was beside the point. Cici had completely screwed us.

'I do not like to use curse words, but yes, I think you are right,' Virginie agreed, feverishly flicking through Cici's other suggestions. 'This is the place, I have checked.'

'Are all the places she's suggested like this? Completely shat?' I asked, really not wanting to know the answer. I felt sick as a dog and it had nothing to do with mojitos, sangria or cigarettes.

'I don't know what shat means, but I think maybe they are not the best places,' Virginie said, taking out the original pieces of paper. 'I do not know any of them. Some of the cafés, the hotels, they look real. They are in places I recognize, but the stores, I am sorry. I do not know.'

I looked around for somewhere to sit and sank on to a concrete wall. Les Halles was not the prettiest place in all of Paris. Although I could apparently get any image I wanted screen-printed on to a T-shirt for forty Euros. But why would anyone want the naked picture of Kate Moss they had on the T-shirt displayed in the window? Fashion capital of the world my arse.

'Oh, here is one I recognize!' Virginie piped up suddenly.

'A good one?' I asked. Hoped. Prayed.

'Erm, no.' She bit her lip and looked up from the bit of paper. 'It is a shop called Tati in Montmartre. You do not want to go there.'

'*Tati*? Seriously? It's not an ironic name, is it?'

'I do not think so. Tati is bigger than Mim. It has separate jewellery and wedding stores, but they are both . . . not what you are looking for.' Virginie sat down beside me. 'I am sorry, I should have checked these notes. Perhaps we can do some of our own research online?'

I looked around, trying in vain to find something

worth writing about. I had a feeling that a fast-food place called Flunch was not going to be it. What was that? Were people eating in there? Oh God. I had left Paris and entered the seventh circle of hell.

'Good idea, but I've got no charge on my laptop.' I couldn't believe I'd forgotten to look for an Apple store. I was practically handing Cici my cock-ups on a plate. 'And it's what, almost five? I'm completely buggered.'

'We have tomorrow,' Virginie suggested, trying her best to talk me down. 'And some time on Saturday maybe?'

'Tomorrow is Alex's birthday.' I shook my head. 'I promised I'd spend the day with him. But maybe Saturday, I'm meeting my friend for lunch, but I've got some time. I can't ask you to work on Saturday though.'

'But I want to help,' Virginie offered cheerfully. 'And I worry that you cannot manage in Paris without me.'

'You're probably right,' I admitted, somewhat relieved. 'If you're sure you don't mind.'

'*Non.*' She hopped up from the wall and gave me a half hug. 'I say I want to help.'

'No big weekend plans? No hot dates?' I checked. Not that I was that bothered to be honest, if she wanted to help, I was not going to stop her. I was this close to cancelling Alex's birthday, lunch with Louisa, the festival and Christmas to get this article finished.

'I am all yours,' Virginie promised. 'Now, I do not believe we are going to find anywhere else today. We should go home and make you very beautiful for the party tonight. The shops they are closing and I have very exciting ideas about your hair.'

'Let's go.' I knew when to admit defeat. And I really did want to look good at this party.

CHAPTER NINE

'Oh my God,' I stood in front of Virginie's full-length mirror and stared hard. 'Is that really me?'

'It is!' Virginie clapped her hands together before coming at me with a blusher brush. 'You like?'

I knew it wasn't terribly becoming to stand staring at myself with my mouth wide open, but it was roughly a lifetime since I'd felt so pretty. After listening to me bleat on for two straight days about how badly I missed my hair straighteners, I thought Virginie was answering my prayers when she produced a pair of GHDs. But was my hair straight? No. Somehow it fell in soft, ringlety waves that bounced on my shoulders, while my make-up was better than it had ever, ever been. Virginie might not be into fashion, but she had a God-given gift with an eyeliner brush, and more make-up than Bloomingdales.

'And the dress, it is perfect.' She stepped back, satisfied with her work at last. 'And the blue shoes, they are matching the cat. It is meant to be.'

'I feel really weird about borrowing them,' I said, twisting in the mirror to show the lipstick red soles. She was trusting me with Louboutins? The last person to do that had regretted it. 'Really, they're so expensive.'

'They were a gift, I never wear them.' Virginie dismissed my concerns by pointing to her Converse. 'I would be so pleased if you would wear them. They are perfect.'

'But I'll knacker them, I know I will.' I pouted, torn between wanting to wear the beautiful shoes and the vision of me getting the gorgeous covered leather heel stuck in between paving stones within three minutes of leaving Virginie's flat.

'I insist.' Virginie turned away from the mirror, refusing to engage in the conversation. 'You are so much prettier than Solène.'

I pulled a face not nearly pretty enough for the outfit I was wearing. 'Not quite, but I feel like I can take her on at least.'

'You will fight her?' Virginie asked, concern creasing her forehead. She wanted to stop that before she needed Botox.

'I don't think it's going to come to that,' I said, picking up my bag. Although I couldn't pretend that punching her (hard and in the face) if the worst came to the worst hadn't crossed my mind. Solène might be hotter than me, cooler than me and have all sorts of sexy French history with my ex, but I reckoned I could definitely take her in a fight. She was a twig, I was at least a substantial branch. If not an out and out trunk.

'So, I'm ready,' I said, trying not to touch my hair too much for fear of the curls dropping out before I left Virginie's tiny flat. 'Sure you don't want to come?'

'No, I cannot.' She frowned, wrapping the long cord around her cooled straighteners. 'I promised that I would meet some friends. But you and Alex will have fun?'

'Fingers crossed.' I checked my phone for the fifteenth time that evening. Nothing. 'I told him to meet me at the hotel in a bit, but I'm not sure my phone is working properly.'

There was a slim chance that was true. There was also a slightly more substantial chance that no one wanted to talk to me. It wasn't just Alex who was giving me the silent treatment, Jenny hadn't emailed me back either. OK, so it was a very slim chance. The facts all pointed towards my friends giving me the cold shoulder.

'He will and he will tell you that you look beautiful,' Virginie predicted. 'You would like to call him from my phone?' she offered, holding out a knackered old handset.

'It's fine. I'm just going to stop in for a moment, just to say hello and then leave.' I took one last look in the mirror for reassurance, and then turned, allowed Virginie to spritz me with her perfume and give me a quick hug. 'OK, I'm ready.'

'The taxi is waiting downstairs,' she said, squeezing me back. 'You look too good to take the *Métro*.'

'You are an angel.' I grabbed my bag and headed for the door. 'Thank you so much.'

'Please, no,' she said, hurrying me out of the door. 'I am just so happy to be working with you, Angela. It is an honour for me.'

Oh Lord. And just when I thought I'd snapped her out of that.

I stood outside Solène's apartment for eight full minutes before I went in. It really didn't matter how great Virginie had convinced me that I looked (and for all of ten minutes in the taxi I really had believed it) I just didn't want to go in. I was being stupid, why on earth was I standing outside my boyfriend's ex-girlfriend's party when I could be at dinner with him? And why was I wearing a dress with a great big cat on the front? My phone was in my hand, a new text message to Alex open and ready to send, when I heard someone shout my name across the street.

'Angela, hey!' Craig and Graham crossed the road towards me.

Bugger. And there went my plans for ditching.

'Hi.' I waved half-heartedly and slipped my phone back into my bag. The knackered brown Marc Jacobs satchel didn't really go with my new grey silk mini dress or the baby blue Louboutins I'd borrowed from Virginie, but I always felt better for having Marc around.

'You meeting Alex?' Craig asked, popping a breath mint before offering them around. 'I didn't think he'd show.'

'Erm, no.' I took a mint and tried to find a boy-appropriate explanation for my being at the party of my boyfriend's ex who I had met twice in my life. Without said boyfriend. 'He couldn't make it, but I told Solène I'd come so, you know, I just thought I'd say hello.'

Craig looked confused.

'And then I'll go.'

Graham looked even more confused.

'And meet Alex.'

'Solène invited you?' Graham asked, gesturing towards the front door. 'To the party?'

'Yes,' I nodded, jumping into the lift and watching Craig press the penthouse button. Of course the penthouse. 'We were talking last night, she said me and Alex should come and meet her boyfriend, but you know Alex, he didn't fancy it.'

'Hardly a surprise,' Craig scoffed. 'Dude is not OK about—'

'Craig, man, I don't think Angela wants to get into this right now,' Graham cut him off as the lift pinged and the doors slid open. 'You look great by the way.

Cool dress,' he added taking my hand in his and giving it a squeeze.

Lovely Graham.

'Yeah, is that like, a cat on the front?' Craig asked, giving me a once-over. 'And I'm pretty sure I've said this before, but great legs, Angie. Killer.'

Not so lovely Craig.

'You sure you don't just want to bail? Go hang out with Alex?' Graham asked, holding open the doors. 'I mean, won't it be a little weird?'

'I know she and Alex had a thing,' I tried not to choke on the words. 'But she was really nice the other night and you know, she's got a new boyfriend and everything. I just thought it would be fun to come to a party and stuff.'

'She told you that they had a thing?' Craig asked. 'Wow.'

'It wasn't a thing?' I looked at Graham, who was pulling an entirely unreadable expression. 'Well then what was it?'

Before either could answer, the lift doors slid open right into Solène's apartment. And it was amazing. Stepping out of the lift, sticking close behind Graham, my jaw dropped at the beautiful floor-to-ceiling window in front of me. It was just like Alex's place, except instead of opening out on to the spiky skyline of Manhattan, I could see all of Paris. I had no idea how many floors we'd travelled to get up here, but the view was incredible. The bright blue sky was settling into dusk against the white and grey buildings that rippled up and down along the banks of the Seine, broken by wide boulevards and leafy squares. The Seine was right below us, the Louvre was almost directly opposite, and when I looked downriver, I could see Notre-Dame. The inside of the apartment was almost as impressive. The cool white walls were lined with black-and-white photographs, some of Solène and the band, some of other bands I didn't recognize, a couple I did. None of Alex.

A spiral staircase in the middle of the room lead up to a mezzanine level that had two huge overstuffed cream sofas either side of a low coffee table. Three matching sofas dominated the main part of the lounge and were covered with an assortment of pretty people. And I'd been staring at them for far too long.

'Angela, you want a drink?' Graham asked, still holding on to my hand. 'Come on.'

He pulled me into the busy room, weaving in and out of all the people. Every available surface was covered with half empty drinks, plastic cups, cocktail glasses and bowls of snacks that were really just for show. This was clearly not her first party. I couldn't help but wonder which of the assorted hot, hot men present was her boyfriend. There were more than a few Alex-alikes, but all pale imitations of the real thing.

'You know, I think I will just go back to the hotel,' I said, letting go of Graham's hand. 'I don't feel that well and me and Alex have got a big day tomorrow. The big three-oh and everything.'

'That's cool,' Graham gave me an understanding nod. 'I'll walk you out.'

'Graham, can I ask you something?' I pressed the, button for the lift, feeling a weight come off my shoulders when it lit up.

'Sure,' he agreed, even though he didn't look convinced. 'What's up?'

'How come you came tonight?' I leaned against the wall, taking the weight off the balls of my feet. Best made shoes in the world or not, I would never be a natural high-heels wearer. 'It doesn't seem to me that you're Solène's biggest fan.'

'And that's 'cause I'm not,' Graham admitted. 'But I made a deal with that asshat over there.' He pointed to where Craig already had Marie pressed up against the window, his arm blocking her escape. They were both laughing, but I couldn't help but feel that Marie was laughing at Craig, rather than with him. 'I would come here with him so he can try and get in Marie's pants and then he has to come to the museums and galleries with me tomorrow.'

'Doesn't sound like you get much out of it to be honest.' I really couldn't watch. It was like one of those nature programmes where some awful predator plays with its dinner before it pounces. I couldn't believe that Craig actually thought that he was the one in charge here. 'You don't want to be here and are you seriously telling me you want Craig tagging around after you all day? He doesn't strike me as the museum type.'

'No fair, you saw through my evil plan.' Graham raised a eyebrow and leaned in to whisper theatrically. 'He'll hate it. It's his punishment for snoring all the freaking way here on the plane.'

I laughed and then took a deep breath. There was every chance I didn't want to know the answer to my next question. 'So how come you don't like Solène?'

Graham stopped smiling. 'Look, Angie, I promised Alex I wouldn't talk about this stuff, but it kinda looks like he didn't really tell you about it either and to be honest, I think your being here is kinda messed up, so . . .'

'So what?'

'So, yeah, you know that Alex and Solène dated, right?'

I nodded. 'Following so far.'

'I'm thinking maybe he underplayed the way things went between the two of them.' He turned and pressed the button for the lift, clearly it wasn't coming fast enough for him. 'I guess he's kind of freaked out to see her here. Honest, we did not know that her band was booked to play the festival. I don't think any of us would be here if Alex had known.'

'So it didn't end well? With the two of them?' I asked. Was there even a good answer to that question? Unless it ended when Alex had woken up one morning having had a dream about a transcendentally beautiful English girl who didn't know when to stop asking questions.

'I just don't really think it's my place to fill you in on this stuff.' Graham placed a big, bass-playing hand on my shoulder. 'But don't sweat it Ange, everything is awesome with you and Alex. This is just an unexpected, uh, I don't know, hiccup? One never to be seen again once we're back in New York.'

I nodded, he was right. If we hadn't come to Paris, none of this would be happening and once we got back to New York and Alex and I moved in together, it would be as if it never had. Because I was well known for being able to let things go. Crap. Why had I come here? Why, oh why, oh why had I listened to the voice in my head instead of someone sensible? This was what happened when Jenny Lopez wasn't around to counsel me. Clearly it was her fault.

At last, the lift pinged gently to announce its arrival and I was so relieved to be leaving, that I actually smiled for the first time since I'd stepped out of my taxi. And I absolutely didn't see her coming.

'Graham!' Solène sidled into our path with two cups of beer and planted her customary kisses on his cheeks. 'And Angela, you are here. I love your dress.'

The smile slid halfway off my face, not sure whether the compliment was genuine or not.

'And such beautiful shoes.' She handed us the cups. 'I am underdressed.'

Solène was barefoot. And wearing black jeans and a long black T-shirt. Exactly what I'd been wearing all day long and not in any way a six-hundred-Euro silk dress with a cat on it and borrowed five-inch heels. I felt like a complete tit.

'Your flat is beautiful,' I said, stepping slowly backwards as Solène directed us back into the living room and away from the lift. 'Really, it's gorgeous.'

'Oh, thank you.' She gestured to the arm of one of the giant sofas and practically pushed me backwards until I was sitting down. Would I ever be able to balance properly in big girl heels? 'Graham, please could you get me a drink? Red wine?'

Graham looked from me to Solène and then back to me again.

'Actually, I was just gonna take Angela out to grab a cab,' Graham pulled me back up again. 'Alex has this whole romantic dinner thing planned for her and she needs to leave right away.'

'Does he?' Solène asked, pushing me back down again.

'He does?' I asked.

'Uh, yeah, it's supposed to be a surprise,' Graham said, taking the beer out of my hand and balancing it on a coffee table behind him.

'Then I will call a taxi for Angela,' Solène said, squeezing my hand and giving me a big smile. 'There are not many outside. This is Paris, not New York.'

Graham pushed his square, black glasses up his nose and pushed me up the arm of the sofa, settling down beside me. 'That would be great. As soon as you can, please.'

'The phone is upstairs with the red wine,' Solène replied, flashing another smile. 'You can bring it to me.'

Reluctantly letting go of my hand, Graham practically made a run for the stairs. Solène watched him go, laughing quietly.

'Graham, he is so funny,' she said, dropping lightly on to the sofa beside me. 'I miss him.'

'You spent a lot of time with Graham on tour?' I asked, trying not to feel like a ginormous, overdressed idiot.

'On tour yes, and of course when we all lived together,' she said casually. 'He seems different now. Maybe not so happy.'

'When you lived together?' I had already put two and two together and I didn't like what I was coming up with. 'You lived with Graham?'

'For a while,' she said, twirling a long strand of icy blonde hair around her finger. 'He left his boyfriend and moved in with Alex and I. It was for maybe two or three months.'

Right. Of course. He moved in with her and Alex for two or three months.

When she was living with Alex.

When she was living with my boyfriend.

'I miss so much about Brooklyn, tell me, how long have you been living there?' she asked.

'I, uh, I live in Manhattan,' I managed to say, leaning forward to grab my beer.

'Alex moved to Manhattan? He sold his apartment? With the beautiful views?' Solène asked, plaiting the strand of hair she'd so carefully separated from her elegantly styled bird's nest. 'I cannot believe he would leave.'

'No, he's still in Brooklyn, in Williamsburg.' I was having to think so carefully about my words. Talking really shouldn't be such a struggle. Breathing really shouldn't be such a struggle. 'We don't live together.'

'Oh, so it is not serious?' she asked a little bit too quickly for my liking. 'With you and Alex?'

'It's serious,' I replied, equally speedy. 'It's totally serious. I'm moving in when we get back to New York actually.'

'That is good.' Solène watched as I chugged my beer. 'For a long time he was so hurt. Of course, I know that was all my fault. I am so happy he has found you.'

'He was hurt,' I repeated, not sure if it was a question or not. Where the hell was Graham?

'I know, you must think I am a horrible person, Angela.' She let go of her hair and took the (now empty) cup out of my hand, before holding on to both of my hands. I couldn't help but notice that even though her hands were soft and tiny, she had calluses in all the same places as Alex. 'I just was not ready to settle down. Alex, he was just so desperate to get married, to have babies. I was so young, so far from home. I was very confused. But I realize it was a mistake. I had never wanted to break his heart.'

And I had never wanted to break anyone's face.

Solène hadn't had 'a thing' with Alex, they hadn't dated.

She was the one.

The ex who had cheated on him with his best friend.

'Angela, please, if Alex is not coming tonight, I understand, but I hope you will tell him that I am still very sorry.' Two big fat tears rolled down her cheeks, streaking her porcelain skin with smoky black lines. 'He still will not speak to me and it is years ago. We were happy before, I am too sad that we cannot ever be friends again.'

I gave up on Graham and pulled my hands away,

standing up. 'I'm sorry Solène, I don't think I should really be talking about this.'

She nodded tearfully and dropped her head to her knees.

Not cracking her head open with my shoe was the most civilized thing I had ever done. Which wasn't to say that I wasn't desperately fighting a very strong urge to pull off a Louboutin and play to my strengths, but I was determined to be the bigger person here. For once. That was the plan in the first place, wasn't it?

I left her on the sofa and strode back to the lift as fast as my heels would carry me. My eyes burning only slightly less than the balls of my feet, I jabbed the button over and over until it pinged and the doors slid open.

'Angela,' Graham yelled over the crowds that had now filled the apartment. 'I'm sorry, I got stuck with Craig and then I couldn't find the phone or the wine and, Jesus, are you OK?'

I nodded, holding the lift door. 'Probably would be better if I hadn't just found out Solène and Alex and, well, everything. From her.'

'Probably.' Graham winced. 'Angie, I'm real sorry. But it's history. Ancient, you know? It just doesn't matter.'

'Hmm.' I stepped into the lift. 'Yeah.'

My eloquence astounded me at times.

'I called a cab, it should be downstairs by now,' he said, holding the door open. 'Can I come with you?'

'Um, I think I need five minutes actually,' I said. It was the most diplomatic version of 'piss off, I want to be on my own' I could come up with.

Obviously there was no taxi outside when I got down there and none to be seen anywhere in the street. I wandered around to the front of the building and leaned over the wall, staring out at the river. Notre-Dame was all lit up on the opposite side of the bank. The huge towers were so beautiful, but totally intimidating and just a little bit scary. I wondered if Solène ever clambered around the roof under cover of darkness and jumped about. Or maybe she just clung to the edge like one of the gargoyles. Except, you know, a really beautiful gargoyle who had seen fit to break my boyfriend's heart and then expect us all to play BFFs. Bitch.

There was only one person who would appreciate my rage at that exact moment. Rummaging around in my bag, I found my phone, almost out of charge, and pressed the first speed dial button.

'Jenny Lopez,' she answered on the first ring. Thank God she never checked caller ID before picking up the phone. Or however you answered an iPhone.

'Jenny, it's me,' I said quickly, surprised to hear a few tears in my voice. 'Can we talk? Please?'

'Angie, I'm sorry, I can't right now,' she sounded tense, but not angry. 'I have a ton of problems to sort out so you're gonna have to wait.'

'But I'm having a bit of a crisis,' I started. If I could just get into the bitching soon enough, she'd be powerless to resist.

'Let me guess,' she cut me off. 'Uh, Alex is being an ass or you fucked up the *Belle* job. Which is it?'

Wow. I really did not have an answer for her. It didn't strike me that she'd be too impressed if I replied with, well, it's a bit of both really.

'Can't do this right now, sorry,' Jenny went on. 'I'll call you later.'

'But Jenny,' I tried to stop her, but apparently that was a bad idea.

'Ah, you didn't have time to talk to me when you kept diverting my calls yesterday, now I don't have time to talk to you. Go take care of your crisis, I have stuff to do.' And then she hung up on me. Actually hung up.

I stared up at Notre-Dame again. No chance of divine intervention? Apparently not. Possibly because I'd never stepped foot in a church in my life unless there was a promise of cake, a three-course meal and a free bar at the end of it.

I fought the urge to break out into a chorus of 'On My Own' from *Les Mis* and looked back at my phone. I didn't really know who else to call. I couldn't cope with a panicking Louisa and I was seeing her in a couple of days anyway. Erin would tell me I should have put a shoe through Solène's skull, and I just didn't feel like I could talk to my other New York friends about this stuff. They didn't need to know the ins and outs of Alex's sexual history. Of course, I was forgetting the one person who wouldn't need a brief. I was pretty sure Alex was familiar with all the details.

I pressed the second speed dial button and waited for it to ring through. And it did, straight to voicemail.

'Hey, it's me.' I started walking towards the bridge and over towards the cathedral. Surely there would be taxis around there? 'I'm on my way back to the hotel, sorry I've been such an idiot today. I blame Paris, it's so pretty I can't think straight. Plus, I haven't had a hot dog since Monday and I think it's done something strange to my brain. I'll be back as soon as I can. Or call me and I'll come and meet you. Or, well, whatever you want to do. I love you.'

Hanging up, I convinced myself he was in the shower, making himself all pretty for me, and continued on my mission to find a taxi. On my own. Pretending he's beside me.

Sniff.

One hour and several blisters later, I hobbled into the reception of The Marais looking incredibly pitiful. Pale grey silk might look beautiful in a shop window or at a terribly stylish cocktail party (there was no classier accessory than a good caipirinha), but after an hour's mad wandering around a strange city on a sweaty August evening, it wasn't the most becoming outfit a lady had ever worn in Paris. But then there was a pretty strong case to suggest I wasn't that much of a lady. Apart from the fact that I hadn't smacked Solène in the face, which was very reserved of me. The second I stepped through the sliding glass doors that lead to the reception, I threw myself into the nearest chair, a big plush, red velvet affair this time, and fought with the tiny straps on Virginie's Louboutins. Damn the fabulous craftsmanship.

'Oh, for fuck's sake,' I wailed, dropping my head on to my knees. I couldn't go another step with these torture devices strapped to my feet. Beautiful torture devices though they might be.

'*Madame?*' a voice asked across the room.

'*Mademoiselle*,' I barked back. Really, how many times?

'*Mademoiselle*, can I help you, please?'

I looked up to see my good friend, Alain, from the concierge desk. Along with a familiar look of concern, he was also wearing a coat and a backpack.

'I'm not drunk,' I said too quickly. Not that he would have believed me anyway. 'I just had to walk back from this party and I didn't really know where I was going and, well, I had a map, but I'm not very good with maps and I kept getting confused with *gauche* and *droite* and the battery on my phone ran out and I don't have my charger and—'

'You would like to borrow a charger?' He looked incredibly relieved to have a reason to cut me off. 'We have many different kinds. May I see your phone?'

I handed over my BlackBerry, so mad at myself for not thinking to ask at reception before now.

'Thank you so much,' I said, finally managing to wrestle the shoes off my feet and gingerly trotting after him. 'Honestly, that's amazing. You're just like my friend Jenny, when I first met her she had everything in the world in her little office at the hotel.'

'*Et voilà!*' Alain held out a neatly coiled BlackBerry charger with an almost smile. 'May I help you with anything else?'

'Not unless you've got a super secret insider's guide to Paris in there,' I smiled back, slipping the charger into my bag. 'Or a charger for my laptop.'

'I am sorry, no.' Alain looked back in the drawer again, just in case. 'But there are many computer stores in Paris.'

'Oh, I know, but it's for my Mac and my friend didn't think I'd be able to get one very easily,' I replied, trying to ignore the burning in my feet long enough to get through one sensible conversation with Alain. It was a shame he lived in Paris, Jenny would have loved him. Tall, blonde, bright blue eyes and an unwavering commitment to the art of the concierge. Also, totally handsome, but I'd had enough problems with hot hotel workers to last me a lifetime. I was staying well clear of this cutie. 'It'll be a relief just to get my phone working again.'

'There is a store very nearby, it specializes in Apple products, I am sure they will be able to help,' Alain suggested, taking a map of the city from the desk and marking on a very short route. 'It is open quite late, I think.'

'That's amazing, thank you so much,' I said, staring at the map. 'Maybe it opened while Virginie was in New York or something. She mustn't know about it.'

'Of course,' he said, swinging his rucksack back on to his shoulder. 'My shift is over for today, but if there is anything else we can help you with, please let my colleagues know.'

'This is brilliant, thanks again.' I stepped lightly from foot to foot. At least the marble flooring was cool. 'I'll bring the charger back in the morning.'

'*D'accord.*' Alain went for a full smile and just about cracked it. 'Have a lovely evening.'

'You too,' I said, tiptoeing backwards towards the door. 'Oh, and Alain, erm, I'm really sorry about being in a bit of a state last night.'

'Not at all *Mademoiselle.*'

'Ahh, thanks.' He'd called me *Mademoiselle.* About bloody time.

'Hey, Alex? I'm back, I'm so sorry I took so long,' I shouted through the door, fiddling with the lock. 'I swear I'm not leaving this room again unless I'm with someone who knows exactly where they're going or I'm getting in a cab.'

But the room was empty. Alex wasn't there.

'Alex?' I called out, flicking on all the lights. 'Are you in the bathroom?'

He was not in the bathroom. I pulled the shower curtain aside, as though he might be hiding. Why did people always do that? I flopped down on to the bed, half relieved to be off my feet and half freaking out about Alex's mysterious absence. It was almost ten, I should have been home at least an hour ago and there was nothing, no note, no phone message, nothing. I plugged in my borrowed BlackBerry charger and waited for the battery icon to flicker on to the screen.

'Come on,' I said quietly, staring at the screen. Nothing. 'Bugger.'

I pressed the speed dial button to try to call him, but it just wouldn't connect. Probably not enough charge in it, I told myself, setting the phone down on the bedside table. I wriggled out of my dress and lay back on the bed. He'd be back soon enough, Graham and Craig were at Solène's and besides, Graham would have called me and left a message if Alex was with them. There was nowhere else for him to be. I closed my eyes for just a moment, willing my feet to stop throbbing, my stomach to stop rumbling, my head to stop aching. The sheets were so cool and the bed was oh so soft, I couldn't help but let my eyelids flicker once more. Reaching out to the bedside table, I turned on the TV, settling on a noisy translation of *Grey's Anatomy*. It didn't seem to matter what language certain shows were in, it was hardly difficult to follow.

'Oh, McDreamy,' I mumbled quietly at the screen. 'Make up your bloody mind.'

I reached over to grab my BlackBerry, only managing to knock it on to the floor. The homepage was back up, but there was no signal at all. I waved it around with one feeble, half-raised arm, but nothing was happening.

'Crappity crap.' I dropped it back on the bedside table with a clatter and rolled over on to my back. Alex would be back soon, hopefully with the number of a takeaway, there was no way I could manage to be vertical again today. In fact, he'd be lucky if I was even awake when he got—

* * *

I had no idea how much time had passed when my eyes snapped open, fresh from a dream about desperately needing the toilet, but finding them all occupied by Solène lookalikes, but I found myself both desperately needing the toilet and asleep under the sheets in my underwear. The TV was off, the lights were out, but Alex wasn't in bed beside me. I sat up, waiting for my eyes to adjust to the darkness, and the globs of mascara that were gluing them shut. Worried that I might actually wet myself, I hopped off the bed and into the bathroom, pushing the door shut and peeing in the dark. I washed my hands and blinked back into the bedroom, not quite managing three steps before I tripped over something in the middle of the floor and went flying across the bed.

'Fuck!' I squeaked, planting my face on the corner of the bedspread. Heat started to spread through my left cheekbone and I pressed my hand on to my face until the sharp pain dulled to a slow throb.

'Fuck, fuck, fuck,' I said through gritted teeth, kicking whatever it was I'd tripped over. As my only open eye adjusted to the half-light, I realized that it was a pair of Converse. Alex's Converse.

'Angela?' Alex's voice asked from a dark corner of the room.

'Alex?' I mumbled from the floor.

A lamp clicked on showing the whole sorry scene. Alex was all curled up in an armchair in the far corner of the bedroom, still wearing his jeans and T-shirt, while I was stretched out on the carpet in my bra and knickers, a pair of trainers wrapped around my ankle and a small pool of blood collecting next to my hand. Fortunately it wasn't on the carpet. Unfortunately, it was on my brand new, *über* expensive, grey silk dress.

'What are you doing over there?' My voice sounded

weird and nasal and nothing was really making sense. Why was Alex in the chair? And why was I on the floor again? 'What happened?'

'Can we start by cleaning up your bloody nose?' He unfolded his legs and scrambled out of the chair, at my side before I could unravel his shoes from around my ankles. 'Jesus, Angela, I'm gonna have to put a bell on you. What are you doing?'

'Peeing?' I winced as he lifted my chin and took my hand away from my cheek. 'Why were you in the chair? Where were you?'

'Let's get you fixed up first.' He pulled me up to my feet, one arm wrapped around me, the other sweeping my hair out of my face.

I perched on the edge of the bath, staring at my bloody hands while Alex ran the cold water and gently dabbed at my face with a damp flannel. 'You are definitely going to have a black eye tomorrow,' he said, squatting in front of me. 'I don't think your nose is broken though.'

'Are you sure?' I asked, trying not to pull away. 'It feels broken.'

'You ever break it before?'

'No.'

'Then how would you know? It's hurt, it's not broken.'

'Feels broken,' I muttered, trying not to think about any incidents in the past where I may or may not have broken someone's hand.

'When you've toured with Craig for six months straight, you'll know when a nose is broken.' Alex swapped the bloody flannel for some clean tissue. 'I fixed that boy up more times than I want to remember. Come on, let's get you in bed.'

I stood up on wobbly legs and let Alex lead me back to the bed. He took out a button-up shirt and slipped it on me, fastening the front few buttons and then popping out two Advil and placing them in my palm. 'Let me get you some water,' he pushed me carefully on to the bed and disappeared back into the bathroom.

Through my not-quite-with-it haze, I spotted the glowing clock on the bedside table. It was just after two a.m.

'Alex?' I called as loudly as I could with the shooting pain that ran all the way across my cheekbone and up into my forehead. Ouch.

'Yeah?' he replied, back at my bedside, glass of water in hand.

I swallowed the Advil with a swig from the glass that Alex held out. Clearly he didn't trust me to hold it. Which was, I supposed, perfectly understandable.

'It's after midnight. Happy birthday.'

'Thanks,' he said quietly. 'Try and get to sleep.'

'OK,' I whispered back, feeling a bit weird. And not entirely because of the bed frame to the face incident. Alex turned off the light and I heard him unfasten his jeans.

'You're coming to bed?' I asked, blind as a bat.

'Yeah,' he said as his weight hit the other side of the bed.

Relieved, I tried to roll over, but the pain on the right side of my face wouldn't let me. I waited a second for Alex to cuddle up, but he didn't. Reaching out, I traced down his forearm until I found his hand, curled my fingers around his and squeezed. He wrapped my hand up in his, but didn't squeeze back. instead, I heard a quiet sigh and felt his body pull away slightly, rolling towards the window. I stared up at the dark ceiling with my good eye and tried to breathe evenly. What a great start to his birthday.

CHAPTER TEN

'Oh my God, what happened to my face?' I moaned
as sunlight poured into the room. I prised open my
right eye, unable to open the left. Alex stood by the
window in his boxers and a T-shirt with his back to
me. 'Did I try and take a drink off Lindsay Lohan or
something?'

'You don't remember?' he said, turning to face me
with something like a smile. I noticed there was a big
rusty streak of blood down the front of his shirt. 'Jesus
Christ, I leave you on your own, you get in trouble. I
bring you with me, you get in trouble. You tripped in
the middle of the night.'

My brain still hadn't quite processed everything that
had happened in the previous twenty-four hours, but
I knew I was relieved to see that smile.

'I did?' I shuffled upwards into a sitting position. Alex
came over and sat on the edge of the bed with a glass
of water.

'You did,' he confirmed, taking a bottle of Advil from
the bedside table and shaking a couple of tablets out
into his palm. 'You really don't remember?'

Looking around the room, the memory flooded back.

I took the tablets, swallowed and nodded. 'I'm such a clumsy cow.'

'It was my fault, I shouldn't have left my shoes in the middle of the room, I'm sorry.' He took my hand in his, turning it over and running his forefinger over the bloody trail that marked the back. 'Does it still hurt?'

'My hand?' I was confused. Not for the first time.

'Your cheek,' he said, lifting his hand to trace tenderly along my cheekbone. I pulled back slightly, it was so sore. 'Aw, man, you're not going to like it.'

'It looks bad?'

'Looks painful,' he offered diplomatically. 'Maybe you should just stay in bed. I'll get some ice or something.'

'I'll be fine,' I said, trying to convince myself more than anything. I'd never actually had a black eye before. I couldn't believe how much this hurt. 'It's your birthday, we're going to go out and do Paris.'

'Yeah, uh, about that,' Alex pulled a face and ruffled the back of his hair so that it stood up in soft, spiky peaks, 'I kinda have to go and do some band stuff today.'

'But I thought we were going to spend the day together?' I was confused again. Wasn't spending his birthday together the whole point of my coming out to Paris? 'It's your birthday, Alex.'

'I know,' he stood up and picked his jeans up off the floor. 'I wish I could get out of it, but the record company said we'd do some more interviews, meet with some of the European execs. It sucks, I know. I would have told you last night, but—'

'But?'

'You weren't here.'

Ouch. I wasn't sure what hurt the most, my face or

Alex's low blow. I bit my lip and chose to ignore it. An early birthday present. To go with my moving in announcement and the lovely vintage watch that had been blown up. It had been lovely.

'I suppose if you don't have any choice,' I said. I really wanted to pull a face, but my aching left cheek wouldn't let me. 'Can we still have dinner together?'

'Absolutely.' Alex folded up the jeans and placed them on the foot of the bed. 'Look, why don't you go back to sleep, I don't know, maybe do some shopping or something this afternoon, and then we'll do dinner tonight. It's totally my fault that I ruined our day so, take my credit card, go crazy.'

If I hadn't been suspicious before, I was now. 'You want me to go shopping with your credit card?'

'Yeah.' Alex shrugged. 'It's my fault you're on your own with nothing to do, it's my fault you have a smashed-up face, and I want to make it up to you.'

'You can't do that with a credit card,' I said, narrowing my eyes. This wasn't Alex talking and I was over playing dumb. 'What's going on, Alex? Where were you last night?'

'I was here,' he said, his head inside the wardrobe, 'waiting for you.'

'You weren't here when I got in.' I kicked off the covers, hot and bothered all of a sudden. 'And you weren't answering your phone.'

'Uh, no? You were the one not answering your phone,' Alex said, closing the door and turning to stare me down. 'And you were the one who went to a party at my ex-girlfriend's place instead of coming out to dinner with me. Sure, I took a walk after I'd been sitting here waiting for you for two hours, and then I get back and you're passed out on the bed. I don't think you're in a position to be pissy with me right now, Angela.'

'I'm not being pissy,' I protested, pissily. 'I told you I was going to stop in for two minutes and then I was coming back. And I left you a voicemail to say I was on my way back at like, eight-fifteen or something.'

'Well, I didn't get it.' He pulled a faded black T-shirt roughly from its hanger and threw it at the bed. 'Can we please not argue today?'

'I'm not arguing,' I said, throwing myself back down on the bed. And immediately regretting it when a sharp shooting pain coursed all the way down my cheekbone and into my eye socket. Ow ow ow ow ow.

'Good.' He threw a pair of socks and clean boxers on top of the T-shirt and then vanished into the bathroom, slamming the door.

I folded my arms and pouted. Maybe I wanted to argue. Maybe I wanted to know why he thought it was perfectly acceptable to give me the silent treatment and not be where he said he would be, and then wake up the next morning and pretend that everything was rosy. And maybe I wanted to know why he thought he could buy me off with his credit card. That was so weird. I lay on the bed, listening to the shower running and tried not to think about Alex being all soapy and naked. It was difficult to be mad at a naked soapy man you were in love with. Especially on his birthday. Well, any time really.

He emerged from the bathroom with a towel wrapped around his waist, wet, black hair dripping down his face. I folded my arms and stared. It wasn't any easier, naked man in a towel was equally as difficult to be mad at. He stopped in the middle of the room and held out his arms.

'What?'

'Nothing,' I replied, turning over and flicking on the TV.

'Good.'

I burrowed back under the covers. It didn't matter whether or not I was far too hot, it was the principle. And the principle was that I was being stroppy.

Alex dressed in silence while I sulked in bed. I tried to think of something to say that would be funny, alluring and yet show that I was mature enough to put this squabble to one side in honour of his birthday.

'So, do you feel old?'

Alex stopped dead, one leg in his jeans. 'I feel great, thanks for asking.'

Probably not quite the reaction I'd been hoping for. Or the question I should have asked.

'What time do you want to meet for dinner?' I asked, flicking my toes out from under the sheets. It really was warm in there. 'Are you coming back here?'

'Sure,' he said, rubbing at his hair with a towel. How come he could treat his hair so incredibly badly and still have it be so very soft and shiny, while I could condition myself stupid and treat my hair as delicately as a newborn kitten and it still looked like crap?

'Uh, eight?'

'Eight?' I repeated, except in a really rather high-pitched voice. 'You won't be back until eight?'

'Angela, it's almost twelve now.' He pointed at the alarm clock beside the bed. What did you know, he was right. 'I have to meet these record company guys for lunch and then do a bunch of interviews and meetings. I'll be back at eight.'

He sighed, leaned over and kissed me on top of the head. 'Get some rest, feel better and I'll send room service up with some ice for your eye.'

For the want of a better idea, I lay in bed for another ten minutes, waiting for my eye to stop hurting. When it didn't, I frisked the bedside table for my BlackBerry, unable to tear my good eye away from the quite terrible French soap opera on TV. I was making up my own storyline since I couldn't translate, but I wasn't very good at it.

Although it was fully charged, my BlackBerry still wasn't showing any emails or phone service at all. Frowning, I tried to open the web browser, but it just wasn't happening. Tossing the tiny black box to the foot of the bed, I gave a huge dramatic sigh. Flicking the TV over to MTV, I decided that sitting in bed, feeling sorry for my Alex-and-his-hot-ex situation and ignoring the nagging panic that I was never, ever going to get this article finished wasn't going to help me in any way, so I stood up, stripped off and headed into the bathroom singing along to classic Britney as loud as humanly possible. At the exact same time Alain arrived with my bucket of ice.

'Pardon, *Madame*, ah, *Mademoiselle*,' he stuttered, pulling the door closed as I scrambled for a towel. 'Monsieur Reid asked me to bring up some ice. You did not answer when I knocked.'

I flailed around for a moment, trying to wrap the towel around myself, but only succeeding in flashing him a couple more times. I settled for holding the towel in front of me like a slutty matador, and backed up towards the wardrobe.

'I had the TV on loud,' I tried to explain, brushing over the part where I was singing along like a tuneless goat. Who had lost its hearing in a particularly nasty farmyard brawl. 'You brought it up yourself?'

'Yes, you left this on the desk last night.' Alain handed over my map to the Apple store. 'I think you might need it.'

'Oh, I will, absolutely,' I replied, taking it and setting

it safely inside my handbag. I didn't really have any pockets in my towel. 'Thank you so much.'

'My pleasure,' he said, looking away quickly while a very impressive blush spread from his neck all the way up to his pale blonde hairline. He really was cute. 'If there is anything else, please call the front desk.'

'I will,' I promised, automatically edging forward to see him out before I realized my backside had been on full display in the mirror the whole time.

Thankfully, Alain was in almost as big a rush to get out as I was to get rid of him and the door slammed shut in record time. Hovering by the bathroom mirror while the shower ran, I couldn't help but sympathize with the poor man. My hip was turning a fetching shade of yellowish-green from where I had fallen through the bed, and my face was a giant purple mess. And that's without getting into what had happened to my beautiful tousled curls overnight. I looked like an extra from *28 Days Later*. Except, twenty-eight days after that. What a picture-perfect couple Alex and I would make on his birthday. The hot hipster and his zombie love.

After a good twenty minutes of delicately dabbing my entire limited cosmetics stash over my eye and a good five minutes sniffling over my ruined Paul & Joe cat dress, I pulled on my skinny jeans, borrowed another of Alex's shirts and thanked the Gods of Man Fashion that my boyfriend did not travel light.

Thankfully, Paris was insanely bright and sunny and so I was able to camouflage my eye Olson style, carefully perching my sunglasses on the bridge of my battered nose as I trip-trapped out into the cobbled street in the new flip-flops I'd picked up the day before. According to Alain's map, the Apple store was only a few streets away. I crossed the wide main road and practically skipped into the narrow, windy streets of the Marais. I had decided I was in love with this part of Paris, it was just too lovely. Everything was charming and quaint and elegant and all those other lovely words that I wished would one day be attached to someone's description of me even though I knew they never, ever would.

I stopped to stare into the windows, scribble down the names of the cutest stores and generally dash from one side of the street to the other, oohing, aahing and sighing at the general beauty of the pretty Parisian things. There were just so many beautiful boutiques, and even the chain stores seemed to have more of an individual charm about them. I stalled for just a moment longer than was healthy outside a ridiculously expensive bridal salon, staring at the dresses in the windows. One was a long, slender column of elegant silk, a high neckline that draped down low in the back with delicate, floating angel sleeves. In the other window was a more structured, crisp white dress, almost a straight replica of the dress Audrey Hepburn wore at the end of *Funny Face*. A low, wide neck, three-quarter length sleeves and a fitted bodice with a full-knee length skirt. It was beautiful. I realized I'd been staring for far too long when the owner of the shop came to the door and smiled glowingly at me. Then glanced at my ring finger, tipped her head to one side, turned around and closed the door. What a bitch.

'Maybe I don't want to get married anyway,' I said under my breath, turning and marching off down the street, red-faced. Patting my trusty, but knackered satchel, I tried to work out how many Marc Jacobs bags I could buy for the cost of an average wedding. It was surprisingly and upsettingly few. I tried to clear my mind by taking another look at Alain's map. According to his scribbles, I was in the right place and, come to think of it, the road was looking slightly more familiar. Had I doubled back on myself?

'I'm so going to get lost,' I muttered, glancing back at the map. Every street looked the same to me and I had absolutely no internal compass to direct me. Stupid BlackBerry, where was GPS when I needed it?

I paused on a corner for a moment, took off my sunglasses and, ignoring the horrified stares my face was receiving, looked around. And then I realized why the street was so familiar. The store that made handbags out of leather jackets, Virginie's top-secret Parisian find, was directly opposite me. I frowned, turning the map around a couple of times. It definitely told me to pass that store. Following the street down and enforcing the discipline not to go into the chocolate shop opposite, I reached the end of the road. And found the Apple store. Turning back, I could still see the handbag place, it was crazy, we had been so close. Relieved to be one step closer to an internet connection, I almost ran into the shop, narrowly avoiding being run down by a man on a scooter. It was disgusting how quickly I'd got used to looking only one way when I crossed the street. God, I was New York dependent already.

After a couple of minutes of aimless wandering around from computer to computer, a very young sales assistant sidled up to me, clad in the internationally recognizable aqua shirt of someone who is going to help you, but also make you feel really, really stupid in the process.

Realizing my ability to order coffee, croissants and wine weren't going to get me through the purchasing of a power cable, I took out my laptop and pointed at the outlet.

'Hi, I um, God, sorry,' I gesticulated wildly with my free hand and pulled my best 'I'm a really stupid tourist, I know' face.

'You need a power cable? Or an adaptor for your cable?' he asked in a clear Californian accent. 'People always forget them when they travel.'

I pulled a tight smile. Wow, he really wasn't going to have to work at making me look stupid, I was doing quite a good job of that myself. 'Power cable, please.'

While the child prodigy busied himself looking for a cable to work with my 'wow, practically antique' laptop (it was two years old), I hopped on to a stool and immediately logged on to one of the store's MacBooks. The site of a browser window opening up in front of me was far more exciting than it should be, and I actually felt my blood pressure drop from 'definitely-about-to-have-a-stroke' to a 'will-live-through-the day' level as I clicked into TheLook.com.

There were about five emails from Mary, each one slightly more pissy than the last that I was ignoring her. And any number from Donna. My heart rate started to creep back up as I clocked through to the last message from Mary.

Dear Angela,

I realize you are far too important to acknowledge me now that you're writing for *Belle*, but if you want to keep your blog, please email me immediately.

Regards,

YOUR EDITOR, Mary

Panicking, I pressed reply, hashing out a quick overview of what had happened to my case, my BlackBerry, my everything. Reading it back, I really didn't feel 'and it's all because of that psycho bitch of an assistant, Cici. She's totally mental' was overly harsh. Spotting aqua-shirt man approaching with my cable, I pressed send and hurried over to the checkout only to have him wave his portable card reader at me. Seriously, was being a smug little bastard part of the Apple recruitment policy? I silently vowed never to be peer pressured into another Apple product again. Except for maybe a new iPod, who could live without that? And maybe an iPhone. Once I'd replaced my laptop with the new MacBook Pro.

The mid-afternoon streets were boiling compared to the ice-cold air conditioning in the Apple store and I was achingly hungry. I wasn't sure if it was my bashed-up face or the terrifying noises coming from my stomach that was scaring women and small children, but people did seem to be crossing the street to get away from me. Steeling myself, I walked into the nearest café and bought an orange juice and a croissant. The lovely, tiny grey-haired man behind the counter did a really great job of trying not to stare at my bruises and within a minute, without any major miscommunication problems, I was out of there. With the items I had gone in to purchase. It was a proud moment.

Going back to the hotel felt like admitting defeat on the article front, and so I trekked around a few more streets, looking for somewhere to sit and eat my bounty. After crossing a couple more streets, I spotted a group of French people walking along with bags of food. Following them through a giant set of wrought-iron gates at a safe and not stalkery distance, I found myself in a beautiful walled courtyard, all stone archways and manicured gardens. A small sign by the gates read *Musée Carnavalet*. I glanced around, trying to spot somewhere to pay, but I couldn't see anything. Feigning ignorance, I bagged a spot on the steps and tore into my croissant.

For the first time since I smashed in my face, maybe since I'd got to Paris, I began to feel relaxed. Without the assistance of alcohol. I'd jotted down the names of lots of stores and taken crappy little pictures on my BlackBerry as I'd walked around, yes it was still very Marais-centric, but who at *Belle* was to say that the Marais wasn't the coolest, hipster hangout in all of Europe? Virginie would help me take better pictures, but *Belle* knew I wasn't a photographer. Their brief was just to get snaps and if we needed anything fancy, I was sure they could send a photographer out to get better shots. I was just the writer. A really, really good writer.

And Jenny couldn't stay mad at me for ever. I would do whatever I needed to do to help her, and we'd sort things out. We always did. And Alex, well, my problem wasn't really with Alex, when I thought about it. My problem was the fact that he'd dated a spectacularly beautiful woman before me and that spectacularly beautiful woman just so happened to be here, in Paris, with us. There wasn't very much I could do about that. It wasn't as if Alex was interested in her and it wasn't as if she was interested in Alex, so what was I getting wound up for? Aside from the obvious 'because I'm a girl' reason, obviously.

The garden was so peaceful and ridiculously pretty. Tearing off a big chunk of croissant, my mind wandered off and I imagined myself solemnly entering the garden in the gorgeous *Funny Face* wedding dress carrying hot pink gerberas, my hair loosely curled and half pinned up, half falling around my shoulders. I had my dad at my side, Jenny and Louisa behind me. In something horribly unflattering. Like canary yellow Bo Peep dresses. My mum was sitting at the front of the congregation, complaining that we should be doing this in church and that I'd always been awkward. And at the front of the garden, under the archway, was Alex. And since it was my fantasy and not my mother's, he was wearing a slim-fitting Dior Homme suit, a skinny black tie and his beat up black Converse. But he had brushed his hair to acknowledge the solemnity of the occasion. I walked slowly up between the two rows of seats, full of our nearest and dearest who had of course travelled to Paris for our wedding, and I smiled at him, and he smiled back and— woah! I blinked a couple of times and actually shook my head. Where did that come from? I'd been off weddings ever since Louisa's debacle. It was way too early to start fantasizing about chasing Alex up the aisle. I'd only just decided I wanted to move in with him, there was no need to rush. As difficult as it was to accept, Beyoncé wasn't always right, you didn't have to put a ring on it.

My hands were empty before my stomach was ready to accept that the croissant was gone, so I forced myself to stand up and headed back to the gate, giving the group of late lunchers a quick smile as I passed. And got weird stares in return. Which reminded me to put my sunglasses back on.

After another hour of getting to grips with the Marais and adding several charming little cafés and bakeries to my notes, I declared my afternoon a success and attempted to find my way back to the hotel, only getting lost twice. Happily sailing past an Alain-less reception desk, I headed up to the room to plug in my laptop. The Apple logo glowed reassuringly and I kicked off my flip-flops, settling in for a lengthy blogging session.

The Adventures of Angela: Sacré bleu!

It's safe to say that my first twenty-four hours in Paris were not entirely what I had been hoping for. There hasn't been a single tandem bike ride down the Left Bank in Breton shirts and black Capri pants. And would you believe it, not a single beret in sight? But I've decided to take a more positive attitude from here on and be very laissez-faire, je ne regrette rien, *and so on.*

And I have to be honest, aside from the fact that I have a killer black eye (I fell over my boyfriend's shoes – no, really, I did. Our relationship has not taken a dramatic turn for the worse) I think I might love Paris. Compared to London and New York, everyone seems very chilled out. Every other building is a bar, and the ones that aren't bars are cafés and restaurants pushing wine and beer on you. No wonder France has a reputation, hic. The city really is beautiful though, I saw Notre-Dame all lit up last night and I thought I might cry. And that wasn't just because I had to walk back to the hotel with no idea where I was going in borrowed, but not broken-in four-inch heels. I felt as if it was floating on the river and it might sink at any moment or melt away or something. It was just too magical to be real. To clarify, I didn't feel as if I was floating, I felt as if I was walking on hot coals and smashed glass. Ouch.

Don't worry, I haven't gone all romantic on you, the only thing that brought me back down with a bump of course, was me. On my face. Serves me right for getting up in the night to pee. Or, serves me right for drinking so much that I had to get up in the night to pee, I'm not sure which.

Anyway, I just wanted to check in and let you all know I'm OK. Sorry I've been AWOL, but there was a problem getting a cable for my laptop (bloody Macs) and my BlackBerry isn't working (anyone ever had trouble getting Verizon service in France?), but I'm back now and still in desperate need of your top tips. It could end up in Belle magazine! Have to go now, I have approximately three hours before Brooklyn Boy gets back from his long hard day of interviews (poor lamb) and I have to take him out for a slap-up birthday dinner. And at least two of those hours will be spent trying to cover up my black eye, otherwise there will be no gazing lovingly over dinner. In fact, I would imagine he'll struggle to keep anything down at all.

Ah, c'est la vie . . .

I posted the blog and flipped the computer shut. There was no reply from Mary even though I knew she would be at her desk, and the other emails, including an urgent request from the bank of Paraguay, would wait until I'd had a very long, very hot bath.

Before I'd moved to New York, it took me about three minutes to decide what to wear on a date with my boyfriend. Usually, whatever was on the top of the ironing pile that didn't actually need ironing. After almost a year living with Jenny, I couldn't decide between a pair of black jeans, a pair of black leggings and three identical V-neck T-shirts in black, white and grey. After trying on all three, I opted for the white, teaming it with my skinny jeans, Virginie's baby blue Louboutins, and a long, delicate silver chain with a beautiful aquamarine stone pendant I'd picked up during my last spin around the shops in the Marais. I wasn't convinced it would pass as an insurance-covered replacement for an essential item in most work places, but this was *Belle* after all. How was a girl supposed to go out to dinner in Paris on a Friday night with her boyfriend on his thirtieth birthday unaccessorized? The extra make-up I'd picked up from MAC (*vive la* American world domination!) on the way back to the hotel however, was definitely an essential, whichever way you looked at it. By eight, you could barely see my bruised cheek and black eye. If I set the dimmer fairly low. And parted my hair to one side. And didn't look up. Finally satisfied that I was passable, I sat in the chair by the window, editing the beginnings of my article for *Belle* and waiting for Alex to sail through the door.

Thirty minutes later, I was still waiting. I closed my laptop and flicked through the TV channels, trying to be reassured by the fact that the chair still smelled like Alex and not unnerved by the fact that it smelled like him because he'd slept in it for half of last night. Ten more minutes of French *Wheel of Fortune* (starring Victoria Silvstedt!), I worked out that I could call Alex's mobile from the French hotel landline. Cross-legged on the bed, my mobile in one hand, the handset of the hotel phone in the other, I attempted to work out how to put through an international call. When the door clicked open five minutes later, I had got as far as bashing the receiver into the mattress, while repeatedly calling it a piece of shit.

'Ahh, Kodak moment,' Alex said from the doorway.

'Where were you?' I half shouted. 'It's nearly bloody nine.'

'Didn't we say nine for dinner?' he asked sheepishly, brushing down the back of his hair.

'You said eight,' I replied, emphasis and finger-pointing on the 'you'.

'Shit, Angela, I'm sorry.' He winced. 'I guess I got caught up with everything. You ready to go now?'

'Yes,' I said, feeling bad right away. He'd had to work on his birthday after all, I ought to give him a little bit of leeway. And if he really did think we were meeting at nine, he was fifteen minutes early. I stood up and gave him a twirl. 'Do I look ready enough?'

'You look awesome,' he said, crossing the room and wrapping his hands around my face. He kissed me gently and peered at my injuries. 'How's the face?'

'Painful.' I pressed my lips together to redistribute what gloss there was left on them. 'Does it look awful?'

'I can't even see it.' He brushed my carefully arranged hair out of my face. 'Really, you look beautiful. And really, I'm sorry I'm late.'

'Don't worry.' I kissed him again. 'It's your birthday, you can do whatever you like.'

'Thanks. I'd done a great job of forgetting about that.' He ran a finger from the fine, short hair at the nape of my neck all the way down my spine and back up again. 'I can do whatever I like, huh? Sure you don't want to celebrate in here?'

Looking up at his high cheekbones, his dark eyes, I paused for a moment.

'They have room service,' Alex promised, his finger on the base of my spine making figure of eights all the way back up again.

'I think I'm offended that all it takes to get in my knickers is the promise of room service,' I said with closed eyes, my back melting.

'They have *steak frites*.'

'Doesn't matter.'

'*Saignant.*'

154

'What does that mean?'

'Just cooked on the outside, bloody as all hell on the inside.'

'Oh.'

'And I'll let you sing happy birthday to me.'

'I don't think that's going to help matters, do you?' As difficult as it was, I wriggled out of his arms, trying to solidify my spine. 'We're going out for dinner whether you like it or not, it's your thirtieth birthday.'

Alex stuck his hands in his pockets and gave me a defeated half-smile. 'And you'd think I'd get to do whatever I wanted to do on my own birthday, wouldn't you?'

'And you will later,' I replied, blushing at my own brazenness. 'But you promised to show me Paris.'

'So if I show you mine?' Alex never blushed.

'Take me out for dinner and we'll talk.' I picked up my bag and headed for the door with a great big smile on my face.

CHAPTER ELEVEN

'So how was everything today?' I asked, ripping into the bread basket. Bread first, booze later. I'd learned my lesson. 'Did all the meetings go OK?'

Alex nodded, sipping a glass of red wine. I'd suggested champagne, but he had insisted he had nothing to celebrate. Boys are so touchy.

'You saw all the record label people?' I thought I may as well carry on asking questions, even though I knew he wasn't going to answer. The second we'd walked out of the hotel, it was as if someone had thrown a switch on him. I could barely get two words on a subject. And it wasn't as though he was the world's most chatty individual, but he was definitely being weird.

'Yeah, all done,' he said, reaching for a piece of bread and then thoughtfully tearing off the crust. 'Tell me about your day.'

'Got up, got a power lead for my Mac, came home, blogged and waited for you,' I briefed him. 'Come on, spill. What interviews did you have today? Did you tell all of France how much you love me?'

'Ah, come on Angela!' Alex pulled a face. 'I've been

talking all day. Can we just go an hour without questions?'

'OK,' I said, trying to keep up with his mood swings. 'Um, what are we going to do after dinner?'

'That's still a question.'

'Oh yeah.' I bit my lip, thinking for a moment. 'I found this really beautiful little garden in the Marais this afternoon.'

'Oh yeah?' Alex nodded at the waiter as he placed two plates full of *steak frites* in front of us. 'Tell me about it.'

'It was lovely.' I tried not to be distracted by the giant piece of meat on the plate in front of me. Good God, I loved food. 'There was this really gorgeous court-yard, surrounded by these really elegant archways, and through them there was a garden with really low mani-cured hedges that were in like, swirly patterns. It was so peaceful and pretty. So different to New York.'

'Was it the Musée Carnavalet?' he asked in between mouthfuls.

'Yes! I loved it.' I nodded enthusiastically. 'We should go if we get the chance. I keep forgetting that you know where stuff is.'

'Yeah, I don't know.' He looked down at his plate. 'I mean, you have lunch with Louisa tomorrow, right? And it's the festival on Sunday and, well, then Monday we're going home.'

'It's such a shame,' I said, letting my knife slip into the steak as if it were butter. Oh, this was going to be good. 'I really wish we'd been able to do more stuff.'

'All I know is that I can't wait to get home.' Alex poured us both more wine. 'This wasn't as good an idea as I'd thought it would be.'

'Oh.' At that moment, I may as well have been eating a tin of Stagg stewing steak. 'You're not having fun?'

'Hey, I didn't mean I'm not glad you're here,' he started to backtrack. 'I just hadn't thought we'd be doing so much work.'

'Yeah, it's awful being popular, isn't it?' I wanted to raise an eyebrow, but ow ow ow.

'It sucks,' he relented with a small smile before his face fell again. 'And, you know, well, I should have figured that Paris wasn't strictly speaking, my happy place. I'm just not feeling myself.'

It didn't take a genius to guess what he was talking about, but I had made a promise with myself that the name 'Solène' would not be passing my lips this evening.

'I'm really glad you're here right now,' he added, putting down his knife and fork. 'I'm sorry we haven't spent more time together.'

'We're together now,' I said, forcing a smile. 'But you are going to have to talk for a bit so I can eat this amazing steak.'

'How about we both eat and then we can talk?' Alex bargained, his foot rubbing up the inside of my leg. 'Just listen to everyone else for a while.'

'That's all right for you to say,' I said through a mouthful of bloody meat. I held my hand over my mouth, but really, we were a long way past that. Thank God. 'You can understand what everyone else is actually saying.'

'And it kills you that you can't,' he said with the first genuine smile I'd seen in over an hour.

'I'm a writer, I'm inquisitive,' I protested.

'You're nosy,' he bounced back.

'And I thought we weren't talking while we were eating?'

Alex speared a piece of steak with his fork and grinned.

* * *

'So, does it feel different?' I asked later as we walked through the streets eating ice creams. It was still warm and Alex paused to lick an escaping trickle from the back of my hand.

'Does what feel different?' he asked, going back to his own cone and swinging my arm happily. The second bottle of red and the champagne I ordered while he was in the bathroom seemed to have loosened him up.

'Being thirty,' I explained. 'Do you feel different?'

'Nope,' he replied quickly. 'How's that ice cream?'

'It's not a good enough liar to distract me that easily,' I came back just as quick. 'You must feel a bit different, surely.'

'I don't think so,' he said, pulling me down a narrow cobbled street lined on either side with small shops filled with bright fabrics. 'Do I look different?'

I took a big lick of my ice cream and stopped to look at him. Same shiny black hair, short and ruffled in the back, one chunk always slightly stuck up from where he'd been running his hand through it all day. Long and shiny in the front, parted slightly to the left so one side fell just below his eyebrow, fluttering in front of his eyes, a bright and vivid green. They looked a little tired, but it was late and I was guessing that spending half the night in an armchair wasn't conducive to clear eyes. A few laughter lines reminded me that, despite the last few days, he spent a lot more time smiling than he did brooding and sulking. The other side of his hair fell longer, past his high cheekbone, highlighting the contrast between his black hair and pale skin. His lips were just as full and red as ever. As they stretched into a small smile, I could see that they were stained with the red wine we'd been drinking.

'So, do I look old to you?' he asked again.

I shook my head and reached up on tiptoes to kiss him, ignoring the ice cream that was melting all over my fingers. 'You look OK.'

'Well, thank God for that. Come on.'

'Where are we going?' I asked, my heart skipping along faster than I could in my borrowed Louboutins and tossing my messy almost empty cone into a bin while Alex munched his.

'You wanted to see Paris.' He pointed up a set of steep steps. 'So let's go see Paris.'

I looked upwards and saw a beautiful church with a gorgeous domed roof. 'Sacré-Coeur?' I asked, channelling my inner *Rough Guide*.

'Sacré-Coeur,' Alex confirmed. 'Can you take the stairs in those shoes?'

'I love that you know me well enough to ask,' I said, looking down at the pretty instruments of punishment I'd buckled to my feet. 'And I love that I am comfortable enough with you to say no, no I cannot.'

'Come on,' Alex laughed, pulling me towards a little tram-looking thing. 'We don't have long until they close up.'

Once we'd run the gauntlet of men trying to sell us plastic Eiffel Towers and Sacré-Coeur snow domes, and squeezed into the rush of people clicking their cameras before they'd even got in front of the church, I turned and stared out over Paris. It was so breathtakingly beautiful, a pitch black sky dotted with stars reflected in the city below it. Once I'd got my breath back, I turned around to take in the church, if you could call it that, it seemed so inadequate a word. It was so beautiful. Prettier than Notre-Dame, more welcoming than imposing, but still so dramatic, I couldn't find words for it. The white stone seemed to glow in the darkness, floodlights shining from below the building and carefully placed spotlights illuminating every beautiful feature. If there were any flaws, I couldn't see them. Jenny would kill to find out who had designed the lighting on this place and get them to do her next headshots.

'You like it?' Alex asked, placing his hands on my shoulders from behind me.

'I love it,' I said, switching my eyes back and forth from the city to the church. 'Thank you for bringing me here.'

'I know you like a view,' he whispered. 'And I'm pretty sure it's the only thing in Paris that's older than me.'

'Yeah, you do look a similar age.' I punched him lightly on the arm.

'I'm getting tired of having to tell you to shut up,' he said, hopping lightly on to the low wall in front of us. 'It's beautiful, right? I used to love coming here, having Paris all laid out in front of me.'

'Better than the Eiffel Tower?' I asked, looking around for the landmark.

'It's on the other side,' Alex said, reading my mind again. 'And yeah, better. Parisians hate the Eiffel Tower you know.'

'Snobs,' I said, clapping his hands between mine. 'This is gorgeous though. I love how Paris ripples.'

'Ripples?'

'Yeah, you know,' I said, trying to find the words, but only gesticulating randomly. 'It's like, up and down. The buildings are round then square, high then low. It feels, I don't know, curvy.'

'And how does New York feel?' He looked bemused. It was fair, I was supposed to be a writer after all.

'New York is skinny,' I decided. 'Everything is tall and thin and holding in its breath. It's the one thing I

161

miss about London, there aren't nearly enough little green spaces in New York. It can be so claustrophobic. Not enough places for you to just sit down and have a minute.'

'People don't have a minute,' he rationalized for me. 'Manhattan is always busy.'

'True.' I nodded, trying to work out how to bring the conversation around to my moving in with him. 'But I feel like I would never get anything done here. It's a city made for wandering around, holding hands, eating ice cream.'

'And for getting drunk, did you notice how many bars there are here?' he pulled me towards him, resting his head on my chest.

'I'm trying not to notice,' I said, thinking back to how much I drank when I was in LA. Not good. In fact, I'd had the same bottle of vodka in the apartment since I got back and I'd actually had a bottle of wine in the fridge for over a week. How things had changed since Jenny had moved out.

'So maybe London is the perfect mix of the two?' he suggested.

'It's not perfect,' I disagreed. 'It's missing a few vital New York ingredients.'

'Yeah?' he asked as I rested my forehead against his.

'Yeah.' I pressed my lips to his for as long as I could without breathing. He tasted hot and warm like red wine, but with a cold ice-creamy sweetness.

'So, seriously,' I said, nestling in between his knees and resting my hands on his shoulders. 'You don't feel any different at all? About being thirty?'

'I honestly haven't thought about it,' Alex said, taking a few strands of my hair away from my face and brushing them back. 'But no.'

'Fair enough.' I shook them back again. He might

have forgotten about my black eye, but I hadn't. And neither had the American tourists at the side of us who were whispering and pointing. But since they were both over forty and wearing baseball caps and bum bags (or fanny packs, tee hee) I wasn't too concerned about their opinions. 'So when you were younger, what did you want to be doing when you were thirty? What did you think you'd be doing?'

'I don't know.' He pushed up off the wall and stood staring past me, up at the church. 'I guess I stopped thinking about it a while back. Thirty creeps up on you so fast.'

'You talk like you're so old already,' I said, leaning in to rest my chest between his shoulder and his chin. 'You must have had ambitions, you must have wanted to do stuff.'

'Yeah, I did.' He nodded, brushing his lips against the top of my head. 'I wanted to make music for a living and I was lucky, I got to do that pretty young.'

'And you wanted to do soundtracks, music for films?' I asked. His body was always so warm, even as the night got cool around us. 'You said that ages ago.'

'I do, I'm looking into it,' he said. 'James Jacobs actually emailed me about some stuff yesterday. I should get back to him.'

'You should,' I replied, letting myself feel a little bit pleased that I could take at least a bit of credit for helping him. I sometimes worried that there wasn't much I could give Alex, nothing that he didn't already have or couldn't get for himself. 'But there's nothing else? Nothing you wanted?'

'What do you want?' he asked, his arms tightening around me. 'By the time you're thirty, where do you want to be?'

Hmm, wasn't expecting him to turn the tables. 'I don't

really know either, maybe I'd like to write a book? I'd like to be writing for more magazines, not just the blog, but more stuff like this, like I'm doing for *Belle*.'

'In New York?'

'Yes, in New York.'

In Williamsburg, in your apartment with you, I added in my head. Why couldn't I say it out loud? Now was the perfect time.

'Cool. For one really scary minute I thought you were going to say married with babies,' he laughed. 'Phew.'

'Yeah, phew,' I repeated.

Hang on a minute, what?

'Alex?'

'Yeah?'

'What would you have said if I had said married with a baby?'

He didn't say anything for a moment, but I felt his arms and his jaw tighten. 'But you don't want those things. Do you?'

'Not necessarily by the time I'm thirty,' I said, choosing my words as carefully as humanly possible. 'But I wouldn't say I'm not ever going to want them.'

'OK,' he said diplomatically.

'Don't you?' I said, staring hard at one of the buttons on his shirt. 'Want those things?'

'I did once,' he said slowly. I knew he was putting just as much thought into his words as I was. Not that it made me feel any better. 'But I stopped thinking about them and they just sort of fell off the radar a while back. I would say I don't think I need those things to be happy.'

My hands loosened around his waist and dropped on to the wall behind him. 'Right,' I said quietly, hoping that tears wouldn't come. I would not be that girl. As much of a surprise as it was to hear him say that, my reaction was an even bigger surprise. It wasn't on his radar? He didn't need those things to be happy? Did he even need me then?

'You're not freaking out, right?' he asked the top of my head. 'I mean, with you not wanting to move in and everything, I figured that you wouldn't be thinking about those things either.'

'Uhmm,' I mumbled, hoping it sounded non-committal. What the hell? I was a girl, of course I was thinking 'those things'! Maybe not morning, noon and night and maybe not in my immediate future, but how was I supposed to not have 'those things' cross my mind? While sitting in a gorgeous Parisian garden, fantasizing about how gorgeous I look in my *Funny Face* wedding dress, while Louisa and Jenny look like crap in canary yellow.

'I guess that's one thing that's been good about coming here,' he sounded relieved. 'I totally realize I was pushing you on the whole moving in thing and I just want you to know that I'm happy to wait as long as you need to. It is too soon, you're right. Rushing stuff like that just ruins everything.'

I pressed my fingertips into the cold stone of the wall until I felt the tension all the way up in my shoulders and my hands started to shake.

'Are you cold?' Alex asked, tipping my face up towards his.

I looked away quickly, trying to turn brushing away a tear into a yawn. I nodded into the hands covering my face. 'And tired.'

'Let's head back,' he said, scooping up my hand and squeezing it. 'We'll get a cab, we're kind of a long way from the hotel and I know, birthday or not, you'll kick my ass if those shoes get ruined.'

If he could tell there was something wrong he was

pretending he hadn't noticed. I kept level with him, my face straight ahead. So I'd promised myself I wouldn't say it, but I hadn't promised I wouldn't think it. He had wanted to get married and have babies once. It didn't take a genius to work out when once was. He had wanted to get married and have babies with Solène. But he didn't want them with me.

'Alex?' I said as we crossed the street to a taxi rank. 'I've actually been thinking a lot about the moving in thing.'

'Angela, it's OK. *Rue Amelot, s'il vous plaît*?' he added for the cab driver. 'I told you, I know I was being pushy. Moving in is off the table, you don't have to worry about upsetting me any more. I get it.'

'But I was thinking that maybe I was ready to, well, to move in,' I said, crawling across the back seat. Even I wasn't convinced by my tone of voice. How could I be now?

'Yeah?' He sounded even less convinced. 'Let's just talk about it when we're back in New York. Not tonight.'

We rode back to the hotel in silence. Alex staring out of the window, one hand pressed against his temple and his forehead leaning on the glass, and me staring at the back of his head, trying to work out where the evening had gone so very wrong. So, he didn't want to move in with me any more? And he didn't need to get married and have babies? I breathed in deeply. I was making a bigger deal of this than it was. I must be. I was tipsy, I was tired, I was stressed. I wasn't going to be getting married, moving in or having babies with Alex.

'We're here,' he said eventually, tapping me on the thigh. 'You awake?'

'Hmm, yeah.' I opened the car door into the street, narrowly missing a passing scooter. The rider beeped

166

his horn and barked out some French expletive while I pressed up against the car door, now actually awake and paying attention.

'Hey.' Alex scooped me up as the driver pulled away, leaving me in the middle of the road. 'You trying to get run over? Come on inside.'

I let him put his arm around me and we walked quietly through reception, which was again Alain-less. Alex was talking at me about the warm-up gig on Saturday night, what time we'd need to leave for the festival on Sunday, how much he was dreading the flight back. I nodded along, but it felt as if I was watching myself rather than participating in the conversation.

Once we were in the room, I took my time in the bathroom, scrupulously removing every last trace of my make-up instead of sneakily leaving on some mascara, which would be removed 'after', and brushing my teeth for the full three minutes. After my second wee, I couldn't put it off any longer. Oh my God, was I really putting off going to bed with Alex? Opening the bathroom door, I saw he was already in bed, all the lights out except the one on the bedside table. I crossed the room and slipped under the covers, assuming the position, my right arm across his stomach, my head resting on his collarbone. We lay there in awkward silence for a couple of minutes, his hand trailing up and down my forearm while I absently played with the sleeve of his T-shirt. Well this was a first. Not just that he'd got into bed in a T-shirt, but that I wasn't tearing it off. And he was hardly ravishing me. And I wasn't entirely sure I wanted him to. After a couple more minutes, I rolled over and flicked out the light. The clock on the nightstand flashed one-thirty a.m. I'd been awake for over twelve hours without a nap, no wonder I was so tired.

Before I could roll back, Alex turned against me, pushing his body closer to mine and wrapping his arm around my waist. I felt a warm kiss on the back of my neck before he yawned loudly.

'I can't believe we're in Paris on my birthday and we're just gonna go to sleep,' he said into my hair. He didn't sound as if he couldn't believe it. He sounded as if he was making sure I knew that's all we'd be doing.

I didn't know what to think. He wasn't even going to make a move for me to awkwardly rebuff? I didn't want to have sex with him because I was pissed off and confused, but what the hell? He didn't want to have sex with me? He should always want to have sex with me! Wasn't he genetically programmed always to want to have sex? Isn't that what the Y chromosome was for?

'It's probably because I'm so old.' He yawned again and gave me a squeeze.

A couple of minutes later, I felt his breathing even out, and his grip around my waist slackened. I squinted at the bedside clock until my eyes adjusted to the light. One forty-seven. I knew things always felt worse in the night. I wouldn't feel half as bad in the morning. My stomach would stop feeling like a family of hamsters had set up home in there and were having their housewarming party. And I wouldn't want to cry until my eyes fell out. I'd definitely feel better after I'd slept on it.

CHAPTER TWELVE

It turned out I didn't feel great the next morning. Possibly because I didn't technically sleep on anything. I'd checked the clock every fifteen minutes, occasionally drifting off into tense dreams that ended in me falling off a kerb or a wall and once, most appropriately, the top of the Eiffel Tower, before snapping wide awake. Eventually, I slipped out from under the covers without waking Alex and showered quickly. It was only seven, I wasn't meeting Louisa until twelve-thirty, but I just wanted to get out and clear my head. Literally and figuratively since I must have drunk more than I'd realized at dinner, my brain was fuzzy and my head was sore. The morning-after mirror was rarely my friend, and today was not an exception. My busted cheek wasn't purple any more, but it had taken on an attractive yellow tone. The eye pretty much still looked like I'd gone ten rounds with, well, I didn't know any boxers, but that was the general look. Not sleeping hadn't exactly helped, my nose was red and my eyes all narrow and piggy-looking. Sexy.

I dressed in the bathroom, slapping on my make-up and pulling on the jeans I'd worn the night before.

To be fair, there was no need for the overly dramatic routine, until his alarm went off Alex would sleep through absolutely anything. The number of times I'd laid awake in his apartment, listening to the builders putting up new apartments across the road while he snored right through the clanging and clattering. But this morning I just didn't want to take any chances.

'Good morning, *Mademoiselle*.'

'Alain!'

Happily, I snapped out of the continuous cycle of asking myself 'What the fuck?' and 'Why doesn't he love me' long enough to give him a semi-cheery grin.

'Is there anything I can do for you this morning?' he asked. At least he didn't look scared of me any more. Wary, but not scared.

'You couldn't tell me where I can get on a boat trip could you?' I dug out my map and laid it on the desk. 'One of the ones that goes around the city?'

'The *bâteaux mouches*?' He leaned over to look at the map and narrowed his eyes. 'It is here.'

'That looks pretty far away,' I said, following his pencil. 'Oh! Alma Marceau! I've been there.'

'You are sure I cannot call you a taxi?' Alain looked at me doubtfully. 'You will need to change trains twice.'

'It's fine,' I said, sticking the map back in my bag. 'I've got a really good sense of direction. Once I've been somewhere once, I can always find it again.'

'*D'accord.*' Alain nodded, giving me a supportive smile. 'Have a good day.'

Nodding back, I strode out to the *Métro* station, confident and keen to distract myself with a happy trip up and down the Seine.

But a positive mental attitude and the will to succeed are not always enough. Within fifteen minutes of getting on a train, I was completely lost. I really did think it was incredibly mean to disguise the horrors of the labyrinthine underground system of Paris with the pretty wrought-iron signs at the entrances. It made you think you were wandering on to some cute 1960s film set when in reality, you were descending into the seventh circle of hell. And how come the doors opened before the train had stopped? I nearly fell out twice before I realized it happened at every stop, no matter how many times I dashed out of one carriage and threw myself into the next. My first unaccompanied journey from St-Sébastien to Alma Marceau had taken me an hour. My second took an hour and a half, half of my fingernails and all of my patience. At least this time, people seemed to take pity on my black eye and I'd had a seat for most of the journey. Even though that meant I'd missed my stop twice because I couldn't wrestle my way out in time.

At least, when I finally made it out of the *Métro* tunnels, the *Bâteaux Mouches* was well signposted and well served with stalls selling disposable cameras, cold water and ice creams. Once I was loaded up with all three, I clambered up on to the front of the boat, away from the couples already smooching in the back rows, away from the families, tactically positioned near the toilets, and close to the groups of pensioners, wrapped up warm against the ninety-degree heat. They gave me an acknowledging nod and I smiled back, taking a seat across the aisle. I wasn't ready to make friends with old ladies just yet. Give me another six months and then we'd talk.

After an awkward couple of minutes of me hoping no one was going to sit down next to me, the boat pulled away, and after a couple more minutes of trying to decipher the English commentary from the French,

German, Spanish and Japanese, I swapped over to my iPod. In the great tradition of everything going tits up at once, the first song that came up was one of Alex's. Usually, I loved listening to his band, I'd been a fan before I was a girlfriend (but bypassed groupie, I was always very clear about that), but now it felt as if all the lyrics had double meanings. Which songs were about Solène? The happy ones? The sad ones? I couldn't even listen to the ones I knew for a fact were about me, I was just comparing against the others. They suddenly felt less emotive, less compelling and it wasn't just a first album versus third album thing. Skipping through my play lists, I settled on the best of Girls Aloud. No way to misinterpret that.

I wasn't entirely sure what I was hoping to achieve on my boat trip, but if it was depressing myself even more, it was working. The boat sailed up and down the river, past all these amazing, historical buildings that occasionally set off little flashes of A level history, mainly concerning violent and bloody deaths, and yet I couldn't snap out of my foul mood. OK, I had to be rational about this. Alex had every reason to believe that I didn't want to move in with him. He'd been asking me for months, and I'd kept on making excuses. And I supposed, if I put my pride aside, I could under-stand why he wasn't exactly keen on the idea of marriage. I knew his parents were divorced and the last relationship he'd had had ended horribly, he'd been completely betrayed.

No need to worry about him not wanting kids yet, the collection of little terrors enjoying their playground-en-Seine was enough to scare me shitless, let alone the idea of being responsible for one of them for ever. Didn't help though. As we sailed up towards Notre-Dame, I tried desperately not to turn around and stare up at Solène's apartment, but I couldn't help myself. I spotted it right away and it was just as stunning from the river as it was inside. Bitch. But she wasn't my problem right now, convincing Alex that I really did want to move in with him and that he'd been right, living together would be a great idea, was my problem.

Maybe I should do it after Paris, I thought, snapping away at the Musée D'Orsay and clicking on to make sure I got the Louvre. Just let the dust settle, head home and once we were back in his apartment, he'd remember why he wanted me there in the first place.

Chugging my lukewarm water, I leaned back in my seat and tried to enjoy the boat ride. Rounding the Ile de la Cité, we pulled back on to the main stretch of the river, passing the *Paris Plage*. I really wasn't much of a sand person, preferring Erin's pool to the private beach at her Provincetown house, but you had to admire the commitment of the Parisians laid out on the sand. It was bikinis and swim shorts as far as the eye could see, they were taking this shit seriously. I rested my chin on the railings of the boat and watched all the pretty couples smothering each other in sunscreen and kissing extravagantly. Those that weren't laid out on sunloungers in the sand were strolling down the bank, holding hands and smiling. Was it possible to walk around Paris in a bad mood? Did they make you take some sort of romance test? I had read some-where that they could test for levels of love chemicals now, perhaps there was some sort of pee on a stick test they made you do before you could cross the Pont Neuf.

It was so hot on the boat, I was relieved when we docked and I was able to dash off faster than the fam-ilies and the immobile. It was almost twelve and I was going to have to make a move if I wanted to beat Louisa to the Eiffel Tower. Which, given that I didn't have a working mobile phone, I really did. The sense of panic at not having a phone was bizarre. People had managed without them for centuries, but take mine away for two days and I felt as if someone had chopped off an arm. I just hoped Louisa would actually be where she'd said she was going to be on time. But of course this was Louisa we were talking about. Louisa, who wouldn't even break to pee when we were revising until the allotted time. Louisa, who was at the church before Tim on her wedding day. We'd had to circle for some time and the driver was not amused.

True to form, as I approached the ticket booth just before twelve-twenty, I spotted my best friend there waiting for me. Blonde hair pulled back in a practical ponytail, freshly ironed vest tucked into her freshly ironed shorts, cardigan slung over her arm and small Radley bag strapped across her body in front of her. She was a born British tourist.

'Angela!' she yelped as I ran up and scooped her into a huge hug. She'd put on a little bit of weight since the last time I'd seen her, but given that our last hug was immediately after her wedding and immediately before I broke her husband's hand, that was understandable. Between the boning in her wedding dress and her extreme diet, it felt good to be hugging an actual person. And she smelled right. She smelled like Pantene shampoo and the same Calvin Klein perfume she'd been wearing since the sixth form.

'Oh, it is so good to see you,' she said into my ear while I crushed her harder. 'But you can let me go, I'm not going to run off.'

I released her reluctantly, partly because hugging her felt so bloody good and partly because I hadn't wanted her to see that I'd already started crying.

'Ange, are you OK?' she asked, brushing my hair out of my face. It was a gesture so familiar that felt so strange, I managed to set myself off again. I nodded unconvincingly and tried to stop crying,, but the harder I tried to control myself, the worse it was. I just kept hiccuping and letting out terrible, honking sobs. All around us, tourists, ticket sellers and policemen turned to stare at me. Which wasn't particularly helpful.

'Bloody hell, babe!' Louisa pulled me back in for another hug and carted me off, away from the crowds. 'I thought I was supposed to be the emotional one.'

A good five minutes later, I'd more or less pulled myself together and we were safely seated at a small, overpriced café. I took a tissue from Louisa and dabbed at my face, trying not to poke my black eye unnecessarily, but effectively wiping away all of my carefully applied make-up.

'Oh my Lord, what have you done to your face?' Lou asked, snatching my hand away. 'Is this why you're upset? Has someone hit you?'

I shook my head, still not quite able to make words.

'Angela, babe, you know you can tell me anything.' Louisa's voice was deadly serious. She held my hand and gave me a level stare. 'Did Alex do this?'

The very thought of Alex raising a hand to me made me splutter with laughter through my tears, which Louisa apparently mistook for hysterics.

'I will kill him,' she started, pulling out her phone. 'I'm calling the police, don't get upset, you have to do this.'

'No, Lou, please,' I tried desperately to compose myself, waving her hand away from her phone. 'I fell over, I tripped on my way to the loo in the night. Honestly, Alex would never hit me. Honestly, stop.'

Louisa looked at me suspiciously for a second and

then set her phone on the table. 'You are a clumsy old cow,' she said, weighing up my story against my injuries. 'Bloody hell, you gave me a scare then.'

'I'm sorry,' I choked, pushing away the last of my tears. 'I can't believe how badly I overreacted. I hadn't expected to be such a mess. I'm just so happy to see you.'

'Whereas I had thought I'd be the one crying my eyes out,' she said, accepting a menu from the waiter who had been hovering at her side, waiting for me to finish blubbering before he approached. 'You're the one that's supposed to be all practical Ms Clark. What's happened to you in New York? Have you gone and got all in touch with your emotions?'

'Apparently.' I shrugged, looking at the menu and ordering a Diet Coke. Would it be bad to have steak again? 'Must have been that week in LA. I don't have a therapist though. Yet.'

'Maybe you should get one,' she suggested, ordering still water. 'So, tell me everything.'

I smiled tightly, not really knowing where to start.

'Why don't you tell me about these anniversary plans? Did you get a marquee sorted?' Ah-ha, deflection. Always a winner.

'We did,' Louisa started, excitedly waving her hands around. If there was one thing I knew about my friend, it was that she would talk about wedding or wedding-related activities until the cows came home. There was no reason why her first anniversary wouldn't be treated with the same enthusiasm. Without hesitation, she rattled on about the size of the tent, the chocolate fountain she'd hired, the band Tim had picked and the dress she was wearing until the waiter came back with our drinks and to take our order.

'Shall we get a bottle of wine?' I asked, trying to

convince myself that a hair of the dog would be a good idea. And it would go well with the steak I was absolutely about to order.

'Ah, no, I don't think I'm going to have a drink,' she declined. 'But you should.'

'I'm OK,' I replied, eyeing her closely. 'Saving yourself for tomorrow?'

'Actually,' Louisa handed her menu back to the waiter. 'I'm not really drinking at the moment.'

'You're not?'

'No.'

'Right.'

'Yes.'

I set down my Diet Coke and looked at my friend. She had put on weight since the last time I'd seen her, but she didn't look fat. She looked healthy. She looked glowing.

'Louisa?'

'Angela.'

'Are you pregnant?'

She covered her face with her hands, peeping out at me through her fingers. 'Yes?'

'Oh bloody hell!' I jumped out of my seat and ran around the table to give her another almighty hug before the tears started again. At least this time it was both of us.

'I wanted to tell you,' she bleated. 'But I only found out last week and then when you said you were coming I thought it would be better to tell you face to face and oh, you're not mad at me?'

'Why would I be mad?' I asked, finally putting her down and wiping away the last traces of make-up from my black eye. Who cared if it put other people off their lunch? 'Oh, Lou, I'm so pleased for you.'

'I thought you might be mad that I hadn't told you

yet, but you're the first, apart from Mum and Dad. And Tim's mum. And his dad. And well, his brother, but then you,' she rattled on, sipping her water. 'I'm so glad I got to tell you in person.'

'Me too,' I agreed, reaching across the table for her hand and trying to stop my tears. 'And I don't mind that you told his brother, he's hot.'

It was easy to tell myself I wasn't homesick when I was in New York, so far away and constantly busy. Regular phone calls, reluctant Skyping (did anyone look good on that thing?) and constant emails meant that I always knew what was going on in Louisa's life, but seeing her now, face to face, it was a lot harder than I'd thought it would be.

'I just can't believe you're not going to be around to be a full-time godmother,' she said, giving my hand a squeeze.

'Godmother? Really?' I asked. What was she trying to do? Have me dehydrate completely? 'Are you sure there isn't someone more, well, adult that you'd want to pick?'

'Don't be bloody stupid!' Louisa laughed out loud at my concerned expression. 'It'll be you and Tim's hot brother. God knows you're more adult than he'll ever be.'

'But I blacked my eye on my way back from the toilet,' I protested. 'And that's just my most recent cock-up.'

'Angela,' Louisa stopped laughing and gave me an even look across the table, 'there is no one else in this world that I would pick to be godmother to my baby and you can keep chattering on about it all day, but I am really quite aware of your catalogue of disasters. I've been present at most of them, if not involved one way or another. You're going to be the godmother. Accept it.'

'I don't even know what to say.' I pursed my lips to staunch a fresh flow of tears. 'Of course I'll do it. And I'll be amazing. I won't buy him or her booze until they're at least seventeen and I promise not to swear in front of them or anything. I'll do anything you want me to.'

'It's a start, I suppose.' Louisa moved her knife and fork to one side to make room for her steak. Good girl. 'Now, how about you make a start by coming home for my anniversary party tomorrow?'

I looked up from my bloody steak. 'Lou, you know I can't. Tomorrow is Alex's show.'

'I know,' she sighed, carving up her meat. It was so well done that it took some serious work. How could she? It was steak sacrilege. 'But I had to ask. You know your mum is going to kill you. She reckons she's been leaving you loads of messages and you haven't replied.'

'You told her I was here?' I shrieked far too loudly. Staring around the café, I half expected to see her charging over in her M&S finery, ready to bash me with her holiday handbag. It was slightly smaller than her regular handbag, but just as formidable a weapon. 'Jesus Lou, I told you not to!'

'Not me.' She held up her hands in her defense, a piece of charred steak going flying into our neighbour's bread basket. 'Tim mentioned that I was coming out here when he saw her in Tesco. You know he's a rubbish liar, he would have only buggered it up if I'd told him to keep quiet.'

'Oh, crap.' I took a big swig of Diet Coke. I should have got the wine. 'I'm going to be in so much trouble.'

'Not if you come back tomorrow,' Louisa suggested. 'Just come for the party. We're having it in the afternoon, surely Alex's thing isn't until the evening?'

'It's a festival, I think he's planning on being there

all day,' I muttered, trying to remember what he'd told me at dinner. Before he'd told me he didn't want to live with me, marry me or have babies with me.

'So you have to be there all day?' Louisa raised an eyebrow. Some of her slyer expressions reminded me so much of Jenny, it was scary. 'Really, Ange, you never used to follow Mark around like such a helpless puppy.'

'As I remember, Mark didn't want following because he was shagging your tennis partner,' I replied quickly, stabbing a piece of steak and biting down too quickly, getting the fork. Karma was bloody fast around these parts.

'Fair enough.' Louisa didn't look as if she was about to give in that easily. 'Shame you can't come, you look so amazing and I know everyone is dying to hear about your adventures. I'm forever telling them all about you and Alex and everything. They're so jealous.'

'Louisa,' I started slowly, 'when you say everyone, are you talking about someone in particular?'

'Tim's hot brother?'

'Anyone else?'

'I don't know.'

'Louisa?'

'All right, Mark's going to be there,' she admitted, putting down her fork for a moment. 'Tim invited him because he's been so bloody pathetic lately. I wasn't going to tell you, but apparently things aren't going very well with that Katie girl and he's just drunk at the tennis club all the time. Turning up for work late, same clothes as the night before, all that. And don't tell me that seeing him now you're looking all fancy and glamorous hasn't crossed your mind. Let alone with the rock star live-in lover.'

'Firstly, this is not me looking my most glamorous,' I pointed to my black eye and bruised cheek, 'and secondly, I'm not so sure I can be bragging about the live-in rock star right now.'

'I thought you were going to be moving in with him soon?' Lou asked, a milder version of the 'has your boyfriend been punching you?' concern in her eyes. 'Is everything OK, babe?'

'It's been better to be honest,' I admitted, trying to work out how best to paraphrase our last conversation. 'Um, it was his birthday yesterday and we went out for dinner and he told me he didn't want to marry me or move in together.'

Given Louisa's news, I didn't think I needed to include the 'and he doesn't want kids' part of the conversation just yet.

'What? He just came out with that?' she asked, her voice getting slightly higher with each word. 'What did you say?'

'Well, no, not exactly,' I munched thoughtfully on a *frite*. 'OK, basically, he had this ex who messed him around a few years ago, and because of that, he said that he doesn't think he needs marriage and kids to be happy.'

'He doesn't want to have kids?' she shrieked.

Bugger, I'd forgotten that I wasn't going to mention that.

'No, he just said that he doesn't need them to be happy,' I repeated. I couldn't help defending him, even if I didn't understand what he meant any more than Louisa did.

'And what about the whole moving in thing?' she asked, her lips pressed together into a tiny cat's bottom. Not one of her more attractive expressions. 'How come he's gone off that idea?'

'I think that's my fault. I kept saying we'd talk about it later because well, I was a bit scared given what happened the last time I lived with someone, and now he's decided it's a bad idea and that it's too soon. Even though I've decided I want to. I suppose it's ironic.'

'So, you're not allowed to be worried about moving in with him because of what happened in your last relationship, but he's allowed to keep you dangling by a thread for the rest of your life because of what happened to him in his last relationship?' Louisa demanded.

I stuck out my bottom lip. Well, when you put it like that . . .

'Oh, Ange, it's just like *Sex and the City*—'

'Don't start,' I cut her off quickly. Her eyes were dangerously glittery and excited. 'Just because I live in New York doesn't mean everything that happens in my life is just like *Sex in the* bloody *City*. I've got enough of my own real problems without piling on Sarah Jessica Parker's.'

'I still think he's out of order.' Louisa shrugged, annoyed at being cut off mid-Miranda flow. 'He's allowed to be messed up by his past, but you're not? And what's brought this on all of a sudden anyway? Hasn't he been all super keeno?'

'Yeah, the thing is,' I took a deep breath, 'his ex is sort of here.'

'Here in Paris?'

'She's from Paris.'

'And he knew she would be here?'

'No.'

'Whatever.'

'He didn't,' I protested. 'Yes, she's from Paris and she's in a band, but he didn't know she'd be here. Or performing at the festival.'

'Oh come off it,' Louisa scoffed. 'Listen to yourself Angela. Your previously adoring boyfriend has suddenly gone off the idea of living with you and has gone out of his way to tell you he doesn't want to get married, even though it wasn't even on the cards, at the exact same time the girl who broke his delicate little heart reappears on the scene?'

'Lou, you're making it sound so much worse than it is,' I sulked. But the problem was, she wasn't making it sound worse. She was making it sound like the truth.

'Angela, I'm not trying to upset you,' she insisted. 'I'm trying to look after you. I stood by and let you get hurt last time, I won't do it again. Now, I know that I haven't met Alex, but I also know I've never seen you this upset about anything. It's written all over your face. And I want to believe those tears were just for me earlier, but they weren't, were they? It was about him, wasn't it?'

I nodded a little bit, not especially ready to speak. Because if I spoke, I'd have to admit that she was right.

'Please come home, Angela,' Louisa sighed. 'Even if it's just for a little bit. I know you've got work and friends and stuff out there, but it might help you see things a bit more clearly. Just come for a week. For the day.'

Looking up to the sky, I closed my eyes. How could she be feeling so sorry for me when I hadn't even told her about the crappiness that was work? My boss was pissed off with me, her assistant was trying to sabotage my big break, and said big break wasn't exactly going according to plan. And that was without even getting into the Jenny situation. Maybe a quick trip home would help clear my head. If only to remind me why I left in the first place.

'I can't just up and leave,' I decided, pulling my hair back into a ponytail and then letting it drop. It was getting so long. 'I'm sorry, Lou.'

'You did it once,' she countered.

I pushed my plate away and sniffed. For the first time in possibly ever, I wasn't hungry.

'I miss you, Angela,' Louisa said quietly. 'I just wish you'd come home.'

'Me too,' I said. 'I'm just not sure where home is right now.'

We sat in silence for a few minutes, letting the waiter clear away our half full plates and bring over coffees. Clearly they'd decided either we looked as if we needed them or at least I did, and hadn't waited for us to order.

'Well, we're a right pair, aren't we?' Louisa said, sitting up and rearranging her hair. At least two hairs had escaped her ponytail and she wouldn't be having any of that.

'We are,' I agreed. 'Honestly, I'm so excited about your news. You're going to be an incredible mum, you know.'

'Yeah, well, I've had twenty-seven years of practice on you, haven't I?' she said, sipping her coffee.

'Piss off!' I smiled, relieved that our fight was over. If breaking her husband's hand and spoiling her wedding didn't ruin our friendship, I was pretty certain that not coming to her party wasn't going to see her off.

CHAPTER THIRTEEN

After lunch, Louisa and I wandered around for a couple of hours, crossing the river and taking dozens of pictures of each other from the Trocadéro, me holding up the Eiffel Tower, Louisa with it coming out of the top of her head. I'd need to be on point to stop these from making an appearance online. I was fairly sure this wasn't the image *Belle* writers were supposed to present. It was tricky though, Paris was made for impromptu photo shoots. We had no choice, but to take a very serious series of 'mean and moody girl in beret' under-neath the Arc de Triomphe. I did mean and moody a lot better than Louisa, she was far too blonde and bubbly for serious Parisian photography.

'I wish you'd change your mind and come back with me,' Louisa said, mid-hug as I packed her off into a taxi. 'Oh, I completely forgot, I brought you this.'

She handed me an envelope, with a big cheesy grin. I smiled back and started to open it up, but the taxi driver tooted his horn. Apparently it wasn't OK to sit in the middle of the road with the engine running in Paris. Actually, it probably wasn't OK anywhere.

'Open it later.' Louisa threw her handbag across the

backseat. 'I miss you babe. I can't believe I'm going to have to do all this baby stuff without you. You're sure you won't come back? You're breaking my heart, you know.'

'I know, I promise I'll come back soon,' I swore, stuffing the envelope into my abused handbag. 'But I can't now. I need to sort this Alex thing out if nothing else.'

'You really love him, don't you?' she asked, pushing her hair back behind her ears and staring at me hard. 'He'd bloody better be worth all this, Angela Clark.'

'He is,' I sniffed, half of me in the taxi with her for one more hug, half wishing I could jump in with her and leave all my troubles behind. Again. 'And when you meet him, you'll know.'

'Can't wait.' Lou stuck her head out of the taxi window. 'But you realize you have to bring him before I'm the size of a house or wait until after the baby is born. I'm not having you and your gorgeous boyfriend trotting around London while I look like Shamu trussed up in maternity gear.'

'Got it,' I saluted, waving madly as the taxi pulled away.

I stood at the side of the road, staring at the flow of traffic for far too long, waiting for my mood to balance out. I was so happy to have seen Louisa, but so incredibly sad to see her go. I really hadn't registered how much I missed her. And she was having a baby. It seemed incredibly rude that her life should go on without me in it, but I was undeniably relieved that we had picked up exactly where we had left off. Well, about an hour before where we left off really, when she was still my best friend in the whole world, to whom I could tell anything. Not the sobbing, heaving mess of a woman who'd just had her wedding ruined by a mentalist, aka me. A huge part of me wanted to jump in a cab and go after her, reinvent myself as Auntie Angela, the favourite auntie who let you play with her make-up and always has sweets, but really, that wouldn't help me. It might help me eat fewer sweets, but apart from that, it wouldn't solve my present predicaments.

Luckily there wasn't too much time for me to dwell on my cock ups, past, present or future. It was already after seven and I was meeting Virginie at some random bar she'd picked between seven and eight and since I didn't have a working phone, I wanted to be there as early as possible. There was no way on God's green earth that I was dealing with the *Métro* again, so I hopped in a taxi and gave him the address Virginie had helpfully written down for me, before I pulled out my black eyeliner and got to work. It turned out applying it in the back of a taxi was apparently how all the girls in Paris got that messy, smudgy look down to a tee. Combined with several lashings of mascara and a liberal powdering of the nose and chin, I was pretty passable, given the amount of sobbing I'd done earlier in the day. And it wasn't quite dark yet, but the light was happily forgiving on the narrow, dim streets of Hipsterville-en-France, which made covering up my injuries so much easier.

I hopped out of the cab, throwing what I hoped was enough money at the driver, and looked around for Virginie. She was nowhere to be found, but I soon spotted the sign for L'Alimentation Générale, the place where we were supposed to meet. Annoyed that it mocked me and my GCSE French (it wasn't a general store at all, it was a bloody trendy bar – why would the French lie to me?), I ventured inside to look for my new friend. It was early for a Saturday, but the bar was already busy and the music loud.

Taking a seat at the bar, I ordered a mojito like everyone else and spun around on my stool to watch out for Virginie.

The bar looked fun and was lined with more of the same beautiful people I'd seen in Café Charbon on our first night. It was pretty cool and kitschy, with china cabinets lining the walls and weird lampshades. The crowd lapped it up regardless, already dancing and laughing. The Saturday night feeling was infectious as I sat back with a smile and indulged in some guilt-free people watching. It really was madness how clichéd the world was. New Yorkers all wore black and thought it was acceptable to wear trainers to walk to the office. Parisians all smoked and looked like characters from *Amélie*. And my most important observation, people in both cities drank like fishes. Of course, it was possible that I was spending far too much time amongst the hipsters in both of these countries. Not a healthy pastime.

'Angela?' a voice called from the door. Standing on my tiptoes, I could just about make out the top of Virginie's head, or at least the giant neon pink floppy bow that was on top of it. She raised a hand from the doorway where she was talking on her tiny phone. I waved manically, bashing at least three people in the eye with my frantic elbow. Virginie slipped her phone into her bag, looked around the packed bar and gestured for me to come out to her.

'It is too busy,' she declared after a brief hug and two perfunctory air kisses. 'I am sorry, I was coming early and got held up.'

'It's fine, let's just go somewhere a bit quieter,' I said, trying not to worry about the grandma-like implications of my statement. 'It's going to be loud enough at the gig later.' I was going to be a godmother after all, I needed things like my hearing now. So I could fully enjoy all the wailing and screaming of my forthcoming godchild.

We wandered down the street a while until we found a smaller, slightly less crammed bar. Somewhere right in the back, dangerously close to the toilets and the cigarette machine, we found a tiny table and slid on to the stools on either side of it.

'I will get wine,' Virginie announced, throwing her bright purple sweater at me and venturing back out to the bar.

I couldn't help but take a quick look at the label. Sonia Rykiel, nice. Between this and the Louboutins, Miss Virginie wasn't quite as clueless as she claimed to be when it came to fashion, but then, working on a magazine like *Belle*, I guessed that it would be impossible not to pick up anything, whether you were into it or not. A year ago, I'd have struggled to tell the difference between Prada and Primark if I couldn't see the price tag. And she really did seem wedded to her jeans and ballet flats, which might have been why I loved her.

She reappeared almost as quickly as she had vanished, grasping a bottle of red wine and two not-so-clean-looking glasses, but given the venue, I supposed I should have been pleased we weren't supposed to swig it out of the bottle. I was all for dive bars and low-key venues, but good God this place was rough. While Virginie poured the wine and began to rattle on about how she'd spent her day rereading some of my blog posts for inspiration (I still hadn't quite kicked her off the hero worship wagon), I stared at the flaky red walls, plastered with posters for past shows and random pieces of framed pop art.

I also noticed that the crowd was slightly different to L'Alimentation Générale. The out-and-out party atmosphere was somewhat stifled by a very obvious desire to see and be seen although, God forbid anyone should look like they were trying. Also, I was absolutely certain they would never play Britney here, in an ironic sense or otherwise. A couple of carefully put-together girls leaned against the window, tossing their hair from side to side, occasionally rolling their eyes at each other and desperately trying to pretend they weren't checking out the tall dark-haired boy in the corner with his back to the room. Apparently, he was the only one who really didn't care who was or wasn't in the bar. Clearly, he won 'coolest person' prize for the evening.

'So you met with your friend?' Virginie asked loudly.

I turned back to face her and was met with great big, wide questioning eyes. Good God, she was always so interested in everything. It was quite unnerving.

'Yeah.' I glugged back a mouthful of the wine. When in Rome, right? Or, well, France. 'We had lunch, it was really nice to see her. She's just found out she's pregnant so it was a bit weird. Good weird, but weird.'

'You miss her?'

'So much,' I nodded hard and my hair bounced up and down. 'I didn't actually realize how much until I saw her. It's her wedding anniversary tomorrow, which means it'll be a year since I last saw her. And a year since I moved to New York.'

'You don't think about going home at all?' She glanced over my shoulder as she spoke, I presumed towards Mr I-Don't-Give-a-Shit in the corner behind me. Ha, she was just as at risk to a hot boy as the rest of us. 'A year is a very long time to be away from your friends, from your family.'

'I know. And honestly, I have hardly been homesick at all, but after today I don't know, I feel a bit weird.

Different.' I contemplated. 'Louisa is having a first anniversary party tomorrow. It's so strange to think that more or less everyone I know will be in one place, all together, two hours away on a train and I'm not going to be there.'

'You don't want to go?'

'I actually sort of do,' I admitted quietly. 'I know it's not a good idea though, it's only because I'm having a bit of a downer on stuff back in New York.'

'But your life, it is so amazing,' she protested for what seemed like the millionth time. 'I would kill—'

'It doesn't matter how many times you say that,' I warned, 'it doesn't actually make it any more true right now.'

Virginie shook her head. 'I am sure that London is a great place, but New York! It is the best place in the world. So tell me, what is so bad that would make you want to go back to England?'

'Just, well, loads of stuff.' I took another sip of the wine before I tried to explain. 'Me and Alex are sort of in limbo, Jenny isn't speaking to me and there's just something he said the other night that's been playing on my mind.'

'It might help to talk to someone?' she offered cautiously. I wrinkled up my nose and stalled for a moment. Virginie wasn't that likely to give me objective advice and the last thing I needed right at that moment was all my scary opinions bounced right back at me. On the other hand, talking to Louisa had helped, and she hadn't exactly been pro-Alex. Maybe my own cheerleader-slash-pitbull was exactly what I needed.

'OK.' I decided to go for it. There was something about that pink floppy bow that really made me want to confide in her. 'He made this totally flippant comment about me being on my own at his gigs all the time and it just got me thinking. He's right, I suppose. I haven't made that many friends in New York outside Jenny and her friends. I mean, I'm used to having a small circle of friends and I'm totally fine with that, but I'm worried that the circle just seems to get smaller and smaller all the time and before I know it, I'll be left with no one, but Alex. And that's what happened in London, there were millions of us at uni and then a group of us in London, and after a couple of years, it was just me and Mark, Louisa and Tim. And as of right now, I don't even really have a Louisa in New York. I can't let that happen again. If me and Alex break up, I'm not sure I'd have anything to stay for.'

'And you really think you might break up?' Virginie refilled my glass quickly and then gave me an embarrassed smile. 'I'm sorry, I drink too fast, I know.'

'No, it's fine,' I lied, making a mental note not even to attempt to keep up. 'I'm just not a very good drinker. One too many hangovers when I was in LA, I've sort of tried to avoid getting completely hammered since then.'

'Hammered?'

'Fall down, throw up, pass out and wake up with a stranger in your bed drunk,' I elaborated, sipping my wine slowly. 'And I really can't even think about the breaking up question.'

'Did you work on your article today?' Virginie changed the subject expertly. 'I feel so bad. I hope you will still be able to complete your assignment with only two days left in Paris.'

'There are only two aren't there?' I couldn't believe this week had gone so quickly. Not that it had been without incident. 'It'll be fine,' I reassured her (and myself). 'I actually put some notes together yesterday and felt a bit better about it. Not that there isn't more to add, but I can stick in the bars from tonight. I reckon it'll be OK. What's this place called again?'

'UFO.' Virginie looked over at the bar where the crowds were starting to gather. 'It does get very busy, perhaps it is not so secret?'

'Not to you, but I bet there aren't many Americans in here,' I said, following her gaze. The other half of the room was like a different bar, the clientele were completely different to the moody hipsters in the back. Everyone was talking, waving their hands around, laughing, touching each other on the shoulders, kissing.

'I think perhaps there is one American,' Virginie pointed her almost empty wine glass towards the tall dark haired boy with his back to us. Except he didn't have his back to us any more. He was standing up, ducking his head slightly to the left to avoid the low ceilings, a guitar case in his hand. It was Alex. And following him across the room and out of the bar was Solène.

'Isn't that . . .' Virginie pointed as they paused outside the window, just inches away from us.

'Yes,' I said, trying not to freak out on a monumental scale. 'It is.'

Solène magically produced a packet of cigarettes from her skintight jeans and placed one carefully between her lips, lifting her chin for Alex to light it. She gave him the lit cigarette and repeated the process, just in case I hadn't seen it clearly enough the first time around. Taking a deep drag on the second cigarette, she flicked her long fringe across her face and cocked her head to one side, smiling up at my boyfriend before they set off down the street. Before I could decide what to do, Solène looked back over her shoulder, straight at me and gave me the most smug, self-satisfied smile

I had ever seen. Turning away, she slipped her hand through Alex's arm and carried on down the street and out of sight.

'Angela?'

I stared out of the window, ignoring the quiet voice at my side.

'Angela, please, you will break the glass.'

Snapping out of my trance, I realized that I was gripping the stem of my cheap wine glass so tightly, it really was at risk of shattering. Which would make it all the better to stick right through Solène's heart. If she, in fact, had one.

'You did not know that Alex was meeting that girl?'

I gave Virginie a look that hopefully made it clear that she had asked a very stupid question.

'I don't think that he saw you,' she said. 'And I am sure it was nothing.'

I still couldn't actually make words. In the words, or rather, acronyms of Jenny Lopez, WTF?

'They are both in bands, yes? And playing at tomorrow's festival? So it is like a work meeting.'

I couldn't even raise an eyebrow at that. Did she think I was stupid?

'As you have said, there is nothing between them now. It is all history.'

And history sometimes repeats itself, I thought to myself even if I couldn't bear to say it out loud. Mostly because it was too cheesy. I knocked back the rest of my wine and poured a fresh glassful from the now half empty bottle. And knocked that back too.

'Angela, I—'

'Virginie?'

'Yes?'

'No offence, but can you shut up for a minute?'

'Of course.'

We sat drinking in silence for a few minutes while I stewed on the evidence. There must be a perfectly rational explanation as to why my boyfriend had gone out drinking with his ex-girlfriend without telling me. Like, they just bumped into each other and he was being polite. Or that she'd threatened to throw herself in the river if he refused to meet with her. Or he was thinking about giving her a quick one before the show because he didn't want to do it with me any more. Wow, that was helpful thinking.

Another ten minutes of silence went by while visions of Solène and Alex cancaned through my mind, Virginie sat opposite me, concentrating on staying quiet. I could tell it was killing her, but I really didn't want to hear any of her theories at that precise moment. I wanted to finish the bottle of wine as quickly as possible so that I had a handy and easy-to-wield weapon.

'Angela?'

I turned my head slightly to look at Virginie. 'If you're going to tell me how harmless that all looked, really, it's not going to help right now.'

'Actually, I was going to ask if you wanted to stay with me tonight,' she said hesitantly. 'If perhaps things do not go well.'

'Oh.' I was a little bit shocked. Shouldn't she be bouncing around and yelling about what a slut Solène was and how awesome I was and how Alex must be a fool if he even looked at another woman?

'Because, and I do not know your Alex at all, but I do not trust that Solène. I know I have said this before,' she added, topping up my wine until the bottle was empty.

'Right.' I accepted the drink and swilled it down. I really was past tasting it now, which I had a feeling would be both a blessing and a curse. It really wasn't good wine. And I really shouldn't ever drink red. 'Well, I should talk to him. It could just be that they bumped into each other and he was being polite.'

'I thought he did not care about being polite to her?' Virginie reminded me unnecessarily. 'And that is why he would not go to the party with you.'

'Oh yeah.'

I pretended I'd forgotten, but clearly I hadn't. I couldn't think of a single good reason for Alex to be in a bar with Solène at a time he knew I had plans with someone else, without having told me anything about it. Not one. Unless he'd just found out his mother needed a kidney transplant and Solène was the only matching donor in the entire world. No, not good enough. He never saw his mother.

'Maybe you do not want to go to the concert? You would like to go and get a bag from the hotel?' she suggested, finishing up her wine. 'You have been through so much with cheating boys already, you will not go through that alone again.'

'Oh God, no!' I shook my head quickly, trying to ignore the fact that the room seemed to spin with me, just ever so slightly. 'No, really, this is stupid. I'm being stupid. I should just go over there and ask him. This is ridiculous, getting all worked up when I have no idea what is going on.'

Of course, I did have an idea and that was the problem. It was a really graphic idea and I didn't like it one little bit.

'*D'accord*,' Virginie pouted. 'If this is what you want. But you must come and stay with me if you do not want to go back to the hotel.'

'Virginie, really, it's fine,' I tried to convince us both. I wasn't sure that if the worst came to the worst, sobbing on the floor of a girl I hardly knew was going to help matters, even if she was my very own, very chic, Parisian version of Mary Poppins. Practically perfect in every way. 'You're supposed to be helping me with an article, not taking me in for crisis counselling.'

'But I want to help,' she insisted, reaching across the table and squeezing my hand. And immediately realizing that was a little bit too much, even for three glasses of wine on a half-empty stomach Angela. She dropped it and shrugged, trying to look more casual. 'Or perhaps you could visit your friend in England. I am sure she would be more help to you anyway.'

'You have been an incredible help,' I reassured her, relieved to be worried about someone else's feelings for a second. 'Honestly Virginie, you've been brilliant. And you know, if you ever want to come and visit New York, you will always have a place to stay with me.'

'Thank you,' she muttered, pulling on the length of her long brown hair and checking for split ends. She didn't have any, of course.

'Really, I totally appreciate what you're trying to say.' Oh God, she couldn't even look at me. Bugger it, I hadn't meant to offend her. 'You're brilliant, Virginie. You really are. Oh, and I asked Alex to put you on the guest list for the festival on Sunday, I'd love it if you'd come. I'm guessing he's done it, but he is a bit crap.'

'It is not a problem, I have press pass. More wine?' She looked up, her invisible happy switch flipping into the 'on' position.

I smiled tightly and stood up to go to the bar. She was back. As would be my lunch if we carried on drinking at this rate.

CHAPTER FOURTEEN

As my head started to get foggy, I switched back on to a mojito to try to speed the bar part of the evening along. For some reason, drunken logic persuaded me that it was the wine that was the problem, not the generic alcohol. Not that I was feeling terribly logical. Since I'd decided, with the wisdom of a few drinks inside me, that I wanted to talk to Alex about what I'd seen, I was sort of in a hurry to get it over with, but Virginie was really taking her time with the wine. She seemed to be back in cheerleader mode, but there was something that wasn't quite right. The edge had gone off her irritating perkiness and she seemed preoccupied. I tried to tell her about the work I'd done on the article, but she just responded to my semi-drunken enthusiasm with nods, smiles and the occasional monosyllabic muttering, and when I tried to draw her on to the subject of when she might move over to New York, she actually squeaked, shrugged and looked out of the window.

Giving up, I went back to my mojito, although I'd drunk it so quickly, all that was left was extremely sweet minty iced water. My feet were still a little sore from the previous night's high-heeled marathon through the city, but I'd be OK to stand for a while at the gig, and Virginie had said the venue was close by. And it was. It turned out we were just a couple of minutes away, and not only that, but Nouveau Casino was right next door to the café where I'd met Alex on our first night. Hipster Paris was really teeny tiny, a fact that made my feet very happy. Virginie however, hadn't cracked a smile since we hit the street. Maybe she was pissed because I still had her shoes, I thought. Glancing over at my tiny companion, I saw that she was busily tapping away on to an iPhone I hadn't seen before.

'You got an iPhone?' I asked, trying to start a conversation. 'That's cool.'

'Oh, yes,' she looked up, flustered. 'I was looking for a store so I could find a power cable for your computer. It was stupid of me, of course there is now an Apple store in Paris. I got the phone then.'

'Weren't you on the other one earlier?' I asked, enviously eyeing up her myriad apps. Honestly, Apple addiction was a genuine sickness.

'Uh yes.' She dropped the phone in her bag carelessly. I couldn't bear to look, it was going to be scratched to buggery in a heartbeat. 'I am still using both numbers for now. Not everyone has saved the new one.'

'Yeah, I was using different phones for ages.' I nodded, willing her to finish her drink. 'I had my phone, then the work BlackBerry. But of course as soon as I decide to just use the BlackBerry, it goes and breaks so that's bitten me right on the arse, hasn't it? I should get an iPhone.'

'I suppose so.' Virginie took the tiniest sip of wine. 'Did you call the office? To get it fixed?'

'Cici deals with all my phone stuff,' I explained.

'And clearly she's not going to help me out. I emailed the IT department after I charged my laptop, but they never get back to me, it always takes days. And I emailed my editor at *The Look*, Mary, to tell her Cici had fucked me over, but she hasn't replied. Or she hadn't the last time I checked.'

'You emailed your editor?' Virginie looked alarmed. 'What did you say?'

'It's fine, we're fine. Mary is my boss on the website not *Belle*, Cici's her assistant. I didn't say anything to anyone at *Belle*, don't freak out, you're not going to get in any trouble. If anything, you're a bloody hero anyway. I'm going to be telling them how you saved the day and everything.'

'OK.' She finally flashed me a big smile. 'You know how the *Belle* girls can be, but I will not worry.'

It seemed like my promising to put in a good word had cheered her up and she practically skipped down the street ahead of me. I picked up the pace behind her, the still raw balls of my feet protesting through the medium of intense burning. She really did walk incredibly fast for a short girl.

After a couple of minutes, Virginie came to a sudden halt and turned back to me, to point at a queue of people outside a big dark door. It was only just after ten but people were already lining up for the show. For a moment, I forgot how pissed off I was with Alex and just felt incredibly proud. I couldn't imagine how it must feel to see people queuing to see you do something you loved. No one was ever likely to stand in line to watch me inhale a tub of Phish Food and settle in for a three-hour *America's Next Top Model* marathon. I made a mental note actually to get around to doing something relevant with my life. Or at least have a think about it.

Approaching the door, Virginie explained, in French, to the fashionably disinterested girl with a scribbled-up guest list that we were both on the list and that yes, we were aware that the doors weren't open yet and no, we didn't give a shit because I was in fact the lead singer of Stills' girlfriend. I tried not to wonder how much longer I'd be able to use that label, while simultaneously giving the door girl a raised eyebrow 'yes, that's right' look. It wasn't my first time, but I still wasn't very good at it.

Stumbling through the near darkness into the main room of the club, I just about managed not to knock myself out on a huge iron staircase in the middle of the floor. There were a few people milling around, journos and friends of friends I guessed, and the support band was still working on their sound check.

'I'm going to try and find Alex,' I yelled to Virginie over the deafening feedback. Ouch, that sound check was definitely needed. 'Meet you back here at the bar?'

She nodded and leaned against the wall, assuming a stony, 'don't even think about talking to me' face for the benefit of the pair of giggly boys already whispering and pointing at her from beneath the stairs.

After a quick aimless walk around the venue, I finally spotted someone who looked vaguely as if they worked there and flashed my access all areas sticker (how cool was I?). The unimpressed French roadie pointed up the metal staircase and shook his head at me. Well yeah, OK, it was the only place I hadn't looked. I took a deep breath, steeling myself both for steep stairs and a conversation I really didn't know how to have, and mounted the staircase to find a small seating area, full of leather banquettes and low tables. Another flash of the AAA pass at another miserable-looking bald man and I was in. Unfortunately, Alex was not. No one was.

I leaned over the balcony, trying to attract Virginie's attention. My mojito-fuelled bravado was disappearing quickly and now I was here, my heart beating hard, I really didn't want to confront Alex about anything. Not here, not now. I just wanted to hang out with a friendly face. The VIP area had a great view of the stage and, more importantly, free drinks, but Virginie wasn't looking. In fact she was studiously not looking, tapping away on her iPhone again. The boys who had been hiding under the staircase like a pair of hipster trolls, had sidled up to the bar and were clearly trying to get her attention, but it just wasn't happening.

I was kneeling on one of the leather sofas, trying to wave at Virginie and wishing for the millionth time that hour that I had a mobile phone that worked, when I realized that the music had changed. It wasn't bland indeterminate indie rock support band any more, it was Alex. I paused mid-flail to see him centre stage with his guitar, checking the tuning, strumming a few chords and then asking the sound engineer some questions in French. It weirded me out to hear him speaking another language so perfectly, as if he were someone else. Although thinking about it, if the fact that he spoke fluent French had been the only thing I'd discovered about Alex on this trip, I'd have been far happier. Graham and Craig appeared behind him and started to tinker with their instruments while Alex carried on strumming, singing and stopping until the sound was just right.

'I remember when he wrote that song.'

I didn't need to look to know who it was, but I couldn't help myself. Solène was kneeling beside me on the sofa, her arms resting on the metal barrier and her chin in her hands. She stared out at the stage, smiling softly.

'We had not been living together long. I was so home-sick for Paris and he tried so hard to make me happy.' She rested her head on her arms and turned to look at me with the same smile. 'It is even prettier when he sings it in French.'

I pressed my lips together and held on to the railings. I didn't have a clever comeback, just a very strong desire to club her around the head, call her a bitch and tell her to fuck off. Which would have been very satisfying, but not very grown-up.

'Sometimes we would sing it together, even love-lier.' She pulled her long blonde hair over her shoulder and combed it through with her fingers.

'Oh, just fuck off, you bitch!' I stared straight ahead. So I wasn't very grown-up. But at least I didn't hit her. 'I thought you said you had a boyfriend?'

'I did?' Like any really good backstabbing harpy, Solène didn't react to my ridiculously childish insult. She just carried on smiling at me. 'Angela, I thought we were friends.'

'No, you didn't,' I said. 'You thought you were going to steal my boyfriend.'

'Oh please, we are not children.' She laughed sweetly. 'I am not going to steal your boyfriend.'

'Really?' I didn't like the air quotes she put around 'steal your boyfriend'. And I liked the implication that I was the one being childish even less. Even if I was.

She sighed lightly. 'Alex is mine. I cannot steal what already belongs to me.'

Starting to shake slightly, my mouth already dry from drinking too much. I turned to face her.

'Are you serious? Did you really just say that?' I asked, incredulous. 'No one really says that you know. And also, he's not yours. Hasn't been for a really long time actually.'

'What did you do to your face?' she asked, putting her hand over her mouth in mock horror and laughing. 'I hope that does not hurt too much.'

I ignored her and concentrated on not crying. But it didn't matter to Solène that I wasn't committing fully to the conversation, she seemed happy to talk for both of us.

'It is sad that Alex and I had to spend some time apart, but now, we are ready to be together again,' she reasoned. 'He is ready.'

'And he's over the fact that you cheated on him like a big dirty slag, is he?' I asked, trying to remain calm. Not an easy task.

'I did a terrible thing, but there was a reason, of course. We have talked about this before.'

'And that's how I know you're a nasty cheating slag.'

'That is such an ugly word.' Solène shook her sparkly blonde head. 'You are a writer, *non*? You have no better words for me?'

The worst part was, I didn't. I didn't have any words. Just a great big lump in my throat and a growing urge to vomit.

'I only did what I did because he was too much for me.' Solène placed her hand over mine. 'I loved Alex so much, but I was so young and he was rushing into everything. After he proposed, I panicked, I got drunk, his friend came over and I was upset. Before I realize, we are in bed together and of course, this is when Alex comes home.'

I snatched my hand away as though it had been burned. How dare she touch me? 'Hang on a minute, go back. What did you say?'

'I do not understand, go back to where?' she asked, wide-eyed and innocent.

'Fuck off, you know what I'm talking about.' I was

starting to veer back towards clubbing her around the head. 'He proposed? Alex proposed?'

'Yes, he did. Several times.' She smiled sadly and flipped herself around, her head resting against the back of the sofa. 'And I wish every day I had said yes.'

Still up on my knees, I looked out at my boyfriend on the stage. He had swapped his acoustic guitar for an electric and was fiddling intently with the tuning pegs, staring at the monitor by his foot. His hair shone blue under the stage lights and his knackered old Nirvana T-shirt, the T-shirt I had slept in the second time I'd ever stayed over at his place (I was a girl, I remembered things like that) was covered up by a slouchy black cardigan. His washed-out, black skinny jeans revealed just a little bit too much of his jersey boxers when he bent down to mess with the monitor. Graham saw me first and waved, mouthing a wordless hi and then calling to Alex. He looked up from the stage and gave me such a shining smile, I couldn't help, but return it. But mine just couldn't compare.

'And so I came back to Paris. Without him, I had no reason to stay in the city. New York was dead and cold to me,' Solène carried on with her sob story while I stared down at the stage, my breathing becoming more uneven and heavy. 'I begged him to take me back, I sent letters, wrote him songs, I even sent plane tickets, but he was heartbroken. And then I am hearing many stories about him with many different girls, and I am heartbroken.'

'I heard that too.' I broke away from staring at Alex and swung my legs around to sit on the sofa. This wasn't happening. It couldn't be. 'But then he met a really nice girl and started going out with her and he was really, really, really happy.'

'He did not seem so happy when we went for drinks

earlier,' she countered. 'I would say he was very unhappy. And confused.'

'I'm not going to sit here and argue with you,' I said, finally finding the strength in my legs to stand up. 'You and Alex are over. He said so. He told me so. I don't care why you were in that bar earlier and I don't care what you think is going to happen. It's not. It's over.'

'No, it is not. I am sorry Angela, you are –' she actually paused to look me up and down '– nice? But I love Alex and he will always love me. I know him, I know what he wants.'

'And what if he doesn't want you?' I asked, not feeling quite so confident as Solène stretched up off the sofa and stood in front of me, blocking the stairway. Her tight jeans clung to her curves without even a hint of muffin top and I was fairly certain that she wasn't wearing a bra under her black vest. With her long blonde hair spilling over one shoulder and perfectly worn-in ballet pumps, it was like looking into the world's most flattering funhouse mirror.

'But he does.' She narrowed her eyes and stepped closer to me. 'He wants me completely. So why would he even be thinking about you?'

I didn't have anything. Pushing her out of the way, I ran down the steps, trying not to fall, but not especially caring whether or not I did. My handbag bashed rhythmically against my hip as I stumbled out of the main room, desperate to get out of there without seeing Alex. It was one thing to hear all of that from her, it would be another thing to see it confirmed in him. To see them together.

'Angela?'

I didn't know who it was and I didn't care. I just wanted to go back to the hotel and after that, God knows what, but I just couldn't be there at that exact second.

'Angela, wait!'

I'd got as far as the narrow entrance to the club before I was faced with a stampede of Stills fans pushing through the doors as they opened. I froze in front of them for a moment before I felt a hand yank me roughly out of the way and through another dark doorway. I felt around the walls for a light switch until I heard a click. A couple of blinks later, I saw Graham standing in front of me. And lots of mops. Apparently we were in a broom cupboard.

'Where are you running?' he asked. 'Didn't you hear me?'

'Yeah, no, I mean, I'm sorry,' I said, looking at my feet. 'I just wanted to get outside.'

'I'd give it a while until the crowd clears up,' he said, resting a hand on my shoulder. 'Uh, Angela, I thought I saw Solène up on the balcony with you.'

For the second time in two minutes, I froze. I really didn't like hearing her name, it felt like seeing a really big spider in the bath.

'So she was there, huh?' Graham asked. 'Alex is going to lose his shit if he sees her here.'

'Or not,' I said quietly, forcing the tears back. I was not going to cry for her. Not while I was with people anyway. Possibly later, in my bed, on my own. For hours and hours and hours and hours. Yes, that sounded suitably dramatic.

'Alex will freak out if finds out she's here, believe me,' Graham looked as if he meant it. 'I'm gonna have to find her and kick her ass out of here before—'

'Before he proposes to her again?' I interrupted.

His jaw dropped for a moment before he tried to cover it up with a cough.

'And maybe instead of finding her, you could go and ask Alex why he was in a bar with her earlier on?' I kicked a stray floor sponge out from under my foot, hitting Graham in the shin. 'And why it is that she's so certain, so incredibly certain, that he is still in love with her.'

'Angela, he isn't,' Graham insisted, kicking the sponge back at me. 'You gotta trust me on this one. I've known that guy for more than ten years and there's no way.'

'Well it's difficult to know who to trust when the only person telling me what's going on is the ex-girlfriend who has decided she wants him back and is going to marry him,' I blurted out, losing control to hysterics at the end. 'And you didn't know he met her this evening did you? Maybe he just isn't telling you because he knows you don't like her.'

'Listen to me. Alex does not love her, he can't stand her,' Graham repeated, although to me, he sounded slightly less sure of himself. 'And you know he's crazy about you.'

'I don't know what I know,' I said quietly, trying to calm myself down. Throwing a fit at Graham wasn't going to help in any way. Well, it might make me feel better for a bit, but it wasn't really a viable long-term solution.

'You want to go talk to him?' Graham asked, slipping an arm around my shoulders and giving me what was supposed to be a reassuring big brother hug. 'He's all done with the sound check. I can get him to come out here or something?'

'I think I just want to go and get some sleep,' I squeezed him back. 'Really. We've got a big day tomorrow and everything.'

'We do.' Graham nodded, releasing me from the hug. 'I, uh, but what do you want me to tell Alex?'

'Don't tell him anything,' I said, stretching and

208

yawning for effect. 'I suppose I don't want to stress him out before the show, we can talk after.'

It was such a lie. If any part of what Solène had said was true, stressing him out was the nicest thing I would want to do to him. It wasn't as if he didn't know that I'd broken men before. Idiot.

'I really don't want to lie to him.' Graham looked uncomfortable. 'If he asks, I'll just tell him you went back to the hotel and he can call you, OK?'

'Whatever,' I said, giving him another quick hug. I felt like I'd actually talked myself into feeling very tired all of a sudden. And he didn't need to know that I didn't actually have a phone.

'Are you sure you don't want to go talk to him?' Graham asked once more. 'I really hate the idea of you heading back to the hotel thinking whatever crap she told you was true. She's fucking crazy, Ange. You shouldn't believe shit that comes out of her mouth.'

'Yeah, I know.' He was right about the crazy at least, but crazy didn't always mean liar. 'I promise I'll talk to him after the gig, don't stress. Go. Play.'

Satisfied that I wasn't going to throw myself in the river, Graham opened the door slowly, checking that we weren't about to be trampled by the entire indie population of Paris. After another short hug, I squeezed out of the doorway, breathing out as I hit the cool air of the dark street. I was so confused, so completely overloaded, I made it halfway down the street before I remembered that I had totally abandoned Virginie at the bar. Making a variety of grumpy sounds, I turned around to go back inside to tell her I was leaving. It would be really shitty just to leave her there on her own, and while I felt as though I deserved a free pass on shitty behaviour, it really wasn't fair on Virginie.

It seemed as if every single person who had been in

such a rush to get into the gig just minutes earlier, had been inside, knocked back a drink and then come back outside to smoke. I tried to push through the crowd politely, heading back towards the bright light with all the noise coming out of it, which I assumed was the door, but the fresh air made my fuzzy head swim. And it was hard to tell through all the skinny jeans, vintage T-shirts and elaborately messy haircuts. On the upside, aside from my hair being genuinely messy and my weighing a stone more than any other woman on the street, I fitted in perfectly. It wouldn't help Jenny at all, but for the first time, I was relieved that I wasn't wearing Giuseppe Zanotti booties and a sequined Balenciaga mini dress. The black eye helped me stand out from the crowd quite enough.

'Hi, I need to get back inside, I just left for a moment,' I explained to the girl on the door. She looked back at me blankly while a very large man stood in my way.

'I'm on the list?' I said, looking at the girl and then back at the man. Equally unimpressed.

'I'm on the list for Stills, uh, *je m'appelle* Angela Clark?' I pointed at the list for emphasis.

'*Je ne parle l'anglais*,' the girl said with a smirk, her eyes fixed firmly on the piece of paper in front of her where my name had been thoroughly crossed out. Brilliant.

Just as I was about to give up and send Virginie a groveling email apology from the hotel, I spotted her shoving people out of her way as she stormed out of the club, her iPhone clamped to her ear. She looked pissed. I followed her down the street, trying to catch up without interrupting her call, but she was really bloody fast for someone so tiny. No wonder she never wore her Louboutins, she'd break her neck moving at that speed in four-inch heels.

'But I cannot do any more,' I heard her yell down the phone. 'I did not help with the article, it will not be good, what else is there?'

I carried on following, but held back slightly, pressing up against the wall. She turned the corner and sighed loudly. 'What else can I do, Cici? Please, I hate this.'

Really, I'd had the wind knocked out of me more times in one evening than was healthy. Cici? She was on the phone to Cici?

'Perhaps,' she said slowly. '*Alors*, her boyfriend, he has someone else here in Paris, an ex-girlfriend. She is very unhappy about this.'

I closed my eyes and tried to remember to breathe. This couldn't be good. They were talking about me? They were talking about Alex?

'She is very beautiful, yes, but I do not know if it is true.' She laughed lightly. 'No, I suppose that does not matter. And she is very sexy, I would guess that he is. He has not been very attentive to Angela.'

Well, that much was true, I admitted to myself. But seriously, what was going on? Virginie was quiet for a few moments, making little agreeing noises while Cici rattled on. I could actually hear her crowing down the phone from around the corner, but I couldn't make out exactly what she was saying.

'Yes, perhaps. She met with a friend from London today and was very sad,' Virginie carried on slowly. 'And I believe she is not talking to her American friend, her name is Jenny, I think? If her boyfriend was cheating also then perhaps. Also, if the article is very bad, then I think she might.'

She might what? She might what?

'I do not think you will be able to convince her to leave easily and I have told you, Cici, she emailed your

Mary to say that you sent her to all the wrong places. Will this not be a problem?'

Of course not, I thought bitterly, nothing was a problem for Cici. She was a Spencer. So sending me that list of crappy places wasn't just her idea of a joke, she was actually trying to get rid of me. God, what was wrong with that girl?

'Cici, you know I do not like this,' Virginie whined down the phone. 'I know what we said, but I like her. Distracting her from the article was not so hard, but this is not fair. It is her life, not just one job.'

I ran my ring fingers under each eye to wipe away a couple of stray tears. She was seriously trying to ruin me? And Virginie was in on it? She really was a *Belle* girl after all. I was so stupid. Of course she wasn't that nice! No one was that nice! And thinking about it, I'd made so many excuses for things that didn't add up just because I liked her. When would I learn my lesson? People just couldn't be trusted.

'Maybe she will decide on her own,' she said. 'There is nothing really for her to stay in New York for. She might be happier back in London?'

I peered around the corner as Cici squealed loudly down the phone, causing Virginie to pull it away from her ear sharply.

'I know you do not care if she is happy, but I am not happy either,' she sighed. 'I have done everything you asked. Have you spoken to Donna?'

She was biting her short nails, nodding into the phone. 'Cici, this was our deal, you will definitely be able to get me the visa, yes?'

The nodding shifted into a shake and her pretty pout turned into a hard, thin line. '*Non*, I can get the interview myself, it is the visa I need.'

I hadn't actually seen Virginie look genuinely angry

before, but weirdly, it was far more reassuring than her super perky super fan act. I recognized this, it was human. Even if it was a human who had shat on me completely.

'You cannot do that!' she shouted at the phone. 'I did what you asked, I cannot make someone to move to another country. Cici, you made a promise—'

I walked around the corner, clutching the strap of my bag for strength.

'Angela!' Virginie snapped back into smily mode, although really not fast enough. 'I came outside to find you.'

For a moment I just stood and stared. Then, all at once, everything just exploded in my mind. My suitcase getting blown up, Jenny not talking to me, tripping over Alex's stupid shoes and bashing my face in, screwing up the *Belle* article, Alex deciding he didn't want me to move in any more, Solène announcing that she was taking Alex back, how much I missed Louisa, her having a baby, and now this. There really weren't words for how incredibly pissed off I was. So I didn't bother with words. I slapped her right around the face.

'Angela!' she yelled, her hands flying up. I stared at my palm, wow, that was way more painful than I thought it was going to be. But ultimately, pretty satisfying. Even the voices in my head were stunned into silence. A small crowd had gathered beside us, split between whispering and whooping. Wiggling my fingers, I looked at Virginie, shrugged and turned my back on the whole sorry situation. Really, I was feeling better by the second. Not that violence solved anything. It just really, really helped sometimes.

'Angela, please wait,' Virginie pleaded, following me down the street. 'Angela!'

'Oh, just don't.' I kept on walking, feeling strangely

light-headed. 'I heard all of it. Just, seriously, leave me alone.'

'No, I wasn't, I – you heard?' she asked, planting herself in the street in front of me.

'I heard,' I confirmed. 'So piss off.'

'But I had no choice,' Virginie protested. 'I will tell you everything. I am applying for a beauty assistant position on US *Belle*, but I cannot get the visa I need. Cici said she could help.'

'Cici never helps anyone,' I said, trying to dodge past her, but she kept weaving in front of me. 'Which I thought you knew.' I stopped, sighed and pushed her out of the way.

'I did not lie, we were not friends.' Virginie ran along beside me. No point trying to lose her, she really was too fast. 'She found out I had applied for the job and asked if I would help you with your article. I really am a fan of your blog, you are my inspiration.'

'What part of my being your inspiration inspired you to completely fuck me over?' I asked, stopping at last. More because I was lost than because I wanted to hear her out. It was so much harder to get lost in New York. Paris might be beautiful, but it was a pain in the arse to find your way around.

'At first I believed I would be helping with your article, this is why I agreed,' she said quickly. 'But after I accepted the job, I spoke with Cici and she said that your boss was worried that *Belle* was bad for your career, that she did not want you to do it, but you told her you would do it whatever, and then she told Cici she would fire you.'

'And you believed her?'

'*Belle* is not good for everyone,' Virginie admitted. 'It is not good for nice people.'

'Do you know what I was about to say?' I laughed.

Ooh, I felt weird. 'I was going to say that you're nice and you work at *Belle*. How stupid am I?'

'I know I am not nice,' she said far too easily. 'But I want to work in New York more than anything. And Cici tells me that you are really a bitch so I was not feeling too bad. Until I met you.'

'Cici said I was a bitch,' I repeated. 'Wow, pot, kettle, black.'

'Sorry, I don't understand.' Virginie reached out to grab my forearm. 'But I know you are not a bitch. I am a bitch, but I can help you with the article still. I am very sorry, I was wrong, but I very much still want to come to New York.'

'I don't need your help,' I lied, pretty certain that I did. 'The article is looking OK, I'll get it sorted. And you can stop trying to get me back on side because you've been busted. You're both buggered, you and Cici bloody Spencer.'

'OK is not enough for *Belle*,' Virginie pointed out. 'Please let me help. I was very stupid to help Cici, I know. I feel horrible.'

'Well, you should,' I said, removing her hand from my arm. 'You made a deal with the devil. I hope it bites you on the arse.'

Fairly certain I was heading in the right direction, I left Virginie in the street and half walked, half ran down the street, back to the hotel.

CHAPTER FIFTEEN

Twenty minutes and a couple of wrong turns later, I found myself back in the hotel reception, panting heavily and trying very hard to look as if I was interested in leaflets for Disneyland while I got my breath back. Behind the reception desk, Alain stood staring at me, a smile on his face, but terror in his eyes. Granted, I must have looked a little bit scary, all smudged makeup and yellowing black eye, but at least I wasn't drunk. Well, I might have been a little bit drunk, technically, but I didn't feel it. I didn't know how I felt.

'*Bonsoir*, *Mademoiselle* Clark,' Alain said after an awkwardly long moment of silence. 'How are you this evening?'

'I'm OK,' I replied, fumbling in my bag for the hotel room key. I knew it was in there somewhere. Because unlike everything else in my life, this bag was the one thing that would never let me down. 'I think I'm OK.'

'Can I get anything for you?' he asked, his tone sounding a little relieved.

'No, I'm good,' I said, finding the key and holding it up triumphantly, shaking off whatever was stuck to it.

'*D'accord.*' He smiled, looking back down at his computer monitor or just possibly away from me.

I reached down to pick up the stray piece of paper stuck to my room key, eager not to have Alain add 'litterbug' to his existing list of 'drunk', 'crazy' and 'naked'. But it wasn't a stray piece of paper, it was the envelope Louisa had given me. I tore it open and pulled out a photograph. It was a candid shot of us from her wedding day. We were outside in the gardens, after the ceremony, and she was tucking a stray strand of hair behind my ear while I held both of our bouquets. As usual, she looked composed and flawless while I looked like an impatient toddler. Formal wear was not where I was most comfortable, she might as well have been spitting on a tissue and wiping chocolate ice cream from my face. The sun shone fiercely behind us, almost bleaching out Louisa's pale blonde hair and glinting off my engagement ring. I was engaged. But the main thing that looked strange were the smiles on our faces. We were happy. Really, really happy.

I sank down on to one of the transparent chairs in the lobby and stared at the photo. It didn't even look like me any more, no matter how hard I stared, I just couldn't find myself in that girl. She looked content and relaxed and her only concern was how much longer she'd be able to stay upright in four-inch heels. Of course, that girl was also completely clueless as to the fact that her fiancé would be shagging his tennis partner in the back of their car in a couple of hours. But she wouldn't be for much longer. I ran a finger over the picture, settling on my diamond ring. Wow, I was engaged. Actually engaged to be married. It seemed like such a foreign, grown-up concept right now. Sliding the photo back into the envelope before it could do any more damage, I looked blankly at the floor. It was only a year ago. A year ago tomorrow and yet it felt like a lifetime.

'*Mademoiselle* Clark?' Alain was at my side with a box of tissues before I even realized I was crying.

'Alain, do you have a schedule for the Eurostar?' I asked, wiping away my tears with the back of my hand and trying to take a subtle swipe at my runny nose at the same time. 'For tonight?'

'I believe the last train has left for this evening,' he replied, pulling out tissue after tissue. Once I'd started, I really couldn't stop. 'Would you like me to check times for tomorrow?'

'Yes, please,' I said, shoving the envelope clumsily back into my bag. He disappeared behind his computer monitor and made some faraway tapping noises. I sat still in the chair, as big, fat tears rolled down my cheeks and splash on to the floor. I didn't know entirely what I was doing, but at least I was doing something.

'The first train leaves at seven-thirteen a.m..` There are seats available if you would like me to book you on this train?'

I stared into my handbag and gripped the envelope tightly. I didn't take the photograph out, I just looked at Louisa's flowery handwriting against the brown paper. It just said 'For Angela' with so many kisses that her pen had started to run out. Louisa always did overdo things.

'Yes, please book it.' I snapped out of my trance and looked up at Alain. 'And can you book me a taxi to get me there on time?'

'But of course.' He nodded curtly. 'You would like a wake-up call to your room also?'

'No, no, I'll get myself up, don't worry,' I said, remembering how to use my legs. 'Thanks Alain.'

'And what time would you like to return to Paris?'

he asked, still tapping away on the computer. Efficiency, thy name was Alain.

'Erm, don't worry about it.' I felt very, very sick even as I said it. 'I'll sort it out from that end.'

Alain looked up, not scared of me any more, and there was definite concern in his expression. 'And it is just one ticket that you will need?'

I nodded. Words were gone again.

'*D'accord*, your ticket is booked for the seven-thirteen, your taxi will collect you from reception at six a.m. and I will have everything printed out for you in the morning. Shall I charge this to the room?'

'Erm, no, stick it on this.' I handed him my company credit card. May as well make the most of it while I had it.

'All booked,' Alain confirmed, handing the card back to me. '*Bonsoir, Mademoiselle.*'

I managed a tiny, tight smile and headed for my room, holding on to the brown paper envelope inside my handbag all the way.

When I was safely inside the room, I stripped off my clothes, everything felt grubby and used. Rifling around under my pillow in the darkness, I pulled out the T-shirt and pair of Alex's boxers that I'd been sleeping in and slipped them on in silence. The room seemed huge tonight. I flicked the lamp on beside the bed and pulled open my drawer. There was my passport. I took it out and dropped it into my handbag. Ahh, my handbag. There really was an argument for that being the only good thing that had happened to me this entire year. I took out clean underwear, a T-shirt and the clean leggings that had been delivered by the hotel laundry and laid them on the back of a chair. As much as I was still heartbroken for all the beautiful things I had lost, this new minimalist lifestyle did have its benefits. No need to worry about what to wear.

My plan was to avoid talking to Alex at all. I would pretend to be asleep when he got back from the concert, and tomorrow morning, I would just sneak out without a word. Graham was right, we did need to talk about all this stuff, but I couldn't, not just yet. Too much had happened too quickly. Less than a week ago, I thought I was coming to Paris with my boyfriend for his birthday and then returning to the States to move in with him. Now, here I was being told that a) he didn't want to move in with me, b) he was getting back together with his ex and c) I might not be going back to the US at all. I needed to get my head together and I couldn't do that here. I could however, do it from Louisa's spare room, watching *Hollyoaks* and eating shitloads of Galaxy Minstrels. Picking up the phone, I prayed that she still turned the ringer off at night, and dialled her number, slightly surprised that I still knew it by heart. Relief, answerphone.

'Hey, Louisa,' my voice sounded flat and crackly, as if I'd been doing tequila shots and karaoke all night long, 'um, I'm on my way to yours. My train gets into London at about eight-thirty or something. I'll call you when I get there. Love you.'

I skipped washing my face for fear of having to look in a mirror again and slid between the cool, white sheets, sticking my BlackBerry underneath my pillow, the alarm set to vibrate. At least it was useful for something. I felt like a zombie. I'd been through so many emotions in one day, I was just all out. It just wasn't possible that it was less than four hours since I'd waved goodbye to Louisa. I turned over to stare up at the ceiling, staring at a pretty print on the wall. If it weren't for the lovely Alain, I would be totally stealing that right now. Closing my eyes, I rolled over on to my side and waited to hear the key in the door.

The next thing I heard was a quiet buzzing underneath my ear. Grabbing blindly, I pulled out my phone and turned off the alarm, frozen in position, waiting to see if Alex had woken. After a couple of moments, I realized something didn't feel right. Turning over carefully, it took a couple more moments for it to sink in. Alex wasn't there. He wasn't in the bed. He wasn't in the chair by the window. He wasn't in the room at all.

Alex hadn't come back to the hotel.

Not even able to think about what that could mean, I clambered out of bed and pushed myself into the bathroom. I had made the right choice not to look in the mirror before bed, it was amazing how much damage a couple of days of trauma could do. Fortunately, the same trauma had more or less left me not giving a shit. Who needed to look hot on a train? I splashed my face with cold water, brushed my teeth and took a quick shower. I might not need to be hot, but I did need to be clean. Even broken people needed to keep up their standards of hygiene.

Back in the room, I stared at the empty side of the bed. I must have passed out as soon as I closed my eyes, aside from where I'd just rolled out, it looked just like it had when I'd climbed in the night before. Forcing myself not to think about where he was and what or who he was doing, I picked up my bag and walked out of the room, closing the door quietly behind me.

'*Mademoiselle*?'

Alain was still on the desk – really, had the last few hours even happened? The sun shone through the window, confirming that it was actually morning.

'Morning,' I said, surprised by the flat monotone of

my voice. I sounded as crappy as I looked. 'Is the taxi here?'

'It is,' Alain confirmed, gesturing to a large black car outside the door. 'Will we see you this evening?'

'Do you ever leave this desk?' I asked dodging the question.

'Sometimes,' he said, giving me a single nod. 'Not often.'

I smiled or at least tried to, and tried to think of something else to say. 'Well, thanks so much. You've been brilliant. Really. Just really great.'

'Your taxi is waiting,' Alain said awkwardly, gesturing towards the door. Apparently not all hotel concierges thrived on excessive praise, I thought, nodding and heading outside. But then my experience of hotel concierges was relatively limited. Perhaps some people really did just love doing things for other people. Weird.

Throwing myself into the cab outside, I asked the driver to take me to the Gare du Nord and popped in the earphones of my iPod, picking something loud and obnoxious. Paris was only just waking up at six a.m., it was nothing like New York. If I'd taken a cab ride through Manhattan this early in the morning, even on the weekend, I'd have seen dozens of joggers, at least the same number of people on the walk of shame back home, and a whole line of sadists coming out of each and every Starbucks on their way to the office. Often via the gym. I would never understand it.

But not Paris, or at least not the parts I was travelling through. It was so still, so calm. I'd always thought of Paris as a night-time city, the sparkling Eiffel Tower, the Moulin Rouge, the bars and cafés, but in the dawn, the city sighed and whispered. It didn't need to shout, it was far too refined for that. Paris was the city I wanted to be when I grew up. If I ever grew up.

It didn't take nearly as long to get to the station as I'd imagined, so, with nothing else to do, I set up shop at a small table outside a café and pulled out my laptop. I really didn't want to be alone with my thoughts, they were not fun travelling companions after all. I tapped into the station's WiFi and decided to blast out one last blog. God knows if *The Look* would actually publish it, but I was determined to have my say while I still had the chance.

The Adventures of Angela: Ooh la blah

OK, I have some stuff to get off my chest and I hope you won't mind while I vent for a moment. I've had issues with girls before, we all have, right? But I have (very) recently had the misfortune to be completely effed over by another girl. And I do mean completely. And actually not just by one, but by two. Actually three. Shit. Three. In one week.

What's going on? Has there been some sort of memo put out that I haven't heard about? Did someone declare it International Shaft Angela Week?

I paused and stared at the screen. Where was this going exactly? What else was there to say? I didn't really want to have an online breakdown. This had to stop before I was shaving my head in public and beating the crap out of a car with an umbrella. Actually, I didn't have an umbrella. Probably best.

After a couple of moments, *The Look* webpage melted away and was replaced with a photo of me and Alex. It was a candid shot Vanessa had taken at Erin's wedding a few months ago. We were leaning over a balcony, watching the party below. Vanessa had caught

Alex whispering in my ear, his tie was undone, the top button of his shirt unfastened, his hair messy and hanging across my face. I was laughing with my eyes closed, one hand on the balcony in front of me and the other on Alex's chest. My cheeks were flushed and my lipgloss all smudged.

Before I could start to cry, the picture faded away to be replaced by a shot of me and Louisa. I was pretty sure it was from my last birthday in London and we were belting out a big karaoke number in her living room, both of us doubled up with laughter and the emotion of the massive power ballad we were performing. Seeing that picture was a bit of a shock. I'd spent so long blocking out all of my happy memories of my life in London, it was weird to see one right in front of me. That night had been so much fun.

I pressed my hands over my eyes. There was no mascara to smudge, but I still really didn't want to start sobbing in the middle of a train station. Breathing in through my nose and out through my mouth, I looked upwards, forcing away the tears. There was no need to cry. This wasn't the same as last year. This wasn't running away. This was making a choice. I wasn't jumping on a plane and hoping for the best. I was walking calmly on to a train and knowing that the best wasn't always the same as what you wanted.

Circling my finger on the computer's mouse pad brought the screen flickering back into life. Rereading my post once more, I saved it and shut up the laptop. I'd get back to it. A very loud announcement that my train was finally boarding snapped me back to my senses. I shook my bag until all the crap moved around enough to reveal my ticket and passport. This wasn't a reaction. It was a decision. It was the right decision.

CHAPTER SIXTEEN

After stocking up on water, Toblerone (well, three Toblerones) and a load of magazines that I knew I wouldn't read, I stalked straight towards the train. There was no turning back now. I was actually headed for home. If it still was my home. If anywhere was.

The train was mostly empty, just one group of young French girls, a few couples and the odd lone reader, so I ignored my seat reservation and threw myself at a table for four, two entire seats taken up by my arse and my bag, and my magazines covering the table. This was as unwelcoming as I was genetically capable of being. I just couldn't bring myself to put my feet up on the seat in front. Across the aisle, a vomit-inducingly cute couple fell into their seats and snuggled up together, giggling, kissing and whispering in French. Romantic daytrip to London? Actually, it made sense. If you already lived in the one city the rest of the world visited when they wanted a dirty weekend away, where were you supposed to go? I pulled my iPod back out of my bag and tried to close my eyes. I just wanted to sleep until we got there. Maybe then I could convince myself the last year had all been a dream. A really expensive, impossibly involved dream.

The rowdy rock I'd listened to on the way to the Gare du Nord wasn't right for the Eurostar, I didn't want to drown out the voices in my head any more, I wanted to lull them to sleep, but nothing seemed to be right. Instead, I left my iPod on shuffle and watched the countryside roll by, trying to zone out. Every time my eyes flickered shut, I got a mental image of the empty hotel bedroom, swiftly followed up by a vision of Alex's faded black jeans on the floor of Solène's beautiful apartment. If only I hadn't gone to that bloody stupid party, it would be so much more difficult to visualize my boyfriend's underwear hanging off the back of the sofa if I'd never seen the sofa. Now, it was all too easy to piece it all together in my all too vivid imagination.

I'd been doing my best zombie impersonation for about thirty minutes when I first noticed that I wasn't alone at my table. Two identical teenage girls, both with glossy shoulder-length black hair and Chanel 2.55 bags perched on their denim-clad knees were staring at me with a tempered excitement, as though they'd just seen a gorilla wake up from hibernation at the zoo.

'It's definitely her,' one whispered to the other. 'Look at her picture.'

'I'm not sure,' the other replied, looking at the maga-zine her sister thrust into her hands and then looking back at me with a wrinkled-up pout. 'She looks a bit, erm, not like her photo.'

'Yeah, she's properly hungover or something,' the first girl rationalized. 'But it's definitely her,'

I blinked at the girls once, twice, and tried to work out what was going on.

'Can I help you?' I croaked. They looked at each other in delight and grabbed on to each other's hands.

'Are you Angela Clark?' the first girl asked.

'Uh, yes?' I rubbed my eyes and yawned, reaching out for the bottle of water on the table.

'Oh, let me,' the second girl snatched the bottle away from me, unscrewed the cap and passed it back.

'Thank you?' I said, taking it cautiously. I wondered if they fancied peeling some grapes for me too. Or at least running to the buffet car for a bacon sandwich. Then I wondered if they were planning on drugging and murdering me.

'We're massive fans,' the second girl went on, still squeezing her sister's hand and gurning at me.

Even if I wasn't in the middle of a total meltdown, it was far too early for this nonsense. 'Of what?'

The girls looked at each other and laughed.

'Of you.'

They flipped over the magazine they'd been looking at. It was the UK edition of *The Look* and a very flattering photo peered back at me from my 'Adventures of Angela' column.

'Oh.' I took a couple of huge glugs from my bottle of water. 'That's my column.'

'And we read your blog.' The first girl held up an iPhone displaying TheLook.com and yet another photo of me that looked much, much better than the real thing.

'My name is Sasha and this is my sister Tania,' Tania gave me an awkward wave. 'We're twins and we're like, totally, totally your biggest fans.'

'We've been to Paris, our mum took us so we could "immerse ourselves in the language",' Sasha interrupted her sister to point across the aisle and down the car. An older version of the two girls sat staring directly ahead, looking slightly shell-shocked. 'We're starting our A levels in a couple of weeks and we're taking French.'

'And we read on the blog that you were going so we got Mum to take us too,' Tania explained. 'We're definitely your biggest fans.'

'Definitely?' I asked.

'Definitely. Like, we both have that Marc Jacobs bag that you used to talk about all the time.'

'This one?' I asked.

The girls looked at each other again, this time with a little sadness.

'Uh, yeah,' Sasha started slowly, 'but ours are like, not completely wrecked.'

'But we're definitely your biggest fans. You're our idol.'

Hmm, not the first time I'd heard that this week, and look how well that had ended. The girls smiled at me expectantly, but I really didn't know what to say. I never really thought too much about the column. The UK edition of *The Look* had launched at the beginning of the year so I hadn't actually seen an issue in the newsagents, or come across anyone reading it. I only knew for a fact that I was published at all when I got my copy of the magazine almost three weeks after it came out, received a tiny cheque, or when my mum emailed to see just what was going on in 'that there New York' because she'd heard from Carol at the library that according to 'that magazine' I was drinking an awful lot. Which to be fair, I was.

'So, your blog didn't say you were coming back to London.' Sasha flicked her finger down the screen of the iPhone. 'Isn't it your boyfriend's big concert today? In Paris?'

'Yes?' I tried to remember mentioning that on the blog, but I couldn't. I didn't give specific details, ever.

I'd learned the hard way that the internet wasn't always my friend. Brilliant, I had my very own mini-stalkers.

'Well, won't you miss it?' Tania asked. 'You can't miss your boyfriend's big show.'

'It's Alex Reid from that indie band, isn't it?' Sasha picked up the baton, not giving me a chance to answer. 'I know you never use his name in the blog, but when there were all those rumours about you and James Jacobs, I mean, it was everywhere. Do you still see James Jacobs? Is he definitely gay? He's like, the hottest man in the whole entire world. Tania is totally in love with him.'

'Totally in love with him,' Tania confirmed. 'So, it is Alex, isn't it? He's hot too. We googled him.'

'Can we do one question at a time?' I asked, looking for any sort of pain reliever in my handbag, Advil, ibuprofen, revolver. I didn't have a headache before these girls had started talking, but there was a blossoming pain in my left temple and I was fairly certain the two things were related. Now I knew why their mother looked the way that she did.

'Why are you going to London?' Sasha asked before Tania could even open her mouth.

'It's my best friend's wedding anniversary,' I said carefully. Not a lie. Score.

'Your best friend whose wedding you were at when you found your ex shagging that girl in the back of the car? Was that a year ago?' Tania expanded, entirely unnecessarily. I made a mental note to stop putting absolutely any sort of personal information in my blog. And possibly change my name. And get drastic facial reconstructive surgery.

'Yes,' I replied, rubbing my temple.

'Do you have a headache? You should drink some water.'

'And take some tablets.'

'But you can't go to sleep.'

My water bottle and a box of Nurofen were pushed towards me from across the table. I took them graciously, trying subtly to check my watch. Jesus, there was another hour and a half of this yet.

'So how come you're going to London instead of going to your boyfriend's gig?' Tania waited for me to swallow the tablets before starting the questions up again, which, given what I'd come to know about her in the last fifteen minutes, must have been really hard for her. 'We wanted to get tickets, but it was sold out. We bought their albums because he's your boyfriend.'

'Tania didn't like them,' Sasha added.

'Shut up.' Her sister gave her a quick punch on the shoulder.

'I'm, uh, I don't know,' I stumbled over my words. Two sixteen-year-olds with an apparently unlimited handbag fund and a mother that took them to Paris at the drop of a hat were not going to be able to help me with this one. 'I'm just going to see my friend.'

'So, how do we get our own blog?' Sasha asked, flicking her perfectly smooth hair away from her perfectly smooth face. 'Because we want to be just like you, with the blog and the boyfriend in New York and everything.'

'Well, you need to finish school first.' I tried to put on my mature grown-up's hat, but it had never fitted especially well. It was difficult to give advice to two super cool teenagers when you felt like an awkward thirteen-year-old yourself. 'And then go to uni and study journalism or English, I suppose. I studied English.'

'Can't we just start a blog and then get, like *Vogue* or *The Look* to publish it or something?' Tania cocked her head to one side. 'We already know loads about fashion and stuff. And my boyfriend is in a band.'

'They're shit though.' Sasha did not mince her words.

'Yeah, they are,' Tania admitted.

'And he's not that hot.'

'Not as hot as Alex.'

'And he's a bit of a knob.'

'But he is in a band.'

'Yeah—'

'Just because he's in a band doesn't mean you should go out with him,' I interrupted. 'Believe me, boys in bands are more trouble than they're worth.'

'Have you broken up with Alex?' Tania slammed her hands down on the table. 'Is that why you're going home?'

'And why you look like shit?' Sasha added, sympathetically.

Honestly, I couldn't remember a time I'd ever wanted to cry more in my entire life.

'We're sort of on a break,' I said slowly and quietly, not allowing my voice to crack.

'Ooooooh,' the girls said in tandem. 'What did he do?'

'His ex,' I replied without thinking. 'Maybe. I mean, I don't know. Maybe nothing. I think we just want different things right now.'

Like, I wanted him and he wanted Solène. That was pretty different.

'He shagged his ex?' Sasha squealed, attracting the attention of the entire carriage with the exception of her mother.

'Is she pretty?' Tania cocked her head to the other side.

'It doesn't matter if she's pretty,' Sasha was indignant, 'it's totally out of order. You should turn around, get back on the next train and kick her arse. And then his arse. And then hers again, just to make sure. Like, properly kick her in.'

'I think she should go home.' Sasha said. 'Sort yourself out, eat loads of ice cream for like, a day, and then get really skinny and be all like "ha, well, I hate you anyway". And never see him again. Or like, shag his mate or something.'

'Yeah, you could shag his mate,' Tania agreed. 'Do you want to borrow some make-up?'

'I'm OK thanks,' I declined politely, ignoring their 'oh no you're not' looks as well as their advice. Even if they were the two best options I'd been able to come up with myself, shagging his friend aside. I really didn't think I was Graham's type, what with the lack of a penis and everything.

'What did your roommate tell you to do?' Sasha asked, offering me a bag of Haribo. It seemed a weird thing to keep in a Chanel handbag, but there you go. This was what happened when you gave teenagers designer goods. Well, teenagers and me. There were about a million stray Sour Patch Kids refugees living in the lining of my publicly shamed Marc Jacobs. 'Her name is Jenny, isn't it?'

'Yes, but she's not my roommate any more.' I felt a huge pang in my stomach at the mention of her name. Worse than I had talking about Alex. Wow. 'She lives in LA.'

'She's awesome,' Tania chimed in, stuffing her face with sweets. 'When we get to New York, I'm totally going to be Jenny and Sasha's going to be you.'

For the first time since I'd left the hotel, a genuine smile crept on to my face. 'You're going to work as a hotel concierge while Sasha gets routinely shafted by shit men?'

'Well, you know, we're not going to be exactly like you.' Tania shrugged.

I laughed. It sounded weird. And reassuring.

'She used to want to be Carrie,' Sasha rolled her eyes, 'and Rachel. And Serena. I always had to be like, Charlotte and Monica and Blair.'

'Blair is the best one,' I reassured Sasha. This was getting more surreal by the moment. 'I'd be Blair.'

'Told you!' Sasha turned triumphantly to her sister.

'Yeah, whatever.' Tania looked a tiny bit pissed off. She was definitely a Jenny. 'Anyway, what did your roommate say?'

'We haven't really spoken much this week.' This was a discussion I really couldn't have without bursting into tears so I skirted around the issue as much as possible. 'My phone wasn't working and she's in LA, there's about nine hours' time difference or something.'

'Well, it's only eight now, that's what, eleven in LA?' Tania held out her iPhone. 'Call her now.'

I took the phone and looked at it. 'Oh no, it'll cost a fortune, don't be silly.'

The girls both burst out laughing. 'It's fine,' Tania spluttered. 'Just call her. And can we talk to her?'

I breathed in. Of course I knew her number off by heart. Of course she would be up at eleven on a Saturday night. Of course she wouldn't want to talk to me. But I really, really wanted to hear her voice.

Taking the phone, I tapped in Jenny's number, messing up the international dialling code twice before I heard a distant ringing. The girls sat across from me, staring intently.

'Would it be OK if I talked to her on my own for a minute?' I asked, standing up and not waiting for a reply.

'But you'll come back so we can talk to her?' Tania

shouted down the carriage, ignoring all the muttering, tutting and sighing around her. 'I need to ask her opinion on boots. It's almost boot season.'

Not knowing exactly where else to go, I slid open the door to the toilet and waited for her to answer. Or not answer. Or answer.

'Jenny Lopez.'

I almost didn't recognize her professional voice. It was really far away from the 'Yo, bee-yatch' or 'Angie, what the fuck?' that I was used to.

'Jenny, it's Angela,' I paused giving her the chance to hang up or at least bitch me out again. But there was nothing.

'Jenny? Can you hear me?'

'Yes,' she replied flatly.

'OK, look, I'm so sorry,' I was quick, trying to get everything in at once, 'I know I messed up with the clothes, but I'm sure they'll be insured through *Belle* or I'll find a way to replace them, I'm just so, so sorry and I hate that we're not talking. It's been horrible these last few days, really, I'm just so sorry—'

'Wait, you're apologizing to me?' Jenny interrupted.

According to the Angela that stared back at me in the mirror, I was confused. 'Yes?'

'Shit, Angie,' Jenny sighed. 'I'm the one that owes you an apology. A big one. A pretty fucking huge apology. I've been trying to call you all weekend, but I couldn't get through to your cell or your BlackBerry and that bitch at your office wouldn't tell me where you were staying.'

'Seriously?' Mirror Angela was confused *and* surprised. And really did need some make-up. 'But the clothes I ruined . . .'

'Oh shut up. I'm so sorry, Angie,' Jenny talked over me. 'I'm not pissed about the clothes. It was like,

234

annoying, but it wasn't your fault. Besides, no one cares, no one ever asks for stuff back. Most of what I sent you was at least a couple of seasons old anyway. I was totally out of line, but then I was pissed that I couldn't get a hold of you and I wanted to talk to you about some stuff and I couldn't and, well, yeah, I over-reacted.'

'My phone hasn't been working, it's, well, there's been this whole big thing.' I waved my hand in the air, remembering that she couldn't actually see me. Which was a good thing given the state of me. 'What did you want to talk to me about?'

'You first, seriously, wasn't there something with Alex?' Jenny asked, her voice warm and reassuring. It felt so good to be speaking to her like this again. It felt just like when Louisa and I had hugged under the Eiffel Tower.

'There is, but we'll get to me,' I said firmly. 'What's up?'

'I've got to move out of Daphne's place,' Jenny said in a quieter voice. 'She's totally hooking again.'

'Are you serious?' I asked, my voice as high as Jenny's was low. 'In your home?'

'In her home,' Jenny rationalized. 'She's been losing styling clients, everyone is scaling back you know, and I guess if you've done it before, it's easy money.'

'But, oh God, Jenny, you have to get out,' I groaned. 'Come home.'

'I can't, things are going so well for me. I think that's another reason she's doing it. I'm getting so much work and no one is hiring her. It sucks. I feel shitty.'

'It's not an excuse and you can't feel guilty,' I said. I was desperate to get Jenny out of that house, I'd never been a fan of her current roommate. 'Can you go and stay at The Hollywood for a while?'

'I hadn't thought of that actually,' Jenny replied. 'I suppose I could still pull some strings, maybe for a week or so.'

'Just get out of Daphne's house, please. You don't know what kind of people she's bringing back.' And I never ever wanted to know.

'You're right, I'll pack up in the morning.' Jenny yawned loudly and I heard bed springs creaking. 'She's "working away" tonight so I'm having an early night. I haven't slept in days since I busted her last week.'

'I'm sorry, Jenny.' I returned her yawn. 'I haven't been sleeping that well either.'

'So what's going on? Hit me with it.'

I pulled a face in the mirror and took a deep breath.

'Right, here's the short version. Alex's ex-girlfriend is here in Paris and she's decided she wants him back. He's been a bit weird and when we went out for his birthday, he announced that he doesn't think he'll ever get married and have kids and he doesn't want to live with me any more.'

'What the fuck?'

'So, yeah, that's half of it.'

'Shit. OK, go.'

'Cici shafted me on the job I'm doing for *Belle*. She set me up with this assistant who took me to all the wrong places, she stopped my phone, and because I didn't have my power cable I couldn't use my laptop, and all my notes were in the suitcase so the article has been a nightmare and basically, she's trying to get me to mess up so I get fired and I suppose she gets my job.'

Jenny exhaled down the phone. 'So, I'm gonna start with Cici.'

'OK.' I bit my thumbnail.

'She's a bitch and she's dead. Do you have evidence?'

'Not really.' I thought back over the last couple of days. 'Unless Virginie, she's the assistant who was supposed to be helping me out, would tell them what happened.'

'Will she?'

'I doubt it.'

'Want me to make her?'

'You're going to fly out to Paris and kick her ass?'

'If I have to.'

I smiled and shook my head. 'It's fine. I think the article will be fine. I hope.'

'I'll call some people, see if anyone knows any places in Paris you can use, but that bitch needs to be fired,' Jenny insisted. 'You have to tell Mary at least.'

'I sent an email already, she hasn't replied.' I'd been trying not to think about my next conversation with Mary. It would not be fun. 'I just hope I don't lose my job.'

'Could you?'

'It's not beyond the realms of possibility.'

'So you'll find a new job.'

'But I'd lose my visa.'

'We'll get married, I'll get you another visa.'

'I'd say that might not sit well with Alex, but I don't know that for sure.' I paused for a moment to listen to and then ignore a knock at the door. 'He might be pleased to have me out of his hair.'

'So, exactly what has happened?' Jenny asked. 'Tell me that asshole hasn't actually put his dick somewhere he shouldn't.'

'You have such a beautiful way with words,' I said, a little more quietly now I knew I had an audience outside. 'And I don't know. He didn't come back to the hotel last night.'

'He still isn't there?' Jenny asked. 'Did you call him?'

237

'No,' I admitted. 'And I'm sort of not at the hotel.'

'Oh Angie,' Jenny sighed. 'You're gonna have to start from the beginning, honey.'

So I started from the beginning. I told her every single thing that had happened in the last week, from the moment I met Solène in the café, right up to our confrontation at Alex's gig, via his disastrous birthday dinner, Solène's party and their secret date that I'd witnessed in the bar. And I did not feel any better for getting it all off my chest.

'Angie, this girl is a psycho,' Jenny decided. 'Trust me, takes one to know one. But it doesn't mean anything is happening. You know I'm totally on your side over this, but there is no way Alex would cheat on you with this bitch. With anyone actually, but especially this bitch.'

'But they have so much history and he loved her and they were going to get married and—'

'Angie, stop,' Jenny interrupted. 'I'm gonna have to play a hard card OK? But it's only because I love you. Weren't you engaged before you met Alex?'

I stopped breathing, just for a second. 'Yes.'

'And didn't that guy cheat on you?'

'Yes.'

'But if he went around behind your back announcing to Alex that he was going to win you back, would that mean for sure that you were getting back with him?'

'But she's really amazingly gorgeous and just super sexy and—'

'Shut up before I come over to Paris to kick *your* ass,' Jenny threatened. 'Angie, you're freaking out. I mean, obviously it's all my fault because I wasn't there to talk some sense into you, but this bee-yatch is obviously just trying to get you out of the way so she can make her move. Alex values his dick and his kneecaps way too much to hurt you and piss me off. I made my position on his looking after you super clear before I left.'

'But what about all the "I don't think I need to get married to be happy" stuff?' I twisted a strand of tangled hair between my fingers. Really this conversation ought to be reassuring, but as the train chugged along, I was starting to feel more and more sick.

'Angie, he just turned thirty, he's feeling his age,' Jenny reasoned. 'And nothing makes guys feel older than the idea of marriage and babies. He's acting out. Also you're the one that's been refusing to move in with him for just about for ever. He's probably confused about stuff and trying to protect himself. Like, he's thinking, well if she doesn't want to move in with me I'm gonna tell her I don't want to marry her, then she'll see I don't care.'

'That sort of makes sense,' I conceded, the sick feeling growing. 'I suppose.'

'Damn, I need to stop spending so much time being the new Rachel Zoe and get back into being the new Oprah,' Jenny said, a dream filling her voice. 'Or maybe the first ever Rachel Zoe/Oprah hybrid . . . sorry, back to you.'

'Thanks,' I muttered, attacking the other thumbnail. 'So what do you think I should do?'

'You go back to the hotel, if he's not there, you call him and you tell him to meet you, the pair of you talk all this shit out and then call me to tell me I was right.' Jenny made it sound so simple. 'And if you want to kick the shit out of this Solène bitch then go for it, although karma will totally have her ass. She's not worth it. Just remember she isn't part of the problem, not really. Any decisions Alex makes, he makes for himself.'

'I know you're right,' I conceded.

'Well, duh,' Jenny snorted down the phone. It was amazing how she could be incredibly helpful and completely obnoxious at the exact same time.

'There might be a bit of a problem,' I said, finally deciding it was time to abandon the train toilet. It really was quite disgusting. Which I didn't think would bother the line of five really, really angry-looking people outside. Bless them for not kicking the door in. Must be English. 'Just with the whole getting back to the hotel thing.'

'Where are you?' Jenny asked over a now crackly line. 'You keep dropping out. Connection in Paris sucks.'

'I'm on a train,' I said, staggering back up the aisle towards Sasha and Tania who were bouncing up and down in their seats like Tigger. If Tigger had been drinking Vitamin Water and eating Haribo for the last hour. 'I think we're about to go into a tunnel.'

'Tell me you're on your way to the festival, Angela,' Jenny had a warning in her voice. 'Say it.'

'Well, no. I'm not. I sort of freaked out a bit and erm, I'm on my way to London,' I admitted, resting my forehead on the metal luggage rack in the middle of the carriage. The scream that echoed down the line was not helping my headache at all.

'You're what?' Jenny yelled. 'Angela Clark, get your ass off that train right now. I do not believe you sometimes.'

'But I didn't know what else to do,' I tried to keep my voice down, but it wasn't easy. 'I thought Alex was cheating on me, I thought you weren't talking to me, I might lose my job – it was just easier to take myself home rather than go back to New York to get dumped, evicted and deported. What would you have done?'

'You freaking asshat,' Jenny moaned. 'Are we actually going to have to schedule a daily call from now on so I can check that you're not doing anything supremely dumb?'

'Yes?' I shrugged. It certainly would make my life easier.

'Angie, why do you always assume the worst?' I could almost see her shaking her head at me. 'Why are you going there?'

I bit my lip. 'Because I didn't know where else to go, so I just thought, you know, home. Isn't that what you're supposed to do?'

'Yeah, but London isn't your home any more, Angie,' Jenny said. 'Is it?'

'I didn't know what else to do,' I repeated, quietly this time and with tears starting to trickle down my cheeks. I turned my back to the twins, ignoring their audible impatience.

'Angie, I'm so sorry,' Jenny said. 'Seriously, I really feel like this is my fault. I wasn't there for you when you needed me.'

'Jenny, no,' I choked over my words a little bit. 'I'm just a total idiot. I was running away again. Thing is though, even if I have a chance of sorting stuff out with Alex, it's still really possible that I'm going to lose my job. I might still be better off in London right now.'

'You know how we *just* talked about you assuming the worst?' Jenny reminded me gently. Well, as gently as Jenny was able. 'Angie, do you want to go back to London?'

I bit my lip and thought about it for a moment. Louisa, *EastEnders*, fish & chips. Yes. Mark, my mum, the number 77 night bus. No.

'Because if you really want to go back, really,

desperately, deeply in your heart of hearts, then go back,' she carried on. 'But if you want to be in New York with Alex, working as a writer, you might have to fight for it this time. But if that's what you really want, it'll be worth it.'

'Oh God, Jenny, I don't know, I just need to think for a minute—'

'Hello?' The line crackled once, twice.

'Jenny, can you hear me?' I shouted down the line before I noticed that the view of the beautiful rolling countryside had been replaced with pitch black. We were in the tunnel. Swearing slightly too loudly for the company I was in, I weaved up the aisle back to my seat.

'I'm sorry, we got cut off,' I said passing the phone back to Tania, not really remembering which twin the phone belonged to. 'But, uh, she said that I should give you her email address and she'll answer all your questions for you.'

The girls made excited mewing noises and pulled out matching Smythson notebooks, to scribble out Jenny's address. She forgave me for the clothes, she would forgive me for this. Eventually.

'And she said you should email her right away because she's going to be busy for the next couple of weeks and she really wants to hear from you,' I lied again. Really, I needed some peace and quiet while I tried to sort my head out, and answering Sasha and Tania's questions about how best to snag a rock star boyfriend was not going to help me get that.

I rested my head against the window and closed my eyes. Crossing my fingers under the table, I hoped that feigning sleep would convince them to leave me alone.

'Angela?' one of them whispered.

'Shut up!' the other cut in. 'Can't you see she's asleep?'

'No need to hit me, you cow,' the other sulked. 'I want to ask her about James Jacobs.'

'Let her sleep,' her sister said after a moment's consideration. 'She really looks like she needs some sleep. Sort her out a bit.'

'Please, Sash, a coma couldn't sort her out,' the first, presumably Tania, giggled. It was pretty much all I could do not to kick her really, really hard under the table. 'I can't believe we met her though. Amazing.'

'Want to go to the buffet and get a Diet Coke?' Sasha said after a short pause.

'Yeah, come on,' Tania agreed, hustling her sister out of the seat.

Once I was certain they were gone, I popped in my iPod headphones and stared at my reflection in the darkened glass of the window. OK, so Tania was right, I looked like living crap. My hair was limp, my skin was grey and my eyes had more baggage than I did, but it was to be expected right? I thought back over what Jenny had said and more importantly, what I'd said to Jenny. When she told me she had to move out of Daphne's place, I hadn't asked her to come back to New York, I'd told her to come home. And I had meant it. It was home.

So, worst-case scenario, if Alex decided to break things off and I lost my job, would I still want to stay in New York? I pouted at my reflection. How would being single and unemployed in New York be worse than being single and unemployed in London? And really, I didn't know that I was going to be fired. Maybe I was going to get a roasting from the *Belle* team, but Mary wasn't going to fire me. I'd explained what had happened, she knew what Cici was capable of, and anyway, I hadn't cocked up that job, I'd still been blogging. Jenny was right, I always assumed the worst.

And if I had to fight to get another opportunity at Spencer Media, I would. Maybe somewhere else even. I was still the girl that got the James Jacobs coming-out story. Maybe I could get him and Blake to adopt. That would be a big story. Probably incredibly unethical and the worst thing in the world that could happen to any child, but still. Well, maybe not the worst thing, it would have impossibly immature parents, but it would be exquisitely dressed.

And as for Alex, Jenny was right about that. I shouldn't be giving up on him easily. The only part she wasn't right about was when she had said it wasn't worth kicking Solène's ass. Given how satisfying it had been to give Virginie a slap around the chops, I couldn't even begin to imagine how great it would be to get into some serious hair-pulling action with Solène. Not that I was a violent person. Well, maybe just for one day a year.

But the pull of Louisa and the baby and *X Factor* marathons was still there. It would be so easy to bury my head in the sand and disappear into suburban south London for a while. As long as I didn't have to deal with my mother. Or my ex. Or my unemployment. Maybe I could be Louisa's nanny. She wouldn't mind that I'd never so much as held a baby without it bursting into tears, would she? I could take it for walks and make sure it took lots of naps and watch *Teletubbies* with it. I just wasn't sure about the dirty nappies. And the crying. And the sleepless nights. OK, I couldn't be a nanny. Maybe I could just work in a coffee shop or something. Work on my novel. Not that I was writing a novel. I could always go on the game like Daphne, I thought for a second. Hmm, probably not my best idea, given that I was already terrified of telling my mum I was out of a legitimate job, let alone considering entering the oldest profession on earth. And with my hair and arse in the state they were in, I was a long way off high-class hooker. Lower-middle-class call girl didn't really have the same ring to it.

I spotted the girls strutting back down the carriage, armed with Diet Coke and even more Haribo. I was pretty sure that was what they lived on. It would make a lot of sense. Chemicals and sugar. I closed my eyes and resumed position against the window, counting down the seconds until the train pulled in to St Pancras. I still had a lot of thinking to do and not a lot of time to do it in.

CHAPTER SEVENTEEN

After exchanging numbers with Sasha and Tania (realizing too late that I'd given them my real number as I was too distracted to think of a fake) and promising to talk to 'people at the mag' about getting them their own blogs, I ran through Customs, and stopped dead in the middle of the station concourse in front of a payphone. Instead of picking up the handset, I looked upwards for inspiration. But instead of seeing some holy light, I saw the world's longest champagne bar.

'Are you really open?' I asked, plopping myself on a tall stool and staring around me in wonder. 'It's not even half-eight.'

'We are.' The girl behind the bar smiled politely and set down the glass she had been polishing. 'We open at seven. And we're busy from seven.'

'I can't believe people just sit here in public drinking champagne at seven o'clock in the morning.'

It was honestly a wonderful thing. I had never seen so many bottles of champagne in one place. And I had seen a lot of bottles of champagne, having lived with Hurricane Jenny for the best part of a year.

'Well,' the girl gave me a terse smile, 'can I get you something?'

'Oh, erm, yes?' I said, not sure what to order. She wasn't going to make me a cup of tea, was she? I picked up the champagne menu, fully aware that none of my all-time great decisions had been made under the influence, but perversely keen to put off making any decisions in any way possible for as long as possible. It wasn't as if I was drinking White Lightning under the slide in the park. I would be enjoying a civilized and elegant flute of champagne. At eight-twenty-two in the morning. 'I'll go with the Taittinger.'

'Absolutely.' The girl poured my glass of champagne expertly then backed away to carry on polishing glasses. It felt strange. If I were sitting alone at a bar in New York, the bartender would always try and chat with me, it was a prerequisite of the job. If you didn't want to chat, they would immediately take the hint (a smile and a nod at their first lame joke), but they would always try. Thankfully, today was a day when I was more than happy for a bit of British reserve.

I watched the bubbles break on the surface of the champagne, a steady train at first and then a slower, one-by-one. Pop, pop, pop. I took a sip. It was delicious. Not what I'd usually go for at this time, but it never hurt to try new things. I thought back to the last time I'd drunk (too much) champagne. Erin's wedding. Alex had been amazing that day, so attentive, so loving. He'd sat through hours of awful banking talk with a smile on his face just to be there with me. Not that he hadn't got his reward, I thought, a small smile breaking on my own face. That was the first time I'd ever really honestly thought about the fact that we might possibly one day do the deed ourselves. Get married, obviously. The other deed was well taken care of. And the last big champagne event before Erin's wedding had been Louisa's. Not nearly as romantic an occasion.

'Oh bloody hell, what am I doing here?' I asked myself out loud.

The girl behind the counter gave me a slightly concerned look that she tried to turn into a smile, only not quite quickly enough. I didn't have the energy to give her a reassuring cheery grin and instead scrunched up my face and rubbed my eyes hard.

'Can I please get the check?' I asked. 'I mean, the bill?'

'Of course, madam,' she passed over a small white receipt on a silver saucer, ignoring the daggers in my eyes at 'madam'. How many more times?

I dropped my credit card on the saucer, only then to spend two minutes faffing around, trying to get back in the habit of a chip and pin system. I picked up the champagne flute, ready to swig it down – ever the classy lady – before setting it back on the bar. Seriously. Just Say No. Before I could change my mind, I stood up, grabbed my bag and sprinted back down the escalators, as quickly as I had come up them.

Planting myself in front of a blatantly barely used payphone, I marvelled at the fact that it took credit cards and picked up the receiver. With the champagne bolstering my confidence, I tapped in the first number, waiting for the call to connect and closed my eyes.

'Hey, this is Alex,' his voicemail kicked in immediately, not even ringing once. 'Leave a message if you want, but you know I never check this thing.'

'Alex, if you get this, it's me, I need to talk to you,' I rambled into the handset after the beep. 'Uh, I guess you're on your way to the festival or something, but oh, bloody hell, I really need to talk to you. Except I don't have a phone. So I'll call you back. Just, yeah, I will. I'll call you back.'

Hanging up, I looked around the station. It was still only eight-thirty in the morning, but it was already busy. It felt strange to conceive that I was actually in England for the first time in a year. There was a WH Smith to the left of me, a Foyles on my right and oh, M&S! I could actually see an M&S. The pang of homesickness that had been popping up every now and then in Paris hit me hard in the gut. There were British accents all around me and football shirts as far as the eye could see – and not just Manchester United ones like in New York. It was beyond weird. Utterly familiar and yet completely novel. But there were still a lot of things that were the same everywhere, Starbucks cups in every other hand, white cables peeping through shaggy haircuts and lots and lots of skinny jeans. But they didn't make me feel better. They didn't make me want to stay. The only thing I felt for certain was that I needed a wee.

Picking up the receiver for a second time, I ran my credit card back through the slot on the phone. The dialling tone gave way to a ringing and the ringing gave way to a click and an answer.

'Hello?'

'Louisa?'

'Angela?'

I smiled, it still felt great to hear her voice. 'Yeah, I, erm, I'm in London—'

'Oh, babe, that's amazing!' Louisa squealed down the phone. 'Annette! It's Angela, she's in London! She's coming home!'

'Shit, Lou, are you talking to my mother?' I screeched. 'Why on earth is she—'

'Yes of course I'll put her on, Angela, it's your mum,' she said as her voice pulled away and was replaced by a very pissed-off-sounding Annette Clark.

'Angela? It's your mother,' she announced, entirely unnecessarily. 'Where are you?'

'I'm . . .' my lips set themselves in a grim line. 'I'm in Paris.'

'Then why is there a London number showing on the phone screen?'

Bugger.

'I mean, I was in Paris. I'm at St Pancras,' I admitted. She'd been watching too much *Morse*.

'Well, you want to get yourself to Waterloo,' she said, as though I was stupid. 'Do you remember how to get there? They've got these special cards that get you on the trains now, Oysters or something. Do you have any money? Can you get one?'

'Mum, they've had Oyster cards for ages,' I sighed. 'I have one. And yes I know how to get from St Pancras to Waterloo. I've done it before.'

'Well I don't know, do I?' she replied, grumpy. 'You've been off fannying around in America for bloody months and it's not like you told me you were coming home, is it? Your dad would have come and got you, you know.'

'I know,' I replied. The idea of my dad rocking up in the Ford Focus right now was too much. He would probably take one look at me and drive me straight to rehab. 'But I'm not actually coming home.'

Which was a fact I wasn't even sure of until I'd said it out loud.

'Yes you are. Louisa told me you were,' she stated. 'What time will you be here? Do you have something decent to wear to the party or should I get the box of clothes out of the loft?'

'What box of clothes?' I asked, completely lost with my mother's train of thought.

'The clothes I picked up from Mark's when you pranced off to New York,' she explained. 'There's probably something in there. Or you can borrow something of mine.'

I let out a silent sob at the idea of turning up to Louisa's first anniversary party in my mum's Dorothy Perkins finest. And then I imagined getting out of a cab in the sequined Balenciaga mini dress and Giuseppe Zanotti heels Jenny had sent me. If they hadn't been blown to very fashionable smithereens, it would almost have been worth it, just to see the look on Mark's face.

'Angela, are you still there?' Mum asked impatiently. 'I don't suppose you'll pass a Waitrose on your way? Louisa's got a caterer doing a spread and I'm sure it's lovely, but there's not a pickled onion to be seen. How do you have a family party without pickled onions?'

'Mum, can you just put Louisa on for a minute?' I bit my lip. She was making this easier by the second.

'I can't believe you weren't going to tell me you were coming home in the first place,' she carried on, ignoring me completely. 'We'll be having a talk about your attitude when you get back, young lady. You'll stay with us of course, but you'd better not think you're going to be running roughshod all over me and your father, coming and going at all hours.'

'Mum—'

'If I hadn't seen Tim in the supermarket, I wouldn't have even known you were in France. And France of all places. I don't know. Why you didn't just come straight back to London, I will never know. Gadding about all over the place.'

'Mum, can you put Louisa back on please?' I was rapidly losing my temper and it really wasn't her fault. Well, it was a bit her fault, but mostly not.

'Fine,' she huffed into the phone. 'Just don't tell her what I said about the pickled onions. Louisa!'

'Thanks Annette,' she said with a smile in her voice before she dropped an octave. 'Did she ask you to bring bloody pickled onions? Seriously Ange, if she doesn't stop going on about it, I'm going to drown her in a vat of effing pickled onions. Not that she needs it, the sour-faced old—'

'Why is she even there, Lou?' I had no sympathy for the girl, my mother had hardly invited herself over at eight-thirty in the morning.

'She invited herself over to help with the party,' Louisa said. 'Can you believe it?'

Oh, fair enough.

'I'm sorry I put you on, but I really thought I was going to kill her,' she sighed. 'And you know, she is your mum.'

'I'm sorry,' I said truthfully. 'Look, Lou, I know I said I was coming back, but I'm not. I've been thinking about it and I need to go back to New York.'

'What? Angela, babe, I thought you said you were in London?' Louisa sounded understandably confused. 'Aren't you at St Pancras?'

'Yeah, sort of,' I said, trying to work out the time in Paris. Eight-thirty here, nine-thirty there. If I could get a train in the next hour, I could make it. 'I'm really sorry, I've been acting like an idiot all week. I just felt really lost, you know?'

'Then come home,' Louisa said firmly. 'You won't be lost if you're home.'

'Exactly,' I agreed. 'So I'm going home.'

'Babe, you've lost me.' Now it was Lou's turn to start

losing her temper. 'Are you coming or what? I need to know if we need to make a bed up.'

'She's staying with me!' I heard my mother bawl from across the room.

As nice as it was to be fought over, that really did settle it for me. 'I'm going back to New York,' I said. 'I'll talk to you tomorrow.'

'Honestly, Angela,' Louisa said with a distinct air of huffiness. 'One of these days you're going to have to grow up and make some adult decisions.'

'I know it doesn't seem like it right now,' I said, looking longingly at a little girl wandering by with a packet of Percy Pigs. 'But that's what I'm doing. Trust me.'

'Always,' she said. 'I'm just gutted I'm not getting you back. You know you're still welcome if you change your mind?'

'I do and I won't,' I promised. 'I'll call you later, have an amazing day and I'm sorry about my mum.'

'Not as sorry as she'll be if she doesn't shut up about those bloody pickled onions,' Louisa threatened. 'Love you.'

'Love you too,' I said, putting the phone down.

Breathing out, I looked up at the clock again and scanned the concourse for a ticket office. Heading for the Eurostar sign, my ballet pumps starting to slob off the back of my feet and making an attractive slapping sound, I pushed through the glass doors and approached the tired-looking man on the desk with my best 'please help me' smile.

'Can I help you, miss?' he smiled back.

I gave him the biggest grin I had in appreciation of the 'miss'.

'Hi. I need a ticket to Paris,' I started, pulling out my wallet.

'Absolutely,' he said, tapping away at his keyboard. I rubbed the sleep out of my eyes, having a total flash-back to doing this with Alain, twelve hours ago. 'And when would you like to travel?'

'Now?'

He looked up from behind the keyboard. 'Really?'

I shrugged and nodded. 'Yes please.'

'Oh-kaaay,' he said, tapping some more keys and scrolling through some more screens. 'Last-minute shopping trip?'

'Actually no,' I smiled brightly. 'I need to go and kick the living shit out of this girl who's trying to steal my boyfriend and then tell him that I love him whether he's having a midlife crisis or an affair or whatever and even if he says he doesn't want to marry me or live with me, I still want to be with him.'

The man stared. It was possible that not everyone he spoke to at this time in the morning was so much of a sharer.

'So I need to get there as soon as possible really.'

He stared for a second longer before breaking out into an impossibly big grin and clapping his hands together.

'Right then,' he yelped. 'We'd better get you on the nine-thirty.'

'The nine-thirty,' I repeated, hopping from one foot to the other in a tiny dance, much to the amusement of everyone else in the ticket office. 'How much is the ticket?'

'Hmm, because it's so last minute I only have busi-ness class available,' he said, scanning the page. 'It's going to be £350.'

I stopped dancing. Wow. That was one way to sober me up quickly.

'Otherwise the first economy seat I have is on the

254

twelve-thirty, won't get you into Paris until three-forty-five.'

'And I still have time to make the nine-thirty?' I asked, looking down at my credit cards.

'Yeah, you've even got time to go for a coffee, just be there twenty minutes before departure,' he leaned over the counter and whispered, 'they say half an hour, but really, twenty is fine. If you wanted to do some shopping or get some breakfast or wash your hair or whatever.'

'What?'

'Nothing,' he looked back at the screen.

'Just book it,' I said, handing him my credit card.

He ran my card through the machine and I waited in front of the keypad, my fingers poised, but nothing happened.

'I'm afraid this card has been declined.' He pulled an exaggerated sad face at me. 'Do you have another you could try? Or you know, a couple?'

I looked back at him with a grimace. This man was rapidly falling down my Christmas card list. Returning my attention to my wallet, I spied my Spencer Media corporate card. If this wasn't an emergency, I didn't know what was. And I could pay it back. It would be fine. Really.

Handing it over with bated breath, I waited for it to go through and after a split second, the machine beeped, buzzed and ran out a small paper slip for me to sign.

'Phew, right?' My new-not-a-very-good friend said, passing me a Eurostar ticket wallet. 'Make sure you pull her hair, bitches always go down when you pull their hair,' he added with some confidence.

'Thanks?' I said, backing out of the ticket office slowly.

Back on the concourse, I remembered just how badly

I needed the loo. Once I remembered, I really, really had to go. Luckily the toilets were right by the ticket office and with even more luck, there was no queue. I thanked the god of the ladies' toilets and hurled myself into a stall. Relief.

Washing my hands, I couldn't help but look at myself in the full, brightly-lit mirror and was forced to acknowledge that the Eurostar ticket man was right, I looked terrible. Even worse than I had on the train. I just wasn't going to cut it in a potential Angela versus Solène face-off, even with the recommended hair pulling. I still had more than twenty minutes before I absolutely had to be on the train and they needed to be used wisely.

And wisdom told me that there was only one place to go. Within seconds, I was sitting at the Clarins counter in Boots, giving the make-up girl an abridged version of events and allowing her to smother my face in a variety of lotions, potions and ultimately, an awful lot of make-up. I figured I'd already crossed the line with the company card, so I paid for more or less all of the make-up (it was only polite) and hightailed it over to the dry shampoo, hairbrush and ponytail holder department. This was going to be a mission the likes of which I had never attempted before, at least not without Jenny, Erin and a small army of hairdressers. Stopping in at M&S for enough packets of Percy Pigs to feed roughly the entire train, I realized it was almost nine a.m. and I sprinted to the train. Only losing my shoe twice.

I got to the check-in line just as they started calling people to the front for the nine-thirty train, wishing I had enough time to try and call Alex again, wishing I had enough time to go and buy some knickers from M&S, and wishing that I had never been so stupid as to come to London in the first place. Clutching my passport and ticket in one hand and ramming delicious sweets in my mouth with the other, I ran my ticket through the check-in machine and followed the slightly peeved-looking attendant towards the waiting train.

I'd made it.

CHAPTER EIGHTEEN

The journey back to Paris was painfully slow, but at least it gave me the opportunity to attempt to do something with my hair. By the time I tore out of the train doors at the Gare du Nord, I'd created something appropriately avant-garde with a skinny black Alice band and an awful lot of dry shampoo, aka the best invention since sliced bread. Actually dry shampoo must have surpassed sliced bread in the world's must-have stakes by now, it was surely saving more women more time.

My taxi driver seemed to understand my urgency, even if he didn't understand my directions. I repeated the name of the hotel three times in an appallingly bad French accent until I decided to write it out on the back of my Boots receipt, at which point the driver huffed, puffed and set off unhappily. The traffic was so much worse than it had been that morning. Paris had woken up and was enjoying a busy Sunday. Honestly, why couldn't everyone be hanging out in cafés eating pastries when I needed to get through town, I huffed, high on anticipation and jelly sweets. This must be how Tania and Sasha felt all the time.

Miraculously, we arrived at Rue Amelot without me leaping out of the car and killing any of the wandering tourists that thought it appropriate to cross the street in front of my taxi when the lights had already changed to green and without the taxi driver killing me for shouting out of the window at the tourists that crossed in front of us. It was a fun journey. I threw money at the driver, possibly too much, possibly not enough, and leaped out of the car and into the hotel.

'*Mademoiselle* Clark?' Alain raised his head in surprise as I dashed through the reception. 'You did not go to London?'

'I did,' I called, jabbing the lift button, 'but there was a bit of a change of plan. I don't suppose you know if my boyfriend, um, *Monsieur* Reid is still here?'

'I believe *Monsieur* Reid left the hotel some time ago,' Alain said, looking really quite confused. Perfectly understandable.

'Oh shit!' The lift doors pinged open, but there really was no time to go upstairs. If he was already on his way to the festival, I had to get there, now.

'Is there anything I can help you with this afternoon?' Alain asked. I could tell by the look on his face he regretted saying the words as soon as they were out of his mouth.

'Thing is, Alain,' I tried the same 'please help me smile' that had been so effective at the Eurostar desk, 'I need to get to Arras. In fact, I needed to get to Arras some time ago, but I made a massive cock up and went to London instead.'

'That is quite the problem.' Alain nodded to show he was following, which impressed me no end.

'Right? But the thing is, I don't know how to get to Arras. There's this festival and I need to be there right away. Can you help?'

'The train goes from the Gare du Nord, I believe the next train is at four-twenty.' He wrinkled his nose, not even knowing it, but channelling concierge extraordinaire, Jenny Lopez. 'And it will take approximately one hour. And then you can walk to the main square.'

'I just came from the bloody Gare du Nord!' I clung to the concierge desk and stamped out of sheer frustration. 'It's too late. How much would it be for a taxi?'

'Very expensive.'

'Very?'

'Very.'

'Shit.'

I put my forehead on the counter and waited for inspiration to strike. And waited. And waited. And—

'Possibly I could help,' Alain's said reluctantly. 'I could drive you to Arras.'

'Are you shitting me?' My face was shining brighter than a Christmas tree. 'I mean, really? Are you sure? Because that would be amazing.' Somewhere in the back of my mind I knew it was a huge imposition, but I was too desperate to decline politely. I hadn't come all the way back to mess up now.

'I live in Arras,' he replied, signalling to another concierge further down the desk and saying something in rapid French. 'I can drive you to the festival. I leave very soon.'

'If you don't mind, it sounds like a great plan.' I waited for him to come around to my side of the concierge desk and gave him a little hug. Which, I realized as he stiffened, was apparently too much. 'Sorry.'

'This way.' He coloured up and gestured out of the door.

Alain listened to my story with polite attention as I was driven through Paris for the third time that day.

I was just at the part where I saw Alex and Solène together, my hands gesturing wildly and practically jumping up and down in my seat when I realized that there was an actual possibility that Alain was just helping me to get out of work for the afternoon. His firmly-set jaw and white knuckles, tightly wrapped around the steering wheel did seem to suggest that he wasn't finding my companionship relaxing. Maybe I shouldn't have eaten two bags of Percy Pigs and a Toblerone on the train back from London. My sugar buzz was worse than any early-morning champagne rush.

'And well, I just really need to talk to my boyfriend, so thanks for this,' I said, cutting the story short and folding myself back into the passenger seat. I checked his expression out of the corner of my eye, wondering if he would be desperate to know what happened next. Letting out a small sigh of relief, Alain stared at the road ahead, relaxed his vice-like grip on the steering wheel and reached across the gear stick to turn on the radio. Loud.

I just about managed to sit on my hands and keep my mouth shut for the rest of the journey, much to Alain's visible relief. For every mile we drove in silence, I could see his shoulders slowing inching down from their previous position, tightly tensed up around his ears. After twenty long minutes of bad French radio (I would never have had Alain pegged as a country fan), we pulled up at the front gate of the festival.

'Thank you so much,' I said, fumbling for the door handle. 'You're a life-saver. Really. I just can't thank you enough.'

'Of course.' He loosened his concierge's tie, confirming that letting me out of the car meant that his working day was really over. 'We will see you back at the hotel very soon?'

'Hopefully not too soon,' I said, clambering out of the car. 'I mean, hopefully not later within the next hour or anything.'

'Yes, hopefully not too soon,' he repeated, his intention pretty unmistakable. Still, he had brought me to the festival, and he hadn't kicked me out on the motorway when I accidentally spilled half a can of Pepsi all over his upholstery, so I needed to be thankful, not pissy.

Closing the door carefully, I waved him off, re-applied lipgloss and walked up to the gate. Unlike every other festival I'd ever had the misfortune to attend, there wasn't a muddy field in sight. The huge stage was set at one end of, well, the main square. I wasn't sure quite what I had been expecting, but this was beautiful. I decided it was a good thing that my guest pass was still waiting for me at the entrance and peered around the ticket gates into the festival. Man alive it was busy. How was I supposed to find Alex among all these people?

'You're such a genius, Angela,' I muttered, pushing through the crowds. 'Get delivered to the middle of nowhere in a country where you can't speak the language, without a bloody phone, and then expect to be able to find your boyfriend in the middle of ten thousand people.'

What made this especially difficult was the fact that at least sixty per cent of the ten thousand people were dressed just like my boyfriend. Every single one of Paris's hipsters had descended on Arras and it looked to me like they'd shipped in some reinforcements, just in case. As much as the very idea of it pained me, I had to head to the main stage and see if I couldn't get into the artists' area. It was super unlikely that Alex would be in there, he was always out watching bands somewhere, but the chances of Craig declining back-stage hospitality? Cold drinks and hot groupies? There was no way he was anywhere else.

'I think I'm on the Stills list, it's Angela Clark?' I said, approaching the two very large men guarding the backstage gate and holding my lanyard out for inspec-tion. It wasn't quite a Jedi mind trick, but it should have worked. Instead, they looked at me, looked at each other and then carried on ignoring me.

'No, really, I'm on there,' I said, hoping it was true. 'I'm looking for Alex Reid?'

'You and me both,' said a familiar voice behind me.

I whirled around to find Graham carrying his guitar case, and threw myself into him for a hug. 'What's going on Angie, where is he?'

'What do you mean, where is he?' I asked, really not wanting to let go as he shook me off. It was so good to see Graham. It felt like for ever since I'd said goodbye to him the night before. 'I came here to find him.'

'But I thought you were back in London.' He waved his access all areas pass at the great big men and they parted slowly, allowing us through. 'You didn't go?'

'Why would you think I was in London?' I asked, spotting Craig leaning against the bar, talking to a cute blonde. Of course.

'Because I have some insane voicemail from Alex saying that you'd bailed on him and gone to London so he was going after you.' Graham dug around in his pocket for his iPhone, pressed a few buttons and passed it to me. 'Care to listen?'

I pressed the hot phone to my left ear, sticking my finger in the other so that I could hear the message over the roaring crowd that were greeting the band just about to take the stage.

'Hey man, uh, I gotta go to London and find Angela, I fucked up and I have to make things right.'

I swallowed hard. He had gone to London? He'd followed me?

'I'll try and be back for the show, but uh, well. I guess I might not be. I'll try and get back. Sorry man.'

I handed the phone back to Graham, all of the colour draining from my face, rendering all of the Clarins girl's hard work more or less pointless.

'Did you call him back?' I asked, frantic. Alex had gone to London? Why had Alex gone to London? How did Alex know I'd gone to London?

'Of course,' Graham said, pushing his glasses up his nose and giving me a not particularly friendly look. 'I couldn't get through to him. I'm guessing the reception isn't that good under the ocean.'

'No, it's not,' I confirmed, trying to ignore the fact that he wasn't looking any happier with me as the conversation went on. 'But it has to come out the other side sooner or later. Can we try again?'

'You try.' He pushed the phone back into my hands. 'I have to go sound check my equipment. In case the rest of my band shows up and we actually get to go on.'

'Gotcha.' I gave his back a quick salute as Graham strode off, physically dragging Craig away from the blonde and the bar. I really didn't like it when he was mad at me. It took me a couple of seconds to work out how to redial the last number on the iPhone and waited for it to ring through. Which, thank God, it did.

'Hey, Graham, man,' Alex answered and launched straight into his apology. I choked up before I could stop him. 'I'm really sorry, I know I've fucked you and Craig over, but I have to talk to Angela, I've let this situation get way out of hand and I just need to get her to come back or to just listen to me or something. I'll be back before we're on. When are we on?'

'I don't know,' I stuttered down the phone. 'But I do know I'm not in London.'

'Angela?'

'Yes?'

There was an awfully long silence on the other end of the phone.

'Alex?'

'Angela, are you in Paris?'

'Arras, actually.'

'You're not in London?'

'No.'

'Were you in London?'

'Erm, just for a bit.'

Another long pause.

'I'm gonna run out of battery,' Alex said finally. 'Can you please just sit your ass down and not move until I get back?'

I nodded emphatically.

'Are you nodding at the phone?' he asked.

'Yes.'

'OK.'

And he hung up.

CHAPTER NINETEEN

I stared at the phone and wondered what I was supposed to do next. I thought about texting him, apologizing for sending him on a wild goose chase to London except I had no idea how to text from an iPhone and I really didn't want to have to ask Graham. And besides, if Alex's phone was out of battery, he wouldn't get it anyway. Damn it. Feeling like a complete spare part, I wandered back to the bar area and asked for a coffee. Dropping into a chair at an empty table, I pulled out my iPod and laptop. All I really wanted to do was sleep until Alex got here and then wake up just in time to see him take the stage, sweep me up in his arms in front of all of Paris's assembled musos and declare his love for me. But given the events of the last twenty-four hours, that seemed about as likely as me getting onstage and filling in for him if he didn't make it back in time for the band's set.

My laptop was still on the same page as when I'd closed it in the Gare du Nord hours ago. I read and reread what I'd written in the morning. It was all still true, I had been completely effed over by a girl this week although no one had really messed anything up quite as magnificently as I had messed up myself. I apple-xed the text until I was left with an empty page and then started again.

The Adventures of Angela: Know Your Enemy

Confession time. This is the second time I've written this blog post in the last twelve hours and I am slightly worried that it might be my last. To cut a really long story short (this is only a blog, after all) I came to Paris this week with visions of bicycle rides by the Seine, skipping through the Louvre hand-in-hand with my Brooklyn boy and generally devouring everything edible that came my way, but instead I got something really quite different.

Rather than La Vie en Rose, *I got* La Vie en Rubbish. *Between transatlantic rows with my best friend, a total psycho trying to steal my boyfriend, another one trying to steal my job and a great big bout of homesickness, I really haven't had a lot of time to steal kisses on the Pont Neuf or inhale macaroons at Ladurée. It's been a bit of a busy week. And now I'm sitting here trying to work out just what the bloody hell went on. I can't help, but feel that if I had just had more confidence in my own decisions and in myself, I really could have avoided at least some of my problems and it's possible that I wouldn't be sitting backstage at the Main Square festival in Arras, looking like something Worzel Gummidge threw up. At least my black eye has more or less gone now – I'll explain that later.*

So I'm trying a new approach from here on. I'm going to actually tell people what I'm thinking, do what I want to do and see what happens after that. Que sera, sera and all that. Hopefully, I'll be able to let you know how that works out for me . . .

I pressed send and hoped for the best, closing up my laptop and sipping my coffee. Graham and Craig were still AWOL, presumed sound checking and so I rested my head on my forearms for just a minute, closing my eyes and listening to the lilting music that drifted around from the front of the stage.

'Angela?' a small voice whispered above me.

I opened my eyes, realizing that I was still face down on the table and from the smudgy black marks on my arms, I'd been there for a while. The music blasting out of the backstage speakers was quite different to the gentle lullaby that I remembered playing and my arms prickled with goose bumps. How long had I been asleep?

'Angela?' the voice asked again.

I looked up, blinking and confused. Where was I again? Standing beside me at the side of the table, but well out of arm's reach, was Virginie. It took me a moment to remember why I felt a burning desire to claw her eyes out, but once I worked it out, the feeling did not go away.

'Sod off,' I said, plonking my head right back on to my arms. I was too tired to deal with her and really, what could she have to say that would help?

'I have sent an email to your Mary to tell every-thing.'

Oh. What do you know?

'Really?' I asked, opening one eye.

She nodded, still standing a fair distance away, with

her arms wrapped around her back. It made me feel a bit weird to think that she might be scared of me, but it also made me feel ever so slightly awesome. I was badass and somewhere in LA, Jenny Lopez would be smiling.

'What about this beauty assistant job you applied for?' I opened the other eye.

Virginie shrugged. 'It has been filled. I do not think Cici was even speaking to anyone about me. I am sorry. I have been stupid.'

Waking up properly and taking a good look at her, I realized Virginie was not looking her sparkly pep-tastic best. In fact, she looked slightly shit. Her eyes and nose were rimmed with red and her hair was pulled back into a messy ponytail and not the stylishly messy kind, it actually looked as if it needed washing.

'They already filled the job?' I pulled out the chair beside me and nodded for her to sit. Instead, Virginie regarded me nervously and ran her fingers along the back of the chair. 'Oh for Christ's sake, sit down, I'm not going to hit you,' I said, holding up my hands in a gesture of peace, 'not again anyway. And well, sorry about that.'

'I would hit someone that did the same to me,' she said, sitting across from me. I made a note never to piss her off. 'And they have filled it, if there was a job to begin with. It is possible that she created the adver-tisement herself, is it not?'

'It absolutely is,' I agreed, refusing to feel sorry for her. 'So you didn't bother to check it out with anyone at *Belle* before you agreed to try and ruin my life?'

'The girl I knew, the old beauty assistant, she was fired,' Virginie explained. 'Cici told me she got fat.'

'They can't actually fire someone for getting fat,' I said, really hoping it was true. 'If she was fired then there is a job?'

'I do not know, but there is so much talk of restructure and lay-offs in the US office it is possible she is not being replaced.' Virginie wiped a stray tear away from a tired-looking eye. 'And yes, you can be fired for being fat.'

'Shit,' I breathed, regretting getting full-fat milk in my coffee. 'Well, I appreciate it. The email.'

'It is the least I can do.' Virginie tried to smile, but didn't do a terribly good job. 'I know I have not helped you this week and I know it has been difficult.'

'You don't know the half of it.' I rubbed at the smudges on my arm and tried not to think what that meant for the make-up on my face. 'I saw Solène at the show last night, before I saw you outside. Apparently she's decided she's taking Alex back.'

'Oh, I am so sorry.' She tentatively reached a hand out and lightly squeezed my forearm. 'I was hoping that we were wrong.'

'Well, I said she's decided, not he's decided,' I clarified for my pessimistic pal. 'I don't know what he's decided.'

'You did not speak with him last night?' Virginie asked, pulling her hand away. Baby steps.

'He didn't come back to the hotel last night,' I said. I really hated telling people that part. 'And I wasn't around this morning.'

'I see.' She pressed her lips together and rolled her silver necklace between her thumb and forefinger.

'Right.'

'Right.'

We sat in silence for a moment, neither one of us knowing quite what to say. There was no point in Virginie leaping back on to the cheer wagon, I wasn't going to believe it now, and I was all out of energy. I just wanted to see Alex.

'What time is it?' I asked, as much to break the tension as anything.

'Six-thirty?' Virginie checked her watch. 'Six-thirty-five. Alex, he is playing very soon. Isn't he here?'

'I don't know.' I stood up, looking for Graham and Craig. If Alex's phone was flat, he couldn't let them know whether he was going to make it or not, and there was no way he would know anyone's mobile number off by heart to call from a payphone. 'I'm going to go and have a look.'

'May I come along?' Virginie asked, leaping to her feet. 'I would like to help, if I can.'

'Why not?' I shrugged. It was just a waiting game now. There was no more damage to be done.

The security around the stage area was conveniently lax and between my guest pass and Virginie's press pass, we managed to make it up to the side of the stage without too much trouble. Graham and Craig were standing with their equipment, looking anxious.

'Did he call?' Graham asked, holding his hand out for the phone I'd completely forgotten I still had. I pulled it out of my handbag, attempting to peel the sticky Toblerone wrapper off it before I handed it back.

'He did, he told me to stay here.' I tried to look apologetic. 'I guess that means he's going to be here.'

'He had better be,' Graham brushed his hair back off his face, 'he's got ten minutes before these guys finish. We're on at seven.'

'What happens if he misses the slot?' I didn't especially want to know, I already felt quite guilty enough, but it seemed polite to ask.

'We get fined and I doubt we ever get to play for the promoter again,' he tilted his head to one side. 'So not great.'

'How often do you come out to Paris?' I held out my arms. 'Really?'

'The promoter is global.'

'Oh.'

'Yeah.'

Craig walked around Graham and folded me up in a huge hug, with only the slightest hint of a pat on the ass. 'Don't worry Ange,' he whispered into my hair. 'And what's with this chick you got with you? She single? Can I hit that?'

I pushed out of the hug and gave him my sternest look. Virginie had already had her dream job taken away and a slap in the face in the past twenty-four hours, hooking up with Craig would just about push her over the edge.

'So that's a no?'

'It's a no, Craig,' I confirmed, looking out at the stage. Wow it was big. And wow, there were a lot of people in the crowd. As in thousands. Directly opposite, there was another group watching the band, waving at us. Craig waved back before he had his hand slapped down by Graham. I looked suspiciously at the boys and then squinted back across the stage, through my smudged mascara, holding my hand over my eyes to block out the early evening sun.

It was Solène.

And she was waving at me.

'Angela, just let it go,' Graham urged, apparently able to see my temper rising through the back of my head. 'She's not worth it.'

'Did you talk to Alex about it?' I asked him, as quietly as possible when you were standing next to a band belting out their closing number to 10,000 screaming fans.

'We didn't get a chance last night, he vanished right

after the show,' Graham yelled into my ear. 'When I got that message I figured you two must have had a bust-up or something.'

'But he didn't come back to the hotel,' I said slowly, feeling the Percy Pigs coming right back up. 'He wasn't with you?'

'Uh, no.' He looked back across the stage to where Solène was dancing with the rest of her band. 'Don't get ahead of yourself, Angie, you don't know what he did. Alex knows this city probably as well as he knows New York, there are a million places he could have stayed.'

'A million,' I repeated, unable to take my eyes off Solène. I wanted to believe Graham, but out of the two of us, I was the one with dirty hair and no idea where my boyfriend had spent the night. If Alex had told her to go to hell, why was she dancing? If I knew that I had lost him for good, I wouldn't be able to dance. I wouldn't be able to laugh or smile or probably get out of bed for a month, so I sure as hell didn't know what she was looking so happy about. Unless . . .

'Ahh, fuck, they finished early!' Craig slapped his hand against his face as the drummer onstage threw his sticks up into the air to announce the end of their set. 'I never liked those bastards.'

The band came off towards us, high-fiving Craig and Graham as they went, while the roadies swarmed the stage, unplugging all the equipment to make way for Stills.

'What do we do, man?' Craig asked Graham, looking panicked. 'You know the words, you could sing?'

'Knowing the words isn't the same as singing.' Graham frowned. 'But we've got to do something. I'm gonna go and find someone, see if we can hold on for a little while. You go set up, you take too long anyway.'

273

Ignoring, or not recognizing the insult, Craig tiptoed through the cables and on to the stage to help his drum tech set up. I couldn't believe this was happening and as much as I was trying to stick to my new positive thinking regime, I was pretty sure it was at least fifty per cent my fault. Possibly slightly more. Or slightly less. Depending on whether or not Alex needed to see me to break up with me or to tell me he had been a dick and that he loved me.

'I am going to find drinks,' Virginie announced loudly, apparently sensing an impending meltdown and wanting to be out of harm's way. 'I will bring back wine.' Regardless of her previous betrayals, there was no disputing the fact that she was an intelligent and intuitive girl.

I paced the limited space I had beside the stage, willing Alex to burst through the doors, take the stairs two at a time and storm the stage just in time, but the clock kept on ticking and no one came up the stairs except for a tall blonde – oh, brilliant, just what I needed.

'Angela,' Solène greeted me, as usual, with a smile. Stage-ready in a stripy black-and-white mini dress I was pretty sure I had owned pre-exploding suitcase, black over-the-knee boots and perfect make-up, she was not a sight I wanted to see. 'Angela, have you slept at all? You do not look well.'

'Whatever,' I replied eloquently, looking past her to where Craig was struggling with a particularly tricky snare drum. I did not want to get into this. There was no way I was listening to another word out of that woman's mouth until I'd spoken to Alex.

'Of course, I did not get too much sleep myself,' she shrugged. 'But perhaps I am glowing. Where is my Alex?'

My heart fell right to the floor, my stomach and my handbag following closely behind. She hadn't? He wouldn't? They didn't?

'All right,' I breathed out, remembering too late that my laptop was in the bag I'd just dropped. 'You can stop. I'm sure this is all hilarious to you, but until I've spoken to Alex, I don't want to see your face. And I'm fairly certain that even after I've seen him, you're going to be the last person I want to talk to, ever again.'

'You have not seen him?' she asked, her bravado drooping slightly. 'You have not spoken to him?'

'I'm not talking to you.' I folded my arms to stop them from doing anything I might regret. One slap per trip was my limit. 'So whatever it is that you're dying to tell me, you can just piss off until I've heard it from him.'

'But he said he had to talk to you,' Solène faltered. 'Last night. He said we would speak when he had spoken to you.'

'Well that's very chivalrous of him, isn't it? He dragged himself all the way over to London, so he could break up with me before you carried on your epic romance.' I couldn't believe this was happening. Had they spent the night together? And that was why he needed to speak to me? Of course he needed to speak to me. He couldn't be with Solène without breaking up with me first, that way he could convince himself he hadn't cheated. I was so stupid. Positive thinking, my arse. Delusional was a better word for it.

'London?' She looked confused. 'He is in London?'

'I can't actually explain any of this to myself so I'm not going to try and explain it to you,' I snapped, desperate to be away from her. 'Please just go away. You've got what you wanted, haven't you?'

'Yes.' She shrugged, the self-assured arrogance

reappearing on her face. 'Where is he? There is no way Alex would miss a gig.'

'Apparently, he would.' I waved my arms around, tears prickling in my scratchy, dry eyes. 'Can you see him anywhere?'

'This is your fault.' Solène's eyes narrowed and she prodded me in the shoulder. 'Alex has never missed a show before, not for anyone. I cannot believe he would risk his career for you.'

I paused for a moment. Why was she so pissed off if they were back together? 'What, he never missed a show for you?' I asked.

She froze, her mouth set in a hard line. 'He would do anything for me.'

'Except, it was me he chased to London.' I tipped my head to one side and pursed my lips. 'When you come to think of it, that's a weird thing to do if you're going to dump someone, isn't it?'

'No.' She didn't even sound as though she'd convinced herself. 'He said that he could not see me until he had spoken with you.'

I breathed in sharply. They hadn't spent the night together at all. 'You've said that once. So you haven't even seen him?'

'I am sure that once he has spoken to you—'

'Oh my God!' I pushed some loose hair behind my ears and took a step towards her. 'This was all in the bar, wasn't it? You didn't even see him after the gig last night.'

'He said—'

'Stop telling me what he said and tell me the truth.' I took another step as she stumbled backwards. High heels and stage cables do not mix. 'Did you spend the night with my boyfriend or not?'

'Maybe not last night, but—'

'Piss off, Solène,' I said with as much venom as I could muster given how incredibly relieved I felt. 'You're pathetic.'

I hadn't thought she would break down in floods of tears exactly, maybe more of a defeated skulk back to where she came from, but really, the last thing I'd expected was for her to let out a terrifying battle cry and throw herself at me, pulling at my hair, and generally behaving like a complete psycho. I tried to fend her off, flashing back to my last full-on girl fight, with Janet Martin on the school playing field in year nine. Only this time, there was no Louisa around to kick her in the shins while I ran away.

'What the—' I panted, trying to push her away. But compared to her, I was an amateur. I might have got one unexpected slap away on Virginie, but this was not Solène's first time in full combat. The Alice band had been my first mistake. She ripped it out of my hair and began attacking me with it like a claw. There must have been a full minute of battle before anyone even attempted to break us up, most likely because the first person to spot the fight was Craig, and I saw him actually hold one of the roadies back so he could watch. If I lived through this, he was next on my ass-kicking list.

Before Solène could attempt to pull any more of my hair out at the roots, I felt someone swoop in behind me and pick me up by the waist. Luckily, the elevated height meant that I was able to land a good kick to her jaw as I was snatched away and then dropped unceremoniously on to my backside.

'Angela, what are you doing?' Graham hissed, attempting to hold Solène away with one arm. 'Everyone can see you.'

'I'm going to kick her arse, Graham, leave it,' I said,

scrambling to my feet and pushing him out of the way. But I shouldn't have launched myself at such a skinny target with so much vigour. As soon as I hit her, we both barrelled backwards, landing in an undignified heap, only stopping the scrapping just long enough to ascertain that we were right in the middle of the stage.

The crowd whooped and screamed as we appeared on the big screens set up at either side of the stage. I sat up, straddling Solène, and stared out at the sea of people.

'Oh shit,' I said, blinded by the flashes coming from the photo pit.

'Stupid bitch!' Solène wailed, knocking me off balance and rolling over on top of me. The crowd cheered us on as Solène sent a flurry of tiny fists my way while I wriggled underneath her, slapping away her hands and kicking my legs wildly. It only took someone who would forever be on my shitlist a couple of seconds to turn on the stage mics so that the crowd could hear the running commentary of bi-lingual cursing, and, even though it felt as if she'd been clawing at my face for hours, it was probably only seconds before I felt her foot in my stomach as she was pulled up and away.

Opening my eyes, I saw that it wasn't a roadie or Graham or even Craig removing Solène, but Virginie, who was dragging her backwards across the stage. Even though she was considerably smaller than my nemesis, Virginie had the element of surprise. And a good handful of her hair, right at the roots. Solène's dress had ridden up around her waist and one of the heels of her thigh-high boots had snapped off. She wasn't really looking her best for the cameras. The two girls screamed at each other in French, to the delight of the hometown crowd, Solène trying to twist out of Virginie's vice-like grip and Virginie kicking her feet forwards to the edge of the stage. I propped myself up on my elbows to watch and try to get my breath back. Fighting was the best aerobic exercise I'd ever tried.

Just as Virginie was about to push Solène backstage, she managed to weasel herself free and started attacking my would-be saviour. I jumped up, making sure my own T-shirt covered everything it was supposed to, and leaped back into the fray. I pushed Virginie out of the way, as gently as possible given the heat of the moment, and turned back to give Solène the slap she so sorely deserved. Solène looked surprised to see me back up on my feet, but not surprised enough to forget what we were doing. Before I could even draw back my hand she planted a fist in my cheek, exactly where I'd blacked my own eye.

'Oh, you bitch,' I squealed, doubling over and pressing a hand to my face. Solène gave me a triumphant smirk, shuffled her dress back into place and flicked her hair back over her shoulder. Before I could even think to react, I heard a loud wail behind me and saw a flash of brunette hair barrel by. I staggered out of the way, falling back down on my arse just in time to see Virginie smack Solène full in the face. She wavered for a moment, teetering backwards and forwards on one flat foot and one four-inch heel, and then took a step backwards on to the stage to steady herself. Unfortunately, there was no more stage. I held my breath, waiting for her comedy windmilling arms to propel her forward, but nope. She dropped off the front of the stage like a brick, right into a huddle of photographers, all trying to get a good shot of the bitchfest. I waited to hear her start screaming before I breathed out and she didn't make me wait long.

Virginie and I crawled to the edge of the stage and

peered over to see Solène slapping away the helping hands that tried to pull her upright. I waved down at her with a cheesy smile, able to laugh now I knew she hadn't accidentally broken her neck. Which probably would have been a bit harsh. She pushed through the popping flashbulbs and out of the photo pit, vanishing into the crowd, who cheered as she went by.

I shook my head, gingerly rubbing my cheek. I couldn't believe she'd actually gone for an all-out punch. And I couldn't believe that Virginie had KO'd her off the stage.

'Thanks for that,' I said, pushing my cheekbone in as I spoke.

'I am not normally violent,' Virginie blushed, 'but I feel better.'

'You don't need to explain to me. I completely understand that sometimes, you just need to slap someone. Or hit them with a shoe. Sorry about that again, by the way.'

'You did not hit me with a shoe?' she said, confused.

I turned to look at the side of the stage where Graham was still standing, openmouthed and staring at the chaos. Craig was beside him, but looking far less concerned, in that he was making rock signs at me while drinking a beer.

'No Alex?' I mouthed, not knowing whether or not the mics were still turned on. Graham shook his head and shrugged, pointing at his watch. The band should have gone onstage five minutes ago.

Without the impromptu entertainment to keep then occupied, the crowd began to get restless. A small section at the front began chanting for Stills, and the cry soon rippled all the way to the back of the square. Graham threw his hands up in the air and turned away, holding his phone to his ear.

'Erm, is this still on?' I asked no one in particular, picking up a stray microphone from the floor. A high-pitched squeal from the monitor in front of me confirmed that yes, it was. And without knowing what I was going to say, I suddenly had the crowd's attention, whether I wanted it or not.

'Hi,' I said slowly. 'I'm Angela. Sorry about the whole fighting thing.'

The crowd was suddenly silent. And all looking at me.

A lone voice in the photographers' pit coughed and shouted up to the stage. '*En Français?*'

'*Je suis desolée, je ne parlez vous la Français?*' I stuttered my stock phrase into the microphone against a wave of boos. 'But I'm sure Stills will be on in just a minute.'

The boos faded out to some confused mass chatter.

'Ah, *Stills seront sur la scène dans un moment,*' Virginie grabbed the mic out of my hand, and the crowd responded with a cheer. 'Say something,' Virginie urged, her hand over the microphone. 'I will translate.'

I took the mic back and stared out. Really, that was a lot of people.

'So, my name is Angela and I'm a huge Stills fan,' I put the microphone back in its stand.

There was a brief delay while Virginie translated, followed by a huge roar.

'Angela, what are you doing?' Graham yelled offstage. Craig was too busy shouting along with the crowd. It seemed he was a huge fan of his own band.

'I don't really know,' I shouted back. 'I want to say I'm buying you some time, but I might mean making myself look like a complete dick.'

'Yeah, the second one sounds right,' he shouted back.

'The band are having some technical issues,' I said back into the mic. 'So they'll be on in a minute.'

A murmur travelled across the square. The cameraman at my feet called something out to Virginie, bypassing me altogether. And she replied into the microphone, eliciting a loud whoop, followed by a mass giggling from the female festival goers.

'What did you just say?' I hissed across the stage, blinded by a sudden outbreak of flashes at my feet.

'He asked who you were,' Virginie said, backing away from the cameras slightly. 'I told him you were the girlfriend.'

'You didn't?'

This was not good. I was not in a state to be photographed as 'girlfriend of the lead singer'. I could possibly pass as 'drug dealer of the lead singer', but that was about it. A fact not lost on the girls in the audience, who did not seem too keen on Virginie's revelation. I was seeing a lot of arms folding in front of me and even hearing a few boos. Harsh, ladies.

'They want to know why the band aren't onstage,' Virginie translated the random screaming coming from the front few rows. 'I think you should tell them, it is a very sweet story.'

'No it isn't!' I replied, trying to think of more diversionary tactics, but all I could come up with was flashing the crowd, and that wasn't going to win anyone over. Certainly not the girls, who already hated me. This was not one of my best ever days. 'I'm not telling them why Alex isn't here.'

'Then I will tell them.' Virginie gave me a sly smile. The new Virginie had more in common with Jenny than enough. 'They also want to know why we were fighting with the girl from Stereo.'

'Fine.' I looked out at the thousands of people one

last time before someone turned a spotlight on above me and made them all disappear. 'OK, basically it's like this.'

Somewhere offstage to my right, I heard Graham cursing. Onstage to my left, I could hear Virginie's fast translation.

'So at least when I got to Paris, I was Alex's girl-friend, Alex from the band,' I clarified by pointing at the huge, blown-up Stills album cover hanging from the stage rigging behind me. 'But he didn't tell me his ex-girlfriend lived here, that was the girl that I was sort of talking to onstage a moment ago.'

'You want me to say "talking to"?' Virginie stopped translating mid-sentence and gave me a 'really?' look. 'They are French, not blind.'

'Just say it.' I gave her look right back and continued with my story. 'So yeah, she was hanging around, pretending she wanted to be my friend, inviting me to parties and stuff, but it turned out she just wanted to break us up so she could get Alex back.'

I couldn't see the crowd, but I could hear them ruminating this twist in the tail. The photographer, acting as their representative, shouted a question up to Virginie.

'He wants to know why they broke up in the first place,' she repeated in English.

'Oh, because she was cheating on him,' I said, waiting for the appropriate response. And I got it. Ten thousand sharp intakes of breath and unmistakable 'bitch!' comments echoed around the square. 'Yeah, she was really awful. And this was a couple of years ago, before I ever met Alex. She totally broke his heart.'

I realized the murmuring had stopped. There was nothing, but silence while everyone waited for me to go on with the story.

'So yesterday, Stills played Nouveau Casino in Paris,' I paused for a couple of 'I-was-there-whoops' to die down. 'And she announces that they're getting back together. And I didn't know what to think because I'd seen them in a bar together before the gig and Alex and I had sort of had a misunderstanding about us moving in together—'

'You're moving in with him?' Craig asked from offstage. 'Dude, that's sweet!' Graham punched him in the arm and smiled at me, shaking his head.

'Well anyway, I was really upset because I didn't know what was going on and I'd cocked up my job a bit.' I looked over at Virginie who winced as she translated. 'But I think that's all going to be OK, and I was really homesick for my friends back in the UK and so I decided to leave and go back to London. And well, basically, Alex followed me to London except I changed my mind at the last minute and came back to Paris to find him. Which is why he's not here.'

The crowd let this sink in for a moment before the confused chatter started again.

'Perhaps it was not that sweet a story,' Virginie said, stepping back from the stage as the crowd started to get rowdy. 'Or perhaps we should not have told them that he is in London looking for you.'

Before anything could turn nasty, the photographer yelled something out and the crowd began to laugh, chanting something over and over.

'Angela?' Virginie tried and failed to suppress a smile.

'What?'

'They want you to sing.'

I stepped out of the spotlight for a moment, trying to get my eyesight back. It didn't change anything. There were still 10,000 people shouting '*chantez*' at me, over and over and over. And looking over to Graham and Craig, they weren't helping. In fact, Graham was clapping along with the chant and Craig was running to his drums, shouting something about playing along.

'No, really. I don't sing.' I laughed nervously. 'Unless you've had several drinks and I'm going to do "Hungry Like the Wolf" on karaoke, you don't want me to sing.'

'They like "Hungry Like the Wolf",' Virginie confirmed as the photographer gave me a thumbs up.

My heart was pounding so hard, I could barely breathe. How was this happening? At what point did I think addressing the crowd at a music festival and joking about singing a Duran Duran song was a good idea?

'Really, it's not a good idea,' I said into the microphone, but Virginie had already set hers back into its stand. She held her arms up in a helpless gesture, but I was fairly certain she was enjoying this.

Opening my mouth to speak, the crowd roared, and I closed my eyes.

'She means it guys, it's really not a good idea.'

Another voice came over the loud speaker, followed by a 'da-dum-ting' comedy drumbeat. The spotlight shifted away from me, over to a tall dark-haired man, striding on to the stage with a microphone in one hand and a guitar in the other.

'You absolute bastard,' I said, throwing my arms around Alex's neck.

'OK, maybe I deserve that,' he said, kissing the top of my head before I let go and punched him in the shoulder. 'I'm not sure about the punch though. What was that for?'

'For not coming back last night.' I stared at his face. Was he really there or had I actually passed out? It was my first time in front of a capacity crowd after all.

'I know, we have a ton of stuff to talk about,' he said, suddenly serious, but still with light in his dark green eyes. 'Just promise you won't take off while we play?'

'I promise,' I said, remembering that the crowd weren't here to see me. 'But it's a tough crowd, it's going to be difficult.'

'We'll do our best,' Alex said, swapping the mic I'd been using for his, and plugging in his guitar. 'I usually play better when I haven't been on a wild goose chase to another country, but I'm pretty sure we'll do OK.'

'You say that now,' I said, tiptoeing offstage with Virginie, 'but I just killed it.'

'You're a tough act to follow,' he shouted after me with a grin.

'Believe it,' I shouted back, squeezing Virginie's hand.

'Ow,' she yelped, snatching it back.

'Sorry,' I said, gazing out at my boyfriend, pretty certain that he was still my boyfriend, as the band began at last.

CHAPTER TWENTY

It was a good few hours before we were back in Paris, back at the hotel and finally alone. Virginie had gone for a drink with Craig, ignoring my repeated but subtle shin-kicking in the van on the way back to the city, and Graham had gone to lie down. According to him, my impromptu one-woman show had brought on a migraine. Nice. I was scared to think what might have happened if I had sung. A stroke? Keen to avoid any and all discussion of my performance, I had played my favourite 'pretend to be asleep' card for most of the journey, resting my head on Alex's chest, delaying the inevitable 'conversation'. Everyone in Arras knew the ins and outs of our bust-up, but not even I knew what was going to happen next.

Alex held the bedroom door open and I scuttled back in, suddenly nervous to be on my own with him. I placed my handbag carefully on the bedside table, pretty pointless given the bashing that it and my laptop had taken already, but still, it was nice to be nice. Sighing loudly, I turned to face Alex, who was still standing by the door.

'You're not coming in?' I asked awkwardly.

'Do you want me to?' He raised his shoulders with his question.

'I want to know where you were last night.' I sat down on the bed and looked at my knackered shoes. 'And I want to know why you followed me to London.'

'I followed you to London because when I got back this morning your passport was missing and you'd left a print-out of your itinerary,' he replied, crossing the room to sit in a chair. 'And I spent the night with a friend.'

'Why were you looking for my passport?' I had decided to park the 'friend' thing for a moment.

'I check your passport every day.' Alex shrugged. 'Don't take offence, but you tend to lose stuff pretty easily. Who do you think puts your keys back in that bowl by your front door every night? Because it sure as hell isn't you.'

'Oh,' I said, quietly touched.

'And I know you're freaking out about it, but you're not going to ask, so the friend was actually Solène's brother,' he went on. 'They don't get along, but he and I always stayed in touch. He's a cool guy. I had a lot to think about and Graham said you'd come back to the hotel because you had a migraine and that I shouldn't call you. So I went there.'

'He said that?' I asked. Bless Graham for lying when he'd said he wouldn't. Except, if he hadn't, Alex might have come back to the hotel and none of this nonsense would have happened. Excellent! The whole festival debacle was Graham's fault!

'He did.' Alex looked up at me from behind a stray lock of black hair that had escaped from behind his ear. 'But I'm guessing it's not true. You spoke to Solène at the show, right?'

'I did,' I said. 'And I saw you together in the bar before.'

'Jesus, why didn't you just come over?' Alex ran his hands up over his face and through his hair. 'So that's why you took off. Honestly, Angela, how many times do we have to have the same conversation about talking to each other?'

'So talk to me now,' I replied quickly. 'Tell me why you were even in a bar with your ex-girlfriend who you hate so much.'

'Because she wouldn't leave me alone. Because she wouldn't leave you alone. Because I needed her to know that it was over, for ever, and that I was in love with someone else and that nothing she could say or do would change that fact.' He stood up and crossed the room towards me, kneeling at the edge of the bed and taking my hands in his. 'I'm sorry I didn't tell you, but it was kind of a personal message to leave at the front desk. I *was* going to tell you afterwards. She's not part of my life, Angela, no matter what she told you. She hasn't been part of it since the day she cheated on me, and she will never be part of it again.'

'Good to know.' I sniffed, determined not to cry. I still had more questions. 'So what happened the other night? On your birthday?'

'You tell me.' He twisted himself around until he was sitting cross-legged in front of me. 'You're the one that went all weird.'

'Nuh-uh,' I squeaked. 'It was totally you. You said all that stuff about not getting married or having kids and then you said you didn't want to move in with me any more.'

'Oh. That.'

'Yes. That.'

'Well,' he looked down at the floor, 'you kept saying you didn't want to move in with me, so I just thought it would be easier for my ego if I took away the stick for you to beat me with.'

I frowned. I hated when Jenny was right about stuff like this.

'But I do want to move in with you,' I said in a tiny voice. 'I was just scared about, you know, the last time I lived with someone.'

'And I'm scared too. The last time I lived with someone didn't go so great either,' Alex said, looking back at and me, and brushing my hair behind my ears. I though it was very sweet of him not to comment on how gross it was. 'But I want to live with you. I want to do everything with you.'

'But you said—'

'I know what I said, and I was being a dick.' He held his hand against my twice-bruised cheekbone and shook his head. 'I guess seeing Solène fucked me up more than I thought it would. I don't think I ever told you, but I actually asked her to marry me. It was dumb, things weren't working out, she was having problems with her visa, and I thought it would make everything better. It wasn't the strongest foundation for a lifelong commitment, I know.'

'You didn't tell me, but she did,' I said, pressing my hand against his. 'But you know I was engaged before, I would have understood.'

'Yeah, like I'm not totally jealous every time I remember that.' He raised an eyebrow and smiled. 'And really? You would have been totally cool with it?'

'I would have understood eventually,' I admitted. 'Really, I do get that it's not a big deal. I suppose I wondered why you never mentioned it, but I do get it. I wouldn't go around spouting off in favour of marriage if someone waved my ex around in my face.'

I chose not to mention that I'd only realized that

once Jenny had pointed it out. Let him think I was wise and empathetic, he could work out whether or not it was true in his own time.

'Yeah, well that was some of the stuff I was thinking about,' he said quietly. 'Saying that I didn't want those things kinda made me think about them.'

'Oh?' My mouth was suddenly very dry. 'And what did you decide?'

'That maybe, I do want them,' he said, raising his face up towards mine. 'With you.'

'Really?' I whispered against his lips.

'Really,' he whispered back. 'This is it for me, Angela. I'm yours, however you want me. If you want to get married tomorrow, we'll fly home via Vegas. You want to move back to London, I'll get Graham to pack up my stuff and we'll go right now. You want eighteen kids and a white picket fence, shit, I'll get a job in advertising, slick back my hair and we can go totally *Mad Men*. Except without the philandering and prescription meds. Whatever you want. As of now.'

'Maybe we can just start with the whole living together thing before we get on to talking about marriage,' I suggested, my heart pounding so hard I could feel my pulse in my bruised cheekbone. 'Or kids.'

'Let's just hope that when we do have them, they aren't as dumb as me and as clumsy as you or they're screwed from the start,' he said, ending the conversation with a kiss. I pulled him up on to the bed, never taking my lips off his and, as I felt his familiar weight above me, the warmth of his body against mine, all the voices in my head finally went quiet.

Later, curled up around each other in the darkness, a thought crossed my mind. 'Alex?' I said, stroking lazy circles on his chest with my fingers.

'Yeah?'

'What were you going to do when you got to London? I mean, how were you going to find me? You knew I didn't have a working phone.'

'Oh yeah.' He yawned, rolling over on to his side and wrapping his arms around me. 'Tomorrow morning, we need to call your mom and tell her you're OK.'

'You called my mother?' Suddenly I was very awake.

'In the morning,' Alex replied, kissing the back of my hair. 'Sleep now.'

'Easy for you to say,' I whispered, as angry as it was possible to be with a man who had just been doing something incredibly rude to me not fifteen minutes earlier. 'I cannot believe you called my mother.'

'I cannot believe you didn't call me!' my mother screeched down the phone at the top of her voice. 'First you're coming home, then you're not. Then I've got strange American men ringing me up and asking where you are. Then you're calling me up and telling me everything's fine. Well it's not fine, Angela. You bloody well get your arse home right now. I've been up all night, sick with worry, no idea how to contact you. We tried that Facebook thing and you didn't answer, we called Louisa, we called your flat in America, I called that Jenny girl and she told me to "chill out". Chill out! You tell me Angela Clark, what was I supposed to think?'

I closed my eyes and made a mental list of all the people I needed to call and apologize to. 'I'm sorry Mum,' I said once she'd stopped to breathe. 'Yesterday was a bit mad, but I'm OK and I'm going back to New York this afternoon. I actually really need to go, we've got to get to the airport.'

'Oh no. No, you're coming back here immediately,

292

young lady. My nerves have had all they can take. First you're running off to New York, then it's gallivanting around LA, next you're in Paris, then you're in London. No, you're coming home.'

'Mum—'

'Don't mum me—'

'Will you please just let me finish?'

'There's nothing else to say! Get on a train right—'

'Mum, will you just shut up for a minute?'

She shut up for precisely one second.

'Did you just tell your mother, your own mother, to shut up?' she breathed out slowly. 'Well. Honestly, I can't believe—'

'Oh, don't start!' I was really, seriously thinking about hanging up and telling people I was an orphan, but I knew this was all just because she cared. Somewhere, somehow I knew that. And had to keep reminding myself. 'And it wasn't strange men calling you, it was Alex, so don't make out like I've got random blokes ringing you constantly.'

'Get off the phone, get off it,' my mum was ranting, her voice getting quieter as she went on.

'Mum?' I asked, ignoring Alex, who was laughing at me from the bathroom. 'Mum, are you there?'

'Angela, it's your dad.'

My mouth dropped open. I hadn't heard my dad's voice in months. According to my mother, he 'never had much to say', but I was more inclined to believe that she hadn't left him anything to say. And besides, she didn't like him talking on the phone in case he got 'ideas'.

'Dad?'

'Yes, Angela, love?' he replied, calm as anything despite the clattering and commotion that was going on around him. I could still hear my mum rattling on in the background, louder than before if anything.

'It's really nice to talk to you,' I said, crying before I realized. 'Are you all right?'

'I am,' he said. 'Now, are you all right?'

'I am,' I replied. 'I really, really am.'

'And you're going back to New York, you say?'

'Yes.'

'And you know you can come back whenever you like?'

I couldn't hear my mother any more and had a strong suspicion that he had locked himself in the cupboard under the stairs. I'd always wondered why there was a bolt on the inside of that cupboard.

'I do, Dad.'

'Then you get yourself back off home and we'll see you when we see you,' he said. 'Love you angel.'

'Love you too.' I didn't want him to know I was crying, but it was hard to stop. 'Look after Mum.'

'Will do,' he said and hung up.

Alex had stopped laughing and was looking on from the bathroom doorway. 'Are you OK?' he asked. 'Do we need to go back to London? I can take you home, you know.'

'We are going home,' I nodded, wiping away the tears, 'not to that home though, our home.'

'You're sure?' he asked.

I hung up the receiver. 'Positive.'

CHAPTER TWENTY-ONE

Twenty-four hours later, I was sitting outside Mary's office, jet-lagged out of my tiny mind and fairly certain I was drooling. But this had to be done. I'd called and left a message on her machine as soon as we'd got back into New York, Monday evening, telling her I'd be there the following morning. I knew she got in early, usually earlier than Cici, so it was my best chance of seeing her without having to get past my New York nemesis. Wow, from no nemesis to two in one week. I really had been busy.

At eight on the dot, the lift doors pinged open and she strode in, coffee in one hand, BlackBerry in the other, a look of annoyance on her unlined fifty-something face.

'Angela,' she said, walking right by me, her steel-grey bob bouncing as she went.

I followed, trying to fight the urge to vom, and sat down in the chair opposite her desk.

'Shoot.' Mary set everything down on her desk and shook off her hoodie to reveal a cute black cashmere tank top. She had unfeasibly toned arms for a woman of her age. Or you know, for a woman.

'It's hard to know where to start,' I admitted. 'But to keep it brief, Cici screwed me over. Really badly. She cancelled my BlackBerry, she set me up with an assistant from French *Belle* who was trying to stop me from getting my article done, she sent over a list of rubbish places to visit, and then she tried to convince the assistant to convince me not to come back to New York at all.'

'Right.' Mary sipped her coffee and looked at me over the top of her glasses.

'I don't know what else to say, Mary.'

'And I don't know what you want me to do. Is the piece done?'

'Not yet, but it will be,' I said. 'No thanks to Cici.'

'As far as *Belle* will be concerned, whether or not you get the piece in really isn't anything to do with Cici,' she said. 'She doesn't work for *Belle*, she wasn't assigned to you by *Belle*, anything she did with, for or to you is on your head.'

'You believe me, don't you?' I was feeling sicker by the second. 'About what she did?'

'I do.' Mary nodded. 'Unfortunately, there's not a lot I can do.'

'What do you mean?' I asked. 'Not a lot you can do about what?'

'Not a lot I can do about the fact that Cici forwarded some email you sent cursing her out on to her grandfather,' she said, flicking her computer monitor into action. 'You want to read your own rather colourful words?'

What. The. Fuck?

'But I didn't send an email to Cici?' I said, leaning across the desk. I didn't send an email to Cici. Did I? I was sure that was something I'd remember, jet lag and France's vast quantity of booze aside.

But there it was, a forward from Cici to 'Grandpa Bob', her sob story all in caps, labelling me a bully and a tyrant, claiming she hadn't said anything before because she was trying to be my friend. And then a much shorter email from Bob to Mary, the gist of which was 'get rid of her'. At the bottom of the page was the email supposedly from me. And, I had to admit, it was littered with lots of very colourful words, all aimed at Cici.

'I didn't send this to her,' I said, recognizing some of what was written on the screen. 'I sent this to you. But not this, it's been changed.'

'You sent me an email bitching Cici out?' Mary asked, sliding her glasses on to the top of her head. 'To my work email address? Are you serious?'

'Um, yes?'

'Angela, who is my assistant?'

'Cici?'

'And so who has access to all of my emails?'

'Cici?' Shit.

'And who, it would seem, really, really does not like you?'

'Cici?' Double shit.

Mary rested her hands on the desk in front of her. 'To say that Bob is no longer your biggest fan would be something of an understatement.'

'Am I fired?' I whispered, definitely about to be sick.

She nodded. 'It's safe to say that you will no longer be writing a blog for TheLook.com.'

Triple shit, shit, shitty shit shit.

'But they still need your *Belle* piece, it's too late to fill the pages with anything else,' she went on. 'And who knows, if that's really good, after the heat has died down, I might be able to rehire you. You certainly bring in a lot of traffic and that brings in advertisers. But right now, you're too hot for anyone at Spencer Media to touch you.'

'What about my visa?' The room was spinning fast and it had nothing to do with my jet lag. This wasn't happening. It couldn't be happening.

'You're not completely fucked,' Mary clarified. 'You're still a contributing editor for *The Look* in the UK. Your visa isn't going to be revoked immediately. I spoke to one of our lawyers and she seems to think that you can stay for a couple of months before anyone from Immigration makes enquiries. Even if they did, you could appeal that you're technically still an employee of Spencer Media. But if they make a check and they don't agree with what could be a costly appeal, you could be deported. The lawyer suggested you head back to the UK and apply for a new media visa that's not tied to an employer as soon as you can.'

'How long will that take?' A new visa? Go back to London? Was she serious? I'd just bloody come from London.

'I'm not the US Embassy, I have no idea.' She shrugged. 'But if you need a reference, I will be more than happy to give you one. Look, I'm sorry, this is a really shitty situation.'

'But Virginie, from French *Belle*, she said she would call you?' I said desperately. 'She was the assistant who was helping me, she said she would explain everything.'

'And she did,' Mary took another look at her computer screen, 'but one rambling voicemail from a junior assistant at French *Belle* isn't going to mean much to Robert Spencer when he has a sobbing grand-daughter on his hands and an email from some random employee, calling his pride and joy a, and let me quote this directly, "crazy fucking psycho bitch who needs to be put down like a rabid dog".'

'I did not say that in the original email,' I protested.

'I said she was a bloody crazy psycho bitch who needed to be put down like a dog. Not a rabid dog. And no eff word.'

'I'm touched that you thought to hold back on the f-bomb for me,' Mary said, 'but really, you're going to have to give me some time. Wait until Bob has calmed down, let me talk to him. I like to think I have a little influence there.'

Ha. I was right, they'd definitely been doing it. Ew.

'Maybe I can even send a few freelance things your way if you can write under a pseudonym.' She shrugged. The conversation, as far as she was concerned, was clearly over.

'What if Immigration do check up on me?' I asked, not really needing her to tell me the answer. 'What if Cici sends them after me?'

'Cross that bridge when you come to it,' Mary suggested. 'And leave Cici to me. She's got what she wanted, she'll leave you alone now.'

'You think she will?'

'Leave her to me,' Mary repeated.

'OK, well, I suppose I should leave my BlackBerry and stuff,' I said, digging around in my handbag, trying not to cry in front of Mary. I knew it wouldn't help my case with her. I had to hold it together.

'I know this sucks, but leave it with me.' She waited for me to stand up and then leaned in for an awkward hug. 'I'm not saying I'll be able to save the day, but I'll try. I'm not losing a good writer because that snot-nosed little bitch cried to Grandpa.'

'You think I'm a good writer?' I sniffed over her shoulder.

'Get out, Clark.' Mary pushed me away with something that almost looked a little bit like a smile. 'I'll be in touch.'

I stumbled out of Mary's office, not knowing when or if I'd ever be back there, and took a moment to try and compose myself. You never knew who you would bump into in *The Look* offices. Of course, on this occasion, I was only ever going to bump into the one person I really didn't want to see.

'Oh, hey, Angela!' Cici sailed through the double doors and sank into the chair behind her desk. 'Would you like me to call security to escort you off the premises, or can you drag your tragic ass out all by yourself?'

There was a time and a place to be the bigger person in life and, as I turned to face Cici, who was sipping a giant vat of iced coffee through a hot pink straw, I knew that this wasn't it.

'A friend of mine always says that people like you will get what's coming to them,' I said, simply shrugging my shoulders. 'What do you think?'

'I don't know?' she said, the straw still in her mouth and a confused look on her face.

'Can I ask you something?' I sat down on the edge of her desk, enjoying watching her squirm. Which was difficult in skintight Herve Leger. An interesting choice for the office.

'Yeah?' Cici finally put down the coffee. Maybe Virginie had told her how handy I was with my fists and she wanted to be prepared.

'Why do you think you went so out of your way to mess things up for me?' I asked, dropping my hands between my knees. I wasn't going to hit anyone in this country. Hello, lawsuit? 'I mean you really went to a lot of trouble.'

'I don't know.' She tipped her head to one side, her long ponytail of strawberry blonde extensions following shortly afterwards. Really, someone should tell her that Lindsay Lohan was not a role model. 'I don't like you?'

'That's funny because I don't like you that much either.' I rapped my fingers against her desk. 'I wonder why that is?'

'Because I'm younger and hotter and cooler?' she asked. And the worst part was, she actually seemed to mean it.

'Maybe,' I nodded, 'maybe. Hey, isn't it weird how you can be hot and cool at the same time? That's weird, isn't it?'

'I guess,' Cici said, looking at me as if I'd gone mad. Which was quite possible.

'One of those weird little semantic things I suppose,' I said, hopping up from the desk and making her jump. 'Or like iced coffee. I don't get it, I suppose because we don't have it in England. Do they make it hot to start with and then put ice in it or is it always cold?'

'I don't know, freak.' Cici turned up her nose and reached for her Starbucks cup. But I was faster.

'It does feel cold through the plastic,' I said, shaking it up to watch the ice swirl around. 'How does it feel to you?'

'Huh?' Cici was far too slow to avoid the shower of iced latte that rained down all over her extensions. All over her dress. All over her, ouch, suede boots. 'You bitch!'

'I'm a bit too impatient to wait for karma sometimes,' I said, dropping the cup into the bin at the side of her desk. 'Or maybe that was karma. I'm not sure.'

'Shame about all your shit getting blown up,' Cici shouted as I turned to walk away. 'I heard that it burned up extra quick because your case was full of manmade fibres.'

'That's the best comeback you have?' I shouted, still walking away. 'Really, I've seen *Ugly Betty*, I expected better.'

'I guess I'm not as good at insults as I am at talking to airport security people,' she shot back. 'And not nearly as good as I am at getting you fired.'

I pressed the button for the lift just as the penny dropped. My suitcase had been blown up because of Cici? Looking at the finger reaching out for the lift button, I saw that my hand was shaking. Trying to screw me over at work was one thing, but destroying all those clothes? My beautiful blue handbag? My perfect-fitting Top Shop jeans that they didn't make any more? My irreplaceable Louboutins? This was serious. This was shoeicide.

'Are you kidding me?' I asked, turning around slowly and facing off against her like John Wayne. Or Sharon Stone in that cowboy movie she did with Russell Crowe and Leonardo DiCaprio. I figured that was a more flattering comparison.

The lift pinged open behind me to reveal half the staff of *The Look*. And they looked mighty confused.

'What are you going to do?' Cici asked, throwing her arms open wide. 'Your sorry ass is out of here. You can't prove anything. My grandfather won't believe a word you say.'

Before I could react, Mary's office door slammed against the wall making everyone jump.

'No, but he'll believe me,' Mary said behind her. 'Cici, get in my office. Angela, I'll speak to you later.'

Cici's face flared red. She crossed her arms tightly over her soaking dress and spun on her ruined heels, marching into Mary's office.

'Mary,' I wailed, pressing my hands to my heart. 'She blew up my shoes. My *shoes*.'

'And she'll be replacing them,' Mary replied, with all the certainty of a headmistress. 'Angela, go.'

I pushed through all the gawkers and jabbed the

lobby button, holding tightly to the metal rail that ran around the inside of the lift. My poor, poor shoes. No longer just innocent casualties of airtight security, but senseless victims of a vindictive tit. I had to mourn them all over again.

Alex was waiting for me outside the building, dressed in jeans and a sweatshirt that was far too heavy for the already sweaty sunshine. Paris had been hot, but New York was just humid. Ick.

'What happened?' he asked, ready to grab me as I barrelled into his arms. 'Is everything OK?'

'Cici blew my suitcase up,' I yelled into his chest. 'I mean, she arranged to have it blown up. It wasn't an accident.'

'Really?' He whistled. 'Wow, you really must have pissed her off in a previous life.'

'I know,' I said, letting him squeeze me tightly. 'My shoes!'

'It's going to be OK, we'll get you new shoes.' Alex kissed the top of my head. 'So your job is OK?'

'Oh, that.' I screwed up my face. 'Not really. I've sort of been fired.'

'What?' He held me at arms' length and stared at me. 'You got fired? And you're complaining about your shoes?'

'I know,' I sighed, closing my eyes. 'But I just can't think about it now. If I do my head will explode, and I am so tired. Please, can we just go home?'

'Fine.' He wrapped an arm around my sweaty shoulder and we started off down 42nd Street. 'But I can't believe you're not freaking out.'

'Oh my God, I'm freaking out.' I sat on the edge of my sofa, rocking backwards and forwards, before standing up and pacing over to the window. I tapped my fingers against the glass, shaking my head. 'I got fired, Alex. Fired. I've never been fired. And oh my God, I'm going to lose my visa, I'm going to have to go back to London. I mean, what am I going to do? I'm not qualified to do anything else. I'll have to be like a bin man or something. No, they'll never let me on the bins. I'll have to be a postman. Oh my God, I'm going to have to be a postman.'

Alex folded his arms, staring at me from across the room. 'Are you done?'

'You don't understand! Postmen have to get up so early. And I'll have to ride a bike.' I sat down on the windowsill. 'I can't believe I'm going to have to be a postman.'

'Right.' Alex walked over to the window and held my shoulders in his hands, squeezing until I looked up at him. 'Angela Clark. You don't have to be a postman.'

'I don't?'

'No,' he replied. 'Or a bin man. Whatever that is. All you have to do right now, is calm down, remember what Mary said, and chill.'

'You know I can't "chill",' I frowned, 'I'm English. We don't know how to chill. At best I can try to keep calm and carry on.'

'If that's what works for you.' He slid his hands up from my shoulders to cup my face. 'You're going to be fine. It's all going to be fine. You just need a distraction.'

'Really, not right now,' I said wearily. Honestly, I was shattered, was he trying to kill me?

'Not that,' Alex laughed and sat down next to me on the windowsill. 'I was thinking about something else.'

'It's going to have to be a pretty big distraction.' I scooted up the sill so he would have room to sit. It helped that his arse was about half the size of mine. 'What have you got in mind?'

'Packing.' He laced his fingers through mine. 'You're moving in with me today.'

'I am?' I asked. A tiny thrill raced down my spine, cutting through the jet lag and the stress.

'You are,' he confirmed. 'You're gonna go lie down while I get some boxes and shit, then we're going to start taking stuff over to my place. Our place.'

'Is that right?' I felt a tiny smile start on my face. And it wasn't just because he'd said I could have a nap.

'It is.' Alex closed his bright green eyes and planted a kiss on the tip of my nose. 'So go get some rest. You're gonna need your strength to cook my dinner tonight, woman.'

'Don't you "woman" me,' I warned, striding off into the bedroom. And silently planning his dinner. I was a terrible feminist.

CHAPTER TWENTY-TWO

'And this is the living room,' I said into the computer, carrying it out of the bedroom. 'We're getting new couches so don't look at those, they're covered in all sorts of crap.'

'New what, Angela Clark?' Louisa laughed through the computer as I placed my laptop carefully on the coffee table. 'I'm sorry, I don't speak American.'

'Settees,' I over pronounced. 'Apologies, I'm bilingual now. I also say trash and candy and sweater. You have to be. If you come over here wanting to buy a courgette or an aubergine, I've got to tell you, you're going to be struggling.'

'Whatever.' She gave me the finger. Skype was the best invention ever. 'Well, it looks like a lovely apartment. Those views of Manhattan are amazing.'

'Right?' I said, cracking open a bottle of white wine. 'It's awesome.'

'Right?' Louisa parroted. 'Do you have to say it at the end of every sentence? We're losing you. I'm so concerned about your influence over this baby.'

'I will be nothing, but perfection around my godson-slash-daughter,' I promised, pointing to the scan I had printed out and stuck to the fridge. 'See how dedicated I am already? Alex asked me to take it down because it was putting him off his food.'

'I just think it's weird that you have a picture of your best friend's insides taped to the place we keep our food,' Alex defended himself, yelling from the bedroom. 'Hey, Louisa.'

'Hello Alex,' Louisa shouted back. 'Sorry we interrupted your shower.'

I blushed at the screen, laughing as Lou winked back.

'You realize I can see you both, right?' Alex stuck his damp head around the living-room door.

'Right?' Louisa cackled.

'Aw, screw you guys!' Alex vanished back into the bedroom.

'Ignore him,' I said, settling on a couch with my glass of wine. 'He should be dressed by now anyway.'

'I'm gutted I couldn't come to your party.' Lou sulked through the screen. 'But Tim couldn't get away, and he didn't like the idea of me flying without him. I know it's rubbish, I'm sorry.'

'Not at all.' I waved away her apology. 'I'm glad he's taking care of you and my godson-slash-daughter.'

'If I tell you what we're having, will you please stop calling him or her that?' Lou sighed. 'Honestly, I've known for nearly a week and it's killing me.'

'I told you I don't want to know!' I shouted, covering my ears. 'Seriously, it's so exciting! I want it to be a surprise.'

'I'm glad it's exciting for you,' Lou rested a hand on her practically non-existent bump. 'Finding out I was nearly five months along was a big enough surprise for me.'

'That's fair enough,' I agreed, gutted that Louisa had missed out on months of knowing she was pregnant, but secretly delighted that I would have a baby to spoil so soon. The new Little Marc Jacobs line was so incredibly cute. 'I'm sure there will be more to surprise you later on.'

'Don't say things like that,' she said, holding her hand up to her forehead. 'Let's just get this one out of the way first.'

The doorbell buzzed, making me jump and spill half my glass of wine on to the sofa. 'Shit,' I whispered, rubbing it frantically.

'I won't tell,' Louisa promised. 'Just pull that throw over it. Didn't you say you were getting new sofas anyway?'

'Good point.' I pointed at the screen and then followed her advice. Good as new. 'I'd better get the door.'

'I'd better go anyway, it's really late,' Louisa said, waving through the computer. 'Have a lovely house-warming party, me and the baby wish we were there.'

'Love you both,' I said, blowing kisses into the monitor. 'And I suppose Tim.'

Closing the laptop up and sliding it under the sofa to avoid any further damage to its cracked casing, I jumped up, rearranged my gorgeous pink and orange Marc by Marc Jacobs striped party dress (Alex had suggested it was overkill for a house party with a bunch of our friends, but I had politely declined to take his fashion advice) and went to the door.

'Alex, people are here,' I shouted into the bedroom, buzzing a whole group of people up. Holding open the door, I kissed them all hello. Graham and his boyfriend. Craig and his latest, well, I wouldn't say girlfriend, but she was a girl and they seemed very friendly. Vanessa and some of the girls from The Union followed, with Erin and Thomas and about a dozen of Alex's other friends from around Brooklyn.

'Alex, can you put some music on?' I asked, about to shut the door when a gorgeous pair of leather flip-flops blocked it.

'You're gonna shut the door on me?' a voice wailed from the hallway.

'Jenny!' I screeched, grabbing her by the neck and wrapping her up in a huge hug. 'I didn't know you were coming!'

'Can you believe that we actually managed to keep a secret from you for almost a whole week?' Alex leaned against the other side of the door frame, looking extraordinarily pleased with himself.

'Oh you great big pair of bastards,' I said, so happy I could have cried. 'You should have told me. Do you have any bags?'

'Nope, they're all at the apartment,' Jenny said, taking in my outfit. 'Cute. Very cute.'

She wasn't looking too shoddy herself, her tiny tanned frame just about covered by a slip of aqua silk. 'Vena Cava,' she confirmed, not waiting to be asked. 'Awesome, right?'

'Absolutely,' I agreed, taking another glass of wine from Alex. 'So you've been back to the apartment? How long are you staying?'

'I have, and well, maybe for good?' she said, peeking at me from behind a cascade of unruly curls. 'I was thinking, maybe New Yorkers should only do LA in small doses.'

'Honestly? Oh Jenny, that's amazing!' I tried not to splash wine on the pair of us as I went in for a second hug. 'I am so so happy. Yes, stay, don't go back.'

'You just want me for the discounted shopping.' She laughed, but I could tell she was happy for the warm welcome. As if I would ever give her anything else. 'I figure I can work just as much in New York as I can in LA. There are still people here with too much money and not enough sense, right?'

'Definitely,' I nodded. 'Oh, I'm so happy. But I'm sad that we won't be roommates.'

'I'm not moving you back over the river,' Alex butted in. 'I can't believe how much shit you had. And that's after half of it got blown up.'

'Please, I'm not having her back,' Jenny said, chugging her first glass of wine and passing the empty back to a passing and already smitten Craig. Apparently his date was forgotten. 'Van is moving out this weekend and I kinda thought it might be nice to live by myself for a while. You know, after Daphne's escapades. I'm gonna turn the spare room into an office.'

'Well, I'm still coming over for *Top Model*,' I declared, hugging her again. I knew that I was grinning like an idiot and I didn't care.

'Damn right you are,' Jenny agreed, brushing my hair over my shoulder. It was getting so long. 'But you're bringing the beers. Damn, I missed you, Angie.'

'I missed you too,' I said, getting the same pang I had the last time I hugged Louisa. Except this time, I got to keep Jenny. 'Now let go of me so I can go and pee.'

'Don't you dare pee on this dress,' Jenny said, releasing me instantly. 'It's one hundred per cent silk.'

'And it would look even more beautiful on my bedroom floor,' Craig purred in her ear, holding out his hand. 'I don't think we've met. I'm Craig.'

'Tell me you didn't just say that?' Jenny stared at Craig with a blank expression. 'Damn boy, you are going about this in all the wrong ways.'

I dashed off to the bathroom, closing the door behind me. Smiling into the mirror, I held a piece of tissue underneath each eye, trying to catch the tears before they fell and spoiled my carefully applied messy make-up.

It was almost a week since we'd got back from Paris, I was all moved in to Alex's apartment and nearly all healed from my double black eye. I still hadn't heard anything from Mary about getting my job back, but I had received a written apology from Cici and a cheque for two thousand dollars. It wouldn't nearly cover what had been ruined, but I appreciated the effort that Mary must have gone through and it gave me hope that I'd be able to get my job back somehow, some day. Until then, I was pitching my arse off to UK magazines and getting by on my column. And generally not thinking about the immigration issue.

There was a quiet knock before the handle turned, and Alex stuck his head through the door before I realized I hadn't locked it.

'You OK?' he asked with a soft smile. 'I'm sorry I didn't tell you about Jenny, I thought it would be a nice surprise.'

'It is,' I said, flapping my hands in front of my face. 'I'm so happy.'

'And so you're crying because?' he slipped into the tiny bathroom and shut the door behind him.

'Because I'm happy,' I repeated. 'Honestly. Moving in, having Jenny back, they're happy tears.'

'You don't regret not staying in London?' he asked, wiping a stray tear away with a gentle thumb.

'Nope,' I said, my voice thick and popping on the p. 'I do miss Lou and I suppose even my mum, but I want to be here. I felt an awful lot worse when Mary said I could lose my visa than I did when I got back on the train to Paris.'

'We'll figure it out,' Alex promised. 'We will. It's just paperwork. It's nothing.'

I nodded, hoping he was right.

'Are you two rutting in there?' Jenny yelled through

the door. 'Because you have guests, so it's really fucking rude. And I need to pee.'

I shook my head and pushed past Alex, opening the door to Jenny, hand on hip, one eyebrow raised so high I was worried it might fall off her face altogether.

'Dude, control yourself when you have company,' she said, slapping Alex lightly around the head. 'She's living with you now, it's like you have hot and cold running Angela, twenty-four-seven. You can't wait until we go home?'

Someone had turned off the big light during our intermission in the bathroom, and switched on the fairy lights I'd hung earlier in the week, despite Alex's concerns that they might make the apartment look like the Playboy grotto. But they did not. They looked awesome. Twinkling around the window, they framed the blinking lights of Manhattan, the Empire State Building lit up green, the Chrysler building glowing like an upside down ice-cream cone, and the rest of the city flashing away, just to let us know it was there. Life went on.

'Do you need anything?' Alex asked, putting a hand around my waist while I looked at the happy scene in our apartment.

'Uh-uh.' I shook my head, turning in towards him for a kiss. Lipgloss be damned.

'You don't want anything?'

'I have everything I need and everything I want,' I replied, squeezing him tightly, watching Jenny roll her eyes at whatever bullshit story Craig was telling her, glancing at Louisa's scan photo stuck up on the fridge.

And for that moment at least, it was absolutely true.

Angela's
Guide
to Paris

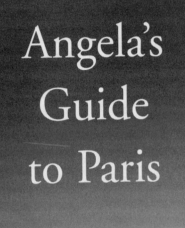

Hands down, Paris is the most beautiful city I have ever, ever visited. Everything is gorgeous – the shops, the restaurants, the people – everything. It doesn't matter where you look, every angle is breathtaking. My best advice is to take flat shoes for walking, lip gloss so you don't let the team down and a brown paper bag for when you start hyperventilating. You can only let out so many sighs before you start to feel a little bit faint.

Unlike New York and LA, Paris is a city you're supposed to get lost in. Pick an area to explore, get a good breakfast and then put away your watch, your phone, your sense of direction and just wander. There's no way you won't have a wonderful time. Despite my experiences, I'm told by lots of other people that the Metro is perfectly negotiable as long as you know your route and it's definitely the most convenient way to get around – taxis aren't as easy to hail as they are in New York or even London but if you do manage to grab one, they're relatively reasonably priced. If you really don't fancy navigating the Metro, ask your hotel for the number of a trustworthy taxi company and use them to get around. This is an especially valid point when you've been on le vin. All. Day. Long.

HOTELS

Hotel Les Jardins du Marais

74 RUE AMELOT, 11TH
75011 PARIS, FRANCE

This is a great hotel for a weekend away in Paris with your girlfriends. The homely rooms aren't nearly as glamorous as the sexy, minimalist foyer and the sexy, minimalist foyer isn't as fantastic as the bright, airy courtyard but when you add up all the parts and then throw in a brilliant location, Hotel Les Jardins du Marais is a great option. Hipster hangout, Bar Pop In is directly opposite, it's just a ten-minute walk to the centre of the Marais and ten minutes in the other direction will take you right to the Oberkampf area, full of cool bars, cool restaurants and even cooler boys and girls.

Hotel du Nord

CANAL ST MARTIN
102 QUAI DE JEMMAPES, 10TH
75010, PARIS
01 40 40 78 78

Hotel du Nord always pops up in Cool Hotel lists, thanks to its location on Canal St Martin and its regular hipster clientele. Even if you don't decide to stay at Hotel du Nord (and a whole lot of people tell me you really should consider it), try and pop into its yummy restaurant for dinner – it's all very low ceilings and candle light so Hotel du Nord is a great romantic option if you're looking for a traditional French-based menu. The bar is nice for a cocktail (Paris' omnipresent mojitos are great here) but it can be tricky to get in the bar if you're not eating dinner – the pains of popularity…

Hotel Amour

8 Rue de Navarin, 9th
75009 Paris

Should you be looking for a, cough, 'romantic' weekend away (and by romantic, I mean dirrrty) the appropriately named Hotel Amour is the one for you. It's teeny tiny with just 20 rooms and once upon a time, you could rent the rooms by the hour. Now, things are a little more respectable but there are still no phones, TVs or internet hook ups in the bedrooms – far too distracting for lovahs. There are iPod connections though so make sure you've got your Sexy Times playlist organised before you arrive. And if you really must let all your friends know what a mindblowing time you're having, there is wi-fi in all public spaces. Just don't start writing on my Facebook wall.

Hotel Athénée

Plaza Athénée
25 Avenue Montaigne, 8th
75008, Paris
Tel 01 53 67 66 65

If you're looking to splash out on Parisian glamour, big time romance and just a touch of Carrie Bradshaw fabulousness, Hotel Athénée is the place to be. Especially if someone else is paying. A byword for luxury, the rooms are beautiful and chockfull of every amenity you could ever need – CD player, remote control air con and even a pillow menu. If you can draw yourself away from the super comfy bed, the views to be had from this hotel are absolutely beautiful, the Eiffel Tower on one side and Avenue Montaigne on the other (Avenue Montaigne = amazing designer shopping which is why a regular street view really does rival a picturesque vision of the Eiffel Tower). If you make it out of your room, all cuisine in the hotel is overseen by Alain Ducasse and even me, who can't tell the difference between Dominos and Pizza Hut, realises that this is a Good Thing.

BARS & RESTAURANTS

Le Bar Dix

10 RUE DE L'ODÉON, 6TH
PARIS, 75006
01 43 26 66 83

Le Dix is teeny tiny and about as far away from chic Parisian glamour as you can get but if you're looking for an authentic piece of Left Bank character, you'll find it here in this dark basement bar. Grab a jug of sangria, order some delicious snacks and embrace the old school jukebox. It's one of those bars where you stop in for a quick drink and end up spending the entire night talking to your neighbour and before you know it, they're chucking you out at closing. Just one note though, take some loo roll in your bag – the toilets leave a little to be desired.

L'Alimentation Générale

64 RUE JEAN-PIERRE TIMBAUD, 11TH
75011, PARIS

I LOVED L'Alimentation Generale and wish I'd spent more time there. It's a big bar with a kitschy general store theme. It's packed out every night and there's usually dancing although the DJs change every night. If you're looking for somewhere to start a big Friday night with the girls, look no further… It shuts pretty early though so have somewhere in mind to go after. And be aware that the men in here can be a little aggressive so keep your girlfriends close by.

Pop In

105 RUE AMELOT, 11TH
75011, PARIS

This is hipster heaven without having to venture deep into the Oberkampf, Pop In is right opposite the Hotel Les Jardin du Marais. On an average night you'll find more plaid shirts in here than you can shake a stick at, checking out up-and-coming indie bands downstairs and knocking back pitchers of beer while setting the world to rights around the crowded tables upstairs. If you like your bars (and your men) scruffy but cool, this is the place for you.

UFO Bar

49 RUE JEAN-PIERRE TIMBAUD, 11TH
75011, PARIS

UFO bar has more than a little in common with Pop In but enjoys a more central Oberkampf location making it a good option on your hipster bar crawl. DJs keep the atmosphere alive with current indie and classic rock and roll and yay, there's dancing in the basement. Stick to your battered Converse and vintage slouchy boots though, this is not the place for your sexy heels. There's a pretty good happy hour here and the mojitos are strooooong. Hic.

Nouveau Casino

109 RUE OBERKAMPF, 11TH
75011, PARIS

Open midnight-5am Wed-Sat. One of the things that really surprised me about Paris was how early everything closed. It's possible that living in New York has spoiled me completely but when I come out of a bar, I sometimes want to get my dance on. Happily, Nouveau Casino caters to those needs. They have a mix of live music, great DJs and very strong but pretty pricey drinks. And again with the aggressive men.

Le Pick-Clops

16 RUE VIEILLE DU TEMPLE, 4TH
75004, PARIS
01 40 29 02 18

A delicious café open super late, serving yummy, yummy food, free popcorn while you wait and at least the last time I was there, they were playing the second Yeah Yeah Yeah's album. When is that not a good thing? I recommend the burger. Surprisingly.

Berthillon Glacier

31 RUE SAINT-LOUIS EN L'ILE, 4TH
75004, PARIS
01 43 54 31 61

Best. Ice Cream. In the World. EVER.
Really, I don't know what else to say. You can get a million different flavours but my money is on nougat au miel, chocolat au nougat and gianduja aux noisettes. Oh lord, someone put me on a plane right now. And the gorgeous Ile de Saint-Louis setting doesn't hurt the delicious glaces go down either.

SHOPPING

Antoine et Lili
95 QUAI DE VALMY, 10TH
75010, PARIS
01 40 37 58 14

A mini Paris chain that I fell in love with right away. It's pretty hard not to spot the shops with their bright pink store fronts and you can expect to find just as much exciting colour inside. Gorgeous girly dresses, cute accessories and carefully selected homewares shout out as you wander around but what really grabbed me were the shoes. The pretty, pretty shoes...

Matières à Reflexion
19 RUE DU POITOU, 3RD
75003, PARIS
01 42 72 16 31

This is such an amazing shop. The lovely, lovely owners work vintage leather jackets into brand new handbags and wallets, each one absolutely unique and so, so beautiful. You can even take in your own old leather jacket and have it transformed – yay! They also stock lots of lovely little accessories in case you need a quick fix...

Alice Cadolle
4 RUE CAMBON, 1ST
75001, PARIS
01 42 60 94 22

This lingerie boutique has been passed down through generations of the Cadolle family, back to Hermine Cadolle who claimed to be the inventor of the bra. All hail Hermine... today, Poupie Cadolle produces some of the most gorgeous lingerie in Paris. Perfect for your romantic weekend away...

Free 'P' Star
8 RUE SAINTE CROIX DE LA BRETONNERIE, 3RD
75003, PARIS
01 42 76 03 72

One of the best vintage stores in all of Paris, there is always something to buy at Free 'P' Star. The prices are a little more affordable than many of the other vintage boutiques in the city and there's a good selection of stuff from all eras. I especially liked the battered leather bags and belts, even if I had to practically fight a fashionista to get my mitts on what I wanted. Totally worth it though.

Chanel

31 RUE CAMBON, 1ST
75001, PARIS
01 42 86 28 00

You can't talk about shopping in Paris and not mention Chanel, right? Whether you're just after a bottle of No. 5 or you're there to invest in an iconic 2.55 bag (black leather for me, thanks) no trip to Paris is complete without sticking your head in this flagship boutique. This amazing four storey building houses the boutique on the ground floor, the Haute Couture rooms on the second, Coco Chanel's apartment on the third and her workshop on the fourth. Style, like cool, trickles downwards, ladies. Soak it up in this temple of fashion.

Colette

213 RUE ST-HONORÉ, 1ST
75001, PARIS
01 55 35 33 90

Everyone's heard of Colette, right? One of Paris' most famous stores, this beautiful space houses a bazillion super cool, on trend brands and so-hot-you-haven't-even-heard-of-them designers. In case the prices make you feel a little faint, you can always hit the Water Bar in the basement. No really. A bar specialising in water. Every glass of wine in Paris shudders in shame.

Log onto
www.iheartparis.co.uk
to find out more about
the *I heart* series and read
extracts from previous books

You'll also have a chance to enter
competitions, keep up-to-date
with Angela's adventures through
her blog, read top tips for where to eat,
drink, shop and sleep in Paris,
and much much more!

In case you missed the start of Angela's fabulous adventures, here's a taster from

I heart Hollywood ♡

The wedding was perfect.

Just ten people at City Hall, no hymns, no readings, no fuss; and then over to Alta in the West Village for the reception. Tiny candles flickered in the faces of my favourite people: Jenny, Vanessa, Erin. And Alex. God, he looked pretty in a suit. I made a mental note to get that boy a three-piece more often. Like maybe at our wedding . . . no, bad Angela, too soon to even think it. Dum-dum-dee-dum . . .

'So you don't think I'm making a ridiculous mistake?' Erin whispered over my shoulder, bringing me back with a bump. 'I mean, it can't be six months since I was telling you I would never get married again.'

I shook my head. 'Not at all.' I glanced over at the new Mr Erin, or Thomas as he was known to his friends. Or 'that mad hot piece of ass' as he was known to Jenny. 'You wouldn't be doing this if it wasn't absolutely the right thing to do.'

'Uh, which it totally is. Hello?' Jenny Lopez swung in and planted a great big kiss on the bride, smudging Mac Ruby Woo lipstick all over her face. 'He's a super-hot, super-rich lawyer and super in love with you. I'm pretty sure they are the main three factors to take into consideration before you hitch your wagon. Plus, wow, classiest wagon ever. Even better than your last wedding. And way better than the one before that.'

'My God, you are so rude,' Erin playfully slapped Jenny's mass of chocolate brown curls. 'But you're right. I couldn't not marry him. He's so sweet.'

'Yeah, sweet. I'm totally only getting married when the guy can rent out my favourite restaurant for an entire Saturday evening.' Jenny sighed and sank a full flute of champagne. 'Doesn't Thomas have any single friends? And I do mean, single, rich lawyer friends?'

I couldn't stop smiling. The last wedding I'd been to hadn't been such a roaring success. I had started the day as a blushing bridesmaid with a devoted fiancé and ended up a high-heel-wielding hand-breaker, whose devoted fiancé was at it with some tart in the back of their Range Rover.

After leaving everyone in the wedding party in tears and/or hospital, I had hotfooted it over to New York only to be taken in by Jenny: an entire family, best friend and therapist all in one. It hadn't been a walk in Central Park but I'd found my way eventually. A job blogging for *The Look* magazine, great friends, an actual life, all the things that had been missing for so long. As a hand slid around my waist and pulled me close, I was reminded of the other thing I'd found in New York: Alex Reid.

'So this is the nicest wedding I think I've ever been to,' he gently pressed his lips against my skin. 'And I have the hottest date here.'

'Firstly, there are only eight girls in the entire wedding and secondly, it's still not even true,' I said, turning to brush Alex's long black fringe out of his eyes. 'Erin looks stunning, Jenny is ridiculously pretty in that dress and Vanessa—'

'Will you please just take the compliment?' Alex shook his head. 'And I don't care what you say, there's not a girl in the whole city that could compare with you right now.'

I wrinkled my nose and accepted a kiss, silently thanking my lucky stars. We'd met just after I had arrived in New York and got far too serious, far too quickly. He had put the brakes on and I had spent six months cooling my heels, pretending I wasn't ready to start dating but really wondering when it would be OK to call him. Eventually, I'd picked up the phone, cashed in all my karma chips and, thank God, Buddha and Marc Jacobs, he'd answered. Now I was just trying to have fun and ignore the constant burning feeling in my stomach, that this was it, that Alex was the one. There was no way I wanted a repeat performance of last time. I'd spent ten years with my ex and not once, not for a moment, had I felt so scared to lose him as I did when I lay wide awake at night, watching Alex sleep.

For the last two months, he had been the most attentive, thoughtful, heartbreakingly wonderful boyfriend I could ever have imagined. He bought me little gifts, like the beautiful sunflower, my favourite flower, he'd brought to pin to my olive green Cynthia Rowley shift for the wedding. He surprised me with indoor picnics when I was on deadline, ran out to pick up breakfast before I woke up and even trekked all the way over from Brooklyn to Manhattan with the handbag and keys I'd left at his apartment as well as a huge hangover-friendly pizza when Jenny and I had both managed to lock ourselves out of our place at three a.m. We never did find out where Jenny had left the keys . . . But, most impressively, when I'd drunk far too much at a wine tasting I was supposed to review for *The Look*, he'd held my hair back while I threw up. Outside a very fancy restaurant. While everyone was watching. On his shoes.

And it wasn't just that Alex was competing for the title of World's Best Boyfriend, there was also the little fact that he was also a total rock god to take into consideration. His band had released their third album while we were on our 'break' and, despite a little commercial and a lot of critical success, he was still being a complete angel. While Jenny was loudly insisting that he should be out snorting coke out of groupies' belly buttons, Alex was lying watching America's Next Top Model, eating Chinese takeout on our sofa.

I peered up and down the table as we sat down for dinner and couldn't remember a time I'd felt so happy or so at peace with myself. So what if these weren't the people I'd grown up with, or the people that had taught me to ride a bike? They were the people that had taught me to ride the subway and to stand on my own two feet. Or at least how to get back on them after I fell on my arse, drunk.

I heart New York ♥

It's official. Angela Clark is in love –
with the most fabulous city in the world.

Fleeing her cheating boyfriend and clutching little
more than a crumpled bridesmaid dress, a pair of
Louboutins and her passport, Angela jumps on
a plane – destination NYC.

Holed up in a cute hotel room, Angela gets a
New York makeover from her NBF Jenny and
a whirlwind tour of the city that never sleeps.
Before she knows it, Angela is dating two sexy guys.
And, best of all, she gets to write about it in her
new blog (Carrie Bradshaw eat your heart out).
But there's one thing telling readers about your romantic
dilemmas, it's another figuring them out for yourself…

Angela has fallen head over heels for the big apple,
but does she heart New York more than home?

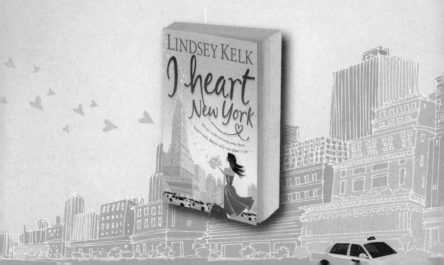

I heart Hollywood ♥

Angela Clark can't believe her luck...

She's living in New York, the most FABULOUS city on earth. And, she's bagged the perfect job at hip magazine *The Look* along with a sexy boyfriend – singer Alex Reid.

When Angela's editor sends her off to Hollywood to interview hot actor and fellow Brit James Jacobs, she doesn't exactly jump at the chance. The trip is going to test her new relationship with Alex to the max.

Angela doesn't fall for Hollywood right away. It's not as glossy and shiny as she had imagined and she doesn't feel like she fits in. Despite his lady-killer reputation, the only person who seems genuine is James Jacobs and Angela is suprised to discover they have lots in common.

But then a paparazzi snaps Angela and James in a very compromising position. Will the people Angela trusts come through – or will they believe everything they read?

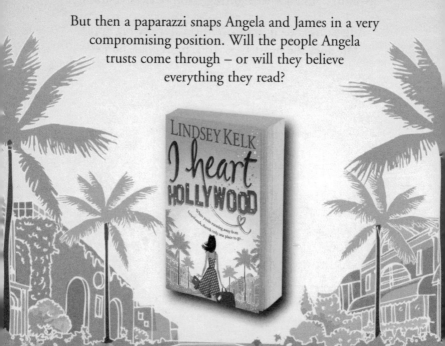